Praise for
HOW TO LIVE WITH A GHOST

"Haunting yet heartfelt, this story breathes life into an old Iowa farmhouse where one ghost clings to the past and one woman won't stop until she sets it free."
— Ninya Feltz writing as Blair Bryan
Author of the best-selling *Midlife in Aura Cove* Series

"*How to Live with a Ghost* is a nuanced blend of romance, mystery, and the paranormal—with just the right amount of humor. Melinda Wichmann delivers a refreshing twist on the classic whodunit that's perfect for fans of ghost stories, home renovation, and anyone who's ever whispered, 'Did you hear that?'"
—Nick Narigon
Author of *The F-Man Himself*

"I was completely captivated with *How to Live with a Ghost*. Jess's desire to quietly start over is interrupted at every turn with mystery, humor, danger and love...The authentic rural Iowa setting, local references, and traditions are refreshing. I can't wait to see what Melinda Wichmann writes next!"
—Debbie Tindle Parker
Author of the Hope Series

OTHER BOOKS BY PEARL CITY PRESS

Married, Living in Italy by Misty Urban

The Last Voyage of the Marigold by Dan Moore

The Adventures of Bobby, Iowa Farm Boy by Bob Bancks

Penny and the Woodland Fairies by Bob Bancks

Silent Sam and Other Stories by Alan Arkema

Escape on the Silk Road by Dan Moore

HOW TO
LIVE WITH A
GHOST

MELINDA WICHMANN

MUSCATINE, IOWA

Pearl City Press
An imprint of Writers on the Avenue
Muscatine, IA
www.writersontheavenue.org

Cover image licensed from
Cover design by Christoph Truemper, C. True Designs
Book design © 2017 BookTemplates.com

This is a work of fiction. All characters, incidents, and events are products of the author's imagination or are used fictitiously with no relation to actual persons or events.

No AI or AI-assisted elements were used in the creation of this book or cover.

ISBN-13: 978-1-969511-00-4

For my grandmother,

Mary Christine Mills,

who read to me

The boundaries which divide Life from Death

are at best shadowy and vague.

Who shall say where the one ends,

and where the other begins?

—Edgar Allen Poe

CHAPTER 1

Sunday, Oct. 21

Two weeks was plenty of time for the ghost to introduce itself. It hadn't, which confirmed my suspicion the tale attached to my new—old—house was nothing more than a local legend.

Since late September, I'd spent hours here after work and on weekends in a pre-move cleaning marathon. I hadn't encountered a single misty form floating around, rattling chains, or engaging in any other kind of paranormal nonsense.

Today was moving day, and anything already living here was going to get a roommate whether it wanted one or not. I parked my Jeep Cherokee and gazed through the windshield at the structure's peeling white clapboards.

Ornamental lightning rods with colored glass balls spiked up from the roofline, and flame-colored leaves drifted down from the huge maple tree that stood by the back door like a sentinel.

The house was built in 1910 and looked solid enough to stand for at least another one hundred and eight years. This was reassuring because I'd been running on iced coffee and dreams since signing the papers for the acreage.

While those substances were doing a fine job of holding me together, the resulting buzz made me question a few life choices.

Especially this one.

I got out of the Jeep and released Raider, my Belgian Malinois, from his crate. He trotted to the enclosed back porch and stood, tail wagging and ears up hard, as leaves swirled and collected behind the worn, wooden spindles of the screen door. That ornamental trim was one more item on a checklist of things that needed to be repainted, repaired, restored, or removed.

The twang of country music blasted up the lane, and a minivan pulled up next to my Jeep. Kerri Grimm, my accomplice in all things from dog show road trips to kennel club political maneuvering, shifted her vehicle into park but didn't get out. She stared at the house. She turned the radio down, as if that would help her see better.

I pulled a box containing the final remnants of my previous life out of the back seat and braced myself for what was coming. My reflection in the window stared defiantly back at me as I bared my teeth. Generous smile, slightly feral at the moment. Great skin for mid-thirties. Okay, late thirties. Medium height, medium build, curvy in the right places. I have my mom's wavy auburn hair and my dad's dark hazel eyes. My folks would have loved this house.

My name is Jess McCallister. Not Jessica. Absolutely not Jessie. The only person allowed to call me Jessie was my Grandma Wallace, her gentle tone chiding me for whatever bad decision I was sleeping with. Eleanor Wallace died two years ago, and I'm sleeping alone these days, my dog notwithstanding.

"I can't believe you bought this place."

Kerri's tone, somewhere between impressed and horrified, didn't invite a reply. Together, we gazed up at two-and-one-half stories of early 1900s architecture.

Original millwork trimmed the wrap-around porch, and faded, blue-gray fish scale shingles at the roof peaks reminded me of the house where I'd grown up. That echo of my childhood was only one of the reasons I bought it. Four bedrooms, two baths, original woodwork, front and back staircases, pocket doors, and oak and walnut inlaid floors had me making an offer before the realtor finished the initial walk through.

Plus, the house held a permanent place in the history of Lenox County. I pushed that out of my mind.

"Questionable curb appeal," Kerri said in her best it's-your-funeral tone. "Although Halloween is coming so the haunted look is in."

"It's not haunted. It's just old." I handed her the box of dish towels and coffee mugs and pulled out another one.

She didn't move. "You can't argue with its history."

"I'm not. Every old house has a history."

"Not like this one."

We were not having this conversation again. I started toward the back door along the jigsaw puzzle of broken cement and dead grass that called itself a sidewalk. Clumps of scarlet and gold gaillardia bloomed madly near the foundation, confirming a previous owner had been an avid gardener. Another previous owner put a new roof on both house and barn.

Yet another brought all the wiring and plumbing up to code. I was eternally thankful for the former owners and their infrastructure upgrades. They'd saved me a lot of headaches, and that was a blessing because there were a lot of headaches left.

The late afternoon light softened the air of neglect that hung over the place, letting the house present itself as rustic, the word realtors use when they want to make "fixer-upper" sound more attractive. Thanks to a string of short-term owners who didn't stay long enough to address cosmetic issues, the farmstead had descended into the genteel shabbiness decorators capitalized on in six-figure cul-de-sac homes in nearby Cedar Rapids.

Fox Hollow Farm didn't look superficially old and battered.

It *was* old and battered.

"This is a lot," Kerri said cautiously as she looked around. With a scattering of freckles across her nose and her walnut brown hair pulled into a ponytail, she looked more like a high school sophomore than the mother of two teenage boys, partner in a family construction business, avid dog obedience trainer, and volunteer at the county historical society.

"House, outbuildings, and forty-five acres." I gestured eastward, where gently rolling land reverting to native prairie gave way to old-growth timber edging the Iowa River. I'd sold my unimaginative, Mid-Century Modern ranch in

Cedar Rapids with zero regrets and bought Fox Hollow against Kerri's and her husband Matt's advice. My realtor hadn't even been excited when the previous owners accepted my low-ball offer, but this timeworn old property at 1984 Cat's Back Road, Sand Creek Township, Lenox County, Iowa, was going to be my happily ever after.

"I still don't get why you bought a place that's going to be nothing but work."

Kerri's words poked at the tiny grain of doubt that embedded itself in my mind the minute I signed the papers making me Fox Hollow's official owner. The place was a lot. And I was alone. I straightened to my full five-foot-six-inches and glared at her. Juggling the box, she raised her hands, palms out in a gesture of peace.

"Hey!" she said, glancing at the house. "Raider's going to tear the back door off the hinges, and then you'll have something else to fix."

Raider was ricocheting happily off the porch door, which rattled violently with each impact. At three years old, Raid is sixty pounds of hard muscle and gleaming mahogany and black fur wrapped in a wicked canine sense of humor. He's the only guy in my life now. I'm good with that.

The back porch smelled pleasantly of dried flowers, and the floorboards were worn but clean. Raid danced in front of me, air snapping with Malinois happiness, like moving out here had been all his idea. I twisted the key in the lock, turned the white porcelain knob, and stepped over the threshold.

My stomach dropped like I was on a roller coaster in free fall. My boots remained planted firmly on the floor, yet I was weightless, soaring on a rush of euphoria that threatened to knock me off my feet. My vision blurred, like looking through old, wavy glass, and I stumbled into the kitchen, coming up hard against the oak table. Ouch.

"Are you all right?" Kerri grabbed my arm. "Have you had anything to eat today besides coffee? You're not coming down with something, are you?"

"Stop mother-henning. I'm fine." The dizzying rush of happiness affirmed I was doing the right thing despite the annoying little doubt that lurked where I could never get a good look at it. I really was fine. I was so tired of failed relationships and worry about ending up alone, the decision to deliberately be alone was a huge relief.

I set my box of moving day detritus on a counter, dropped my bag and keys next to it, and breathed a repeated, silent thank you to the former owners who kept the kitchen's restoration true to the house's heritage. The ceiling was ten feet high. Bead-board wainscotting circled the room above a floor of sealed fir planks. The refinished floor-to-ceiling Shaker-style cabinets retained the original flour and potato bins. The farmhouse sink with its attached draining board was four feet of gorgeous vintage porcelain.

McCallister family heirlooms completed the kitchen's turn-of-the-century look: a Hoosier cabinet, a tin-punch pie safe and the oak table with hand-turned legs that had contributed to the bruise now blooming on my thigh. The result was a single room that looked like a layout in a home decorating magazine. The real estate ad described the rest of the house as a DIYer's dream. That was a little optimistic, but the first time I saw sunlight slanting through the tall windows, casting the echoing rooms in gold dust and promise, it had been so easy to ignore the cracked plaster and sagging wallpaper.

"You told me it needed work, but this is way more than I imagined," Kerri said as she peeked into the dining room. "I think you're nuts."

That wasn't news. When I bought Fox Hollow, Kerri started referring to it as my "situation," like I had a condition you shouldn't talk about in polite company. Even though she thought the house was incredibly cool from a historic standpoint, she'd never understood the dream that drove me to make it mine.

"Raider and I like it," I said. At his name, the dog leaped up and put his paws on my chest. I scratched his ears while he showed a little fang in a canine smile.

"This house is fifteen miles from town!" Not giving up, Kerri waved a hand toward the dining room. "And the plaster is falling off the walls."

"Only in a couple of places. Most of the repairs are cosmetic. Besides, you and Matt are Mr. and Mrs. Construction Company. You've got connections if I need to hire out the bigger jobs."

"What about the ghost?"

And here it was. I took a deep breath. "There is no ghost. You're spending too much time at the historical society. Those people have a legend for every square inch of Lenox County, and no sensible person would believe half of it."

Kerri refused to admit defeat. "If it pushes you down the stairs, don't say I didn't warn you."

I ignored this. The ghost had plenty of time in the last two weeks to push me down the stairs if it wanted to. Since it hadn't, I figured it either couldn't be bothered or didn't exist in the first place.

A pickup pulled up in front of the house, and I opened the door for Matt Grimm. He staggered in, the upper half of his stocky frame obscured by a teetering stack of plastic storage totes. He looked around as if expecting the ceiling to fall in momentarily.

"Where do you want these?"

I love Matt like a brother, but he'd joined Kerri in trying to talk me out of buying Fox Hollow, finally resorting to, "Why in the world do you want to live in a big old place all the way out there by yourself?"

I'd long passed the point of explaining it. Besides, no one was going to believe me if I told them the house liked me as much as I liked it. This house and I were more compatible than my ex-husband or any of the guys I'd dated recently.

I'm not one of those sage-smudging New Age witches who believe houses are sentient beings, but the first time I walked through the rooms, something clicked, as if the walls recognized a kindred soul. The days that followed confirmed that feeling. The owners accepted my offer with alacrity. The house passed the requisite inspections with flying colors, and the sellers cooperated at every turn. It was as if it was meant to be. Kerri said it was as if they couldn't get rid of it fast enough.

I directed Matt to leave the boxes in the dining room and went outside for another load, pausing on the wrap-around porch to admire my little kingdom. Locals still call it the old Cameron place even though the last Cameron to live here died twenty years ago. It's a Lenox County landmark, the only thing left standing after a tornado leveled the area in 1919.

The house and out buildings sat at the end of a long farm lane, surrounded by acres of cropland and timber in eastern Iowa. The house was late folk Victorian style with Craftsman elements. It was built when the clean lines of the Arts and Crafts movement were slowly replacing Victorian fondness for uber ornamentation.

I deposited a box of books in the cluttered dining room and stepped into the open hallway adjoining the living room. The inlaid walnut and oak floor of the entry was dull with wear, but the front staircase gleamed. The scent of Murphy Oil Soap lingered from my cleaning campaign.

"That porch is fantastic." Kerri wandered into the living room and looked out the picture window. "You could sit out there in the summer and watch the storms roll in from the west." She gave me a sideways look, daring me to take the bait.

"You like my house after all," I said. I'd heard the tornado story so many times I could tell it in my sleep. It was a great story, up to a point.

"I never said I didn't like it. I said you're crazy to

take it on by yourself." Her gaze fell on the oak fireplace mantel. "I'm amazed no one painted the woodwork. The ghost must have driven all the other owners out before they could wreck anything."

"If it's living here rent free, it might as well make itself useful," I countered.

"Jess McCallister, you'd better take that story seriously. Spirits don't like to be mocked."

Invoking my last name meant she was in full-on mom mode despite our being the same age. I rolled my eyes. Kerri loves a good ghost story, and here I was, moving into one.

She let the ghost go. "Have you met your neighbor yet?"

"I've been too busy to meet anyone," I said. "Selling the Cedar Rapids house and wrapping up projects for the *Times-Tribune* were their own special nightmares. I thought Josh was going to cry when I quit. You'd think I was the only freelance writer on this side of the state. Besides, I don't have a neighbor. It's just farmland and river bottoms out here."

"Mare says you do."

Mare MacGregor is a mutual dear friend who operates a bookstore and bakery in North Willow, fifteen miles away.

"Have you two been talking about me?" I tried to sound indignant, but it was hard to fault my two best friends for caring.

"Yes." Kerri beamed, unrepentant. "I don't know the guy, but she says you really need to meet him."

"I need to meet someone who can teach me how

to repair plaster and restore old tile. Aside from that, I don't need to meet anyone unless they have a contractor's license."

Kerri made noncommittal noises and headed out for another box. I lingered, turning in a slow three-sixty, admiring the grain of the hardwood floor and the leaded glass doors of the built-in bookcases flanking the fireplace. The jarring, acid blue paint on the walls made my eyes water, but the room felt like home. I've been in old houses where shadows collected in corners like sullen things, but these rooms were filled with an almost tangible sense of welcome.

There was no ghost here. Or if there was, maybe it wasn't the pushing-down-the-stairs type. There were friendly ghosts, weren't there? Or was this one just waiting until I was one hundred percent moved in to start levitating my bed?

"Where's this go?" Matt reappeared, hoisting a box labeled Bedroom. I pushed Kerri's ghost story out of my mind.

"Up. I'll show you." I trotted up the wide front staircase, my footsteps muffled by a faded floral carpet runner.

The second floor held four bedrooms and another full bath. Matt deposited the box in the bedroom I'd chosen and left without comment. Like the rest of the house, the room was gracefully proportioned with high ceilings and tall windows. My previously delivered antique metal bed frame and eclectic mix of early 1900s furniture fit perfectly. Fox Hollow wasn't the well-maintained farmhouse of my youth, but it carried the same vibe. It had sheltered people who were stewards of land and livestock, who made their living gambling against the whims of Mother Nature. You can take the kid out of the country, but you can't take the country out of the kid. A rural property had been my number one priority when I started house hunting.

The view out the windows encompassed the lawn east of the house that extended to an enormous barn with a limestone foundation nestled into the slope of the bank. The numerals 1893 were painted in white under the loft overhang. The running-horse weathervane atop the cupola pointed southeast in the afternoon breeze. The barn sported a sleek steel roof and traditional red paint with white trim, but clumps of weeds around the foundation reflected the same sense of abandonment as the house.

A smudge of topaz and crimson in the distance marked the tree line along the Iowa River bluff. According to Susanne Bartachek, my real estate agent and a fellow dog trainer, the river formed part of my property's northeast boundary. The hilly pasture and timber included with the house weren't worth nearly as much per acre as the surrounding arable farmland, which was why I'd been able to afford it.

Paws scuffed across the bare wood floor as Raider trotted in. He chomped contentedly on the tennis ball he'd liberated from a box and butted his head under my hand. I stroked his ears, happy he was happy, and gazed out the window.

"Here's another box of bathroom stuff."

I turned, feeling guilty for letting my friends do all the work while I daydreamed. I took the box from Kerri, and she followed me down the hall, not sharing my guilt at leaving Matt to continue hauling boxes without either of us.

I set the box atop the toilet seat. The room could have been a 1910 advertisement for the wonders of indoor plumbing. The cast iron clawfoot tub and pedestal sink with its brass and porcelain knobbed taps were worn but original. The floor was laid with one-inch black and white hexagon tile with a traditional Greek key pattern border.

Some of the tiles were loose, and some were missing. I'd found an architectural salvage business in Iowa City where I could buy replacements, but I had no idea how to relay them without making them look like they'd been installed by a pack of intoxicated gnomes. I was praying YouTube held the answers.

We left the bathroom and Kerri shook her head adamantly as I started down the back staircase.

"Those things are suicide stairs," she said. "They're practically vertical."

They were. And they were all mine, along with the broken tile and hideous paint and the furnace of indeterminate age clanking away merrily in the basement. I launched down the narrow stairway, hands braced on rough plaster walls for balance. Generations of feet had worn a groove in the center of each tread. Bare wood showed through gray-blue paint. At the bottom, the steps dog legged to the left, and I twisted the doorknob to emerge in the kitchen with Raider at my heels.

"You're bat shit crazy," Kerri called from the dining room. She'd taken the front stairs. "There's no other explanation." I found her poking at a section of exposed lath. Her affectionate tone took any sting out of the words.

"I'm living the dream," I said with confidence I didn't feel as a chunk of plaster fell to the floor. Kerri gave me an I-told-you-so look.

I'd always wanted to restore an old house but had come up short on finding someone to share that dream. My savagely invested divorce settlement, added to the inheritance from my parents' estate, let me make that dream a reality, no partner needed. I would have happily returned to my home farm in the northern part of the state, but the Iowa Department of Transportation put an end to that idea with two words: eminent domain.

One year after their deaths, Rich and Carol McCallister's Century Farm, including the rambling American foursquare house where I grew up, disappeared under a four-lane bypass for motorists who couldn't be bothered with the slower pace of two-lane county highways. Land values topped $12,000 an acre that year, making the State of Iowa's fair market value offer a truly unfathomable windfall for me.

Raider flung his front paws onto the sill of the dining room bay window and let out a single, deep bark, his alert to something unknown. An old Chevy pickup rolled up the lane.

"Welcome wagon?" Kerri joined me at the window.

The truck's paint, barely visible amidst mud and dents, was faded blue. Rust etched the wheel wells, and the tailgate rattled. The vehicle stopped in front of the house.

Raider growled as a man got out of the cab. My four-legged security system is numbers one through ten on the list of reasons I'm not afraid to live by myself.

The man surveyed the house, barn, and outbuildings with unhurried interest, then reached into the truck bed and lifted out a box. He strolled up the sidewalk, his gait slightly uneven from an almost imperceptible limp. The silhouette of a dog with alert ears remained framed on the pickup's passenger seat.

I gripped Raid's collar with one hand and opened the kitchen door with the other. The man extended his right hand, then looked at my dog, whose lips quivered in warning. He took a step back and slowly dropped his hand to his side.

He was a lean six feet of faded denim and flannel. Dark hair curled from under the edges of a battered cap, and a two-day beard covered his cheeks. A trace of gray showed in the stubble on his jaw. Time had burned away any semblance of youth, leaving a rough patina that invited my eye to linger.

A gold stud glinted incongruously in his left ear. I put him somewhere in his early forties. Storm-blue eyes studied me with amused interest, and white teeth flashed in an easy smile as I struggled to say something sensible.

"Hi," I managed.

"Is your dog going to bite me?" His whisky-rough voice didn't sound concerned. He just stood there and avoided eye contact with Raider. Whoever he was, he wasn't a complete idiot.

"That depends on you." Malinois are excellent judges of character. If you pass the test, you've got a friend for life. If not, you've got a problem.

"Dan Sinclair. I live on the first place west of here. I'd shake your hand, but Fangs might not approve."

Dan Sinclair. The name was oddly familiar, but if I'd ever met him, I would've remembered.

Raider quit growling and fixed the man with a speculative stare.

"Be nice," I said and released his collar. He stepped forward and sniffed the man's leg.

"Are you talking to him or me?" Dan Sinclair asked as my dog continued his slow, sniffing inspection. He raised his eyebrows but didn't move.

"Both of you." I extended my hand. "I'm Jess McCallister. This is Raider."

His grip was warm and firm, his palm calloused, a working man's hand. No doubt he was a farmer, come to make the obligatory welcome-to-the-neighborhood gesture just to see what variety of nut bought the house this time.

"You're number six," he said.

"I'm what?" That wasn't what I expected.

"The sixth owner since Sarah Cameron died." His eyes swept from my Iowa State Cyclones hoodie to my faded Levis, and his lips curved upward in a lazy smile. "And you're the fifth owner in the last six years."

Raider found Dan acceptable and poked his muzzle into his hand. Dan scratched the dog's head. Raid gave a contented sigh and gnawed at his coat sleeve.

It's generally not polite to let your dog chew on someone's clothes while they're wearing them, but I could only think about one thing at a time. Fifth owner in six years? I didn't know the turnover was that high.

Dan indicated the box at his feet. "Brought you a housewarming gift. The couple before you barely lasted six months."

I couldn't tell if that was intended as a helpful fact or a challenge to my ability to live here, but my brain was so busy figuring out why his name sounded familiar I didn't think to ask about all the previous owners' departures.

The box sported a label from Oak Falls, a local craft brewery. Fancy beer for a guy whose truck looked like it was one sparkplug away from the junkyard.

"Thank you, that's very generous."

His grin broadened. "Ready for things that go bump in the night?"

I rolled my eyes without thinking, and he burst out laughing. "Don't tell me you haven't heard the story."

I'd heard the story all right—Kerri wouldn't shut up about it. Oh dear God, what if there were other stories she hadn't told me? Ones only the people who lived out here knew? And what if they were worse? Or worse yet, what if they were true?

Before I could succumb to a panic attack, a small, dusty SUV arrived, adding to the traffic jam in front of the house.

Dan detached his sleeve from Raider's teeth. "I'll go, you're busy. Nice meeting you. Great dog."

"Nice meeting you, too." I mouthed the words automatically.

He turned to the door, and I allowed myself a lingering look at his back side because it would have been a sin not to.

A tall, spare woman made her way briskly up the sidewalk. A veteran of thirty-five years as business manager at the local Field and Farm store, followed by five years as owner of an independent bookstore and bakery, Mare MacGregor sparkled with the energy of someone half her age. Her white curls were held in check by a rolled blue bandana, and she carried an enormous pizza box with a cake box balanced on top of it.

Dan held the screen door open. "Good to see you again, ma'am." He looked back at me. "See you around, McCallister." He tossed off my surname as if we'd been friends for years.

"See you, Sinclair," I echoed, my mind scrambling to return the farewell and suddenly wondering if Mare had anything to do with this. I narrowed my eyes at her. She smiled innocently.

Kerri stepped onto the porch and studied Dan with unapologetic interest as he walked to his pickup.

"Lord have mercy, he's hot. And that earring!" She bit her lip.

"Does Matt know you go around ogling strange men?" I countered.

"I'm married, not blind," Kerri said, then gave a guilty look over her shoulder. Matt was in the dining room, making the hole in the wall bigger but safely out of earshot.

"He's my neighbor." I dismissed the incident as the scent of pizza wafted by me, and my stomach growled.

"Glad you two met." Delight etched Mare's words, as if she'd discovered a long-sought first edition. "You know who he is, right?"

I shook my head. "Should I?"

"D.W. Sinclair."

When that got no response, she looked at me like I was impaired. "The writer!"

The name clicked into place.

"Historical fiction, World War II in the South Pacific. I bought his first novel at your shop," I exclaimed.

Whoa. Wait. Novelists were supposed to be pale, nerdy guys who wore horn-rimmed glasses and shapeless sweaters with leather elbow patches, right? D.W. Sinclair had just disabused me of that stereotype.

"He does book signings for me now and then," Mare said. "Super nice guy, not keen on the public spotlight. He's lived out here for a few years."

I vaguely remembered Mare hosting the best-selling author at her shop several years ago. I was living in Cedar Rapids, caught up in the perpetual deadline lifestyle of a freelance reporter while keeping newly acquired Raider from eating my house. My schedule had been too insane to add one more commitment, so I hadn't made the seventy-mile roundtrip to hear him speak, although I'd enjoyed the novel very much.

"You should have asked him to stay for dinner," Mare said.

"I didn't know we were having dinner." I looked at the boxes.

"My treat. Sorry I couldn't get away from the store to help you today." Mare looked around the kitchen. "It's not every day a friend moves into the most famous haunted house in Lenox County."

CHAPTER 2

I scooped Raider's evening rations into his old blue and white enamelware pan and refreshed his water bowl. To celebrate launching this new chapter of my life, we humans ate pizza off paper plates in the living room. The fellowship of friends filled the room with a welcoming ambiance the awful blue paint couldn't diminish.

Mare's pizza peace offering was followed by one of her homemade cakes. The dark chocolate topped with buttercream frosting put me in such a mellow frame of mind, I made a mental note to forgive Kerri's obsession with the local legend.

"I'm glad you've found a place to put down roots," Mare said. "This is a lovely old house, even if you do have your work cut out for you."

I returned her smile. I'd put her and Kerri through so much crap in the last few years, I should be baking them a cake.

Their stalwart friendship had carried me through the implosion of my marriage to Michael The Jerk and our subsequent divorce, followed by the loss of my parents. Mom was killed by a drunk driver going the wrong way on Interstate 35, and Dad was gone within the year. The doctors said it was heart failure, but he and Mom were so close, I think he just faded away without her. In the end, I was glad neither of them saw the bulldozers take down the house and barns at what had been the three-generation McCallister farm.

After that, I drifted without purpose. The only thing that kept me sane was Raider. Channeling his adolescent Malinois behaviors into something socially acceptable while laying his competitive obedience foundation required so much energy there wasn't much left for anything else. I let my dog and my job encompass my life as I pushed through a revolving door of disasters involving the Y chromosome. Committing to Fox Hollow was my new awakening. I smiled, remembering the joy that filled me when I stepped over the threshold.

Kerri stomped on my reverie. "I ran into Brad at Brewed Awakenings yesterday. He asked about you."

My pleasant reminisces vanished. Brad Jennings had lit the final dumpster fire that convinced me to declare a moratorium on relationships. Lit it, pushed it down the street at high noon, called a press conference, and blamed me for everything.

"I told him you bought this place," she continued. "He said to tell you hi. You ever think about giving him a second chance?"

I didn't say anything, mostly because there was nothing to say. I'd made sure there wouldn't be a second chance when I stormed out of his house in April.

Looking thoughtful, Kerri said, "You two were good together. Bev's a piece of work, though. It might have been a good strategic move, getting away from that family."

I couldn't argue with her assessment. Brad and I had been good together until we weren't, but his mother, Beverly Jennings, was an absolute pain in the ass. Her hobbies were obsessively pursuing the family genealogy and trying to control her kids' lives, as well as the lives of anyone involved with them. When Brad's brother, Adam, and his family moved three states away for a new job, I thought Beverly was going to spontaneously combust or have an aneurysm or both.

"I traded the Jennings dynasty for a house where I can live happily ever after," I said. Fake it until you make it, right?

After Brad and I parted company, I decided I'd had enough: enough of my soul-draining job, enough of being emotionally exhausted by doomed relationships, enough of my unimaginative Brady Bunch era house. None of it was what I wanted from life. I had a heart-to-heart with my financial guy, quit my job and bought Fox Hollow.

It's a fixer-upper, but all of the original architectural elements are still intact. It has functional plumbing, and a structural inspection determined it wouldn't collapse on my head. It's not that I couldn't afford a brand-new house; it's more like I wanted to make this one mine through my own vision and sweat.

I put myself on a self-imposed deadline. Six months sounded like a reasonable amount of time to decide if I was cut out to go solo on the DIY lifestyle with a realistic expectation of restoring the house before I died of old age. If it turned out the success of my dreams relied on having a partner to share them with, I could always sell and move on. My realtor made it clear she knew plenty of lovely turnkey homes ideal for a single woman and her dog.

Sitting contentedly, listening to Mare and Kerri discussing paint colors, I covered a yawn. In addition to several weeks of cleaning, I'd been running a marathon of scheduling appliance deliveries, satellite dish hook-ups, and a dozen other pre-move details that kept me driving back and forth from Cedar Rapids to Fox Hollow for the last month. If I didn't slow down, I'd start seeing ghosts whether they existed or not.

As if she'd read my mind, Mare said, "Tell us the ghost story."

She's a Lenox County native, and her grin indicated she wanted to hear my newcomer's version to see if I got it right.

"I don't think there is a ghost." I wondered how many times I'd have to tell people that when they found out where I lived.

A ripple of energy danced across my skin, then was gone as fast as it came, but a gossamer swirl of something lingered like invisible smoke on the air. I couldn't shake the feeling someone was taking my measure, but no one else acted like they noticed it.

I seriously needed to back away from the coffee.

Kerri raised her eyebrows. "Susanne was talking about the haunting at open training last week. She said the previous owners told her the lights went off and on by themselves."

In addition to being my real estate agent, Susanne Bartachek is a fellow member of the Heartland Dog

Training Club, based in Iowa City. Overwhelmed with selling my former house and orchestrating the move to Lenox County, Raider and I hadn't gone to the weekly group training night since September.

"She told me about the lights," I replied. "Probably just a wiring glitch. It's an old place. I expect it to creak and groan a little."

"Don't tell me nothing weird has happened while you've been here alone," Kerri persisted.

"Nope. Nothing." But my day trips to Fox Hollow had been so fractured by movers, delivery guys, and technicians waving cables and climbing ladders, I'd rarely been here alone. Plus, I'd been desperation-packing, having agreed to be out of the Cedar Rapids house by three o'clock this afternoon, a deadline I'd made with exactly six minutes to spare. For the last few weeks, I'd barely known what day it was, let alone been of a mindset to commune with ghosts.

None of this crazed schedule explained that triumphant surge of joy that nearly knocked me off my feet when I stepped into the kitchen. Or that odd little current of energy that drifted through the room like a summer breeze. Neither were scary. Ghosts were supposed to be scary; therefore, it couldn't have been a ghost.

"Susanne said the last people who lived here left after six months." Kerri echoed what Dan Sinclair said earlier. "They told her the house didn't want them here."

I looked at the noxious blue walls. "If they're the ones who painted this room, no wonder it didn't want them here."

"So, who's the ghost?" Matt asked. It was refreshing to hear the skepticism in his voice, although, being married to Kerri, he'd probably heard the topic dissected over the dinner table more than once.

I gazed around the room with its scarred oak floor and leaded glass windows. It was just a story, and it was totally believable—to a point.

Everyone stared at me expectantly. I took a deep breath and told them what I knew.

"Gavin and Moira Cameron were immigrants from Scotland. They bought this land in 1893 and had two children, Sarah and Ian. They built this house in 1910." I felt like a historic home tour guide delivering a practiced spiel to obedient tourists, but saying the words aloud was an affirmation that consecrated my ownership of Fox Hollow. I knew its history. I wanted to be part of it.

"On the afternoon of July 4, 1919, a thunderstorm spawned a massive tornado that historians estimate was an EF5. It stayed on the ground for nearly twenty miles and destroyed the town of Walnut Bluff and all of the farmsteads east of the town. When it got here—" I waved my hand, indicating the house—"it stopped like it hit a wall. Ten people were killed that day, including one guy whose body was never found.

"That storm put Fox Hollow on the map. People back then didn't understand how severe weather systems developed and decayed, and a rumor started that this farm had supernatural powers protecting it. Anyway, Sarah Cameron helped her parents farm and took over after they retired. She never married. She lived here until she died of old age in 1998." I looked at Kerri and tried to sound blasé. "But people say she's still here."

"That's so romantic," Kerri sighed. "She loved this place so much, she never left."

"Old house, catastrophic natural disaster, lingering spirit—check, check and check. But why would she still be here?" I was so not giving this tale any credibility. Fifteen years as a general assignment reporter and editor left me skeptical of stories with only one side. Since Sarah Cameron had gone to her just reward, I was unlikely to hear her version of it.

Kerri shrugged. "Ghosts stay in places where they have unfinished business. She wasn't murdered, so she doesn't need someone to find her killer. Maybe she's guarding something."

I didn't say anything. One of us was nuts and it wasn't me.

Mare cleared her throat. "Speaking of guarding things, have you heard about the gold that's supposedly buried out here?"

I stared at her. "Stop it. Now you're making stuff up."

She shook her head. "No, really. Last spring, my book club hosted Dr. Peter Aldrich from the University of Oklahoma. He's writing a book about Midwest treasure hunting, and he gave a talk on local folklore, like when Jesse James and his gang robbed the South Amana General Store."

I held up a hand. "That's not folklore. The James

gang *did* rob the South Amana General Store. It's documented."

Mare ignored me and continued.

"One of the stories he told was about two slaves who fled Georgia at the end of the Civil War."

"Wait," Kerri interrupted. "You can't call them slaves anymore. It's dehumanizing."

"She's right," I said. "That was one of the words the Associated Press red flagged."

"So, what do we call them?" Mare floundered briefly.

"Enslaved peoples," I said automatically, wondering how in the world my house could be connected to the racial, political, and social upheaval that was the American Civil War.

"Enslaved peoples," Mare agreed, "although they decided to change that condition. Their owner was a wealthy Atlanta businessman who hid his money to keep it safe from the Union Army, but then suffered a stroke. He was a widower with no children. The, uh, enslaved man and his wife assumed their owners' death was inevitable. They took the money and ran."

"Are we talking Confederate States of America scrip?" Kerri asked. "Or actual coins?"

Mare shook her head. "Dr. Aldrich specified gold coins. Paper bills would have been easier to carry, but CSA money was worthless by the end of the war. The man was injured in a fall from a horse after reaching Iowa, so he and his wife stayed briefly with a family named Bishop at a stop on the Underground Railroad here in Lenox County."

She paused. "The station was at a farmhouse in Sand Creek Township. It may have been on this exact property. Anyway, word reached the couple that their former owner had survived and hired a detective to track them down.

"They knew they'd be hanged if they were caught, so they took off for Canada. They needed to travel light so they hid the gold, intending to return for it after the war ended. They made it as far as Duluth, Minnesota, where they died in a cholera outbreak. Whatever they hid is still out here."

"And Dr. Aldrich knew this how?"

I had liked going to book club at Mare's shop with Brad's mom. A shared love of reading and history was one of the few things Beverly and I had in common. I missed book club. I did not miss Beverly.

"I think I've heard this story," Kerri mused. "We have archives from the Bishop family at the historical society."

"You have archives from half the families in the county," I muttered.

"Private letters," Mare answered my question. "Dr. Aldrich found correspondence between the former owner in Atlanta and the detective. They detailed how much gold had been stolen."

"Like how much?" Matt looked like he was considering buying a metal detector and taking up a new hobby.

"Gold is heavy so they'd only take what they could easily carry, but in today's collector's market, coins stamped with the CSA seal would literally be worth more than their weight in gold," Mare said.

"How did anyone know the runaways hid it?" Kerri asked.

"They told the Bishop family they'd hidden valued belongings near the trading post out on the river bluff," Mare added, "but they didn't specify where. The detective tracked the couple to Duluth, where he confirmed their deaths. He sent a letter with this information to his employer but in the interim, the old man had died for real." She made a dismissive motion with her hand. "That was the end of it."

"What kept the Bishops from digging up the gold themselves?" Matt asked.

"Absolutely nothing, except they allegedly didn't know it *was* gold, and they didn't know where it was buried. That didn't come out until the detective came sniffing around after the couple moved on. There was an advertisement about the search for them in the papers and word got out about the vanished gold." She winked. "Makes a great tale, doesn't it?"

"That's absurd," I said. "This house wasn't built until 1910 and there aren't any gold coins hidden in the attic." At least I didn't think there were.

"Dr. Aldrich said it was buried near the trading post on the bluff," Mare corrected. "That happened in 1865."

I like history as much as the next guy, but I'd never heard of a trading post out here, let alone buried gold. This story was one fire-breathing dragon short of a fairy tale.

"Are you two done?" I asked. "Got anything else?

Maybe a coven of witches dances around in the timber under the full moon?" I love my friends, I really do, but sometimes they're too much.

"CALL IF YOU need anything." Kerri pulled on her coat to leave.

"Let me know if you want help painting. Or treasure hunting," Mare added.

"You guys have businesses to run," I protested. "This is my mess now."

"Your mess is more fun than my day job," Kerri said. In addition to keeping up with their sons, Ryan, 16, and Garrett, 13, she worked as the office manager for Grimm Construction, the family business. She also bred, trained and showed Australian shepherds under the kennel name Firefly Aussies. Kerri lived with a travel mug of coffee in one hand and her cell phone in the other. I'm not sure she sleeps.

"I can take time off if I want to," Mare said. "It's a perk of owning my own business."

Mare ran her shop with a frighteningly efficient staff who called themselves the book commandos. A member of the North Willow Chamber of Commerce, she was a staunch promoter of not only her own business, but also the town's thriving commercial district.

If there was a community activity taking place, Mare's fingerprints were on it. In the spare time she spun out of thin air, she was an Iowa State University certified Master Gardener and opened her beautifully landscaped home to the public during the Lenox County Garden Club tour every summer.

"I'll call you tomorrow. I want to know if you see the ghost tonight," Kerri said.

I rolled my eyes and waved goodbye.

With Raider at my heels like a furry shadow, I unpacked a few essentials in the second-floor bathroom, then washed my face and brushed my teeth. Padding back down the stairs, I trailed a hand along the banister, reveling in the peace of the moment. The quiet of the old house was like a warm embrace at the end of a long, cold journey.

I waited on the porch as Raider trotted the perimeter of the newly fenced yard, marking his territory. The sensor-operated security light between the house and barn had come on at dusk. Beyond its pool of light, the farmstead sank into deep shadow.

My eyes drifted past the barn toward the timbered river bluff. As if a ghost in my house wasn't enough, there'd been a trading post on my land in the 1800s? And a tale of hidden gold? What else was out here I didn't know about?

An owl hooted from the timber, the sound hanging on the chilly air.

Ready for things that go bump in the night? Dan Sinclair's comment strolled lazily through my mind. Had his teasing meant he didn't believe the ghost story either? Or he did?

Whatever. My brand new happily ever after did not involve things going bump in the night or any other time of day.

CHAPTER 3

Raider dropped the tennis ball on my head and clacked his jaws in delight.

Sputtering, I put on the bedside lamp. Outside the window, morning was a soft pearl glow above the eastern tree line. Raid grabbed the ball off my pillow and chomped happily. My eyes focused. It wasn't a tennis ball.

"What have you got?" The dog's tendency to repurpose objects to suit his own ends meant nothing within his reach was safe. Raid dropped the ball onto the quilt, then stared at it with a proprietary gleam in his eye. It was the size of a softball and made of strips of dark blue calico fabric.

"Where'd you get this?" I'd never seen it before.

Raider wagged his tail and play-bowed to the ball. When it didn't move, he spun in a circle, pounced, and bared his teeth at it.

"Okay, you win." I swung my legs out of bed, shrugged into my flannel robe and shuffled downstairs to embrace my first official day as caretaker of Fox Hollow.

In the kitchen, I put the fabric ball on the table next to my car keys, then did a double take. I'd put those keys on the counter yesterday after the bout of dizziness that nearly flattened me when I entered the house. Kerri must have moved them so they didn't get caught in the clutter when Mare showed up with dinner. I tossed them back on the counter near my bag.

I let Raid outside and watched as he enjoyed his morning constitutional. The scent of coffee brewing in the kitchen and the sound of warm air whistling up through the ornate metal floor registers filled me with contentment. Just me and my dog and my house. When I whistled, Raider loped across the frosted grass, looking as happy as I felt.

Back in my bedroom, I dressed in my standard autumn ensemble of jeans, T-shirt, hooded sweatshirt, and boots. I started toward the front stairs but stopped short. The door to the narrow staircase to the upper half story stood partially open. I must have forgotten to close it after taking Kerri, Matt and Mare on a tour of the house last night. Raider stuck his head into the doorway and wagged his tail in excited swoops.

The dog didn't move as I crowded past him into the stairwell. Gray light filtered down through air thick with the smell of dust and unfinished wood, certainly nothing that would merit tail wagging. I looked at Raid. Still wagging.

"What?" I said.

He looked past me and wagged harder, dancing on his front feet now.

I tried to open the door the rest of the way, but it scraped against the floor, then stuck. I pulled up on the knob with both hands and put my shoulder into it, which sent the door crashing back into the wall. I'd just set foot on the first step when a round object hurtled down from above. I said a few four-letter words and slammed back against the wall, heart racing.

A calico ball identical to the first one landed with a soft thud and rolled to a stop at my feet. Raider pounced on it. I reviewed the symptoms of a heart attack and decided I wasn't having one.

I craned my neck upward as I took a tentative step, then a second. The stairs creaked under my boots, but nothing happened. Not even the hint of an annoyed ghost, throwing things in a pique.

I was eye-level with the bare wood floor when a tattered cardboard box came into view. It had been tipped onto its side at the top of the stairwell, and scattered odds and ends from previous residents spilled out.

I took a few more steps upward. Pawprints marred the dust where Raider had nosed around and pushed the box over. This must have been where he found the first cloth ball. The vibration of me yanking open the stairwell door had jarred a second ball over the top step's threshold, and gravity did the rest. No ghost tantrum required, although none of that explained the dog's cheerful interest in the stairwell in the first place. If he'd wanted another ball, he could have just trotted up and gotten it. It had almost looked like he was waiting for someone to toss it to him in play. Except that was ridiculous.

I surveyed the dim confines of the attic. There was definitely no ghost there. With my dog carrying his new treasure, we went downstairs to the kitchen. I traded him a dog biscuit for the lumpy fabric ball and set it on the counter.

I fed Raider his breakfast, then poured coffee and cut a leftover piece of Mare's cake, pondering the second ball. Kerri would have a heyday if I told her the resident haunt was throwing things at me, but I didn't believe that for a minute. The episode had been the result of my nosy dog and the laws of physics.

I spent the morning unpacking kitchen stuff and organizing the butler's pantry. I was thinking about going out to explore the timber when my phone rang.

"How's it going?" Kerri's tone was all innocence.

"Fine. I've almost got the kitchen unpacked." A report of domestic endeavors should put a halt to any expectations of encounters with the undead.

"Hey, you want to learn more about your house, right?" Kerri launched her agenda. "Let's go see if Mare has anything. She's got more books on Iowa history than Amazon."

I didn't remember telling Kerri I wanted to learn more about Fox Hollow, and I didn't know if *anything* constituted information about the tornado or my house's rumored permanent resident. I appreciated her interest even if her enthusiasm for the alleged haunting was tolerable only because this was the week before Halloween. I'd stupidly thought my disinterest in ghost talk would put an end to it, but seeing the house in person last night had gotten her fired up again.

That was all fine and good for her. She didn't

have ten rooms to paint, wallpaper to strip, plaster to repair, hardwood floors to refinish, and a summer's worth of yard work to deal with before winter, including a pile of broken tree limbs the size of a Buick on the front lawn. I agreed to meet her in town in thirty minutes.

I WAS LATE BECAUSE I couldn't find my car keys. They weren't where I'd put them on the counter. I found them eventually, dangling from the coat hooks near the back door. I didn't remember putting them there.

Kerri was waiting in front of A Likely Story, Mare's shop, when I got to North Willow. The shop was in one of the original 1800s brick store fronts in a commercial district so picturesque it had been featured in more than one Midwest tourism magazine. The trees in the city square blazed with autumn hues and mums bloomed in colorful profusion, courtesy of the Women's Garden Society.

At an age when many folks would have thought about retiring, Mare took her late husband's life insurance benefits and her favorite recipes and opened the town's only bookstore and bakery. The ever-changing variety of home-baked goodies in the glass display case meant I'd get something good to eat out of this, even if I had to listen to Kerri talk about ghosts.

A bell tinkled as we pushed through the wooden front door with its dual arched windows. The shop was quiet, the morning rush having come and gone.

Mare's disembodied voice called, "I'll be right with you!"

Pumpkins and gourds entwined with burlap ribbon and sparkling purple and green fairy lights decorated display tables. Wooden folk-art witches and black cats carved by a local craftsman danced atop the bookshelves, and elegant little ghosts styled from lace-trimmed handkerchiefs fluttered in the breeze from the open door. Mare loved to celebrate Samhain—the Celtic high holy day the rest of America calls Halloween. With a last name like MacGregor, she believes firmly in embracing one's Scottish roots.

Mare and I met five years ago while watching a sword play troupe at a local Highland games festival. She'd just opened A Likely Story and invited me to stop in. I did, and we bonded over chocolate layer cake covered with half-inch thick ganache.

As it turned out, we share a Scottish heritage and even a common ancestor's surname, but amidst the tangle of McCallisters, McGregors, Wallaces, Chisolms and Kincaids, it was impossible to tell if we were genuinely related or just trees in the same forest.

I'd dabbled in genealogy briefly, but not seriously enough to find any answers. When Brad and I were dating, Beverly's laser focus on the Jennings family to the exclusion of all else had squashed any budding interest I might have had in pursuing my own roots. Mare encouraged me to follow up, but I never made it a priority.

A decorated chalkboard inside the front door

announced an October special of ten percent off any book about the paranormal. I groaned silently. Ghosts were in vogue no matter where I went. The scent of butter and cinnamon reminded me I could tolerate ghost stories for a chance at whatever had just come out of the oven.

"Hey, guys!" Mare appeared from the small commercial kitchen at the back of the store. "Sit down. I tried a new recipe and need taste testers."

She led Kerri and me to a café table in the bakery area and served slabs of spice cake laced with raisins and nuts and topped with a buttery powdered sugar glaze.

I took a bite and closed my eyes in bliss. "This is better than sex. Less awkward, guaranteed satisfaction."

"Then it's time you start dating again," Mare said. "There's no substitute for a good man." She and her Thomas had been married 41 years before his death.

"I'd rather be alone than hooking up to pretend I wasn't alone." I kept my voice neutral. Love worked out great for some people. I wasn't one of them. It wasn't just my ex-husband, Michael "Can't Keep It in His Pants" Parker. I was tired of doing post mortems on the parade of failed relationships that followed my divorce—work got in the way, too few common interests, overbearing family, no connection outside of the bedroom, no connection inside the bedroom...

"Michael was a Grade A dick. Sawyer needed a bottle of bourbon to be functional, and Colt had a boyfriend on the side. A boyfriend!" I dragged my hands through my hair. "I don't even want to talk about Brad."

"Not all men are like that," Mare said mildly.

"I'm tired of kissing princes and watching them turn into frogs," I said, driving my point home.

She let it go. "What are the two of you up to?"

"We came to see if you have any books that mention the Fox Hollow haunting." Kerri didn't hesitate.

"There is no haunting." I sounded like a broken record.

"Then what made all the previous owners move out so fast?" Kerri challenged. "Nobody buys a house and moves out after just one year. Repeatedly. I bet—"

"Every old house that sits empty for more than ten minutes gets a reputation for being haunted," I interrupted before she could go haring off into more wild supposition. "But I'd like to know more about the tornado."

The awe and terror inspired by those violent storms ran in the blood of everyone who grew up in Tornado Alley. As a child, I'd seen houses ripped in half by twisters that left pictures hanging on the remaining walls and cars dangling from trees. A huge tornado losing strength and lifting abruptly wasn't unheard of, but it was the sort of thing people loved to embellish, transforming a meteorological event into something supernatural. Add a hundred years of retelling the story and you get folklore polished to a high gleam, with my house sitting right in the middle of it.

I wanted facts. How did the surviving residents of Walnut Bluff manage with the town's infrastructure destroyed and no Red Cross to show up with blankets and housing vouchers? What passed for FEMA in 1919? Why had the residents chosen not to rebuild their town?

This was nothing more than simple curiosity, but I was living in a house that achieved local landmark status because it survived that day, even though it stood directly in the path of the devastating storm. It would be nice to have a more thorough background in Sand Creek Township history. So far, the place was rife with killer tornadoes, ghosts, and buried gold.

"Ever hear of Fox Hollow Belgians?" Kerri continued her mission to feed me information I didn't know I needed.

"Yes," Mare said.

"No." I groaned at the reminder I was the new kid in town, having lived in Lenox County for exactly less than twenty-four hours.

"Sarah's parents raised Belgian draft horses. That was their stable name," Kerri explained patiently. "Sarah took over when they retired."

"Name your sources, professor," I said.

"I worked as a docent at the historical society this summer, remember?"

I didn't. I'd spent the summer wallowing in a hot mess of disillusionment and anxiety, thanks to post-Brad fallout.

She turned to Mare. "Didn't the historical society publish a book on Lenox County ghost towns a few years ago? Maybe Fox Hollow is mentioned because it was close to Walnut Bluff."

Mare considered this. "I forgot all about that book. I might still have one in the back room." She vanished into the back of the shop.

I turned to Kerri. "Why this interest in my house? You volunteer at the museum. You already know all about it. Even if my house has a ghost—which it doesn't—what am I supposed to do about it?" My mind clicked through a checklist of things I could be doing instead of having this conversation.

Kerri had the decency to look guilty, but her voice was firm. "I don't know everything about it. It's not like I've had time to sit around reading the archives in the museum. I just know what I've heard people say."

"What people?"

"Friends of friends of the people who've lived there. You know how gossip gets around in a small town. I just thought if you had more information, maybe you'd be able to find out why Sarah Cameron is still there, like they do on those paranormal research shows on TV."

Before I could tell her that wasn't even on the first ten pages of my to-do list, Mare reappeared and plunked two books on the table.

The top volume's black and white cover showed an abandoned one-room schoolhouse. The building's broken windows and peeling paint enhanced the title, *Shadows of the Past: Ghost Towns of Lenox County*. I opened the cover and scanned the table of contents, then flipped to the chapter about

Walnut Bluff.

Kerri looked over my shoulder as I turned the pages. Photos showed families posed stiffly on porches of Victorian homes. Horses and buggies were tied to hitching posts on brick streets around a tree-lined square. Churches' whitewashed bell towers stretched heavenward.

Kerri pointed. "There!"

The picture of Fox Hollow had been taken on the front lawn in 1927, eight years after the tornado. In the foreground, a woman wearing trousers, boots, and a tweed newsboy cap held the lead lines of four Belgian draft horses. The horses gazed calmly at the camera lens, their coats gleaming even in the grainy black and white rendering. I read the text under the photo.

Sarah Cameron is shown on Fox Hollow Farm with her Belgian horses. The farm is a notable Lenox County landmark by merit of being the lone house standing in Sand Creek Township following the July 4, 1919, tornado.

"Funny that she never married," Mare observed. "Fox Hollow was a showcase in its heyday. Sarah would have inherited substantially when her parents died."

I felt a sudden, unexpected pang of kinship with Sarah Cameron. Had she never fallen in love? Had she loved someone her parents didn't approve of or perhaps someone who rejected her?

Maybe she decided men were idiots and let her love for her horses overshadow the need for a husband. Draft animals would have been in high demand in the 1920s, and a strong-willed, hard-working woman could have made a go of running a farm, although doing it without a partner would have been a monumental effort. Day laborers could be hired, but they wouldn't share the same investment as those whose name was inked on the deed.

As a single, female landowner, Sarah would have been courted relentlessly by men who cared nothing for her but wanted to gain ownership of the Cameron farmland. I allowed myself a brief romantic explanation. It must have been unrequited love that kept her single.

Maybe she'd given her heart to a man who was pledged to another, or worse, had died young. America had been involved in World War I at the time many girls her age were marrying. Had her sweetheart left her with a promise, never to return from front-line trenches? But unless she was a workaholic ghost, still rising for chores each morning, that wasn't any reason for her to still be there.

"Your place is mentioned in this book, too." Mare indicated the second volume. The cover of *Wind and Shadows: Eastern Iowa's Pioneer Cemeteries* wasn't any more cheerful than the ghost town book. Another black and white photo showed half-toppled tombstones enclosed by a rusted iron fence. The book had been written by the State Association for the Preservation of Iowa Cemeteries.

She flipped it open and tapped the correct page. There wasn't a reference to my house at all. Instead, two paragraphs referenced a mid-1800s trading post located "near the river bluffs in Sand Creek Township, Lenox County" and its "adjoining burial ground which served early settlers and travelers." It went on to note the cemetery remained part of the modern-day Fox Hollow Farm parcel.

Which I now owned. What the actual hell?

"There's a law about disclosing gravesites on a property, but Susanne never mentioned a cemetery," I stammered. My confidence in the real estate agent's professionalism didn't quell my unease at this unexpected discovery.

"It might only be a couple of unmarked burials everyone forgot about," Kerri said. "It says the trading post burned to the ground in 1887, and the Bishop family didn't rebuild. Gavin and Moira Cameron bought the land in 1893."

"Susanne didn't tell me any of this." Annoyance replaced unease. Why hadn't she disclosed it?

"Look at this map." Mare pointed at the page depicting Sand Creek Township, circa 1870. I recognized the Iowa River and Sand Creek confluence from the modern plat version I'd studied prior to buying the property.

Two sepia-toned stars denoted sites near the river bluff downstream from where the creek flowed into the river. One was labeled Bishop Trading Post, the other, Bishop Cemetery.

Skepticism rising, I shook my head. "If the cemetery was still there, wouldn't it be fenced off or something?"

"If it was still there?" Mare laughed. "If it was

there in 1870, it's still there, whether it's marked or not. Unless a private landowner takes an interest, a lot of pioneer cemeteries get reclaimed by nature and forgotten. Once in a while, you hear about them on the news when skeletons start showing up in the middle of a state's new road project."

Lovely thought. Next thing I knew, Kerri would be telling me there were ghosts in the timber, too. I told Mare the coffee cake was still better than sex and bought both books. If nothing else, they'd look good in the bookcases flanking the living room fireplace.

TUESDAY, OCT. 23

WITH THE CHAOS of moving behind me, Raider's competitive obedience career was re-elevated to its rightful status. I abandoned the final boxes of household miscellany that needed unpacking, and we took off for the Heartland Dog Training Club's weekly open training night, both of us eager to get back into the routine.

I've eaten, slept, and breathed competitive dog training since my parents took me to an American Kennel Club obedience trial when I was thirteen. For an awkward teenager trying too hard to find her niche among the high school cliques, the fellowship of dog trainers was heaven.

Twenty-five years of professional lessons, seminars and countless hours of practice later, I'm as in love with the sport as the day I earned my first AKC obedience title.

The HDTC building was a no-frills, rented

warehouse in a light industrial park near Iowa City. The hangar-like space had enough room for two forty-by-fifty-foot competition-size training rings with crates and lawn chairs set up around the perimeter. It was cold in the winter, hot in the summer, smelled like rubber floor matting and felt like home.

Kerri blew in on our heels. She threw her coat over her chair as her blue merle Aussie, Tangle, did sniffy greetings with Raider.

"I'm surprised you're here tonight. Thought you'd be busy painting or something," she said.

"I have to get back to regular training. I don't want to look like an idiot when I show Raid in Utility next spring." Even if we trained every day between now and then, there was a high probability Raider would commit some kind of lunacy anyway. The Utility class is the highest level of AKC obedience competition, and the exercises are a minefield of errors waiting to blow up a performance.

Kerri looked like she was going to use the words *idiot*, *Raider*, and *you* in a clever sentence when Susanne Bartacheck approached. Her stunning German shorthair pointer, Cannon, trotted effortlessly next to her. Cannon was currently the number one GSP in the country, with best of breed wins at national specialties and multiple all breed best in shows.

I blinked, surprised. CaDan nnon gaited and free stacked in the breed ring with precision that took your breath away, but Susanne had never shown much interest in formal obedience training. This weekly ring-prep class was the last place I expected to see her. Cross-training wasn't uncommon among the dog show fraternity, though, especially if owners want performance titles to showcase a stud dog or brood bitch's versatility.

"Hey, Jess, how's it going with the house?" Susanne asked. Without giving me a chance to answer, she added, "I hope you have better luck with the place than the last owners."

Her smile was brittle. While she'd been nothing less than professional through the sale process, I'd detected an underlying distaste for Fox Hollow's genteel shabbiness. Susanne didn't do worn-out things. Even at a dog training class where jeans and hoodies were the norm, her hair was freshly styled from a salon cut and color, and her sportswear dripped expensive labels. She drove a Cadillac Escalade and vacationed at trendy resorts on the rare weekends she wasn't collecting best in show rosettes with Cannon. She was about ten years older than me and her career was well-established, so who was I to judge how she spent her money?

"Let me know if it's too much for you," she continued. "I'll find you something a little more domesticated."

"What was that all about?" Kerri asked after Susanne moved on. Cannon floated at her side with the grace that bore testament to his impeccable structure. "She didn't sound very happy about you buying your place."

"She wanted to sell me the house she thought was right for me, and it wasn't Fox Hollow. The commission was probably so low she thought it was a waste of her time," I said, only half joking. I also suspected Susanne had been taking Cannon and her other dogs out to run in the pasture after house showings and regretted the loss of her private dog park.

If she'd asked, I would have been happy to let her run her dogs out there, but she hadn't asked, and I liked my newfound peace too much to start inviting people into it at random.

There were nine of us that evening, six women and three men. Competitive obedience is dominated by the fairer sex, and Alfred "Alf" Wittrick, Anders Linder, and Kyle Montgomery were what we jokingly called our token males. We all did this because we loved the sport. None of us made a dime from it.

Susanne alone generated income from Cannon's stud contracts, although it went right back out the door for entry fees, travel expenses, and a wardrobe of sparkling St. John's suits. You don't handle a dog to best in show wearing blue jeans.

We helped one another, playing the roles of judge and instructor, and the evening passed in a pleasant whirl. More than once, Alf tried to engage me in a conversation about Fox Hollow, but I politely evaded him. Alf loved to gossip, and I had no desire to burn precious time chatting when I could be training. The last thing I needed to hear was anyone else's opinion about my house.

My training goals for the evening focused on easing my guilt over putting Raid on the back burner in recent weeks. We spent our time revisiting his foundation skills, which appeared to still be in place, if not a bit rough around the edges. Raid was delighted to be working again, and at the evening's end, I was worn out. We were a long way from earning a qualifying score in Utility, but it felt good to be back on the mats.

"Thanks for your help, Jess! See you next week," Susanne called out as she left.

"It's nice to see a newbie so enthusiastic," Kerri said. She gathered up her gear and shrugged into her coat. "But I heard she and Ron are having trouble. She may just be looking for a reason to get out of the house."

"I think she's serious though, not just putting in minimum effort for a Novice title," I said. "Obedience titles will make him even more attractive as a stud dog."

"He's earning his keep," Kerri grinned. "Can you imagine the number of bitches lining up to be serviced by the number one shorthair in the country?"

"I guess someone has to pay for all those Patagonia sweaters." I looked down at Raider, who was gnawing on the corner of my gear bag. He'd never paid for anything in his life.

On the thirty-minute drive home, I thought about Susanne's insinuation that the house was too much for me. Fox Hollow had timeworn character, and that's what I wanted, not a generically pristine new build. That morning, I'd watched Raider's tennis ball roll from one end of the living room to the other. The floor looked perfectly level, but after a hundred years of settling, that was unlikely. I'd talk to Matt about adding floor braces.

It was shortly after nine p.m. when I turned off the highway onto Cat's Back Road and rattled across Sand Creek bridge. After two more dusty miles, I rounded a curve and pulled into my lane. Reflexively, I mashed the brake pedal to the floor, and the Jeep fishtailed in a spray of loose gravel. Raider let out an annoyed whuff.

I stared. Atop its slight rise, the house glowed like a meteor. Every light from attic to basement was on. When Susanne mentioned former owners having problems with lights going on and off, I'd imagined a single fixture malfunctioning, not the whole damn place lighting up like a Christmas tree.

I eased the Jeep up the lane, powered down the window, and stared. Nothing moved. The house sat there, minding its own brightly illuminated business.

A gust of wind sent dry leaves skittering across the hood, and I jumped. Without taking my eyes off the house, I reached behind the seat and opened the side door of Raider's crate. He scrambled over the console into my lap and stuck his head out the window. He sniffed noisily, but his hackles didn't go up. Okay. That was good.

I pulled out my phone, then hesitated. I could call Kerri, but I didn't expect her and Matt to come chase whoever or whatever was causing this out of my house. Ditto for Mare.

What about my only neighbor for miles? Scratch that. I didn't know Dan Sinclair well enough to ask him to encounter a burglar on my behalf, and I didn't have his phone number anyway. With a grimace, I resorted to the logical conclusion.

"Lenox County 911, what is your emergency?" The dispatcher's voice was calm and professional.

"I live at 1984 Cat's Back Road. I just got home, and I think someone broke in. All the lights in my house are on."

I hated sounding like a damsel in distress, but I'd hate it more if I ended up as a headline in the next edition of the *North Willow Sentinel*: "Woman attacked by escaped inmate from Institute for the Criminally Insane."

"I'm sending a deputy now. Are you in a safe place?"

"Yes." The doors on the Jeep were locked. Raider was riding shotgun. I was as safe as I was going to get. The dispatcher offered to stay on the line, but I assured her I'd be okay. I clicked off and looked at the house.

No shadowy figures flitted from room to room. No tormented face appeared at the attic window. In fact, the house looked bright and cheerful, as if a party with invisible guests was underway. Around it, the lawn and trees were as dark as spilled ink.

Within minutes, a white Lenox County Sheriff's Department Tahoe screamed up the lane, lights flashing and siren piercing the night. I shifted uneasily. It couldn't be...surely the dispatcher wouldn't send...no, just no.

My stomach clenched as the deputy got out of the vehicle. In a panic, I almost shouted it was a false alarm. Sorry for the inconvenience, please, just go away. Then a burning dose of self-righteous anger took over. Damned if I was apologizing for this or anything else.

Brad Jennings wore the khaki sheriff's deputy uniform as if he'd been born to it. His hair was cropped in a military cut. In his late thirties, he had the build of a high school football player slightly past his prime. He walked like a gunslinger stepping into the street at high noon, shoulders squared, hands on his equipment belt as he approached my open window.

"Hello, Jessie."

Of course he used the *ie* suffix, like we still shared that degree of intimacy.

"Brad." His name tasted bitter through my clenched teeth. So help me, if he said it was good to see me, I'd put the Jeep in gear and run over his feet accidentally on purpose.

He leaned down to look in the window. Raider growled. Brad took an involuntary step back and shifted to a more professional stance. "Dispatch said you came home and all the lights were on. Looks like you're keeping up the tradition."

"What do you mean?"

He ignored me. Typical. "Did you go inside?"

"No."

"Are the doors locked?"

"They were locked when I left." All the lights had been off, too, except one over the kitchen sink.

Brad swept his flashlight in a slow arc across the barn and trees. "I'll check it out. Give me the keys."

I held them out. If someone was in the house, I was fine with Brad encountering them first. But if someone were lying in wait, it made no sense to turn on all the lights. I couldn't think of anyone who would be lying in wait for me in the first place. I didn't know anyone I'd count as an actual enemy, just proof I made bad decisions about men.

On the other hand, Brad's and my breakup had been a perfect ten on the Richter Scale. If any of my relationships could spawn retaliation, it would be that one, but it was ludicrous to think an officer of the law had broken into my house, turned on all the lights, then made sure he was available to respond to my 911 call. Ludicrous and creepy.

Brad took my keys. The hard set of his jaw said he, too, was reliving the memory of our final blow up. Siding with his mother against me had made the Jennings family dynamic crystal clear. It would always be family first—*his* family—and I was expected to fall in line.

Without a word, he turned on his heel and strutted toward the back door. He always walked that way, like a ramrod-straight spine made his authority beyond question. How had I ever found that alpha male display attractive?

I stroked Raider and considered the bigger issue at hand. Burglary seemed unlikely. I have some lovely pieces of antique furniture, but short of backing a moving van up to the door, there was nothing else in the house worth stealing.

My brain chose that moment to dredge up something I'd read once in a novel about a haunted house. Lights coming on or going out unexpectedly indicated a spirit's presence.

That was absolutely not an acceptable explanation.

I watched as Brad unlocked the back door and let himself into the kitchen. He was visible as he moved from room to room, service weapon drawn. Did he really think someone was in there, or was he pouring on the testosterone to impress me? If so, it wasn't working.

A set of headlights bounced up the lane and stopped behind my Jeep. As boots crunched on gravel, I saw Dan Sinclair approaching in the rearview mirror.

Raider climbed back into my lap, stuck his head out the window, and wagged his entire body in a very un-Malinois-like fashion.

"You're supposed to be aloof with strangers," I muttered. "Didn't you read your breed standard?"

Dan scratched the dog's head. "Everything okay, neighbor?"

"I'm not sure. What are you doing here?" I stammered. The revolving red and white lights from the Tahoe highlighted the rugged lines of his face, and I briefly forgot about Brad and free-ranging lunatics.

"Heard the siren. Came to see if you were all right." His smile reflected genuine concern.

"When I got home tonight, all the lights were on." I felt silly. Who in their right mind was afraid to go into their own house with the lights on?

"You could have called me."

"I don't have your number," I stammered.

"555-0214. Now you do."

The back porch screen door slammed, and Brad crossed the lawn. He looked at Dan as if he'd found something unpleasant on the bottom of his shoe.

"Who are you?" he demanded.

Dan was the same height as Brad, but where the latter had thickened with approaching middle age, Dan's build was whipcord lean. He leaned on the Jeep's fender and shoved his hands in his pockets.

"I live down the road. Heard the siren, came to check on my neighbor." He made it sound like we'd known each other for years.

"I've got it under control. You can leave."

"He can stay," I snapped. Damned if Brad was going to order people around on my property.

Dan glanced at me, and one corner of his mouth twitched up. "She says I can stay."

Brad ignored him and returned my keys. "Doors were all locked, no sign of forced entry, no one inside. The last owners had the same problem with their lights, called 911 a couple of times for the same reason. Guess they never got it fixed. Your sound system's on, too."

I didn't have a sound system. I opened my mouth to point that out, but Brad overrode me with a rote warning about keeping the doors locked. Turning toward his vehicle, he paused. "You've got my number, Jessie. Don't hesitate to call if you need anything."

I stiffened. How typical of him to assume he'd be my first choice if I needed anything. How typical of him to say it in front of Dan, as if he was marking his territory.

"It's Jess," I said through clenched teeth as Brad got in the Tahoe and left.

Dan looked at me through the open window. "Jessie?" He did it on purpose, but the soft spin he put on my name made me unwilling to call him out.

"He was trying to being clever."

"He needs to try harder. You two have a history?"

I scowled. This was not something I was in the mood to discuss with a guy I'd met for ten minutes two days ago.

"Let me guess—you flamed him, not the other way around." Dan arched his brows, awaiting confirmation.

He wasn't going to stop, and I laughed in spite of my irritation. "His mother came unglued on me for not coming to a family reunion because I had other plans. I told Brad his mother wasn't in charge of my life, and he took her side. Again. I may have called him a few names."

"Like what?"

"Narcissistic, knuckle-dragging control freak."

The warmth of his laugh eased the sting of the memory. He gestured toward the house.

"Do you want help turning out lights?"

"No, but thanks for coming to check on me."

Now I just felt stupid. Not only had I called 911 over nothing more than a probable electrical glitch, my neighbor had heard sirens and thought the place was burning down. Should I invite him in for coffee? A beer? Inviting a guy in for a beer at ten p.m. assumed a degree of familiarity we didn't share. Raider was still on my lap with his head out the window. Dan gave him a pat. Raid grabbed his sleeve and tugged.

"You've got my number. Call if you change your mind." Dan extricated his sleeve from Raider's teeth. He turned, his grin wicked. "See you later, Jess."

The omission of the *ie* was deliberate, but his voice did something with my name that made me want to invite him in, just on the chance he'd say it again. Instead, I dug my nails into the steering wheel and watched as he turned his pickup and drove down the lane. The man was either a smooth-talking flirt or a potential stalker.

I pulled the Jeep into the garage and powered down the door, which closed with a reassuring *thunk*. Nothing was in the house and nothing could get in. Everything was fine.

Everything was, in fact, not fine.

I stepped through the laundry room door straight into a swirl of music and froze. I'd forgotten Brad's comment about the sound system. I couldn't identify the tune. It was soft, with a hint of melancholy, and it filled the house.

I lowered my purse and gear bag to the floor and took a moment to regret dismissing Dan's offer to help turn off the lights. Raider trotted ahead of me, tail wagging with a complete lack of concern as I eased toward the kitchen.

I half expected to find a radio blasting WMT, the AM station out of Cedar Rapids that plays old-time music requests on Sunday afternoon. But it was Tuesday night, and I didn't own a radio.

Something rippled against my skin with a feather light pulse, then retreated as if hesitant to overstep an invisible boundary. I stared into the house's brightly lit interior until my eyes burned as the notes danced on the air. Nothing wispy, or misty, or whatever ghosts were supposed to look like floated past.

"Hello?" My throat was so dry the words came out in a barely audible whisper. "Is someone here?"

The hair on the back of my neck was still standing as the music faded to silence.

I STOMPED THROUGH the house, making as much noise as I could, turning off the lights and not looking over my shoulder. Raider carried a tennis ball as he happily accompanied me from room to room. That made me feel better. If he wasn't worried, neither was I.

Despite both Dan and Brad's encouragement to call them if I needed anything, what I needed was the opinion of someone who dealt with house infrastructure for a living. I called Matt Grimm.

"I thought you had the wiring inspected before you moved in." Matt's sensible tone eased my nerves.

"I did. One of the previous owners replaced all the old knob and tube, fuse box stuff. It's on breakers now, and it all checked out." Which in no way accounted for anything, especially the music.

"It wouldn't hurt to have it rechecked. Wiring in those old places can be a nightmare. Hey, Kerri wants to talk."

There was the sound of scuffling as he handed off his phone, then Kerri's voice said brightly, "Maybe your ghost was saying hello."

"Ghosts don't need to turn on lights. They float around in the dark and crap like that." I ignored the random lights equal spirits equation that had settled firmly in my mind, along with the music earworm. I splashed milk into a saucepan and turned on a burner. Hot cocoa was the universal cure for jangled nerves.

"The deputy didn't find anything suspicious?" Kerri pressed.

"Nothing. Dispatch sent Brad."

She made a strangled noise. "How'd that go?"

"As well as you'd expect. Then Dan showed up."

"Dan? Oh, your hot neighbor!"

"He's not my hot neighbor." Well. Yeah. He kinda was.

"Mmph." Kerri made a noncommittal noise.

I added cocoa, sugar, and vanilla to the warming milk and stirred.

"Brad came blasting out here like Bonnie and Clyde were in the attic. Dan heard the sirens and came over to make sure the place wasn't on fire."

"That was nice of him."

I ignored her emphasis on *nice* and mumbled something about people living in the country looking out for each other. I didn't mention the music or the ribbon of energy that slid across my skin like an inquisitive touch. That was a whole different issue, one I needed to come to grips with before trotting it out for anyone else's inspection.

"Do you ever wonder what happened in your house before you moved in?" Kerri asked.

I scowled at the phone. "That sounds like the trailer for a horror movie."

"You could ask Susanne about it."

"That's a long shot. She told me two generations of the Cameron family lived here before it started changing hands, but I don't think she knows much more."

"Call the museum," Kerri suggested, referencing the Lenox County Historical Society. "They keep files on historic properties. I know there's one on your place, but I never had time to sit down with it."

She agreed to come help paint the next day, and we hung up. I poured the cocoa into a mug and dumped in a handful of marshmallows, full-sized, not mini. Raider poked me in the leg. I tossed him a marshmallow, which he caught with an unerring snap and chewed contemplatively.

I built a fire in the living room fireplace while my mind spun in a dozen directions. Was I supposed to embrace the ghost story as a requisite for living here? If I embraced it, would the ghost leave me alone? If I didn't, would the ghost beat me over the head with a skillet until I came around? Could I live with a ghost? None of the previous owners could, apparently.

That was silly. There were no such things as ghosts. But what if there were? What if my un-belief existed only because I'd never encountered anything that made me think otherwise?

When the fire was crackling, I retrieved *Ghost Towns of Lenox County* and settled into my recliner. Raider sprawled in front of the fireplace with his tennis ball. He swatted it with a paw, then watched it ricochet off the baseboard and roll back.

The chapter on Walnut Bluff showed photos of the devastation from the 1919 tornado. A few still-standing chimneys, interspersed with skeletal tree trunks, were all that remained. The once-proud little town had all the ambiance of a bomb crater.

I read the florid text accompanying the photos, but it didn't tell me anything I didn't already know. Once again, it was noted "The behemoth storm ascended into the heavens as it reached the property line of Gavin and Moira Cameron, saving their gracious homestead at the eleventh hour."

I read on. The storm's force altered the course of the Iowa River. Where the Iowa bordered my land, a channel that formerly looped in a horseshoe now made a hard ninety-degree turn and ran straight as an arrow. Mother Nature had certainly unleashed her fury that devastating July afternoon.

A blurry photo of a tombstone on the last page seemed out of place until I read the copy. It had been placed in the Sand Creek Township Cemetery by the parents of the man who'd gone missing in the storm, the one whose body was never found. I squinted at the picture. The granite marker was engraved *Luke Jameson Bauer, March 19, 1899—July 4, 1919, Son of John and Martha Bauer, Beloved of Sarah Cameron*

Holy crapweasel.

Raider's head snapped up as I inhaled sharply. Midway across the room, his tennis ball stopped rolling.

Beloved of Sarah Cameron

Sarah Cameron had known the missing man. Not only known him, but loved him so much his parents included her name on his memorial stone. I watched the fire burn to embers and thought about ghosts with unfinished business.

CHAPTER 4

"THAT'S AWESOME!" KERRI was effervescent when I shared my discovery with her.

"How do you figure?"

"I bet they were engaged. I bet that's why she never married." She beamed. "I bet she loved him so much she spent her whole life mourning him. No body, no closure, there's your unfinished business. It's a classic haunting scenario."

That's what I was afraid of. I applied my brush to the wall before the pale lavender blue paint dripped.

Rainy light flowed through the bedroom windows, smoothing the rough plaster walls and softening the years of wear on the plank floor.

The house had aged with grace. Was Sarah Cameron equally resilient to the passage of time? Was I nuts for thinking this ghost story might have legs?

"You could have told me about Sarah's connection to this Luke guy earlier," I huffed. "You practically lived at the museum over the summer, and you went all nuts telling me about the ghost when I made an offer on the house."

"I didn't know! I just started helping there this year," Kerri said defensively. "And they're so happy to have a volunteer who's under eighty, they have me climbing ladders and rearranging displays all the time. I never get a sit-down job in the archives."

"Have you ever seen a ghost?" I asked. I was afraid to give Kerri too much encouragement, but after last night, I welcomed her insight. She'd given this matter a lot more thought than I had. It was just a ghost, right? If that were the case—and that was a big if—it wasn't like I'd be violating a county ordinance for harboring a spirit without the proper permit. How complicated could it be?

"No," Kerri admitted. "But you don't have to see them to know they're here. They manifest their energy in different ways."

I was not prepared to deal with manifestations of energy.

"After a person's spirit stays in one place long enough, it gains enough power to communicate with the living," she continued.

I kept painting while Kerri fed me information I didn't know what to do with. Ghosts were supposed to be shimmering images in the moonlight or shadows where there wasn't an object to cast one. Although I'd seen nothing last night, something had been there, even if my feeble attempt at communication with it had failed.

"I WONDER IF someone else would have heard the music if they'd been here," Kerri mused, "or if it was only meant for you."

I suppressed a shiver as we ate sandwiches at the kitchen table after the painting was done. There was a fine line between my house being haunted in general and a spirit directing its energy specifically at me.

"Brad heard it," I said, "but he thought it was a sound system." Typical of him not to question why I was playing old-fashioned music. He'd just assume it was what I listened to when I wasn't with him. When I was with him, we'd listened to music Brad liked.

"It has to be Sarah Cameron," Kerri said with finality. "She's still here because of her connection to that Bauer boy."

"So? What does she expect me to do about it?" Saying the words out loud didn't mean I believed. It just meant I was thinking about it.

I tossed Raid the rest of my sandwich as a peace offering. Wet weather had kept us confined to the house, and as a result, the dog had taken to burning off energy by flinging tennis balls around with reckless abandon. He'd flipped one into the paint bucket earlier.

"Speaking of doing things, I've got company payroll to finish." Kerri stood. "I suppose you want help painting the living room, too?"

"Definitely. You in?"

"Why don't you ask your neighbor? I bet he'd help."

"I'm not asking a guy I barely know to help me with hours of manual labor. He's probably busy writing his next best seller."

Before Kerri could make any more suggestions, my phone dinged with an incoming text. I checked the screen and made a face.

Hi Jessie. Everything OK today? Take care.

"Something wrong?" Kerri asked.

"Brad's checking to see if I'm okay after last night."

Her brows shot up. "Maybe last night made him realize what a catch you are. Think he wants to get back together?"

"Oh, hell no. If he wanted to get back together, he'd make it clear he was giving me a second chance to earn Beverly's approval." I typed a polite *Fine thx* and sent it.

Kerri motioned through the dining room. "What's Raider doing?"

My dog was sitting by the front stairs, staring intently at nothing.

"You know animals can see ghosts," she said without waiting for an answer.

"Would you please stop with the ghost?" I tossed a tennis ball to Raid, who caught it and trotted off.

"You should throw a housewarming party," Kerri said. "Let Sarah know you intend to stay."

Ghosts aside, the idea was appealing. It would be wonderful to christen Fox Hollow as my fresh start. Or my last stand, depending on how you looked at it.

"You should definitely invite your neighbor," Kerri added.

"That would be more polite than asking him to paint for hours."

"He's gorgeous, and he lives just down the road. Why would you *not* invite him?"

I could think of a million reasons why, and Kerri and Mare were numbers one and two. They'd both been blessed with strong, happy marriages, and while they didn't view the absence of a ring on my finger as a character flaw on my behalf, they both thought the situation needed to be remedied.

Ironically, it was Kerri who introduced me to Brad last year. In her defense, she had no clue about his family dynamic that demanded perpetual involvement with all things Jennings to the exclusion of everything else. I didn't hold it against her.

"Go do your payroll," I said as Raider circled back into the kitchen to lean against my leg. "I'll call you about the housewarming."

As Kerri let herself out, Raid's tennis ball rolled into the room as if it were following him. Or me.

CHAPTER 5

THURSDAY, OCT. 25

AFTER BREAKFAST, I messaged Mare and Kerri, plus friends Conn Stirling and her partner TJ Meyer, also members of the Heartland DTC, about coming to a housewarming potluck on Saturday night.

New Age flower children, Conn and TJ had backed my decision to buy a run-down property in the middle of nowhere one hundred and ten percent. They deemed it "a bucolic journey that would heal my soul."

They also advised me to have every pre-purchase inspection known to mankind done before closing. Conn and TJ are romantics at heart, but as independent businesswomen, they are eminently practical.

I didn't include Dan on the group message. I'd call and invite him privately. If he said thanks but no thanks, I could deal with it. He wasn't obligated to jump into my social circle just because he lived down the road.

When my friends and I get together, we're that table you don't want to sit next to in a restaurant. Conversation topics range from collecting for artificial insemination to what disgusting thing our dog threw up on the bed at two a.m. We can do it while enjoying a meal and not miss a beat. It's a skill not everyone appreciates.

I spent the morning lost in the tedium of finishing unpacking. When my phone rang, I answered it absentmindedly even though I didn't recognize the number.

"Hey, it's Logan Barnes. I got your number from Kerri Grimm. She said it would be okay to call you. How are you doing?" a rapid-fire male voice asked.

I made a mental note to kill Kerri. Logan Barnes was a reporter for the *North Willow Sentinel*. I'd met him while I was freelancing, and we both ended up covering the same controversial city council meetings. You couldn't have told it by reading our respective stories. My pieces were factual accounts of the long-overdue firing of the public works director for staggering incompetence, while Logan created an inaccurate diatribe that splattered not only the former public works director but also the mayor and multiple city employees with undeserved muck. As a result, it was whispered the council had ordered a hit on him. Just a rumor, apparently, since he was still alive.

I gritted my teeth. "Hi, Logan. I'm good, you?"

"Great. Hey, I heard you bought that farmhouse west of town, the one that's haunted. I'd love to do a story about it, what it's like to live with a ghost, your restoration plans, all of that. It would make a great Halloween piece. Whattaya say?"

My answer was automatic. "I don't think so."

Logan was always looking for his next big scoop, but youth and exuberance only went so far when unaccompanied by any hint of common sense or accuracy. Logan was a loose cannon with a press pass, and my peace and quiet were not going to be the next thing he blew up.

"Aww, please? It would be a great seasonal piece. I'd love to come out at night, shoot some low-light stuff, get a first-hand—"

"No."

"But it's right before Halloween," he protested. "C'mon, the house is on the National Register of Historic Places and—"

"Actually, it's not." Logan hadn't even done the interview and already had his facts wrong.

"It could be. I promise not to take up too much time. I'll be in and out in less than an hour. Please?" I knew he pounded energy drinks like they were tap water, and I could feel his nervous vibe over the phone.

"I'm sorry, but no."

Liar. I wasn't sorry for turning him down, but I couldn't blame him for trying. I understood what it was like to be chasing a story on deadline.

"I just moved in. I'm not even unpacked. And the whole haunted thing really isn't a thing." Liar, liar.

"Oh." The disappointment in his voice was etched with annoyance. "Well, if you change your mind, you know where to find me." He clicked off.

"Idiot." I put the phone down, and looked at Raider. He thumped his tail in agreement.

"Come on," I said, "we're going exploring."

Yesterday's rain had moved out, leaving the air crisp as cider. Raider spun in delighted circles as we set out through the pasture, following faint tracks of a long-forgotten farm lane that edged the fence line.

The hills rolled with a deceptive gentleness that had my thighs burning as I crested the top of each rise, but the view was worth it. Beyond the boundaries of little bluestem and switchgrass, the landscape sprawled in a sienna quilt of half-harvested fields stitched together with the dark lines of fences.

Raider ran effortlessly, circled back to check on me, then raced off again, wild with freedom. About three-quarters of a mile from the house, the pasture gave way to a thick belt of oak, chestnut, and hickory trees along the river bluff. The sweeping expanse of the Iowa River valley spread below.

I stepped over the sagging, woven-wire fence that separated grassland from timber. Raid jumped it easily, and we moved into the trees. Waterfalls of sunlight spilled through flaming copper and scarlet leaves, casting the afternoon in a fairy tale glow. In a few months, the fiery embers of this season would be covered by the diamond white of snowfall, followed by a carpet of wildflowers in the dappled sunlight of spring.

My heart soared at the prospect of watching this kaleidoscope of hues weave one season into the next. The land was mine to enjoy any time I pleased. I could hike with Raider to my heart's content, soaking in the sun and wind like they were sacraments. For a heartbeat, I wished I had a human partner to share it with, a soulmate whose presence would double my joy. Except I was pushing forty, and if I hadn't found that person by now, it probably wasn't going to happen. I dismissed a twinge of emptiness, refusing to let it spoil this golden afternoon.

Raider bounded back and leapt up so his paws were on my chest. I pressed my forehead against his and kissed his nose. He clacked his teeth in happy approval. I had my dog and my wonderful old house. What else did I need?

The ground near the trees leveled to gentle swells that were more user-friendly than the open field's thigh-busting hills. I followed Raider's lofted tail through the tapestry of sunlight and shadow and wandered through a group of massive chestnut trees into a small glade.

I'd tilted my face up to admire the sun playing through the leaves when an unseen object snagged my boot. I pitched forward, landing in a graceless sprawl atop a tumble of leaf-covered rocks.

"Oomph! Ouch—damn it!" The undignified landing left me momentarily stunned. Raider circled me, expressing concern with sniffs and licks.

"Get off, dog, I'm fine." Wincing, I pushed up into a sit.

The outline of what remained of a low stone wall was barely visible under the fallen leaves. It encompassed a level area approximately forty feet wide by thirty feet long. Portions of the wall remained intact while others tilted crazily in defiance of gravity or, like the part I'd stumbled over, had crumbled entirely. Stunted saplings had taken root in several places, and a burnished bronze mass of Virginia creeper was overrunning one corner of the plot.

A hasty inventory of my person indicated bruises but no breaks. As I braced a hand in the leaves to get up, my fingers encountered another stone. Unlike the irregular field stones of the wall, this one was uniformly flat. With Raider pressed close to see what exciting thing I might do next, I brushed away the leaves. A flat slab of stained, white granite with a rounded top emerged. Time had eroded the carved words on the gravestone.

Double crapweasel. I'd found Bishop Cemetery without even trying.

The thrill of discovery lifted me to my knees. I cleared the remaining vegetation from the stone, but exposure to the elements and a crust of gray-green lichen made the engraving illegible. The deceased's name began with an A. The rest was anyone's guess. The date was 1865.

With apologies to Albert or Abigail for crashing onto them, I climbed to my feet. One knee of my jeans was ripped, and my jacket was smeared with dirt. Raider looked at me like he couldn't take me anywhere.

I started toward the opposite end of the small burial ground where a lone intact portion of the wall sported an opening that might have once held a gate. I took two steps and fell in a hole camouflaged by fallen leaves. I landed with a choice swear word, then collected my newly bruised limbs, annoyed at my determination to break a leg. The hole was about six feet long, three feet wide and several feet deep.

I vaulted out of it with a degree of agility inspired by no small amount of shock at having landed in what looked like a grave. I'd watched too many seasons of *The Walking Dead* to wait for a decaying hand to grab my ankle.

I dropped down on a stable section of the stone wall, my heart racing. Abandoned cemeteries should not have open graves. Raider pushed his head into my lap as I sat there, trying to get a grip. Maybe I was reading too much into this. Maybe the hole was the result of a groundhog enlarging its burrow. Yeah. Right. Groundhog burrows aren't coffin-shaped.

I walked back and surveyed the hole. Raider leaped into it, snuffled around and leaped back out. It wasn't deep enough to be an actual grave, unless whoever dug it had stopped without finishing. That begged the question of whether they intended to put something in or take something out. Neither was a comfortable thought.

The dry dirt along the edges crumbled at my touch. The digging wasn't recent. The shiver that ran down my spine was replaced by irritation. Was this some kind of high school Halloween prank? A dare to dig in an abandoned graveyard near a haunted house? It sounded exactly like the sort of dumbass thing bored, small-town kids would do. I'd certainly done my share of stupid things as a teenager.

Calling law enforcement to report this minor vandalism didn't seem warranted. A hole in the dirt didn't constitute real damage even if it was on private property, and with my luck, Brad would be all too happy to take the call. I made another mental note to ask Susanne why she hadn't told me about the cemetery. I'd have probably found it at some point, thanks to Mare's mention, but it was disconcerting to discover someone with a shovel had found it, too.

I let it go. Halloween would soon be over, and with it, any ridiculous pranks involving graveyards.

I whistled for Raid and worked my way to the edge of the bluff. Below, sunlight reflected dizzyingly off the dark surface of the Iowa River. Vertigo reminded me not to be stupid and I stepped back. Buoyed by a sense of adventure on this golden afternoon, my dog and I paralleled the bluff for a quarter mile, then climbed the fence back into the pasture. We discovered a wide stream with crystal water coursing over a rock-strewn bottom. Raid brought me a stick, and I threw it, much to his delight.

We followed the tree-lined creek, me throwing and him fetching, until the shadows began to stretch long and purple. Raid was still vibrant with inexhaustible Malinois energy when we got back to the house. I grabbed a handful of treats and a tennis ball and tried to steal a few minutes of heelwork outdoors before the day faded.

My dog did his part, trotting with his head up, parallel to my left hip, eyes locked on my face as we danced through a choreography of speed changes, turns and halts. My timing was off, though, and my footwork was sloppy as my mind kept going back to the hole in the cemetery. I was almost relieved when the sound of tires on gravel interrupted us.

CHAPTER 6

THE LATE AFTERNOON sun softened the dents and rust on Dan Sinclair's pickup, making it look marginally better than it had in the hard light of day. He parked and got out, rough and unshaven as the first two times we'd met. That's an observation, not a complaint.

He surveyed my ripped jeans and muddy coat. "What happened to you?"

"Went for a walk."

"Sounds relaxing."

"Not the way I did it."

Before Dan could reply, Raider shot past us. He put his front paws on the driver's side door of the pickup and jammed his nose against the window. Inside, a dog bounced on the seat in either a fit of joy or rage.

"Raid, come!" I wasn't worried about him damaging the vehicle's paint—it was long past the point of aesthetics—but it was rude to let him agitate someone else's dog. He spun and raced back.

"It's all right," Dan said. "That's Ruby." The double-masked face of a blue Australian cattle dog peered through the windshield. "Come meet her. Bring Fangs."

We walked to the pickup. Again, I noticed the slight hitch in his easy stride. I'm used to studying canine gait and structure, and it's a skill that easily jumps species, especially when the species in question bears studying. This infirmity did not suggest weakness but instead emphasized a quiet strength. I wondered what caused it.

Dan opened the door, and Ruby jumped out. She was a beautifully mottled mix of gray, white and tan fur with black splotches. She had an athletic build with dark, upright ears and a tail that wagged confidently as she greeted me. She touched noses with Raider, then the two dogs spun in a circle of mutual sniffing.

"She's named after a character in your first book, isn't she?" I said. "Lieutenant Ruby Murphy in *Corsair Dawn*."

Dan leaned against the pickup and crossed his arms. "You figured me out. I hoped I'd just get to be that guy who lives down the road."

"Take it up with Mare. She blew your cover."

"I'll forgive her. You read military fiction?" He looked me up and down without apology. "You don't look like most of the people who come to my book signings."

"And why is that?"

"You're female." His sheepish grin said he felt at least a little guilty for stereotyping.

"Thanks for noticing." I suspected plenty of fans were female, and it had nothing to do with military fiction. He had that Han Solo, scruffy-looking Nerf-herder thing going on, and damned if he didn't make his beat-to-hell pickup look good just by leaning on it.

"I bought your first book at Mare's shop," I said, scrambling for safe ground. "My ex kept it."

Dan's schoolboy grin faded to neutrality, and I

could have kicked myself. References to broken relationships were a guaranteed conversation killer. The silence stretched as long as the lengthening shadows.

"Divorced? Sorry it didn't work out," he said cautiously.

"It worked out fine until he got caught," I said.

Dan tapped the hood of the pickup. "Get in. I'll show you the township."

I blew out a breath, relieved he'd taken my dismissal at face value. "My mother taught me not to get into cars with men who want to show me things." I was only half joking.

"Bring Fangs, if that'll make you feel better."

I still didn't say anything.

He spread his arms in defeat. "I'm your only neighbor. I'd be the cops' first suspect if you disappeared." His mouth quirked in a crooked smile that was as genuine as it was attractive. Damn.

I climbed in, and the dogs piled between us in a happy tangle. The truck's interior was as shabby as its exterior, but when Dan turned the key, the engine purred like it had just come off the showroom floor. He turned left at the end of the lane, then rumbled across the ancient steel trestle bridge over Sand Creek.

"Have you lived out here long?" I asked.

"Five years."

I wanted to know what brought him here, but before I could form the question without seeming nosy, he said, "You've got a lot of house for one person." He kept his eyes on the road and let the unasked question hang in the air.

"Probably," I agreed, which effectively ended that topic. Alone didn't mean available, and if he were testing the waters, the sooner he figured that out, the better.

Cat's Back Road dipped and twisted and made odd turns wherever it pleased while paralleling its namesake, Cat's Back Hill. Trees edged the road, catching the gathering twilight in their branches and releasing it as we pushed through them into open farmland.

"There's my place." Dan pointed to a white farmhouse and a few outbuildings set back from the road, but he didn't stop. "It was built in 1919, after that tornado leveled the original house. You've heard about the tornado?"

"Once or twice."

"The family who lived there had four sons. The oldest one disappeared in that storm, and they never found his body."

I jerked from the scenery to his profile. Dan lived on the old Bauer place, the last property destroyed by the tornado before it reined in at Fox Hollow's doorstep. The night we met, he'd said he lived at the first place to the west, but I hadn't made the connection.

"The guy I bought my house from told me all about it. He bought the place directly from the Bauer family." Dan gave me one of those rogue grins. "You like ghost stories?"

"Oh, stop it. Not you, too."

His grin widened. "People say Sarah Cameron's

spirit won't rest until she finds out what happened to her true love."

I didn't answer, not wanting to encourage him. It didn't matter.

"Legend has it, Luke planned to ask her to marry him that evening at the Walnut Bluff Independence Day celebration, but he was on the road when the storm hit. Sarah never saw him again."

So it had been more than a fledgling romance—they'd planned to become husband and wife. That explained the inscription on the tombstone. *Beloved of Sarah Cameron* I gave up my pretense of disinterest.

"Did she know he was going to ask her that night?" To have one's fiancé die on the day that should have linked their lives together was even worse than finding the man I'd vowed to love, honor and cherish enjoying the charms of another woman in our bed.

"Maybe. She and Luke were childhood sweethearts, and Sarah's brother Ian was good friends with Luke, so there's a pretty good chance she knew." He guided the pickup around a curve, and Fox Hollow's roof showed through the tree canopy in the near distance. "So, what's it like to live with a ghost?"

I looked over the dogs and gave him my best no-such-thing-as-ghosts smile. "Nothing in my house is going bump in the night."

Technically, that was true. There'd been breezes and lights and music, but no bumping.

"Maybe you haven't been there long enough."

"Seriously, stop it."

He laughed, and the husky sound invited me to join him. "You're not having any of it, are you?" he said as he turned into my lane.

I hadn't told him about the music playing from nowhere Tuesday night when the lights came on. Or the almost tangible ribbons of energy that wove their way through the rooms, dancing off my skin and making me wonder if I'd been drinking too much coffee. I was having a little more of it than I wanted to admit.

Dan stopped in front of my house. I took a deep breath. "Are you doing anything Saturday night?" The words tumbled out in a rush, and I kept going before I lost momentum. "I'm having some friends out for a housewarming party. Come around six if you want."

Surprise highlighted his lean face, but he didn't answer.

"Bring your girlfriend," I added hastily, "or whoever."

"It'll just be me. Thanks, I'll look forward to it."

My mind spun. I'd been prepared for the innocuous *thanks but I already have plans* or a promise he'd get back to me, only he never would. Which honestly might be for the best because the more I saw of him, the more I wanted to see of him, and that couldn't possibly go anywhere good.

"I'll bring the wine, if that's okay," he said. "How much?"

"How much what?" I said, trying to figure out why a guy who looked like he did would be available on a Saturday night on such short notice.

"Are you always this difficult? How many people are coming?"

I mentally regrouped and ran through the guest list out loud for his benefit. "Kerri and Matt Grimm, Mare, Conn Stirling and TJ Meyer. They're all dog training friends except for Mare." I thought of her incorrigible Pembroke Welsh Corgi, Poe, and added, "She has a dog but she doesn't train it. Although she should."

"Dog training friends?" Dan mused. "As opposed to normal friends?"

I don't have any normal friends. Brad had tried to remedy that condition by encouraging me to spend time with his sister, Amy, and her gang of gal pals. I'd endured getting my hair and nails done, shopping at boutiques, and squealing over scented candles at home decorating parties. It hadn't been a resounding success.

Fortunately, Amy and her family moved to North Carolina about the same time I ran out of patience with manicures and candles. Like Brad's brother's move six months earlier, Amy flying the coop had created a great deal of angst for Bev. That was when she started pursuing the family genealogy like she was hot on a quest for the Holy Grail. I guess it was her version of therapy.

"We all train and show in competitive obedience." I left it at that. Dog sports are a lifestyle, not a hobby.

"Is that what you were doing when I got here?" he asked. "It looked very...precise."

"Yes. Heelwork. Thanks."

I was flattered he'd noticed but didn't elaborate. People always say they want to know more until you actually tell them. I slid out of the pickup, and Raider bounded off to re-establish his territory.

"Call me if you need help ghost wrangling," Dan said.

I paused in the half-open door. He sat with his left arm across the steering wheel, his face illuminated by the dim light of the dashboard. His mouth curved with the hint of a smile, his eyes as dark and deep as the timber at night. A tingle that had absolutely nothing to do with ghosts ran down my spine and detonated somewhere low in my belly.

"Go home," I said. "I'll see you Saturday."

I TOOK A STEAMING shower and counted the day's bruises, then pulled on thermal leggings and a sweatshirt, fed Raider, made a sandwich, and built a fire. The fireplace was quickly becoming a guilty pleasure at the end of the day, even if I did have to haul wood in and ashes out.

Straightening from the hearth, I came eye to eye with two balls of blue calico fabric resting on the mantel. It had been four days, but I distinctly remembered putting the second ball on the kitchen counter. Raider might have snagged them off the counter, but he hadn't put either one on the mantel.

I poked them tentatively. Nothing happened. Maybe Kerri put them in here when she came to paint. She always says I have zero decorating skills.

I settled into my recliner with my supper and one of the beers Dan had brought. It's not drinking alone if your dog is there.

Flames crackled in the fireplace as I pulled a blanket across my legs and opened a search engine on my laptop. I typed in *D.W. Sinclair author*. I'd read exactly one of Dan's books and knew nothing about him except a few surface level facts. He had a dog, and she appeared well cared for. He was attractive in the understated way of guys who don't give a damn about being attractive. I'd enjoyed the impromptu tour of Sand Creek Township more than I'd expected. I'd enjoyed him more than I expected. And I'd invited him to dinner.

The search rolled up a list of book reviews, and I read the publisher's release regarding his latest novel.

"Following his debut novel *Corsair Dawn*, D.W. Sinclair has taken fans of World War II fiction on one heart-pounding adventure after another. His subsequent novels, *South Pacific Wind*, *Ironbottom Sound*, *Silk Stockings*, and *The Rendova Mission* have garnered resounding response from readers and critics alike.

"The Army veteran's newest release, *Dance Over Bougainville*, showcases his gift for bringing the men and women of the United States' armed forces to life in gritty, white-knuckle tales. The author lives in the rolling hills of eastern Iowa farm country where he is restoring a century-old farmhouse."

Army vet? A combat injury would explain the limp. I tucked the house restoring claim into a mental folder labeled Ways Men Can Be Genuinely Useful. A neighbor skilled in do-it-yourself home repair could come in handy, but if Dan was working on his own house, he probably wouldn't have time to muck around on mine. Besides, Fox Hollow was *my* project.

I skimmed a few interviews in publishing magazines, but Dan's remarks were directed at his craft with an almost deliberate lack of attention to personal details. His Facebook page referenced upcoming book signings and promotions for his latest novel but little else. His profile picture was a three-quarter angle portrait, steely eyed with a three-day beard. Damn and double damn.

I sipped my beer, feeling mildly guilty about enjoying my voyeurism. He was welcome to do the same to me if he wanted. My online life was an open book. The only things he'd find would be the dog-centric ramblings of an Iowa farm kid who'd gone to college on scholarships from the Iowa Cattlemen's Association and the county Farm Bureau. I'd graduated from Iowa State University, started my career as a journalist, and gotten serious about training dogs. My life was absolutely unremarkable.

I continued scrolling Dan's social media. Reviewers praised his books. An announcement noted he would appear on a panel at a writers' conference in New Orleans in February. A photo with the mention of a reunion showed him with several other men, all clad in desert camo fatigues, arms thrown over one another's shoulders. The desertscape in the background suggested he had served in the Middle East. There were no pictures of him with a girlfriend. Or a boyfriend. Fool me once...

I clicked back to the Google search results, scrolled through a dozen more listings and hit pay dirt.

A magazine article dated six years prior showed a photo of Dan with his arm around the waist of an attractive blonde woman. He was devil-may-care in a dark suit. She was elegant in a cocktail dress, her hair swept into an updo and her sculpted porcelain features glowing.

The picture was one of several candid shots accompanying a story about a writers' awards ceremony. The cutline underneath said only Dan Sinclair and fiancée Hannah Wintergarden.

Had Hannah Wintergarden become Hannah Sinclair? If not, why not? If so, where was she now? When I'd mentioned my divorce, Dan's response hadn't indicated he'd endured a similar emotional avalanche. Then again, he wasn't obligated to share his life story just because I referenced the train wreck of my own.

A faint sound pulled my thoughts away from Hannah's unknown status. Footfalls descended briskly down the front stairs.

My fingers froze on the keyboard. The steps crossed the landing in front of the stained-glass window and continued downward. The hallway was lit only by light spilling in from the living room, but from where I sat, I could see the base of the staircase.

I stopped breathing. My eyes strained into the semi-darkness. Each pounding beat of my heart matched the footsteps of whatever—whoever—was coming.

The footsteps stopped. I stared until my eyes burned. The air hummed with expectation. Then with a soft pop, the tension broke, as if something that was invisible in the first place had just vanished.

On the hearth, Raider thumped his tail.

CHAPTER 7

FRIDAY, OCT. 26

I CRESTED A RISE in the pasture and paused to ease my aching thighs. Under the stained-glass sunrise, the surrounding land rose and fell like laundry pinned in a summer breeze. No wonder Sarah Cameron chose to spend her entire life here.

Last night's footsteps echoed in my mind. I uneasily accepted it being Sarah, but was the phenomenon nothing more than trapped energy replaying in an endless loop? Or did it have a purpose?

I was still pondering the purpose of ghosts when Raid and I reached the cemetery wall. The fallen leaves atop tumbled stone created nature's version of an MC Escher print. Not trusting my depth perception and not wanting a repeat of the previous day's theatrics, I started to skirt the plot, then stopped.

Next to the hole I'd stumbled into was another shallow depression, barely discernable under the leaves. Had it been there yesterday but gone unnoticed in my haste to get out of the first one? I stepped in for a closer look.

Mare's buried treasure story flashed through my mind. I couldn't picture any of the book club's plump, cardigan-clad matrons tromping around the woods with a glass of merlot in one hand and a shovel in the other, looking for X marks the spot.

Besides, the tale only mentioned gold buried somewhere near the trading post, not specifically in the cemetery. Unless someone knew something I didn't, which was entirely possible.

I scuffed my boots through the leaves. While the occasional stone lump suggested a fallen grave marker, they gave no sense of orderly rows. If something aside from the dearly departed was buried here, it would be hard to find without digging up the permanent residents by accident.

My boot kicked up a flash of artificial color amidst the leaves. I bent to pick up the neon pink flag, the kind utility companies use to mark underground lines, but it wouldn't budge. The flag's wire was embedded in the ground and bent at a ninety-degree angle under the leaves.

My heart jolted. I was damned sure there were no underground utility lines out here. Maybe X did mark the spot.

I reined in my imagination. It was absurd to think someone had discovered buried gold on my property and was in the process of digging it up. My brain, already on edge with ghost stories thanks to Kerri, was now jumping to conclusions thanks to Mare. I looked around the forgotten little plot that was slowly being reclaimed by nature.

There were laws protecting historic burial sites, not to mention the ethics of digging in one. Was a bit of dog-eared folklore worth risking a prison sentence? Digging up the entire cemetery searching for an unknown quantity of coins would take a ridiculous amount of effort, not to mention the chance of digging up things that were not gold. A metal detector might pinpoint potential targets, but it couldn't differentiate between coins and metal buttons on the clothing of a body laid to rest more than a century ago. The process would be a matter of painstaking trial and error. Yet the site was isolated enough to accommodate just that. People could come and go as they pleased, unseen from either the road or my house.

Irritated, I yanked the flag out of the ground. As I folded the thin wire and stuffed it in my hip pocket, Raider began capering around with the tell-tale body language that indicated he'd found a treasure of his own. Eyes sparkling, he frolicked over to show me his prize. I expected a bone of some long-deceased animal and was surprised when he dropped a chunk of stone into my hands.

I fumbled in my pocket for one of the little biscuits I carry for this exact purpose. He crunched the treat, pleased with his trade, then watched as I examined the object in case I decided to give it back.

I thumbed dirt away to reveal a chunk of pottery slightly smaller than my palm. The jagged edge of a fresh break gleamed in contrast to the age-crackled pale gray glaze. I recognized it as the rim of an antique pickling crock. I had several in my house, heirlooms from my grandparents.

Nothing explained what it was doing in an abandoned cemetery or where the rest of the crock was. I tucked the sherd into my pocket for later consideration and followed the south end of a northbound Malinois through the autumn morning.

I CALLED SUSANNE when Raider and I got back to the house. My request for information about both the previous owners and Sarah Cameron's lingering spirit hit a not unexpected brick wall.

"I only had the listing for this sale." Susanne's voice was friendly but firm. "If you think something's going on, maybe you should hire one of those paranormal investigation groups."

I grimaced. I hadn't mentioned anything going on but Susanne, like everyone else, was determined to put a ghost in Fox Hollow, whether one belonged there or not. Being pursued by people wielding video cameras and electromagnetic recording gadgets sounded like a guaranteed way to annoy a ghost.

I tried to juxtapose Sarah's spirit against the sunshine pouring through the kitchen windows and casting rainbows on the white porcelain sink. The energy that radiated through the house last night had been neutral, neither antagonistic nor friendly. I could live with that. I switched to my next reason for calling.

"Did you know about the cemetery in the timber?"

After a pause, Susanne said, "Yes, it was listed on the property description."

I waited for her to say more. She didn't. Maybe she had mentioned the cemetery, but since it hadn't been a pressing problem, like locating the leach field for the septic system, I'd promptly forgotten about it.

"I'm considering restoring it," I said.

The lie rolled easily off my tongue. If I told Susanne I thought someone was treasure hunting out there, the North Willow grapevine would have it all over town before lunch.

"Lenox County has a pioneer cemetery commission, maybe they could help with a grant," she said. "Hey, are you going to the Midlands shows next weekend?"

I sighed. I'd have to go elsewhere if I wanted to find out, as Kerri put it, what went on in my house before I bought it.

Susanne and I chatted briefly about upcoming dog shows, which I was not attending due to a total lack of preparedness. She said she'd see me Tuesday night at the club, and we hung up.

I washed the potsherd from the cemetery and wiped it dry. It couldn't possibly have come out of one of the graves there—no one got buried with their pickling crocks—yet there it was.

I swaddled it in bubble wrap left over from moving and stashed it in the butler's pantry. It felt like a piece of a larger puzzle, but I didn't have any idea what the finished image was supposed to look like.

Still grasping for sources who could tell me more about the house and surrounding property, I rummaged in the kitchen junk drawer and pulled out an area phone book. I flipped to the residential listings under C.

Cain, Campbell, Carlyle. No Cameron.

Again, with B.

Baker, Banes, Baughman. No Bauer.

The families were gone. Sarah's brother Ian Cameron's descendants and Luke Bauer's brothers' kids and grandkids were of the generation that would probably still have landline phones, but there were no listings for those names in North Willow or nearby towns. Short of calling area care centers to see if they housed elderly descendants of these families, there wasn't anyone I could visit. The names themselves had become ghosts.

AFTER SEVERAL TEDIOUS hours of dusting and vacuuming, during which my mind created and discarded increasingly bizarre scenarios to account for the holes in Bishop Cemetery, I was no further ahead than when I started, but at least the house looked nice.

I arranged three antique glass kerosene lamps and an oval wooden bowl atop the gleaming wood of the fireplace mantel. On a whim, I went back to the attic, found more of the calico fabric balls in the box at the top of the stairs and put them in the bowl. My fingertips tingled by the time I got the calico arranged the way I wanted it. I wiped my fingers on my pants and admired my turn-of-the-century still life.

I finished my grocery and hardware store lists and drove to North Willow. At Jackson's Hardware, I chose paint from a historic homes palette for the living room and stocked up on spackling compound, masking tape, and roller covers while the paint cans jiggled on the mixing machine.

"Jessie! How are things going?"

I looked up to see Brad striding down the aisle. He wasn't in uniform but walked like the world owed it to him to get out of his way. My hackles went up. My things weren't any of his business.

"Fine," I said. Ghostly footsteps on the stairs and open graves in abandoned cemeteries notwithstanding.

"You could sell that place for a profit after you clean it up, then buy something nicer in town." He smiled with the arrogant condescension I'd once mistaken for sincere interest. He'd been interested all right, until he realized I wasn't going to defer to him—or his mother—every time a conflict arose.

He'd never loved me. He'd loved what he thought he could turn me into. To be honest, I hadn't loved him either. I'd blindly mistaken pleasant companionship (as long as we did things Brad liked) and decent sex (as long as we did things Brad liked) for a genuine emotional connection. It still hurt to think even in that shallow commitment, he'd expected me to put him and his family's priorities first, as if nothing about me mattered at all.

"I'm not selling it." The paint mixing machine stopped. I took the buckets from the clerk and wondered what would happen if I dropped one on Brad's foot, accidentally, of course.

He shrugged. "Be careful out there, okay?"

I didn't reply. Brad hailed a passing customer and struck up a conversation about deer hunting. I paid for my supplies and left.

I DROVE AROUND North Willow's town square, past the Lenox County Extension Office and Brewed Awakenings, the coffee shop Beverly Jennings owned and operated. I love a skinny latte macchiato as much as the next girl, but hadn't dared go in there since Brad and I broke up. Bev would probably put rat poison in mine.

A help wanted sign perched in the window. It wouldn't take long to fill the empty position. Among the high school set, Brewed ranked high as one of the cool places for a part-time job.

There was an open parking space in front of A Likely Story, and on a whim, I stopped to see Mare. Bells tinkled as I stepped from autumn chill into the store's fragrant warmth. An undercurrent of chocolate twisted through the blast of pumpkin spice wafting from the kitchen.

"Hi, Jess!" Mare waved from a corner table. My heart skipped to see Dan sitting next to her. Then I remembered Hannah Wintergarden's sleek blonde perfection. If my jeans, faded thermal Henley, and windblown hair made a statement, it was only that I was low maintenance. Or had gone feral in the last week.

Stop it. Dan's taste in women had no bearing on my life, and the exquisitely fashionable Hannah didn't seem to be in the picture now anyway. I jammed my hands into my vest pockets to keep from doing something stupid, like fluffing my hair.

"McCallister." Dan sounded pleased to see me, unlike Brad's aren't-you-lucky-I'm-talking-to-you tone.

"Sinclair," I returned, wondering if we'd ever advance to using one another's first names.

"Dan stopped to sign some books for me," Mare said. "What brings you in?"

When I'd whipped into the parking spot, I'd planned to press her for more details on Dr. Aldrich's research regarding the potential gold stash on my land, but a girl can change her mind. I gestured toward the bookshelves.

I turned to Dan. "I need something to take my mind off ghosts."

With a nod, he rose and walked toward a shelf where a neatly hand-lettered sign proclaimed Fiction: Authors L – Z.

"What did you like most about *Corsair Dawn*?" he asked over his shoulder. No hint of ego edged the words, although as the author of multiple best-sellers, he had every right to expect a gushing review.

"Lieutenant John Hanson." I named the protagonist of the novel set in 1943. "He was torn up about leaving his girl back in the States, then he fell hard for that nurse in the field hospital, the one who didn't tell him she was married, and when he found out, that wrecked him all over again."

"So not the aerial combat or the fights in the officers' club?"

"Those were okay, too."

I bit my tongue. The testosterone-laden action adventure of *Corsair Dawn* had been crafted atop the undercurrent of a bittersweet love story, but I wasn't sure I wanted to go there with a guy whose professional image seemed to hinge on the former.

We stopped at the end of a shelf. Dan pulled out a volume and handed it to me. The dustcover of *South Pacific Wind* showed a girl with generous curves and hair styled in the victory rolls of the 1940s posed suggestively on the wing of a fighter plane.

"This is my second book. Lieutenant Hanson gets involved with Navy nurses running a black-market operation. Trouble ensues."

"Trouble ensues no matter where he goes," I said.

"That's what I like about him. He's not a ladies' man, but women are always chasing him."

"Usually the wrong women, for the wrong reasons." Heat bloomed in my cheeks. The first novel's love scenes had been rendered with a rough sensuality that left me liking Lieutenant Hanson a lot more. I wasn't going there, either.

Looking for an escape, I turned to find Mare waving me back to the table where she'd set a white porcelain mug of coffee next to a slab of sinful looking chocolate dessert.

"Dan's already passed judgment. I want a second opinion," she called.

Grateful for the respite, I took the book back to the table and sampled her offering. My eyes closed in bliss as flavors swirled on my tongue. "Mmmm, dark chocolate, peppermint, and *something*?"

"Espresso." Mare smiled. "I'll bring a pan to your place tomorrow."

I finished the last bite and fought an urge to lick the plate. Dan picked up a pen and pulled the copy of *South Pacific Wind* toward him. He scribbled something in the front cover, closed it, and pushed it back to me. Grinning, he tipped his hat. "Ladies, work calls. See you tomorrow night." He strolled out of the shop.

I flipped the cover open.

For Jess, welcome to Sand Creek Township. Boo! D.W. Sinclair.

He'd added a simple line drawing of a big-eyed ghost, floating under the words.

If you only knew, I thought.

"*See you tomorrow night?* You invited him to your housewarming?" Mare asked as she rang up the book.

"Yeah. Anything wrong with that?"

"No. Just, wow." She winked. "He's not much for the social scene."

"I asked him because he's my neighbor, and it seemed like the right thing to do." I made a face. "He may not want anything to do with me after he spends an evening with you guys."

I WAS IN THE bread aisle at King's Foods, North Willow's only grocery store, when I heard an impatient huff behind me. I turned and came face to face with Beverly Jennings. Oh, joy. It was two-for-one day on people I didn't want to see.

"Oh. I didn't recognize you." Her tone carried the same note of condescension as her son's, as if it were my fault for not being recognizable.

Beverly Jennings was what the Victorians would have called a handsome woman. Like her son, she was tall, her hair colored a precise blonde that yielded no surrender to gray. Despite the youthful boho tunic over leggings, she reminded me of a faded homecoming queen relying on Estee Lauder to stop the advance of time. Her eyeliner was an uneven smudge, and her foundation looked like she'd applied it with a trowel. Her hair was gathered untidily in a clip that would have been cute on someone forty years younger but made her head look like a bird was attempting to nest there.

"Hi," I said.

"I heard you bought the old Cameron place." Disapproval clung to her words.

"I did."

"Brad said you called him the night someone broke in."

"I called 911. No one broke in."

"I don't know why you want to live out there. Alone." Her lips tightened.

I smiled pleasantly but didn't say anything, enjoying not feeling obligated to justify my decisions. That annoyed her, and I realized with a jolt of guilty pleasure, I enjoyed that, too.

While Bev and I had never been besties, I'd respected her as a small business owner. She was a driving force in the North Willow Chamber of Commerce and gave her time generously to promoting the town. The whole Jennings family was a recruiting poster for North Willow citizenship.

Brad's father had served as Lenox County sheriff for nearly two decades before retiring. While we were dating, I'd watched Bev lay the groundwork for Brad to run for sheriff in next year's election. Unfortunately, this status as pillars of the community created a sense of entitlement that didn't take kindly to being rebuffed.

When I didn't answer, Bev demanded, "Why did you buy that house?"

"Because I like it." I picked up a loaf of bread at random and walked away.

IT WASN'T A LIE. I bought Fox Hollow because I liked the idea that the broken things there could be fixed, and its imperfections were what made it one-of-a-kind, not faults that made it inferior. The thought of calling it my home came with a soul-deep sense of belonging even though I hadn't even lived there for a week.

I startled when headlights flashed through the darkness behind me as I rattled across the bridge on Cat's Back Road. The vehicle came up fast, the glare filling my rearview mirror. I edged to the right, giving the impatient driver room to go around. Judging from the height of the lights, they belonged to a four-by-four pickup.

I slowed further. The Jeep's passenger-side tires left the gravel and bumped onto the thick weeds of the verge. Despite my polite relinquishing of the right-of-way, the truck remained yards from my rear bumper, high beams blazing.

I groaned. It was Friday night of North Willow's homecoming week, and no doubt a couple of high school kids were on their way to celebrate at a bonfire, probably with a head start on a case of beer provided by a non-ID-checking convenience store clerk.

To my right, a shallow ditch separated the road from a harvested cornfield. Fifty yards ahead, the shoulder fell away sharply as the road curved hard to the left to parallel Sand Creek. Dropping my tires off the edge there would guarantee rolling down the embankment into the water.

The pounding beat of hard rock music blared as the truck pressed recklessly closer. A tap on the bumper would send my vehicle tumbling.

It was now or never. Bracing myself, I pressed my foot on the accelerator and turned the wheel to the right just before the road curved. The Jeep lurched into the ditch, throwing me against the webbing of the shoulder harness, which locked with a hard click. Paint cans and groceries protested in the back seat. Headlights slashed arcs through the darkness as momentum carried me through the ditch and up the opposite bank.

If there'd been a fence, I would have smashed through it in a scene worthy of the best Hollywood stunt driving. I twisted the steering wheel to the left and the Jeep's tail end spun around, then stopped as I stomped the brake, facing the road. Furious, I flipped on my high beams.

The pickup sat amidst swirling dust. At least the alcohol-fogged driver had enough conscience to check on me. A window powered down.

Between the darkness, the distance and the dust, I couldn't see the occupants. I rolled down my window, but before I could say anything, a male voice yelled, "Get out!" then the truck lurched forward, spraying gravel, and the taillights vanished.

Fury and adrenaline surged through me in competing amounts. Damn kids. I swore at length, adding expletives to the initial accusation until I laughed at my descent into crotchety old-fogey-dom. Then I remembered Brad's words only a few hours prior.

Be careful out there.

I stopped laughing. An invisible band tightened around my chest. This was just a coincidence, nothing more. It hadn't been Brad's truck, and it was ludicrous to think he'd hire someone to run me off the road. It was just stupid kids, doing stupid kid things. *Get out?* Of what? I'd gotten out of their way for all the good it did.

My foot was still jammed on the brake pedal, my leg muscles clenched so tight they hurt. I took a couple of deep breaths and eased the Jeep along the edge of the field. Cornstalk stubble scraped the undercarriage, and the headlights cut silver beams through lingering dust as I searched for the field entrance.

After a minute of bouncing over rough ground, I found it. By the time I got home, my heartrate was back to normal. Teenagers. Homecoming hijinks. Beer. No need to make more of it than that.

Raider met me at the door, all tail and happy dog noises. I unloaded my shopping, fed him supper and slumped in my recliner. Raid took this as a sign I had nothing better to do and dropped a tennis ball in my lap.

"No ball-throwing in the house," I said.

Raider took his ball back, dropped it on the floor, play-bowed to it and smacked it with a paw. It sailed across the room, bumping to a stop by the pocket doors. After a moment, it rolled back, its fuzzy yellow surface bright against the dark boards. Raider caught it, chomped it happily, and repeated the process. Again, the ball returned to him. I still hadn't talked to Matt about floor jacks.

On impulse, I went to the garage and rummaged through a box of tools I'd kept from my dad's farm workshop. I pulled out a worn wooden level and marched back into the living room.

Raid abandoned his ball and helped me, mostly by getting in the way, as I crawled around on the floor, setting the level near all four walls and in the center of the room. The bubble remained perfectly centered every time. The floors were tabletop level.

I pulled a beer from the fridge, drank half of it while staring at the living room floor and decided not to overthink why balls rolled when there was no slant. Then I retrieved the notebook that contained my to-do lists.

No time like the present to finish the room-by-room inventory of supplies I needed. Today's paint purchase was just the beginning. With the notebook in one hand, the beer in the other and Raid accompanying me, I climbed the front stairs.

While the house had survived more than a century without anyone taking a paintbrush to the woodwork, that hadn't stopped a previous owner from slapping fake woodgrain DIY warehouse paneling along a section of the second-floor hallway.

I eyed it with suspicion, hoping it only reflected a misguided aesthetic and wasn't hiding a gaping section of broken plaster and lathe. Maybe there'd been water damage at some point. Maybe the roof still leaked despite previous owners' improvements. Maybe this was only the tip of an architectural disaster iceberg that extended to a load-bearing wall slowly disintegrating.

I reined my imagination in hard. One of the reasons I bought Fox Hollow was because the restoration work was largely cosmetic—time-consuming but no degree in structural engineering required. But with eleven rooms—no, ten, the kitchen was done—the sheer amount of it was staggering.

Facing it alone, I felt a cold wind blowing through my dream of sharing the process with a partner who loved it as much as I did. Mare and Kerri would help without being asked, but I didn't expect them to invest heart and soul in a place they didn't call home. Maybe Susanne was right. Maybe this was too much house. And it was just me. Alone. What had I been think—

No.

"I can damn well do it myself," I said out loud. "At least there won't be anyone telling me I'm doing it wrong."

In six months, I'd know if I'd made the right decision, and if not, I'd pack it in. No harm, no foul. A life lesson learned.

A woman laughed, a clear, pleasant sound, like wind chimes in a summer breeze.

I clenched the beer bottle and whirled around. If Kerri or Mare had dropped in, Raider would have barked to announce their arrival, but he hadn't made a sound. He trotted toward the head of the staircase.

Thanks to the previous owners' aversion to anything higher than forty-watt bulbs, shadows swathed the hallway in murky half-light. Raid stopped at the newel post, ears loosely back and tail wagging as he gazed upward and showed a little fang. I'd seen that body language a thousand times. It was his happy greeting face.

The hair on my forearms rose. I groped blindly for the wall behind me as my knees buckled. My fingers scraped plaster before closing over the wooden finial of the corner protector. I gripped the smooth wood and breathed in the faint dried flower and Murphy Oil Soap scents of the house.

I wasn't alone.

Energy hung in the air, unformed but undeniable. Slowly, I set the beer on the floor. I stepped forward and lifted my right hand, palm out. The air pressed back against my fingers, cool but solid, as if someone was pushing from the other side of an invisible barrier. My hand tingled. I needed to say something, but what did you say to a ghost?

"Are you okay with me living here?" My mouth was so dry the words came out in a croak. I heard the quick notes of that old-fashioned music, then with a dizzying lurch like an elevator rising too fast, it was over. I stood with my arm still raised in a cautious high-five. I flexed my fingers. The air beyond them was again simple oxygen and nitrogen.

Raider trotted back to my side. Electricity crackled on my fingertips, and tiny sparks flashed as I stroked his fur. I picked up my beer, sat down on the top step, and finished it in three gulps. I really should stop drinking on an empty stomach.

MARE WOULD SAY my Celtic heritage predisposes me to seeing ghosts, but I don't believe it. My ancestors may have dealt with banshees and the *bean nighe*, otherworldly creatures who washed bloodstains from the clothes of those doomed to die, but I'd grown up doing Midwest kid things—4-H club, marching band, showing livestock at the state fair, and cruising the hometown strip after Friday night football games. There was absolutely nothing in my past that would serve as a conduit to the paranormal, but here I was, carving another notch on my ghost-o-meter.

I didn't know if I should burn sage, or hold a séance or just nod and say hi when we passed in the hall. Sarah Cameron could keep flipping on the lights and rolling balls for my dog if she wanted. At the end of the day, I could live with that.

After supper, I made a nest in my recliner. Deciding to trade my ghost problem for my cemetery problem—if this kept up, I was going to need therapy—I typed *pioneer cemeteries* into the search engine on my laptop, then clicked and scrolled, skimming the entries.

"A pioneer cemetery is defined by Iowa law as one in which...fewer than twelve burials in the last fifty years...many were established in pastures or wooded areas...modern day upkeep is often carried out by community service groups or private landowners."

If there was a link between Bishop Cemetery and what had driven the five previous owners out of my house, I couldn't see it. I had no proof the previous owners had been driven out. People misjudged their degree of commitment to home restoration all the time, and with a place this big, there were perfectly normal reasons to leave.

Exhausted from rationalizing things I didn't understand, I opened the novel I bought that afternoon. Dan's masterful storytelling was a welcome distraction, and I read well past bedtime, enjoying the peaceful ambiance of the house.

As I fell asleep, the laughter in the upstairs hallway echoed in my mind. The tone had been one of pleased approval. At least Sarah seemed happy I was here. For now.

CHAPTER 8

Saturday, Oct. 27

I dove into prep for the housewarming party with happy anticipation. Having friends gather under my roof for a meal created a domestic high I hadn't felt in a long time.

There was the ever-present concern someone would find a dog hair in their food, but living with a Malinois means you get used to it. Besides, the people coming tonight were so used to finding dog hair in their food, they'd be surprised if there wasn't any.

I'd only known Dan for a few days, but since he lived with an Australian cattle dog, it was a safe bet he was no stranger to dog hair on clothes, furniture, in the cupboards, and occasionally sticking out of ice cubes. He might fit in better than I thought.

By late afternoon, the kitchen was rich with the aroma of chicken and wild rice soup bubbling in a slow cooker and bread cooling atop the stove. I showered and dressed and, for the first time in months, gave my reflection a long, hard look unfiltered by the unasked-for and unwanted opinions of men who'd never hesitated to critique.

My jeans were faded and my boots were scuffed, but I didn't care. They accented my length of leg nicely, and my teal merino wool sweater clung softly to my curves. Recent hours outdoors left my skin glowing, and my hair tumbled to my shoulders in reckless auburn waves.

I pulled out my makeup bag, studied the contents and closed it again. I'd spent years letting men who claimed to love me rebuild me into what they wanted to see. Had I really been that needy? I shoved the bag back into the drawer and went downstairs.

Dan arrived while I was in the garage, loading seasoned maple from the firewood box into a canvas sling. He wore a long-sleeved, navy-blue shirt tucked into jeans. It was the first time I'd seen him without a hat, and his dark hair curled intriguingly at the back of his neck. He carried several bottles of wine.

"Here, let me," he said as I bent to pick up the firewood. He set the wine on the bench by the kitchen door and reached for the sling, then stopped. He pointed at cornstalks dangling from the Jeep's undercarriage. "Been off-roading?"

"I took the ditch last night on my way home to get away from a truckload of crazy kids. Ended up in a field."

"You okay?" His concern ignited a pleasant heat in my stomach. "I'm fine. I think they were pretty lit. Homecoming and all that."

He raised his eyebrows. "So, it was an accident?"

"Had to be. Why would someone try to run me off the road?"

"Why would someone break into your house and turn on all your lights?"

"No one broke in," I reminded him.

"Ah, right, the ghost turned on the lights."

"Stop it." While I gave Sarah full credit for the light show, that didn't mean I was ready to go public with it.

"You don't seem worried. Most women would be shaken up by something like that."

I wasn't sure if he meant by the incident on the road or the incident with the lights. I folded my arms and gave him a look. "I'm not most women."

One corner of his mouth twitched up. "I think you're a lightning rod for trouble."

"You make it sound like someone doesn't want me living here."

"Sorry. Imagination in overdrive. Occupational hazard." He didn't look sorry, but his grin made it hard to hold that against him. It relaxed the sharp contours of his face into something that invited further consideration. And that looked like a bad idea. I stuffed inappropriate thoughts about my neighbor into the back of my mind.

"Besides, it's the ghost who runs people out of here, not drunken idiots," I said.

That got a genuine laugh. I picked up the wine, Dan picked up the firewood, and we went into the house. Raider wove figure eights around our legs, making a happy nuisance of himself.

Dan looked around the kitchen. "You've done a great job with this."

"The kitchen was done when I moved in, and believe me, it's the only room that looks this good. Wait until you see the rest of it. You're restoring your house, right?" I grabbed hold of the conversation, hoping to gauge his degree of commitment to do-it-yourself-ing.

"Against the advice of two contractors, my brother, and the electrician I have on retainer because I don't want to die at forty-two." He ran a hand over the polished newel post. "This place looks nice for a haunted house. Clean. No ghost tracks."

"Shut up," I said and he laughed, an easy, honest sound I could get used to. I gave him the tour, proud I had a clear restoration plan for each room.

"You've got a lot of ambition." He surveyed the living room when we came down from the second floor.

"More ambition than brains?" I didn't intend it to sound like a challenge and was relieved when his reply wasn't defensive.

"I didn't mean it that way. But work on these old places never ends. It's a lot to take on by yourself."

Raider trotted in with a tennis ball. He dropped the ball and watched it roll across the floor.

"I've always dreamed of restoring a place like this." I let it go at that.

Six months. That would be enough time to decide if I could weave a glowing reality out of that threadbare dream or if like the other owners, I'd bitten off more than I could handle.

The tennis ball reached the other side of the room, stopped, then rolled back. Dan watched as Raid pounced on the ball and set it spinning off again. "The ghost story doesn't bother you?"

I'd abandoned my "There is no ghost" mantra twenty-four hours earlier when I felt Sarah's cool fingers pressing back against mine in the second-floor hallway. I couldn't stand in the house that was her legacy and deny her presence.

"No, not really," I said. "Would you mind building a fire?"

He gave me a speculative look but left to get the firewood from the laundry room. I blinked at the balls of calico fabric resting in the wooden bowl on the mantel. Yesterday, I'd put six of them in the bowl. Five remained. One sat on the mantel, a few inches from the bowl. I started forward to replace it when Dan yelled from the hallway.

"What the hell!"

I pivoted and looked through the pocket doors in time to see Raider snatch his tennis ball as it ricocheted off the opposite wall.

"You almost hit me in the—well, you almost hit me," Dan said.

"What?" I looked at him, then Raider, who capered around with the ball, dropping it and grabbing it again as it bounced.

"What do you mean *what*? You threw a ball at me!"

"I did not! Raid probably knocked it out here with his feet. He does it all the time."

Dan looked from Raider to me, then back to Raider. My dog chomped the ball, happy to be the center of attention.

"Fangs did not throw that ball. It was airborne." Dan scowled. "It nearly hit me in the, well, here." He waved a hand in the general area below his belt to emphasize the seriousness of the situation.

It wasn't polite to laugh, but I did anyway. I got the feeling Sarah might be enjoying his company as much as I was.

"Sorry," I managed.

"You think it's funny?" His hot blue glare was severe, but one side of his mouth twitched. "We're talking about ghosts, and then a ball comes flying across the room like a damn missile."

"You were talking about ghosts," I said. "Not me."

"I'm no expert, but inanimate objects flying around your house might mean you've got a problem."

"Prove it," I said and folded my arms across my chest. I was on thin ice. I couldn't ignore Sarah's presence, but I wasn't sure I was ready to come out of the paranormal closet. Would pretending she didn't exist offend her? What happened if you offended a ghost? Had the previous owners found out the hard way?

"How much more proof do you need?" Dan leaned against the newel post, all lean angles in faded denim. "The lights the other night, that wasn't a wiring problem, was it? Your buddy Brad said it happened before."

"It hasn't happened since. And he's not my buddy. And this is the first time she's thrown anything. She usually just moves stuff around. Little stuff. It's no big deal."

I didn't know what was worse—trying to justify my ghost or trying to justify my ghost to a guy who looked as good as he did. I'd never owned a house with a ghost, and I was absurdly protective of a situation that felt as fragile as a soap bubble.

I wanted to tell Dan about the surge of euphoria the day I moved in, music playing from nowhere, random migrations of inanimate objects, footsteps on the stairs, laughter when no one was there, and over all of it, the feeling of expectant energy swirling through the rooms, but I didn't dare. It sounded like a good way to ensure I never saw him again.

I motioned toward the living room. "Weren't you going to build a fire?"

"Truth is stranger than fiction," he said, then collected the wood and went to work.

"HEY, I DIDN'T MEAN to push earlier."

I looked up from slicing bread when Dan returned to the kitchen. Raider trotted after him with his muzzle raised, air scenting. I automatically moved anything edible out of range. The dog is an opportunistic omnivore.

"About the, uh, ghost thing," he clarified. "It isn't any of my business."

"It is now," I said. "She must like you. She ignores everybody else."

Dan took that as well as I could expect anyone to who'd been invited to dinner at a stranger's house, only to find the house harbors a ball-throwing spirit and the house's owner is possibly bat shit crazy. His eyes were drowning pools of dark blue, his mouth set in a line that gave nothing away.

"Have you talked to anyone about—" he broke off and twirled a finger in the air— "things?"

Before I could answer, the air around us shifted, like a thread snapping taut. Energy gathered with a familiarity that gave me goosebumps. I shoved my hands in my pockets to keep from reaching out like I had in the hallway the night before. Part of me wanted to make that connection again, but if cold fingers entwined with mine, I would probably come unglued right there next to the soup.

Dan pushed off the counter and straightened his shoulders as if shrugging off an unseen touch. His gaze flicked around the room before settling on me. His previous poker face was gone, replaced by wariness.

"You feel it, too, don't you?" I felt vindicated. What were the odds we were both crazy?

He didn't speak, but I read affirmation in his eyes.

The now-familiar feeling of the house shifting under my feet threatened my equilibrium. I stepped forward and gripped Dan's wrists. The solid warmth of his muscle under my fingers anchored me in the swirl of rising energy. His hands closed around my wrists in return, pulling me close enough I could smell the faint cedarwood scent of his aftershave. Neither of us moved, our eyes locked on one another as the air crackled with unseen power.

Hoarsely, he said, "How often does this happen?"

"Third time this week."

We stood, caught in a web of expectancy. Dan's pulse beat against my thumbs, his heartrate matching mine. A ribbon of gold dust sparkled across my vision and something clicked between the two of us as if completing a circuit. His sharp inhale told me he'd felt it, too. The energy coursed through me, bright and pleased, as if having achieved a goal.

Raider barked as a caravan of headlights made their way up the lane. The tension broke like the sudden stilling of wind, and the house settled back into itself with an almost audible sigh. Neither of us moved.

"Ouch," Dan said.

I looked down. My fingers still clenched his arms in a white-knuckled grip.

"Sorry." I hastily released him and stepped back. "It—she—takes some getting used to." I bit the inside of my lip, hoping his silence wasn't a precursor to bolting out the door.

"Does anything else ever happen when, uh, that happens?" he asked.

"No." Not yet.

Dan rubbed a hand over his face and gestured toward the door. "We'll talk about this later."

It's hard to act like nothing happened after you've been accosted by a ghost intent on dragging you into whatever post-death crisis she has going on, but footsteps sounded on the back porch and I opened the door to greet Mare. I busied myself taking her pan of brownies and her jacket, and spared a glance at Dan, who had opened the wine and was pouring a very large glass.

Mare was mobbed by Raider, and Kerri and Matt soon knocked and let themselves in. I introduced Dan to the Grimms amidst the chaos of handing off coats and pouring drinks. He and Matt immediately found common ground when Dan mentioned he was restoring his house. Before long, they were engrossed in a conversation about different ways to end up in the emergency room. Given what had just happened, I thought that was a perfectly rational topic.

Ten minutes later, a final set of headlights flashed up the lane. Raider woofed happily as I opened the door to welcome Conn Stirling and TJ Meyer. Conn looked like a Nordic princess, her platinum blonde hair caught up in a neat French braid, while TJ's auburn pixie cut framed her petite features.

I did final introductions for Dan. "Conn is a graphic artist with her own agency, and TJ owns an art glass studio and does window and stained-glass repair."

Conn eyed Dan thoughtfully. I thought she swallowed a knowing smile as she shook his hand.

"I want the grand tour," TJ said, and off we went.

TRUE TO FORM, we were less than five minutes into the meal before Kerri and Conn started a debate about the merits of artificial insemination versus live cover for a breeding Kerri planned in the spring.

I glanced at Dan, who was following the conversation with a look of amused fascination. If a tennis ball-lobbing ghost hadn't scared him off, animal husbandry over dinner probably wouldn't either. After the meal, Mare cut the peppermint espresso bars.

"Any sign of the ghost yet?" Kerri asked as she helped carry them to the table.

I bobbled two plates of the dessert but recovered with help from Conn before I dumped them in her lap.

"She's only lived here a week," Mare said. "That's barely time to get settled, let alone meet the ghost."

I didn't correct her. Conn stared at me expectantly, and TJ looked around the kitchen as if something might pop out of the woodwork. Seeing their puzzled looks, I gave them a quick version of the Fox Hollow legend.

"Wow," TJ said. "How's that working out?"

"It's no big deal." I dared a glance at Dan, who was deep in conversation with Matt. They'd moved on to plumbing disasters.

"Are you sure nothing weird has happened since you moved in?" Kerri pushed.

Dan caught my eye in the middle of a tale involving a backhoe and an unmarked sewer line.

He gestured at his left wrist and mimed clenching it with his right. I hoped I hadn't left bruises. He grinned, and an unexpected sense of friendship rolled through me. Or maybe it was the wine.

I fixed Kerri with what I hoped was a no-nonsense look. "Do you see any ghosts floating around? There's your answer."

Conn changed the subject. "Did you guys hear about Susanne and Ron Bartacheck? She came home from work a few days ago, and he'd packed his things and moved out."

"What?" I exclaimed. "I knew they were having trouble, but I talked to her yesterday and she didn't say a word about it."

Susanne's husband Ron was head of the Lenox County Secondary Roads Department. A burly outdoorsman, he was the complete opposite of Susanne, who flaunted salon manicures and designer labels like they were her God-given right.

"It sounds like he got tired of being a bucket bitch," Conn said. "They're having a huge custody battle over Cannon. He's registered in both their names, so this could get ugly."

"Wait. Bucket bitch?" Dan asked.

"Unpaid kennel help for handlers at dog shows," I said. "Very glamorous."

Matt snorted. "You groom dogs, walk dogs, pick up dog crap, and get yelled at if you screw up the armbands."

"I only yelled once," Kerri said. "It was justified."

As Matt regaled us with a tale about giving his wife the wrong armband and trying to send her into the open dog class with the catalog number for her bred-by-exhibitor bitch entry at a recent show, I studied the faces gathered around the table. It was like looking through a window into the light and warmth of a room I couldn't enter.

Kerri and Matt had been married for eighteen years, ran a thriving family business and were raising two good kids. Mare and her Thomas had been married more than four decades before he passed. She still spoke of him with affection, like he was in an adjoining room watching TV. Even Conn and TJ, whose relationship occasionally caught backlash even in this alleged age of inclusion, had each other for support and companionship.

Then there was me. Mare told me what happened with Michael was just dumb luck and after that, I was so afraid of getting hurt that I kept trying to be someone I wasn't because I didn't think the real me was good enough. She thinks that turned into a self-fulfilling prophecy of dating guys who weren't interested in who I was anyway. Maybe she had a point.

Raider wandered up and put his head in my lap, and I felt better. Dogs don't cheat.

After the meal, I topped off everyone's wine glasses and the party moved to the living room. Dan knelt to light the fire he'd built earlier. On the mantel, all six calico balls were back in the bowl. TJ pointed at the copy of *South Pacific Wind* on the parlor table by my recliner.

"That series is incredible," she said. "I can't wait for the next book."

"It should be out by early summer," Dan said over his shoulder.

TJ's head snapped around as she made the sudden connection. She clamped both hands to her forehead and blurted, "Oh my God! You're D.W. Sinclair! Now I recognize you from the picture in your books. I feel like an idiot."

"You are an idiot," Conn said affectionately.

TJ turned back to Dan. "Your writing is amazing! Sorry. Fan-girling."

"I'll tell you when to stop." Dan's honest smile took any trace of arrogance out of his reply. He settled into a chair near the fireplace, gestured at the book, then looked at me. "I interviewed Henry Bauer, one of John and Martha Bauer's sons, while I was writing that one. Henry flew with the Marine Corps' Black Sheep Squadron in 1943. He's the reason I'm living out here now."

"How'd that happen?" I asked.

"An Army buddy connected us. I lived in Chicago then, Henry lived in Arizona. I flew out and interviewed him over a couple of days. On my way back, my flight got diverted to Des Moines because of weather, so I rented a car. This area was on the way home, and I decided to do a drive-by. The old Bauer place had a for sale sign by the road so I went up and knocked on the door. A month later, I bought it and moved out here."

Turning to Kerri, I said, "See, other people like living in the middle of nowhere, too." She made a face at me.

"I needed a change of scenery," Dan said.

I waited for him to elaborate but he didn't.

"Have you always been a writer?" I asked. I didn't want him to think I'd only invited him for his celebrity status, but it didn't seem nosy to ask when he was already the topic of conversation.

He flashed a schoolboy grin.

"I started as a history major at UW-Madison but, uh, there was a lot of beer involved, and my advisor suggested I bring my grades up or find another career path, so I joined the Army. I did two tours in Iraq and Afghanistan as a systems maintainer for armored vehicles." Anticipating my next question, he clarified, "Mechanic."

"How did you get from there to writing novels?" TJ asked.

"After the sandbox, the Army paid for me to finish that degree in American history," Dan continued. "Figured I'd go into teaching, but I tried it for a year, and it wasn't for me. Then I worked construction for a while and helped a buddy fix cars. I had a great-uncle who was on the *Arizona* at Pearl Harbor, and I've always felt a connection to World War II. One day I sat down and started writing a story that had been spinning around in my head. It went from there."

He made it sound so easy. I wanted to ask more about his writing career, but Kerri pursued her original topic with dogged determination.

"When you interviewed Henry Bauer, did he say anything about his brother Luke and Sarah Cameron?" she asked.

"He mentioned the Cameron family being at the party his parents threw when he and his brothers came home after the war, but that was all," Dan said. "The three remaining Bauer boys sold the family farm and moved away when land prices skyrocketed in the 1980s. I don't think they could live with the story about their missing brother any longer."

"That story is so strange," Mare said. "People

don't just disappear. That boy's body is out there somewhere."

"I could disappear another one of those brownies," TJ said, and we all went back to the kitchen.

As I curled in bed later that night, reveling in the bliss of an evening spent with good friends and good food, I realized Dan hadn't mentioned Hannah Wintergarden in the brief synopsis of his life. The omission didn't bother me. Everyone has a relationship they want to forget. Some of us have more than one.

When my phone rang, my sleep-fogged mind struggled to register the sound. I fumbled the device off the night stand. It was 3:07 a.m. No caller ID on the screen.

"Hello?" I croaked.

Silence.

"Hello?"

More silence.

"Who is this?" I was wide awake now, anticipating some horrible news involving Mare or Kerri and Matt.

Heavy breathing, then, "Get out." It was such a parody of a low budget horror movie, I almost laughed.

I gathered a semblance of composure. "Who is this?"

The caller disconnected.

Well, hell.

CHAPTER 9

I enjoyed one of Mare's brownies for breakfast with a steaming mug of coffee. The ensuing rush of endorphins convinced me the 3 a.m. phone call had been kids playing a Halloween prank, like dialing numbers at random and whispering, "I know what you did."

A little voice in my head pointed out I was blaming a lot of stuff on kids lately. Bored kids digging, partying kids driving recklessly, now prank kids making phone calls. I didn't have any other explanations. As long as nothing inside the house told me to get out, I was good.

What happened in the kitchen before everyone else arrived the previous night wasn't so easy to dismiss. Now Dan was involved, and that complicated things on a whole other level, but we had not, in fact, talked about it later. He said good-bye with everyone else shortly after ten p.m. and showed no indication of wanting to hang around in case Sarah decided to perform an encore.

Raider woofed as Dan's pickup pulled up in front of the house. My heart danced a quick two-step. I didn't expect to see him again so soon. Actually, I wondered if I'd see him again ever.

"C'mon, you've shown me yours, I want to show you mine," he said when I answered the door.

"What?"

"House, McCallister, I want to show you my house. You know, the Bauer homestead, the last place destroyed before Fox Hollow stopped the tornado with its supernatural powers."

I gave him a first-class eye roll, then poured a cup of coffee and cut one of the brownies to go with it. "Here. Sit."

He took both without arguing. Sharing coffee and chocolate in a warm kitchen knitted an unexpected sense of camaraderie. I wondered briefly if Sarah had anything to do with that.

"I got a strange phone call at three in the morning. I think it was kids goofing around," I said.

Dan brushed his index finger along the rim of the coffee mug, then wiped it on his pants. "Dog hair," he said, unfazed. "What did they say?"

"Get out. It sounded like they were trying to be scary, which made it weird but not scary."

"Are you getting out?"

"No." I held my breath and waited for him to say something about last night in general and ghosts in particular, but he didn't, which was fine with me. We talked about the weather until our coffee was finished, then with Raider leading the way, piled into Dan's pickup.

His two-story, white clapboard house nestled picturesquely among maples and oaks. Built after the tornado demolished the original, the new Bauer house was ninety-eight years old now. It mirrored Fox Hollow in that both had been built for families who faded away, leaving strangers as stewards of their legacies.

Ruby welcomed Raider and me with tail-thumping enthusiasm. The tour was brief and didn't stand on ceremony. Muddy hiking boots and an overflowing laundry basket cluttered a small mud room directly off the back porch. The sturdy kitchen table and mismatched chairs looked like they'd come from a thrift store but fit the old farmhouse kitchen perfectly.

Books, dog toys, newspapers, and discarded clothing were scattered haphazardly over battered leather furniture in the living room. A flat screen TV dominated one wall, but the room was barren of further décor. In the dining room, I admired the freshly stripped and refinished woodwork, then raised an eyebrow at the collection of paint samples brushed on one wall.

"Don't ask," Dan said. "When I get stuck on my manuscript, I come in here and work. If I get stuck much more, I'll have it finished by Christmas. The room, I mean."

We'd completed the circuit of the ground floor when he gestured through the doorway of what would have originally been the home's parlor, a graciously proportioned space with tall, west-facing windows. In contrast to the minimalist bachelor style I'd seen so far, this room looked like someone had lobbed a chaos grenade over the threshold.

A computer monitor perched valiantly atop a cluttered wooden desk that had seen at least two world wars. The edge of a laptop peered around the stacks of reference books that tumbled over every available surface, their pages bristling with markers like literary porcupines. These were interspersed with ragged spiral notebooks and random notes scribbled on Post-its. A half-full fifth of Macallan Scotch whisky and a single cutglass tumbler claimed the sole clear spot, safely out of range of the pending avalanche of stacked volumes.

The flood of papers and miscellany extended to the floor-to-ceiling bookcases. The shelves were jammed with books, model military airplanes, rocks, bits of driftwood, and photos, including one of Dan with four other men in desert camo uniforms in a Jeep. A World War II military map of the Southwest Pacific was framed above the desk, and the walls were hung with vintage aviation art.

I turned in a slow circle. A Browning gun safe rested in one corner. A wood-burning stove crouched in the other like a benevolent cast iron dragon, and the soft tang of wood smoke lingered in the air. Framed covers of Dan's books were displayed on a wall next to an oil painting of pheasants in an autumn cornfield. Sunlight filtered in from the adjoining dining room, refracting off the whisky bottle and splashing tiny rainbows over the cream-colored plaster. It was a wildly cluttered, wood smoke scented, whisky flavored man cave, and it fascinated me.

Dan mistook my silence as a critique. "What does your work space look like? By the way, you never told me what you do for a living."

"I was a freelance newspaper reporter, but now I'm not." That sounded awkward, even though it was the truth.

He cocked an eyebrow. "Let me guess. You're a wealthy heiress, living incognito to escape an evil suitor who's trying to ruin you socially so he can force you to marry him and steal your fortune."

I snorted. "You could write tacky romances with a mind like that. I retired early. Like really early."

Where my money came from wasn't any of his business, but I didn't want him to think I was cooking meth in the barn to fund fresh paint and plaster repairs.

"It started with my ex-husband." I grimaced at the memory. "I came home early from a dog show weekend and walked in on him with our neighbor, Brittni, who ran a local yoga studio. It turned out she was also the featured dancer at the Velvet Kitten Lounge."

I thought about pouring a shot of the Macallan to wash away the lingering bitterness, but I wasn't a Scotch drinker and nine o'clock on Sunday morning didn't seem like a good time to start. "You want to know the real irony? I'd just won an Iowa Newspaper Association award for a series on couples rebuilding their marriages. I was writing about rediscovering trust while my husband was fucking a stripper. Fucking *strippers*, plural. Brittni had friends." I bit my lip. "Sorry."

Dan made a dismissive gesture, his eyes never leaving mine.

"Anyway, Michael's father was a congressman, and his family had more money than God. Daddy got out his checkbook and I, uh, negotiated what it would take to keep my mouth shut about his son's involvement with girls wearing nothing but body glitter. Fastest divorce in the history of ever."

I sighed. "Then my parents died, and I inherited the family farm, and the state decided to build a four-lane highway on top of it. They had to pay fair market value, and it was a good year for land prices. So, I guess you could say I'm living on the cheating husband-Iowa Department of Transportation retirement plan."

Dan leaned against the door frame, hands in the front pockets of his jeans as his eyes sketched my body without apology. Sun glinted off the gold stud earring. His dark blue gaze triggered a not unpleasant surge of heat under my skin, and I got really interested in the vintage map on the wall. I appreciated his appreciation but no. I wasn't about to jump into something with my neighbor just to scratch an itch.

"That had to be rough, losing your family's farm, no matter what the state paid for it. And sorry your ex was such a jackass. Why the hell did he cheat on you?"

"Because he liked twenty-year-olds. I was past my expiration date," I said. Hannah Wintergarden's blonde perfection flashed through my mind, and impulsively I asked, "What about you? Ever been married?"

"Once. Almost."

"Sorry. That's absolutely none of my business." What was I thinking? I'd barely known him a week.

"Her name was Hannah."

I turned away from the map. Dan's expression

was guarded, as if he were rationing how many words the subject deserved. "We were going to get married, before everything went to hell."

"You don't have to—"

His eyes fixed on a spot somewhere over my shoulder, and I wasn't sure he heard me.

"Once that ring was on her finger, it was all about her. What she wanted. What she needed. What she thought we should do on weekends. She thought my dog should sleep in the garage."

I looked at Ruby, who'd taken possession of an old leather recliner near the desk.

"That was six years ago, different dog," Dan said. "Ranger was thirteen. I'd had him longer than I'd known Hannah. I said maybe *she* should sleep in the garage."

He swiped a hand over his face. "That was the end of it. She threw the ring at me, and the damn thing went down a heat vent. I nearly had to tear the house apart to find it."

I didn't know what to say, so I said nothing. I got the feeling this was a bandage he'd ripped off repeatedly, the wound never quite healing.

"Do you know how hard it is on a guy's pride to take a ring back to a jewelry store? I won't make that mistake again."

I didn't know if he meant he wouldn't return a ring to a jewelry store or he wouldn't ask a woman to marry him again.

Dan pushed off the wall. "Come on, I'll show you the rest of the house." We couldn't have agreed any louder to avoid the landmines of past relationships.

The remaining tour encompassed four bedrooms of varying sizes opening off a second-floor hallway. Two were empty, swept clean, and echoing. One held storage boxes and assorted miscellany.

The fourth was furnished with the same comfortable indifference to decorating that marked the rest of the house. The floor's wide planks were partly covered by a faded area rug, and a rumpled, hunter green comforter was flung across the bed with zero attempt at neatness. From the Spartan furnishings of the main floor to the ribald disarray of the office and now this bedroom, there was no sign of feminine influence anywhere in the house.

We got back in the pickup, and Dan drove me home. I was reaching for the door handle when he said, "Do you want to talk about last night?"

I froze, then sank slowly back into the seat. When I didn't say anything, he looped his arm over the steering wheel and shifted to face me. "You're just going to ignore your ghost like nothing happened?"

"I'm not ignoring her," I started, cautious. "But I don't know what to do about her."

"She's got unfinished business. Isn't that why ghosts stick around?" Dan looked like he was contemplating a new, unexpected character that brought a twist to the plot. Easy for him. Sarah wasn't in *his* house.

"You sound like Kerri. She thinks Sarah won't rest until she finds Luke," I said.

"Maybe she wants you to find him."

"What makes you say that?"

"Why else would she be connecting with you?"

"She connected with you, too," I reminded him and stopped just short of saying *it's as if she wants both of us to help her.* Damn it. I had a chance at a friendly relationship with a genuinely decent guy, and here comes my needy ghost, dragging him into her crisis. If Sarah wanted us to hook up just because she'd been denied a happily ever after, she needed to rethink that. I fiddled with a loose thread on the seat cover.

"Maybe she needs us both."

My head jerked up. His voice held a gravelly timbre that under any other circumstances would have been sexy as hell. Then he shrugged. "Or maybe it's just because I live in Luke's family home. Guilt by association."

"But I'm the least paranormally inclined person you'll ever meet," I protested.

"You might want to rethink that." His grin was back. "Not everyone has a pet ghost."

I got out of the pickup, refusing to dignify his comment by acknowledging it. "See ya around, Sinclair."

"THAT'S PURPLE CONEFLOWER and this is a hardy geranium." Mare pointed at clumps of withered foliage with confidence born of practice. The perennial border that edged the wrap-around porch was a snarl of weedy neglect, but I could imagine the riot of summer color it must have been the last time anyone cared. Revitalizing the plantings was on my to-do list somewhere after stripping the 1980s shelf paper in the butler's pantry and before cleaning a century of junk out of the barn.

"If you say so," I said, struggling to differentiate between the bedraggled plants.

"This is a thread leaf coreopsis here in front." She paused her flower inventory and looked over my shoulder. "And that's company."

Dan's pickup rattled up the lane for the second time that day. He parked in front of the garage and let Ruby out of the cab. The cattle dog acknowledged me and Mare, then took off on a mad chase with Raider. Dan approached, carrying a chainsaw.

"Is this a good time to work on that mess?" He gestured toward the tangle of broken limbs on the front lawn. I blinked dumbly before remembering he'd mentioned them the night of the house-warming. We'd agreed he would cut them up and take half for his wood-burning stove. At my hesitation, he set the chainsaw down.

"Unless you'd rather do it yourself. I'll just leave this here." He backed away, grinning.

"No! Yes! I mean, please, go ahead." If he wanted me to beg for help, that's as close as I was going to get.

"Once that maple dries, it'll be great in your fireplace." He picked up the chainsaw and walked across the lawn to size up the mess. I took that as a vote of confidence. He thought I'd be here long enough for the wood to season.

"That's nice of him," Mare said.

"He's a nice guy. Don't make it into something it's not."

She opened her mouth to do exactly that, but Dan fired up the Stihl, rendering conversation impossible. I leaned against the front porch and enjoyed the view. Look but don't touch.

His lean build and the way his jeans rode low on his hips drew the eye in a pleasing combination. His faint limp was noticeable only because I knew it was there. He wielded the chainsaw with a practiced economy of motion that quickly reduced the snarl of limbs to a manageable pile.

When the earsplitting racket stopped, I helped Dan load his half of the wood. Mare politely ignored us and continued to work her way through the perennial beds, making sketches with plant IDs in a notebook for future reference.

Dan tossed the final log into the pickup and leaned against the tailgate. A trickle of sweat ran down one temple in spite of the cool afternoon. He took off his hat, swiped an arm across his brow, and settled the hat back on.

"Anything else I can do while I'm here?" he asked, looking around. "Exorcise a ghost?"

"You exorcise demons, not ghosts," I corrected, then jumped in with what I thought about most when I wasn't thinking about why Sarah Cameron was still living, so to speak, in my house. "Do you know anything about the cemetery out along the river bluff?"

"Bishop? Yeah."

"How?" I challenged. "It's not on your land."

"I found it when I was hiking a few years ago. The fence lines back there are pretty sketchy. It's easy to lose track of whose land you're on. Sorry." His grin said he was not sorry in the least.

"I'll be right back." I went in the house and got three beers and the piece of broken pottery. When I came out, Mare was sitting in the sunshine atop the front porch steps. Dan sat one step down, lazing back on his elbows and throwing sticks for the dogs.

I handed around the drinks, then sat next to Mare.

"Look at this." The potsherd's glaze glinted in the sunshine as I offered it for their inspection.

"Where'd you get that?" Dan held out his hand, and I dropped the piece into it. His fingers were strong and rough, more suited to a man who made his living with power tools than a keyboard.

I told him about finding it in Bishop Cemetery.

"It was just lying there?" Dan handed it to Mare.

"Technically, Raider found it, but yeah, it was just lying on top of the ground. Near a hole. It looked—" I paused, reluctant to voice my suspicion aloud—"it looked like someone had been digging in the graves."

To both of their credits, this didn't produce a theatrical gasp. Dan looked at me like he might regard a hand grenade of unknown status. Mare scraped at the curved rim of the fragment. A black substance came off on her nail. It clung together as she rolled it into a ball between thumb and forefinger.

"It feels like sealing wax." She handed the artifact back to me. It was heavy against my palm, a clue in a mystery I hadn't asked to solve.

"What if someone's digging for the gold?" I said.

"You have a ghost *and* hidden gold?" Dan said.

I told him about the man and wife who fled from Georgia with their stolen loot. He shook his head. "You don't do anything halfway."

"Dr. Aldrich didn't say the treasure was buried in Bishop Cemetery, just somewhere near the trading post," Mare reminded. "And digging at random would be pure folly, not to mention time consuming."

"Confederate gold would be worth a few blisters," I said. "Plus, there's nothing stopping them. You can't see the cemetery from either the house or the road."

"If someone was serious about finding it, they'd have a more methodical approach," Dan said. "They'd want to spend as little time out there as possible."

"The Lenox County Pioneer Cemetery Commission would have burial records," Mare suggested. "Assuming your mystery digger believes the gold is in the cemetery, if he knew how the graves were laid out, he could narrow his search area and increase the odds of finding it."

"Maybe he witched it."

Mare and I stared at Dan.

"You've heard of witching?" he said.

"Dowsing?" Mare asked.

"Divining?" I said at the same time. "Finding things underground with wires that pick up disturbances in the soil?"

"Exactly." Dan said. "Witching."

"You're just calling it that because Halloween is in three days," I said, "and because you think my house is haunted."

"I'm calling it that because that's what it's called. And your house is haunted."

We glared at each other for a mutual moment during which I realized arguing with him was more fun than it should be. Mare did a credible job of pretending not to notice. The dogs tired of their mayhem and flopped down next to us.

"I asked my realtor for more information about the cemetery." I pulled my gaze from Dan's. The gleam in his eyes hinted at a challenge, and I wanted to take it without even knowing what it was. "She said she didn't know anything beyond what was listed in the property description, and I don't see what she'd have to gain by withholding information. I'm going to call the historical society. Maybe they can tell me something about the people who owned this place before me. And the cemetery."

"Think there's a connection between the guy who ran you off the road and the phone call and the cemetery?" Dan asked.

"When did you get run off the road? And what phone call?" Mare interjected.

I told her about the series of odd events that constituted my new normal.

"I can't see any connection, and I don't think it's some nefarious plot to drive me out of here," I concluded with more confidence than I felt. Since moving here, I'd found evidence of vandalism on my property, dealt with drunken teen stupidity on the road and been woken up at three a.m. by a prank phone call. Each incident by itself might have an innocent explanation, but all three in a matter of days sent a finger of ice skittering down my spine. Just because I couldn't see a connection didn't mean there wasn't one.

"Maybe whoever was messing around in the cemetery won't be back now that you're living here," Mare offered.

"Maybe they found what they were looking for," Dan said.

We all looked at the broken pottery lying on the step, and I remembered the pink flag I'd pulled out of the ground the same day Raider found the potsherd. Maybe I should have left it and gone out with my own shovel to see what I could unearth.

There were too many maybes in play, and I wasn't holding my breath on any of them. The sun had started to lower. Leaves skittered across the porch on a cold breeze. Dan stood.

"Thanks for cutting up those limbs for me," I said, grateful to be back on theoretically safe ground. "I owe you one."

"So bake me a pie."

"Do I look like Betty Crocker?" I appreciated his confidence that I could knock out a flaky pastry crust without breaking a sweat, but I had more things on my agenda than producing baked goods at his convenience.

A niggling little voice reminded me he had cleaned up my substantial tree mess at zero cost, and homemade baked goods weren't an unreasonable request. It might be the twenty-first century, but living in rural Iowa still meant a dozen home raised eggs or something from the kitchen were traditional gifts to show appreciation for a favor.

Mare stepped into the breach. "She makes a killer lattice crust apple."

That was a stretch, but I'd helped her occasionally in A Likely Story's kitchen when her regular baking assistant couldn't come in. I'm no French pastry chef, but could still channel my days as a member of the Busy Bees 4-H club to produce a blue-ribbon pie, albeit not without some swearing.

"I'll look forward to it." Whistling for Ruby, Dan loaded up the chainsaw and left.

Mare and I watched his truck roll down the lane. It rattled and bounced as it hit the occasional rut, but nothing fell off. Mare turned to me with a gleam in her eye.

"Don't start," I said. "And why did you have to suggest a lattice crust? Do you know how long it takes to do one of those?"

She ignored my protest. "What does it hurt to let him help you with things? He obviously enjoys it."

"It doesn't hurt anything at first, then it turns into a shit show." The straight-forward friendship Dan offered contrasted with the superficiality of every serious relationship I'd ever had, and I honestly wasn't sure what to do with that.

"We all make mistakes. The trick is finding the right person to make them with."

Mare collected her notebooks. After she left, I sat on the front steps, throwing a stick for Raider in the gathering dusk. I bought Fox Hollow to put down roots. My roots. Alone. Where I couldn't get hurt.

That evening, I curled up with *Ghost Towns of Lenox County*. Raider's tennis ball rolled amiably back and forth across the floor as he swatted it around and occasionally when he didn't.

"Hello?" I said to the room in general, just to see what would happen.

Nothing did.

CHAPTER 10

Esther Wetterling's bright blue eyes sparkled with curiosity as she ushered me into the Lenox County Historical Society's research library. Her brisk gait belied her eighty years, and her Harris tweed jacket and matching skirt made me feel seriously under-dressed in jeans and flannel.

When we were seated in a conference room, surrounded by floor-to-ceiling display cases crammed with county archives, she pointed to a worn manilla folder on the table.

She beamed. "I pulled the Fox Hollow file for you. Such a lovely old landmark home. We would love to include it on our historic showcase tour in the summer."

I mirrored her smile, thinking she might change her tune if she saw the home's current condition. Still, I was willing to negotiate with the historical society if they could shed any light on the previous owners. I opened the folder. The cover was soft and dog-eared with wear. Lenox County had neither the funds nor technology to digitize their collections and relied on precisely curated hard copy.

"We keep files on homes like yours because sometimes the owners seek inclusion on the National Register of Historic Places. You may want to consider that. None of the previous owners ever made time." Her tone indicated they were lacking in their priorities.

I held my breath in anticipation as I sifted through photocopied pages of courthouse records showing land transactions as Gavin and Moira bought additional acres of arable ground to expand their farm, then another series of transactions reversing that as the farmland was sold after Sarah's death. Finally, the house and outbuildings had been surveyed into the acreage I now owned. The file also included copies of the deeds when that property changed hands.

I bit down hard on disappointment. I could have found all of this at the county courthouse, although it would have taken a considerable amount of time to dig it out of the recorder's ledgers.

Then I hit the jackpot. Behind all the legalese of surveyors' coordinates, a sheet typed on the historical society's letterhead bore the label Fox Hollow Farm, 1984 Cat's Back Road, North Willow, Iowa. The list of names below began with Clyde and Gertie Bishop, followed by Gavin and Moira Cameron, Sarah Cameron, and five more couples, ending with my own, Jessica McCallister. The committee for historical preservation had a few OCD issues, if not an outright stalker complex, but I could tolerate the latter in hopes of gleaning something helpful from the former.

"Could I get a copy of this list?" I asked.

"Certainly. We have even more information on the people who called your place home, if you're interested," Esther said. She must have seen my ears perk up because she didn't wait for an answer, just rose and produced a battered metal box from one of the shelves. She flipped open the lid, revealing a collection of alphabetized index cards.

"Loretta O'Brien kept notes on all the county's historic homes. It was her passion. She did it for years until she had a stroke and passed away two months ago. She contacted each of the former owners of your home after they left, and well, let me tell you." Esther looked around the room as if spies might be listening. "They told her things."

God bless Loretta. I pulled a notebook and pen from my bag. Sliding into reporter mode, I said, "I'd love to hear more about it."

AN HOUR AND a half later, I exited the research library with pages of notes—Loretta O'Brien would have made an outstanding newspaper reporter—and the photocopied list of all Fox Hollow's previous owners.

Lost in thought, I rounded a corner and nearly plowed headlong into Bev Jennings, who'd paused to study the display of vintage wedding dresses in the museum lobby.

"Doing some research on your property?" she asked, looking over my shoulder where Esther was tucking the Fox Hollow folder back into its appointed cabinet.

The question shocked me so much I had to make an effort to keep my jaw from dropping. Conversation with Bev usually centered around what Bev was doing and how well she was doing it.

"She's going to open her home for the tour next summer," Esther said, emerging from the library. "Isn't that grand?"

I distinctly remembered *not* agreeing to any such thing, but kept my mouth shut.

"Go on in, you know where to find the material you want," Esther said as Bev angled toward the library door. "Call out if you need anything. I have a box of antique ink wells that have to be cataloged. The Everhardt girls brought them in from their parents' estate, and they're just fascinating."

I made my escape, leaving Bev to whatever Jennings genealogical delights she was pursuing and Esther to her raptures over the ink wells. Bev's sleek sedan with its vanity plates reading BREWED sat a safe distance from my gravel dust-streaked Jeep. I checked my phone. It was 12:30 p.m. Didn't the woman have a business to run? Well, like Mare said, taking time off to do what you wanted was a perk of running your own shop.

LATER THAT AFTERNOON, sullen clouds clogged the sky as I pushed through knee-high weeds in the Sand Creek Cemetery drive. The township burial ground was carved out of surrounding farmland a mile north of Fox Hollow. Cemeteries were playing a larger part in my life than I'd ever expected, but the morning's visit to the historical society and the ghost town book I'd read the night before left me seeking a real-time connection with Sarah Cameron. Short of sitting around waiting for her to make a move, this felt like the next obvious step.

I pounded the rusted latch until it came loose, and the gate creaked inward from weathered limestone pillars. Overhead, Sand Creek Cemetery was spelled out in black, wrought-iron script. The plot was enclosed by a fence of the same ageless iron as the gates. Evergreens edged the northern perimeter, their trunks stooped and bent from more than a century in the wind.

Raider ran ahead as I wandered through the field of stones. This site was the only remaining proof of the families who had called the area their home before the tornado. There hadn't been a burial here in years. Many of the grave markers tilted at angles as the earth under them heaved and settled with the seasons. Others lay broken on the ground, a tangled mat of prairie grass slowly obscuring the identities they honored.

It only took a few minutes to find what I was looking for. The black granite marker was set near the west fence.

Sarah Elspeth Cameron, Aug. 24, 1900 – Sept. 27, 1998

No husband. No children. Just a name and dates. I knelt in the overgrown grass and touched the stone, eyes welling with unexpected tears.

Raider's ears swiveled, and I heard the scrabble of running paws two seconds before Ruby plowed into me. I hastily wiped away the unshed tears, gave the cattle dog an affectionate scratching, and pushed to my feet.

"I was on my way home and saw your Jeep," Dan called. He reached me and looked down at the grave marker. "You found her."

A rooster pheasant lifted off in the adjoining corn field, the whir of wings loud in the quiet afternoon. We watched as the bird arrowed over a fence and landed. The scent of rain hung heavy on the breeze.

"I thought if I came out here, I'd get some kind of vibe, maybe a better understanding of how I can help her." I paused. "Sorry. That must sound absolutely insane."

If Dan agreed, he kept it to himself. "Did you? Get an understanding?"

"No." I sighed. "I'm guessing she wants me to find out what happened to Luke, but that doesn't make any sense because they're both dead now anyway."

A spatter of raindrops left streaks in the dust on Sarah's gravestone. Dan and I turned back toward the gate, heads bent against the rising wind. My mind was so occupied with why a dead person would still be looking for another dead person, I nearly fell over when Dan grabbed my elbow and yanked me to a halt.

The gray granite stone that caught his attention was modest, its surface etched with time but still readable. With my laser focus on Sarah, I'd forgotten all about it.

Luke Jameson Bauer

March 19, 1899—July 4, 1919

Son of John and Martha Bauer

Beloved of Sarah Cameron

Dan stared. "Holy shit."

He had the look of a man who'd discovered irrefutable proof of the Loch Ness monster.

"You didn't know about this?" Odd, since he'd taken such delight in teasing me with the Sarah and Luke story when we first met. Or maybe it wasn't. I wouldn't have known about the stone if it hadn't been for *Ghost Towns of Lenox County*, a volume I doubted he'd encountered.

"Honest to God, I thought the whole story was just folklore. You know—start with an old house and a few facts and before you know it, there are ghosts hanging out of every window. I had no idea until the night of your party that the haunting was real, let alone the story behind it actually happened." Dan realized he was still gripping my arm and let go.

"They were literally carved in stone." I swallowed hard as I looked at the names. "I wish I could help her."

That would have been a fine time for some supernatural epiphany to strike, but it didn't. The wind picked up, pushing the rain in from the west, the drops falling faster now. Neither of us moved. Dan looked at me with a blue gaze so intense I wondered if he was still thinking about Sarah and Luke or had moved on to another topic. The dogs crowded around our feet, their ears flattened in annoyance with humans too dense to get out of the rain.

"Be careful what you wish for," he said.

RAIN DRUMMED AGAINST the windows as I settled in for the evening, blanket over my lap, fire crackling, and glass of wine at hand. This was becoming routine, and I justified the alcoholic accompaniment as a reward for the day's labors.

The visit to the cemetery left me edgy with unspent energy, which in turn led to my prying off the fake wood paneling in the upper hallway. I was relieved to find nothing more ominous than a stretch of badly cracked plaster behind it. Fixing that was easily in my skill set, and I spent the rest of the afternoon spreading spackling compound and generally making a mess. Not exactly life in the fast lane, but it filled me with a sense of contented achievement.

Raider sprawled on his dog bed by the fire, paws twitching as he chased dream creatures. The calico balls were now scattered haphazardly across the mantel. I'd put them back in the bowl once already today, but they made my fingers tingle in a way that left me reluctant to touch them any more than necessary.

Dan joined the parade of images of Sarah, Luke, and aged plaster marching through my mind. He was getting awfully good at showing up at the right place at the right time. He was easy on the eyes, and I enjoyed his company, but beyond that, there be dragons. Even if he was interested in being more than friends, he lived too close. When things inevitably didn't work out, it would be beyond awkward to have an ex-lover as my only neighbor for miles. Friends with benefits might have been worth exploring fifteen years ago, but now that idea felt cheap and empty.

Pushing those thoughts aside, I opened a Word document on my laptop and started transposing my notes from my interview with Esther and subsequent dive into Loretta O'Brien's card file.

Bruce and Abby Linden bought Fox Hollow following Sarah's death. They lived here for eighteen years, and the only remarkable thing they'd noted was that the house had an unusual energy. Whatever that meant.

When the Lindens moved to a retirement community, they sold the property to Sheryl and Bob Ryan, antiques dealers who thought the farmstead's huge barn and scattered outbuildings would be ideal for their business. They had the house rewired but noted the lights continued to go off and on for no apparent reason. Doors also opened and closed on their own, which they blamed on the house settling. In less than a year, the Ryans realized the location was so far off the beaten track, antique hunters breezed past on their way to more accessible shops in the Amana Colonies and Kalona. I took a fortifying drink.

The Ryans sold the acreage to Glen and Theresa Jacobs, lawyers with a passion for gardening and two kids who were heavy into extracurricular activities at school. The lights and doors continued to do their own thing. Chronic plumbing malfunctions lead to installing a new septic system.

The Jacobs family swore they heard old fashioned music playing on more than one occasion. Fed up with fixing things that wouldn't stay fixed and making endless trips to town for school activities, they sold the place to Tom and Betty Franklin.

I took another sip of wine. This was turning into a paranormal version of a college party game. Whenever a familiar ghost behavior was mentioned, take a drink. I should have brought the bottle with me.

The Franklins were restoration buffs who set out to bring the house back to its 1910 glory but didn't get further than the kitchen. After a winter of record-setting snowfall and white-knuckled commutes to their jobs, they threw in the towel, citing isolation as their reason for selling. When asked by Loretta, the couple admitted they occasionally felt what they called a presence in the house, but when pressed for details, declined to elaborate. Their teenage daughter said small objects moved around in her room, but she blamed the cat. Drink.

Ben and Courtney Weldon, a young, upwardly mobile couple, bought Fox Hollow at the start of this year. They lasted six months and bluntly told Loretta they sold the house because it didn't like them.

Courtney was quoted as saying, "I was going to paint the living room woodwork, but something pushed me off the ladder and I wrenched my knee."

If Courtney had been responsible for the hideous blue on the living room walls, I thought Sarah should have pushed her off the ladder sooner. I raised my glass. Cheers.

I remembered Kerri's comment on the day I moved in about the ghost running people out before they could paint the woodwork. I drained the glass.

I shut my laptop. All of the owners had perfectly rational reasons for leaving—the property was too big, too isolated, had chronic maintenance issues, roads sucked in the winter, no Starbucks on the corner, blah, blah, blah. While they'd admitted odd things happened, none of them except Courtney Weldon had come right out and said they felt threatened.

But who would admit they moved out because the house scared them? The former residents had been business owners and white-collar professionals. They wouldn't have broadcast any paranormal experiences for fear of damaging their reputations, and just forget about mentioning a mysterious presence when they listed the property. Unexplained phenomena do not sell houses.

I'd never felt threatened. Sarah liked me, or at least she didn't dislike me. She hadn't pushed me down the stairs despite Kerri's dire warnings. Maybe I was on a probationary period. Was Sarah getting better at communicating with the living, whether they appreciated it or not? Or was she just getting better at showing people the door when they failed to help in her quest to find Luke? I'd found no evidence the previous owners even understood that's what she wanted.

I had no idea what I was going to do about any of it. Sarah and Luke's shattered happily ever after intrigued me as a more tragic reflection of my own failures. She and I shared the common thread of living our lives alone. Would finding Luke so she could rest somehow realign my own romantic karma? I wasn't secretly dreaming of wedding bells, but the rest of my life was a long time to be alone, in spite of my vow to do just that.

Halloween was in two days. It was the time of year when Celtic culture believed the veil between the worlds thinned and spirits walked among the living. That felt like an appropriate time for something to happen, but it was anyone's guess what that might look like.

TUESDAY, OCT. 30

I DROPPED MY my gear bag on top of Raider's crate at the Heartland training building and looked at Kerri.

"I need to know more about the guy who disappeared in that tornado. If I don't help Sarah Cameron find out what happened to him, she'll drive me out of the house like she's done to all the other owners."

I kept my voice low as members trickled in for the evening's group session. If anyone heard me, the kennel club grapevine would light up like a Christmas tree. A ghost would even trump Susanne's now-public custody battle for Cannon.

Kerri fumbled the collar she was holding. Her face went through a series of disbelieving contortions, as if she'd bitten into a cookie only to discover it was oatmeal raisin instead of chocolate chip.

"You have got to be kidding me." Her expression was so incredulous I might have announced I'd just won a hundred million in the lottery.

"You've been preaching ghost-this and ghost-that and now you're surprised? I am not kidding you. She's real."

"But—the story was just—I mean—it was fun to tease you, but I didn't really think—" Kerri choked. "Oh, hell, you're serious."

I rolled my eyes. First Dan and now her. It seemed like all the people who loved telling the story hadn't believed a word of it.

"I got a lot of info from the historical society, and all the previous owners mentioned weird things happening, but none of them would say the G word. You know how small towns are, nobody wants to be the topic of gossip around their neighbor's dinner table. Anyway, the ghost has to be Sarah."

I paused. "It could be Luke, since he's the one who went missing, but ghosts haunt the place where they died, so that doesn't make sense because no one knows where he died." I pinched the bridge of my nose. Ghost communication left a lot to be desired.

Kerri stared in mute fascination as I filled her in on my car keys going walkabout, the calico balls' random migrations, the music, the footsteps, and my encounters with that undefinable energy that swirled like a rising storm. I glossed over the fact Dan had been involved in the most recent episode. She gets ideas in her head too easily.

"The historical society has tons of stuff on that tornado." Kerri recovered her composure. "I'll see what I can find."

"Thanks. Look out for Bev Jennings. She was there yesterday when I met with Esther."

Kerri made a face. "She was in the research library all summer, and she's still there a lot when I volunteer."

"What's she doing?"

Kerri shrugged. "Working on her family genealogy, I guess. Last summer she got all excited when she found out the library had family letters from the mid-1800s. She couldn't get her hands on them fast enough."

I vaguely remembered listening to Bev elaborate about her ancestral discoveries when Brad and I were dating. During that winter, she'd found a trunk full of correspondence from her mother's side of the family while cleaning out her great-aunt Maisie Porter's home in North Willow. Maisie married Milvoy Porter, a state senator back in the 1920s. After he served several decades in Des Moines, the couple retired to North Willow, where Maisie's pastime was meddling in everyone else's business.

That family trait had certainly carried through the generations. The only intriguing element of Bev's discoveries had been a veiled hint regarding Maisie's brothers' involvement in bootlegging during Prohibition. Since that didn't fit with Bev's vision of her ancestors as pillars of the community, she ignored it.

Bored, Raider tried to entice Kerri's Aussie, Tangle, into a game of bitey face. Living with a Malinois is like living with a three-year-old who is constantly trying to stick a fork in a light socket just to see what will happen. Giving up any hope of a sensible conversation, I turned to enter the ring just as Susanne approached. She blew out a dramatic sigh.

"I'm sure you've heard my news by now, girls. You wouldn't believe what it's costing me to get custody of Cannon." Her face looked drawn, but her hair was impeccable and her sportswear was fresh from Macy's.

Kerri and I made the appropriate noises. I barely knew Ron Bartacheck. He seemed like an okay guy, patiently schlepping crates, lawn chairs, grooming tables and other gear in his wife's wake. However, the fellowship of dog trainers meant I came down firmly on Susanne's side. She loved Cannon and had handled him through every minute of his spectacular career. I genuinely hoped the dog wouldn't become a pawn in a war between two bitter people bent on spiting each other.

Susanne wouldn't make a living off his stud fees, but they might support her fashion habits. And I gave her credit for tackling obedience training so she would be ready for another show venue once his breed ring career closed.

"How's everything out there in the back of beyond?" Susanne asked.

"I'm starting a few projects," I replied. My most recent one had been taking the first-floor bathroom door off its hinges after the knob fell off in my hand, trapping me inside.

"I've got a great local listing for a two-bedroom ranch with a fenced yard if you change your mind." Susanne turned on her heel and marched off before I could reply.

"I heard you bought that old abandoned place west of North Willow."

I suppressed a groan. Anders Linder stared at me, demanding acknowledgement. He was a short man with a receding hairline, three chins and an ample stomach. His wire-haired miniature dachshund, George, fixed me with bright eyes from the crook of his arm. Anders owned an accounting business in a neighboring town. He'd been a member of HDTC since before God made dirt and served as the club's treasurer.

"I did." I didn't bother to correct him. The difference between abandoned and empty with a realtor's sign in the front yard was not a hill I chose to die on. Behind him, Kerri mouthed "Good luck" and headed into the ring with Tangle.

"I heard it's haunted."

"That doesn't scare me. I live with a Malinois." Among other things.

"I heard that professor from Coe College speak at Mare MacGregor's shop last spring. He said there's stolen gold buried out there."

I doubted Dr. Aldrich had been so bold as to make that claim. From the safety of his master's arms, George looked at Raider and showed his teeth. Raider showed his back. Size matters. George shut his mouth.

"That's the stolen wealth of a dead man," Anders continued. "That means a curse has settled on the ground where it lies."

He nodded with conviction, chins wobbling. Kerri's warnings about ghosts had been in teasing friendship, but Anders' words held the conviction of a zealot.

My mind flashed uncomfortably to the two grave-sized holes in the pioneer cemetery. No. Not a chance. Anders Linder could barely waddle his bulk around a show ring. If he tried digging anything more than a spoon into a carton of ice cream, he'd give himself a coronary.

"That's just folklore. If anyone knew where it was, they'd have dug it up by now." Before he could warn me the ghost of Sarah Cameron would damn my soul, I jiggled Raider's leash, and we heeled through the gate into the ring.

From the corner of my eye, I saw Anders zero in on Kyle Montgomery, the owner of a local landscaping business. With Anders and Kyle deep in conversation, I had a ridiculous vision of tall, gangly Kyle with a shovel over his shoulder, marching into Bishop Cemetery like an animated scarecrow in search of gold, while Anders sprinkled holy water around the site and droned Gregorian chants. I turned my back on both of them.

In the adjoining ring, Alf and Clara Wittrick were arguing about Alf's schnauzer, Winston. I avoided eye contact with either of them. Like Anders, Alf and Clara were founding members of HDTC. They were both in their eighties, and while I admired their dedication to the sport, their constant squabbling meant other members generally gave them a wide berth.

My training session with Raid started with good intentions but quickly derailed because I couldn't stay focused. I kept seeing visions of fellow trainers descending on my property and digging like a pack of terriers while gold coins flew into the air. Which was ridiculous. With a few exceptions, half of the people present were physically incapable of hiking onto my land, let alone digging large holes, and the other half were so crazy busy with families and jobs, they barely had time to train their dogs, let alone sneak off for unauthorized treasure hunting.

But they were all locals who knew the story. I dragged my hands through my hair. Paranoia was not an attractive trait, and no good could come of viewing everyone I knew as a suspect. But that didn't change the fact that somebody had been digging in the cemetery.

When Clara Wittrick stumped up to the wooden accordion-fold gates dividing the ring, I almost laughed. As she leaned on her cane, I simply could not envision her as a trespassing treasure hunter.

"That dog will never be ready to show if you don't work him at least five times a week," she said with authority.

"I've been busy," I said.

"You bought the old Cameron place, didn't you?"

"Yes."

"Strange old place." She dismissed me with a wave of her cane and went back to haranguing her husband, who'd been doing a fine job without her input.

THE APPROPRIATE NUMBER of lights were on when Raid and I got home at nine o'clock. The house was as welcoming as an old friend, the scent of dried flowers hanging faintly on the air and the furnace purring in the basement. I slung my gear bag on top of the clothes dryer and slid out of my jacket, still thinking about the number of people who knew about the tale of hidden gold.

Without warning, the air crackled. Ribbons of energy climbed the walls like invisible fire, not malevolent but demanding. A thousand miniature lightning bolts struck my skin, each one driving home a desperate need for something I couldn't see. Raider leaned against my leg as I stared into the semi-darkness of the hallway. I wasn't ready to meet a ghost.

Sudden, bitter grief engulfed me like rising fog. A sob echoed in my mind, and the room tilted as if the floorboards were dropping from under my feet. I slid gracelessly down the wall. Raider climbed into my lap. He didn't fit, but that didn't stop him, and I clung to him as the storm raged.

Sarah's grief drew my own betrayals to the surface again, sharp and brutal. Her century-old pain and my more recent hurt swirled like the vortex of a building storm. Tears stung the back of my throat as a deluge of despair engulfed me.

I fought the memories of broken relationships as wounds I thought were healed opened anew. The darkness of never having someone to share my life with, of always being on the outside looking in, swirled in an overwhelming cloud of loss and pain and loneliness.

Raider licked my face. Getting no response, he

licked again, then muzzle punched my cheek, cracking the grip of despair.

"Hey! Ouch!"

Raid sat back, a look of satisfaction on his face.

With a monumental effort, I shoved the broken glass of my failures away and sat with my back against the wall, memories reverberating through my bones. Raid stayed on my lap, keeping me from doing something stupid, like standing up too fast and passing out. I wished Dan had been here. Would Sarah have taken him on the same dark emotional roller coaster, or was this a treat reserved exclusively for me?

"I don't know how to help you," I said with as much authority as I could muster.

I didn't expect an answer, which was good, because I didn't get one. Music played faintly from somewhere, a low, sweet tune tinged with nostalgia and loss. I braced myself against the wall, annoyed with these emotional ambushes that laid open my past like a scalpel blade.

"Stop it. We all have our issues."

The music faded into a silence so deep my ears rang. Great. Had I just turned a sad, lonely ghost into an angry one?

She wanted Luke. I'd felt her century-old pain as it overlaid my own more recent losses. I didn't know what constituted appropriate boundaries in a living-dead relationship, but it felt like she had overstepped.

Crazy as it sounded, I wanted to help her. I couldn't expect assisting a ghost would fix my own broken romantic karma, but there was the bonus of possibly getting her out of my house. That hinged on the assumption she'd leave if I found Luke, which I doubted I could do, so we were right back where we started.

Raider snuffled anxiously and pawed at my arm. I kissed his nose.

"Good dog." If he hadn't been there, refusing to let me drown in that nightmare of sorrow, I wondered how long it would have gone on until Sarah released me. If she was a misery-loves-company kind of ghost, we needed to have a talk. I wasn't spending the rest of my life reliving old hurts at her convenience.

Mare says a person's energy attracts similar energy. That's why you become true friends with only a tiny fraction of the people you meet. Did it work that way with ghosts? Had the euphoria I felt when I stepped over the threshold on moving day been a reflection of Sarah's joy in being able to connect with me because we'd both suffered disastrously broken romances? Did that give me a psychic edge in the ghost department?

Tonight's episode felt like a test, something akin to being evaluated to see if I was strong or fearless or just plain crazy enough to welcome the connection. I said the first thing that came to mind.

"How do you expect me to find someone who's been dead for almost a century?"

The only response was the stillness of the old house settling for the night.

I put on my pajamas and went to bed. I only knew

one thing for sure—each time our paths crossed, she was stronger than the time before.

CHAPTER 11

HALLOWEEN—SAMHAIN, IF you choose the Celtic parallel—dawned with a vibrant sunrise in shades of scarlet and purple. No lingering emotional residue from the previous night's episode clung to the house. If anything, the rooms resonated with a bright energy that hummed just beyond audible.

Raider and I headed out for a hike while frost clung to the little bluestem in the pasture. With Anders Linder's absurd prophecy of a curse on the land fresh in my memory, my senses were on high alert as we approached Bishop Cemetery. An image of Anders digging by lantern light like a Victorian-era grave robber danced through my mind, but Raid's exuberance flushed only a pair of hen pheasants.

I paused near the tumbled stone wall. Leaves knocked down by the recent rain covered the burial plot like a tattered quilt. I saw no further damage to indicate the vandals had returned and sighed with relief.

After dealing with a ghost who threw things and specialized in emotional ambushes, buried treasure quietly behaving itself was almost appealing by comparison.

Logic dictated the treasure had already been found if it ever existed in the first place. Any

Indiana Jones wannabe with a metal detector would have had decades to locate the hidden cache.

I whistled for Raider and we moved on. I focused on enjoying my dog's antics and the autumn foliage and managed to ignore the annoying little voice that kept asking, *then why is someone digging there now?*

MAYBE IT WAS my imagination, but the house seemed to sigh with contentment as I applied the first strokes of dusty sage paint to the living room walls. Mare and Kerri had offered to help me, but neither of them could spare time until the weekend, and I couldn't wait. If I had to live with that acid blue color one more day, I'd poke my eyes out.

I was balanced atop the stepladder, cutting in along the crown molding, when my skin tingled. The sensation of being watched was unmistakable. I'm used to being stared at by Raider as a matter of daily life, but this lacked the feeling of innate nosiness dogs excel at. On the contrary, it felt merely observant.

I clenched the paint brush, remembering Courtney Weldon's claim something had pushed her off a ladder. Maybe something had. Or maybe she was a klutz. I looked down at the floor, six feet below me. If Sarah started in with another of her emotional sideswipes, I'd fall off the ladder, and she'd kill me whether she intended to or not.

A swirl of energy, like the faint warmth of early spring, spun through the room. It carried notes of interest and approval, but none of the grief of the previous evening. A peace offering?

It would be rude not to acknowledge her. "This color is called Superstitious Evening. It's from a historic homes palette." I held my breath.

Nothing happened. The sensation faded, returning to the barely perceptible hum I'd come to recognize as Fox Hollow's normal frequency. As far as paranormal apologies went, I'd take it.

An hour later, I'd hit my stride. Trim around a door. Move the ladder. Trim around a window. Move the ladder. Trim. Move. Try not to think about my aching back and arms. Try not to think about how long this was going to take.

I was belting out Bon Jovi's "You Give Love a Bad Name" when Raider barked from the kitchen. I barely heard the knock through the music thumping from my phone. If it was Kerri or Mare, they had carte blanche to let themselves in. If it was anyone else, they could go away. The song launched into the chorus, and I belted out the lyrics like it was two-for-one night at the karaoke bar. Maybe my singing would turn the tables on Sarah and make her leave.

"Is the concert free or do I need a ticket?"

My head snapped around as I yelped in surprise. The ladder swayed slightly, and my yelp turned to a panicked squeak. Dan leaned against the kitchen door frame, hands shoved in jeans pockets and an almost-but-not-quite apologetic smile on his face.

"You scared me half to death!" I loosened my white-knuckle grip on the ladder as my heart rate decelerated.

"Raider let me in," he said, as if that explained everything.

I pulled my phone out of my pocket and paused the playlist. Raid trotted over and presented Dan a tennis ball.

"Do you want something? Or did you just stop to see my dog?"

"Your dog likes me."

"That's not what I asked. Don't you have a book to write?"

"Needed a break."

"So you came to see me?" The part of me that still believed in Prince Charming wanted to be flattered.

"There's no one else out here," he said, sending Prince Charming packing.

I glared. "Are you always this difficult?"

"No. Sometimes I'm worse."

I opened my mouth to say, "That's not possible," but an idea got in the way. I eyed him objectively, looked at the expanse of unpainted walls, then back at him.

"You could help me paint." I said it fast, before I had time to think about the sheer effrontery of asking a guy I barely knew to dive into my labor-intensive project.

Dan took a step backward. "That sounds like work."

"I'll let you use a brand-new roller."

"Are you trying to Tom Sawyer me into this?"

"Whatever it takes." I climbed down the ladder. "Seriously, why'd you come over?"

To date, there'd been legit reasons for his unexpected visits, but there was no particular reason for him to be here now.

"Just checking on my favorite neighbor."

"I'm your only neighbor, as you pointed out. Be serious."

"I am serious. You live alone. You could fall and hit your head, get attacked by a raccoon. You've already been run off the road and had some nut case tell you to get out of the house. I figure someone needs to keep an eye on you." The corners of his mouth twitched upward, but the smile didn't hide the concern in his eyes.

"We could knock this out in no time." I'd forgive Dan the sexist assumption I needed a man to keep an eye on me if he'd help paint. Besides, it was kind of nice to know someone had my back. "It would make Sarah happy."

"Now you know what makes a ghost happy?"

"She likes this color."

"She tell you that?"

"She didn't tip me off the ladder."

Dan pushed off the door frame and walked slowly around the room, gauging the extent of the project. Sensing victory, I ran with it. "I'll give you a beer when we're done."

"From the case I brought you?"

"Yes. It's going to last awhile."

"Then I should come over more often."

My heart skipped a beat. "Now you're just angling for free beer."

"It's not free if I bought it in the first place."

I crossed my arms and matched his rogue's grin with one of my own. "You in or not?"

***

DAN PAINTED WITH such attention to detail I understood how his pile of junk pickup purred like it was brand new. Any reluctance I felt about asking for his help vanished along with the blue walls.

"Any new developments?" he asked after we'd exhausted the weather and the Iowa State Cyclones' current football season.

"You mean with Sarah?"

"You're on a first name basis now?"

"I can't keep calling her 'the ghost'," I said. "This was her home before it was mine." I'd developed an odd sense of protectiveness. My house. My ghost. I told him about the previous night's episode, ending with, "Not knowing what happened to Luke tore her apart. She's still grieving, but I think she's channeling that into determination to find him."

"So what's your plan?"

I pulled my brush along the edge of the baseboard and watched the paint spread evenly over the rough plaster. Just a normal day, painting my haunted house with help from my reclusive neighbor and talking about how to handle the resident ghost.

"I don't have a plan. Apparently, neither did anyone else who lived here, and look how that worked out."

The weight of the situation settled on my shoulders like a cloak. My six-month deadline to prove myself as a competent do-it-yourselfer would be eclipsed in short order if I couldn't appease Sarah. I wasn't ready to talk about my theory regarding her eviction of Fox Hollow's previous residents. Nor was I ready to be the next notch on whatever ghosts carved notches on when the living didn't live up to their expectations.

Dan's appraising look reminded me of another inconvenient truth—she'd pulled him in, too.

"You think the other owners understood what she wanted?" he asked.

"No. You and I are different from any of them." The words were out of my mouth before I could stop. "They were all married couples. Maybe this sounds stupid, but I think she connected with us because we're single, and we can relate to the pain of losing someone we loved, one way or the other."

Dan's jaw clenched, tightening the angles of his face. I held my breath. I had no right to drag up Hannah Wintergarden's memory to satisfy my off-the-wall theory.

"That doesn't sound stupid," he said, then pointed at my brush. "You're painting your leg."

I HANDED DAN a beer and he dropped onto the couch. I collapsed into my recliner and let exhausted muscles go limp. Autumn sunlight streamed through the windows, and from the worn wooden floor to the polished fireplace mantel, the room echoed with comfortable familiarity, like I'd lived here for years.

"Thank you," I said, waving my arm to encompass the finished project. "It would have taken me forever to do this by myself."

"Now you owe me two pies."

Oops. I still owed him one for clearing the tree

limbs. "What kind?"

"Surprise me. You know how to bake a pie, don't you?"

"Of course I do. Did you think I'd get one from Mare and pass it off as my own?"

"I think I might get it sooner that way."

"Smart ass."

He chuckled, unoffended, and we sat in companionable silence. Damn, he was easy to be around, and he looked good sprawled on my couch, all lean and dark and rough. A warning bell went off in my head, but I silenced it. Ignore and override.

"Tell me about that." I tapped my left ear to indicate his earring.

He scowled. "There was alcohol involved."

"Sounds like a good start."

"It was at a reunion with some guys I served with a few years ago. We decided to commemorate it, either a piercing or a tattoo. I figured I could always take the earring out. A tattoo sounded a whole lot more permanent."

"But you didn't. Take it out, I mean."

His scowl changed to a sheepish grin. "It kinda grew on me. Girls seem to like it."

"Kerri thinks it's hot."

"And you don't?"

I flashed back to that night he showed up on my doorstep with a case of beer and a pirate's grin. Yeah. It was hot. And he had absolutely no business knowing I thought that.

He took my silence for agreement and grinned even wider. "Told you so."

I swore inwardly. Look but don't touch and everything would be fine.

Dan took a pull on his beer and rescued both of us. "I like this house. It's got a good vibe."

"Nobody who lived here before thought so."

"You said it yourself, maybe they weren't the right people for the house."

"Maybe I'm not either."

"Thinking of selling already?" His voice was neutral. He scratched Raider's belly as the dog lolled upside down on the couch next to him.

"No. I'm not taking the easy way out. I'm tired of watching my dreams die." That sounded a little over the top, but it was the truth. I wasn't going to break up with the house I'd fallen in love with just because it already had a permanent resident.

"I don't think you'd do anything the easy way." He shifted, then grimaced.

"Pull a muscle painting?" I joked.

He stretched his left leg straight out, flexed the knee, then eased it back down. "I have an artificial knee and a titanium rod in my femur."

That explained the limp. I immediately felt guilty about asking him to do the ladder work even though he hadn't hesitated.

"War injury?"

"Hannah hit me with her car."

I choked on my beer.

"By accident?" I ventured, then winced at the stupidity of the question. How else do you hit your fiancé with a car?

"No." His voice was resigned, as if he were

recalling an unpleasant but inconsequential experience. "On purpose."

"What the hell?" That was all the tact I could muster. "She meant to hit you?"

"She meant to kill me."

CHAPTER 12

"She what?"

"Meant to kill me," he repeated.

"Clearly she didn't succeed."

"Close. I had two surgeries and six months of physical therapy before I could walk without a cane." He slapped his leg. "I'm good as new now. More or less."

"But she was the one who broke your engagement. Isn't that a little dramatic?"

"She was all about drama." His tone held the roughness of old scars that still hurt. "Little girl had a big sense of entitlement." He tipped his head back and closed his eyes. I wanted to change the subject to anything else, but morbid curiosity charged heedlessly forward.

"You wouldn't make your dog live in the garage so she ran over you?"

Dan opened his eyes. Their midnight blue depths were hard as flint. "You know how you think you know a person, then finally have to admit there's a whole other side to them you'd been pretending didn't exist? One you thought wouldn't matter if you ignored it?"

Yeah. I knew it all too well. "So she drove around, waiting for a chance to hit you?"

Dan contemplated his beer bottle. A muscle twitched in his jaw, and I wanted to reach out and smooth away the hurt. I kept my hands to myself.

"She stalked me."

"Stalked you?" This was going from bad to worse.

"Every time I turned around, there she was. At a bar with friends, in the grocery store, once at a book signing. That was awkward."

"Did she want to get back together?" As far as exes went, she sounded more needy than psychotic.

"It was more like 'Look what you're missing, aren't you sorry?'"

"Were you sorry?"

"No."

Silence.

"Were you seeing someone else?" Why couldn't I stop prying into his life?

"Sure." He shrugged. "Caught a couple of rebounds."

"But she didn't try getting rid of them?" I was still struggling with the idea of golden girl Hannah Wintergarden, with her perfect figure and toothpaste-commercial smile, trying to kill the man sprawled on my couch, drinking beer and letting my dog chew on his sleeve.

"Nope. She decided I should pay for my failure to be Mr. Right. About a month after we parted company, I came home from a writers' conference and someone had tossed my house. She still had a key. A few weeks later, someone took a baseball bat to my pickup, beat the hell out of it. I knew she'd done it, but I couldn't prove it."

I glanced out the window, confused. The battered vehicle parked outside was far beyond any concern about cosmetic issues.

"I banked the insurance money and bought that heap," Dan said. "Shit was getting real, and the police wouldn't take me seriously. She was a second-grade teacher, for God's sake. Miss Wintergarden, adored by her students at Jefferson Elementary School." He shrugged in dismissal. "She ran me down one night as I left a restaurant with a girl I was seeing."

"I'm so sorry." I flashed back to my own myriad break-ups. They'd been monumentally ugly, but I hadn't tried killing anyone in the aftermath. Not that I hadn't thought about it. "What happened?"

"A half-dozen witnesses said she veered onto the sidewalk, hit me, and threw me into a stone retaining wall. Wrecked my leg pretty good, plus a concussion and broken ribs. The responding officer said she kept asking if I was dead. When he told her no, she started screaming at him to let her finish the job. Psych evals said she wasn't competent to stand trial for attempted murder, and her family had her admitted to a private clinic. I decided it was in my best interest to find somewhere else to live. That was when I found the old Bauer place."

"So that's why you left Chicago," I murmured. "Have you ever seen her again?"

Dan drained his beer. The familiar half-smile was back. "Nope. She was released about a year later, and there was the usual restraining order, et cetera." His eyes sparkled with dark amusement. "And my lawyer mentioned to her lawyer that I kept a loaded handgun in every room of my house."

AFTER DAN LEFT, I cleaned up the painting mess. The house's energy hummed against my skin like a live thing. Halfway between the autumn equinox and the winter solstice, Halloween had originally been celebrated as a festival to mark the end of harvest season and usher in the cold, dark days of winter. I couldn't have said exactly what I expected to happen today, only that it hadn't.

"By the pricking of my thumbs, something wicked this way comes," I said to Raider.

Only nothing felt wicked. And I was dealing with a ghost, not witches.

Raid barked, and I looked out to see a delivery van from North Willow Floral pull up in front of the house. I met the driver on the porch and took the arrangement of autumn flowers he handed me. The vase was tied with a ribbon featuring sparkly little ghosts dancing with their sheeted hands in the air. This had Kerri written all over it. Smiling, I pulled the card out of the envelope. The familiar bold handwriting wiped the smile off my face.

Thinking of you, Brad.

I dropped the card like it was red hot. The flowers sat innocently on the kitchen table, unaware of the chaos they'd instigated. I glared at them. If I didn't acknowledge the damned things, Brad would call to make sure I got them, and I'd have to talk to him.

I texted a quick message. *Thx for the flowers.*

Four words. No school-girl gushing about how pretty they were. No invitation for further communication. When my phone rang, I flinched, then sighed with relief at seeing Kerri's name on the screen.

"You'll never guess what I found at the historical society," she said.

"Brad sent me flowers," I blurted.

Her pause was so long I thought we'd been disconnected. Then, cautiously, "Why?"

"No clue." I scrambled to collect my wits, which were running around like someone left the gate open. "Sorry, what did you find?"

Kerri hesitated, no doubt wanting to ask more about the flowers but taking the hint and moving on.

"A huge collection of newspaper clippings about the tornado," she said. "It made every paper from Minneapolis to St. Louis, but that's not the best part. We have a photo album that came from Sarah's estate. It's fantastic."

Excitement surged through me, driving any reconciliation agenda Brad might be pursuing right out of my mind. A physical link to Sarah's past would help me understand her better.

"I made copies of all the newspaper clippings." Kerri lowered her voice to a conspiratorial level. "We're not supposed to take artifacts out of the museum, but I'll bring the photo album out tonight so you can see it. It'll save you a trip to town and the chance of running into Bev again."

"That would be great!" My only plans for the evening included sitting in front of a fire with a glass of wine, both of which could be shared with friends. "Hey, why don't you pick up carry-out at Pasta Ranch? My treat. I'll call Mare and see if she wants to come, too. I need to bring you guys up to date on things."

We settled the food plans and I called Mare, who said she'd come as soon as the chamber of commerce costume parade ended. I fed Raider and showered, then opened a bottle of my favorite local red. I'd just taken wine glasses from the cupboard when a vehicle stopped in front of the house and someone knocked on the kitchen door.

Expecting Kerri, I yelled, "It's open."

"Hey."

I spun as Dan stepped into the kitchen. He was wearing his usual flannel, open over a thermal Henley, and faded cargo pants. Caught off guard, I allowed myself a moment of simple appreciation. The working man's fashion accented his lean build, and his hair was still damp from a shower. A smudge of Superstitious Evening clung above one ear. I resisted the urge to brush my fingers through his hair under the guise of pointing it out.

Raider leaped up and planted his front paws on Dan's chest, sending him staggering back.

"Raid, get down!" I said. "Sorry, he has manners, but they're all bad."

Dan thumped the dog companionably. "Nice flowers." He nodded at the arrangement on the table.

"Brad sent them."

Dan pushed Raider quietly off of him. He looked at the flowers, then at the wine and glasses on the counter. "You're expecting company. I'll go." He turned, one hand already on the door knob.

"No!" I said, my mind refusing to stop thinking about the paint in his hair. "Kerri and Mare are bringing dinner. Stay. Please."

His face was inscrutable. "Not many guys send flowers to a girl who called them a narcissistic knuckle dragger."

"I don't know what he's playing at."

"Really?" Sarcasm dripped from the word.

"I kicked Brad's ego square in the balls when we broke up," I fired back. "If he wants to get back together, it's only because he thinks I'm stupid enough to fall for his crap again, not because he realized he's a self-centered ass and decided to change. That whole family has a pretty high opinion of themselves."

We stood there, looking at each other, Dan laughing now, me scowling. Something about him sent Fox Hollow's undercurrent of energy up a notch. I wanted him here with a need so intense it knocked any other thoughts right out of my head.

"Supper is the least I can do after you helped me paint all afternoon," I managed. "Take off your coat and stay. You want a beer or a glass of wine?"

"Anyone ever tell you you're bossy?"

"I prefer to call it assertive. Sit down."

He muttered something that sounded like "Same thing" but slung his coat over the back of a kitchen chair and sat. I took two more glasses out of the cupboard and poured drinks for both of us. My heart beat a little faster than necessary, and the frequency of the house seemed to a purr like a contented cat. I was starting to have suspicions about my resident ghost that had nothing to do with finding her vanished sweetheart.

Dan reached into his jacket and tossed a copy of the *North Willow Sentinel* onto the table. "Have you seen this?"

The headline leaped off the front page, above the fold.

"X Marks the Spot: Lenox County Treasure Featured in Folklore Book. By Logan Barnes, Staff Reporter."

With a sinking stomach, I scanned the story. Even if Logan got half the facts correct, this wasn't going anywhere good.

> North Willow—A tale of Confederate gold hidden in Lenox County is featured in a soon-to-be-published book exploring legends of the Midwest. "Treasure Hunting in the Heartland," by historian and treasure hunter Dr. Peter Aldrich, investigates long-forgotten stories of stolen artwork, stashes of bootleg whisky, and missing dinnerware from a territorial governor's mansion.
>
> Aldrich, who holds a Ph.D. in history and works as a tenured professor at the University of Oklahoma, assembled the volume after years of collecting obscure lore about valuable items that have disappeared without a trace. He turns the spotlight on Lenox County in a chapter about the Bishop Trading Post treasure.
>
> Aldrich explores the story alleging Civil War-era gold coins were hidden near the Bishop

Trading Post, which was located in the north central part of the county. A combination general store and inn, the post served travelers in the period of westward expansion during and after the Civil War. It burned to the ground in the 1880s and was not rebuilt.

The story claims the coins were hidden near the trading post by a man and woman who had escaped slavery and fled from Georgia. They sheltered at an Underground Railroad stop in Lenox County's Sand Creek Township while the man recovered from injuries incurred on the journey. Pursued by a slave catcher and needing to travel fast, the couple buried the coins and continued north toward Canada, intending to return for them after the war. Word of their death in a cholera outbreak was later received by the family at whose home they stayed.

Like many tales of buried wealth, Dr. Aldrich acknowledges it is easy to let the thrill of the hunt overshadow the odds of finding anything.

"I'm not claiming any of these stories are one hundred percent true," he cautions. "But each of them began with an element of truth and it is my purpose to invite the reader to explore the past and consider the possibilities."

Not bad, given Logan's propensity to play fast and loose with the facts. I skimmed the rest of the story, searching for the information I prayed wasn't there.

Crapweasel in a box. Of course it was there.

"The Bishop Trading Post was located on a parcel of property known as Fox Hollow Farm. Dr. Aldrich noted he tried to contact owners of the property for comment and permission to take photos but was unable to reach them.

"The book will be released in early December and available at A Likely Story in North Willow, as well as other retail outlets."

Dr. Aldrich went on to thank members of the Lenox County Historical Society for their help with his research and cautioned would-be treasure hunters against trespassing on private property. He emphasized the importance of contacting local authorities if they found anything of historical value so it could be properly curated.

At least Logan hadn't mentioned my name. Not that it mattered. Everyone knew where Fox Hollow Farm was.

I took a long drink. "He actually published the book."

"You knew about it?"

"He spoke at the book club at A Likely Story last spring. I wanted to go, but that meeting was right after Brad and I parted company, and his mom was the book club high priestess. I didn't want to be in the same room with her."

"She can't be that bad. She runs the town coffee shop. Gotta have people skills for that."

"She's all chamber of commerce charm when she's taking your money, but believe me, if you cross her, you'd better sleep with one eye open."

"How'd you and Brad hook up?" Dan's tone gave

no indication of anything beyond mild curiosity.

"Kerri's husband is a volunteer fireman in North Willow. They hold a big street dance every summer. Kerri invited me to come—I was living in Benton County then. She introduced me to a lot of people that night, including Brad. It went from there. She still hasn't forgiven herself."

"She must have thought the two of you would hit it off."

"We did, until I realized he pouted like a toddler when he didn't get his way."

Dan flipped the ribbon on the bouquet with a finger. "He's still thinking about you."

"He'll stop it if he knows what's good for him."

My phone dinged with an incoming text.

Glad you enjoyed the flowers. Call me next time you're in town. Coffee?

Not effing likely. And I hadn't said I enjoyed them. Leave it to Brad to put the words he wanted to hear in my mouth. I put the phone face down on the table.

"Brad?"

"How'd you guess?"

"You look like you just ate a bug."

That made me laugh. "He wants me to meet him for coffee."

"Do you want to meet him for coffee?"

"No." I wasn't going to make the same mistake twice. I'd rather make a new one.

I forced my thoughts back to the paper on the table. "If that book doesn't come out until December, at least by then it will be too cold for a bunch of nuts to come marching out here with their metal detectors and shovels."

Headlights flashed up the lane, and Raider bounced off the windowsill, barking happily. I let Mare and Kerri in.

Kerri was laden with plastic sacks of carry-out containers and an overstuffed canvas tote bag. Mare staggered in behind her, arms wrapped around a huge jack-o-lantern which she deposited on the kitchen table.

"Please tell me you didn't carve that thing just to bring out here," I said.

"I didn't," she answered. "I carved it to sit outside the shop during the costume parade. I couldn't leave it there because the little heathens in town would smash it tonight."

She produced a book of matches from a pocket and lit the fat white candle inside the pumpkin. The jack-o-lantern's toothy grin beamed into the room, reminding me of the years when Halloween meant nothing more than homemade costumes and a glut of candy. Mare started to unpack the food. Dan rose to help her.

"Are we interrupting anything?" Kerri asked quietly as I took plates from the cupboard.

"No."

"You sure?"

"Yes," I said through clenched teeth.

"Are those from Brad?" She nodded toward the bouquet.

"Yeah." I'd considered tossing it in the trash in a grand gesture of contempt, but the practical side of me insisted it was too pretty to waste. The little ghosts on the ribbon made me laugh as long as I didn't think about where they'd come from.

"He can't seriously want to get back together, not after the way you two ended."

"He wants to meet for coffee."

"Are you going to?"

"Hell no."

"What about Dan?" she whispered.

"What about him?" I glanced over my shoulder.

Dan was pushing take-out containers to the center of the table. Raider was stuck to him like glue. Kerri opened her mouth to say something I didn't want to hear, but Mare asked if we were going to set the table or if we were going to eat with our fingers, putting an end to the interrogation.

We helped ourselves to chicken alfredo, mac and cheese, beef ravioli in red sauce, and breadsticks shiny with garlic butter. No place does carbs like Pasta Ranch. As expected, Kerri brought enough for an army.

"Hey, what was Anders talking to you about at class last night?" Kerri asked. "You looked like you wanted to push him in front of a bus."

"He was carrying on about how my house is haunted and the gold in the cemetery is cursed by a dead man. He probably thought I'd run screaming or put the place up for sale," I said.

"Speaking of gold, did you see the story in this week's *Sentinel*?" Mare asked.

My mouth was full of food. I nodded and pointed to the copy lying on the counter.

"Do you think the book will make things worse out here?" she queried.

I swallowed. "You mean more people poking around in the cemetery?" I wanted to believe the book would fade quickly into obscurity, but the story would inevitably inspire a few treasure-seeking fanatics who'd end up on my doorstep, at least the ones who bothered to ask for permission.

"What do you mean worse?" Kerri put her fork down.

"Jess thinks someone's playing Indiana Jones out in the old pioneer cemetery," Dan said.

I passed Kerri the paper. "This book turned that old legend into front page news."

Kerri scanned the article. "Someone's been digging in the Bishop Cemetery? Do you really think there's Confederate gold buried out there?"

"It doesn't matter what I think, but yeah, there are a couple of places where someone has dug. The holes aren't really deep, though. I mean, not like they're digging up actual graves. Unless they partially refilled them, and I don't even want to think about that."

I got the potsherd out of the pantry and set it on the table. "I found this out there. It must have come out of one of the holes."

Kerri ran her finger along the edge of the broken stoneware. "You don't think that's why Sarah Cameron is still here, do you? To guard the treasure?"

"Dragons guard treasure," Mare corrected. "You're getting your mythologies mixed up."

"I don't think Sarah has any connection to the cemetery. It was abandoned before she was even born," I said.

I told Kerri and Mare about my contact with my invisible roommate the previous night. The aching sadness wasn't as sharp when recalling the incident in a warm kitchen surrounded by friends, but it still lingered in my bones like an old injury.

"It was like she was tapping into my emotions and mixing them with hers." I shrugged. "Maybe she's just trying to make me as unhappy as she is. Misery loves company and all that."

Dan steepled his fingers. I waited for him to say something, but he didn't. The intensity of his dark blue gaze was nearly tangible, and for an instant, ghosts were the last thing on my mind.

"I bet she couldn't connect with any of the previous people who lived here, and that's why they left," Kerri said.

My mind slammed on the brakes before it got in trouble. I directed my thoughts back to the conversation Dan and I had while painting, about the reason why Sarah chose me—and him—to target from beyond the grave.

"I've got a theory about that," I said and turned to Dan. "Would you open that second bottle of wine, please? We're going to need it."

I LIT THE fire as Mare and Kerri settled on the couch. Raider plopped himself happily between them, while Dan slouched into one of the recliners. Once admiration of the room's new paint was finished, I took a deep breath and flipped open my notebook. "I need you guys to hear me out on something. I talked to Esther at the museum a few days ago and got an overview of this place's previous owners."

"Let me guess, Loretta O'Brien's files?" Kerri asked, and I nodded.

"This house has had five different owners since Sarah died," I said. "The first ones stayed fifteen years, but none of the others stayed more than a year. I think the first couple were aware of Sarah's presence, but she didn't have enough power to make them leave yet."

Mare looked intrigued. Kerri's eyes had grown even wider. Dan watched me with the cautious interest of someone encountering an unpredictable animal. I plowed on.

"All the owners told Loretta about odd things happening, like lights going on and off or hearing music. One of the kids said small objects moved around in her room." I forced myself not to look at the calico balls on the mantel. "The wife of the last couple who lived here claimed something pushed her off a ladder." I was this far down the rabbit hole, there was no going back. "It's like Sarah gives people a trial run. When they don't suit her, she makes it so uncomfortable they leave. She's been, um, reaching out to me in little ways since I moved in."

"Maybe she just hasn't found anyone she wants to share the house with yet." Kerri's voice wobbled. "Maybe it's a compatibility test."

I gave her a quick smile, glad for her support.

"She's not going to drive you out. She wants you

here." Dan's tone made the conversation sound reasonable, but he avoided any reference to his own encounter with the spirit.

"It's more than that," I said slowly. "I think she's chosen me to find Luke because I'm single, like her." I swallowed hard. "I don't mean just not married. I mean alone. No attachments. The people who lived here before me were married couples or families. They couldn't relate to what she'd been through."

The only sound in the room was the fire crackling.

"Next year is the one-hundred-year anniversary of that tornado and Luke's death," I continued. "He's been missing for almost a century, and now that she's been dead for twenty years, she's built up enough power to communicate with the living about finding him."

The first-floor bathroom door slammed like an exclamation point at the end of my sentence. We all stared through the open pocket doors into the hallway. Nothing else happened.

"She's not evil, she's not trying to scare me out." Yet. "She can't rest until Luke is found, and she wants me to do it. But I don't have a clue where to start."

Kerri sat bolt upright. "The tornado stuff from the museum!"

She retrieved the overstuffed canvas bag and handed me a thick folder of photocopied newspaper stories from 1919. "There's even an interview with Luke's family. I put it on top," she said.

I opened the folder and skimmed a story

headlined *Missing Man Intended To Propose To Childhood Sweetheart On Day Storm Ripped Through County.*

Luke's parents confirmed he intended to ask Sarah to marry him at the Independence Day celebration. Luke had asked Gavin and Moira Cameron for their daughter's hand the week before. He'd ridden off to Walnut Bluff the afternoon of July 4, 1919, with the engagement ring in his pocket, never to be seen again. Nothing new there.

Then a paragraph at the end of the story caught my eye. The reporter had interviewed Ian Cameron. I read aloud, "Bauer's long-time friend Ian Cameron, brother of the grieving Sarah Cameron, noted he accompanied Bauer when he purchased the engagement ring, a sapphire solitaire set with diamonds, from Locke's Jewelers in Walnut Bluff."

My heart gave a painful stutter. The ring sounded beautiful. Everyone had known about the pending proposal, most likely including the bride-to-be. I turned the sheet face down and sifted through the remaining copies, reading the headlines aloud. "*North Willow Ledger*, 'Walnut Bluff Decimated By Monster Twister'; *Omaha World Herald*, 'Rescuers Work Around the Clock to Free Survivors,' and finally, *The Des Moines Register and Tribune*, 'Ten Dead as Sky Falls in Eastern Iowa.'"

I jogged the sheets together and set them on the parlor table by my chair. "I can read those later. Let's see the album." My fingers tingled in anticipation of seeing photos of the woman who once—still—called Fox Hollow home.

I evicted Raider from the couch and joined Kerri and Mare. Dan stood behind and leaned to look over my shoulder. A subtle blend of soap and warm, clean male drifted on the air, and my focus wandered.

Then I got a grip. Dan Sinclair could look and smell as good as he wanted. He was my neighbor, and that was as far as it went.

I opened the album cover and recognized Sarah immediately, like someone I'd known forever. The girl smiling at the camera was slender, her hair pulled up neatly with a few curls escaping to frame her face. High cheekbones and a long, straight nose accented the contours of her face, and her generous smile hinted at good humor.

By the time she was nineteen, Sarah Cameron had lived through World War I, the Spanish influenza pandemic and the disappearance of the man she'd planned to spend the rest of her life with. She went on to live through the Great Depression and a second world war, all the while managing the family farm and raising the pedigreed draft horses Fox Hollow was famous for. Perhaps lingering after death to resolve Luke's disappearance was simply one more thing she'd set her mind to.

The photos captured the rhythm of her daily life. Sarah and Ian on the day of her high school graduation. The family standing in front of a Belgian team hitched to a wagon piled high with hay. Sarah with a broad-shouldered boy with dark, curly hair, standing next to a Model A flatbed truck laden with baskets of apples. The neat script below the photo read *Sarah Cameron and Luke Bauer, September 1918, cider pressing at the Bauer orchard.*

So that was Luke. He, too, shone with the irrepressible optimism of youth, untarnished by any hint of the future.

I turned the pages. Luke was in so many photos with Sarah or Ian, he might have been part of their family. One picture especially caught my eye. The black and white print showed Sarah and Luke, arms linked around the neck of a sturdy Belgian foal, a shepherd-type dog sprawled in the grass nearby. They looked impossibly young and wildly happy, even the dog. The photo was captioned *Sarah Cameron and Luke Bauer, June 1919.*

I turned the page. There were photos of Gavin and Ian harvesting corn, Sarah quilting with other women on Fox Hollow's front lawn, Moira snapping beans on the porch. There were no more pictures of Luke.

Interspersed between it all were dozens of photos of massive Belgian horses, their flaxen manes and burnished chestnut and sorrel hides gleaming despite black and gray Kodachrome limitations. Sarah was in many of them, accompanied by a variety of dogs and the occasional cat.

I closed the album and set it on the table in front of the couch.

"Let me play devil's advocate," Mare said. "This is a lovely old house, and I've never felt anything but comfortable here. Are you sure a lingering spirit is asking you for help?"

"Yes." The affirmation spilled out without conscious effort. I stood and reached for the wine bottle on a side table. "Anyone else need a refill?"

The energy that had hummed just beyond my range of hearing all day escalated to a frequency that made my ears throb. The bulb in the lamp by my recliner blew out with a crackling pop, plunging half of the room into shadow. Starbursts of energy sizzled bright as lightning in front of the fireplace, and a keening wail filled my ears.

I backpedaled, tripped on the rug and stumbled against Dan. He caught me awkwardly around the waist and set me upright but didn't let go. Kerri gasped. Mare grabbed Raider's collar as the dog sprang to his feet, growling.

Backlit by the fire, the folder of copied newspaper clippings exploded across the room in a blast of paper shrapnel. The wail rose to a crescendo, a lament fueled by a century of grief that nearly split my head in two. The papers swirled on an updraft before slowly eddying to the floor. A single calico ball tumbled from the mantle and landed atop them with a thud. Raider stared at it, ears up hard.

Dan and I stood as if welded together by a bolt of emotional lightning, his heart beating like a triphammer against my back. My fingers tangled with his. I knew what was coming. When the brutal memories hit, I refused to let the element of surprise drag me into the darkness.

But this time, Sarah ripped into Dan's emotions along with mine. I caught a fast, hard onslaught of rejected love with its aftermath of anger and pain. Involuntarily witnessing Dan's memories felt horribly wrong, but they were so tangled with my own and Sarah's, I couldn't separate them as the cacophony of loss swirled around us.

"No," Dan whispered. He wasn't talking to me. I squeezed his hands tighter and tried to channel the razor's edge of those dark memories away from both of us before they reopened too many old hurts. He relaxed marginally as his face pressed into my hair.

The air rippled like a stone tossed into a pool of clear water, and the room came back into focus. Dan's ragged breathing sounded like a half-drowned man gasping for breath. No one moved. A log collapsed in the hearth, sparking embers upward like fireflies.

"I rescind my comment questioning the spirit's presence. My apologies," Mare said quietly.

"Holy. Shit." Kerri had gone milk white, her eyes huge.

Dan exhaled a long sigh and relaxed his grip. He gave my waist a gentle squeeze and let go. In the melee, one of his hands had caught under my sweatshirt, his fingers warm against bare skin.

"Sorry," he said.

"It's all right," I mumbled. A little unintentional groping was the least of our problems. His eyes reflected the same disbelief I'd felt the first time Sarah pulled me into her firestorm of loss. I turned to Kerri and Mare.

"Did you guys feel that?"

Kerri shook her head. "I just saw..." She waved her hand at the paper-strewn floor.

"Feel what?" Mare asked.

I swallowed hard and looked at Dan. "Every time she connects with me, she gets stronger. Now she's going after you, too."

"Going after what?" Mare was still gripping Raider's collar while the dog stared at the calico ball on the floor.

"She was feeding off bad memories, mixing them with her own grief after Luke vanished." Dan rubbed a hand over his face. "Didn't see that coming."

I wanted to throw my arms around him and tell him I knew exactly how he felt, that for some insane reason my ghost had decided to make him part of her lingering personal tragedy, and I had no idea how either of us could make it stop. Instead, I knelt to pick up the scattered photocopies. As I lifted the calico ball, the headline underneath leaped out at me.

Walnut Bluff Man Unaccounted For In Tornado Aftermath; Family And Neighbors Search To No Avail.

The old-fashioned type blurred on the page, then a scene from that deadly July afternoon blasted into my mind's eye as clearly as if it was on a movie screen. I stood amid a ravaged landscape. No birds sang. The earth was torn and raw.

Pendulous mammatus clouds hung in the sky above the bluff, backlit by a bloody sun. Directly in front of me, a massive cottonwood tree had been stripped of its limbs. Only the ragged trunk remained. At my feet, a bronze church bell lay half-embedded in the dirt. I stumbled in the debris and collided with the shattered ruin of a wood-spindled farmhouse door perched impossibly atop a red and yellow striped parlor chair. Yards away, the broken body of a black cow lay on her side. A single, gold-rimmed china plate painted with rosebuds sat delicately in the mud by her hooves.

I tried to move, but there was nowhere to go. Broken trees, pieces of ruined homes and dead livestock blocked me at every turn. A soft, strong hand closed over mine.

Here!

The single word detonated in my mind.

I knew what she meant. I knew it with all the conviction of a love that endured for a century after being ripped apart.

"Jess!" The image vanished as Dan's voice broke into my consciousness. Adrenaline surged through me, and I lurched to my feet, dizzy with discovery.

"Sit down before you fall down." He reached out to steady me. "You look like you've seen a ghost." He glanced around the room. "No offense meant."

I pushed away from the chair where he was trying to plant me and grabbed his forearms.

"She knows where Luke is!" I spun him in a reckless circle as the revelation rose through me like tiny, fizzing bubbles. "She showed me!"

FINDING A BODY, even with directions from a ghost, was not going to be easy.

"He's in the river bottoms," I said stubbornly. I didn't dwell on the fact the river bottoms extended for endless acres on either side of the Iowa. I didn't dwell on the fact I was now having ghost-induced visions, either. Had things gotten to this point with any of the previous owners? Or had Sarah been unable to communicate with them beyond initial attempts, then grown frustrated when they wouldn't respond and changed her agenda to evicting them?

Kerri, Mare, and Dan either believed me or were willing to humor me when I described the scene immediately after the tornado lifted. There'd been no visible landmarks except the river bluffs, and I'd been standing near their base.

My thoughts spilled out. "After Sarah died, Luke must have shown her what happened to him. I don't know why he isn't the one haunting this place, except he didn't die here so maybe the ghost rules say he can't. Or, typical man, he doesn't care where his bones are. Sarah finally knows where his body is, but she can't get anyone to bring him home, and that's what's keeping her here."

I was on a roll. "I don't know where Luke actually died—he could have been haunting the middle of someone's cornfield for the last hundred years—but his body ended up near the river. That storm was massive. There was so much debris his family could have searched for years and never found him. Sarah wants him brought home and buried in consecrated ground. She doesn't want him to be that man who disappeared in the tornado for eternity."

She hadn't said that. Not exactly. But I felt it with every fiber of my being.

Dan lifted his wine glass. "Ghost whisperer."

"I am not a ghost whisperer," I said, even though evidence pointed to the contrary.

The four of us sat up past midnight, trying to define a search area. The river bottom was little more than flood plain populated by water-loving cottonwoods and willows. Its topography changed annually, according to drought or flood. Unable to pinpoint the site I saw in Sarah's vision, let alone expect a body to still be there, my initial euphoria at her revelation drained away, replaced by a sense of aimless wandering.

Finally, Kerri looked at her watch. "I'd better head home."

"Me, too," Mare sighed. "Thanks for the most interesting Samhain I've had in years."

Dan was the last to leave. As he pulled on his coat, I tugged the top off the jack-o-lantern and blew out the candle. The scent of melted wax and raw pumpkin drifted upward, a lingering scent memory of childhood Halloweens.

"You okay?" He made no move toward the door.

"I'm fine," I said a little too quickly. If it hadn't been nearly one in the morning, if my brain hadn't been yelling at me not to do something stupid, I would have suggested opening another bottle of wine and going back to sit in front of the fire. With Mare and Kerri gone, maybe Sarah would have something more to say to the two people she'd chosen to fulfill her quest. At least that was the reason I told myself.

"How about you?" I asked instead. I wasn't sure how deeply Sarah had tapped into his fiancée-turned-attempted-murderer memories. Knowing how she'd accessed the bitterness of my own failures, I could make a pretty good guess.

"I'm bringing a bottle of Scotch next time," he growled. "If she pulls that crap again, I need something stronger."

"She's not being deliberately mean." My heart jumped at how easily he accepted there'd be a next time. "She's using my—our—emotions to push her agenda."

"I liked her better when she just threw things at me," he said. One corner of his mouth lifted slightly, a rogue's smile, open to interpretation. The memory of his hand against my bare skin lingered.

"Good night, Sinclair."

"Good night, McCallister."

I went through the nightly routine of checking the doors and went to bed, but sleep wouldn't come. It was one thing to sit in front of a cozy fire, drinking wine with friends and discussing how to find someone who disappeared a century ago. It was something else entirely to lie in my own bed with a snoring dog and realize a ghost expected me to do exactly that. What happened if I couldn't?

And for God's sake, Dan Sinclair needed to get out of my head. I didn't need him settling in like he belonged there.

CHAPTER 13

THURSDAY, NOV. 1

KERRI FORGOT TO TAKE the photo album with her. When I yawned my way into the kitchen the next morning, it lay on the table, open to the photo of Sarah and Luke with the knobby-kneed foal. I distinctly remembered it being in the living room when everything happened last night.

I made coffee and slumped into a chair. Was there a spirit-imposed deadline for me to find Luke? What happened if I couldn't? I needed an owner's manual: *The Comprehensive Guide to Care and Management of Your Resident Haunt.*

The *Sentinel* Dan had brought lay next to the jack-o-lantern on the table. The chunk of salt-glazed pottery sat atop the story about Dr. Aldrich's book. I stroked the rough ceramic surface with my index finger and re-read the story.

"Aldrich explores the story alleging Civil War era gold coins were hidden near the Bishop trading post..."

That could mean anything from ten feet to half a mile. The cemetery easily fell within those parameters, but it was absurd to think anything other than the dearly departed had been deposited there. I could get a metal detector and launch my own expedition, but with my luck, I'd dig up something that was decidedly not gold. I didn't need more trouble with dead people.

As I contemplated this, headlights cut through the predawn darkness from the east. They stopped at the end of the lane but didn't pull in. I glanced at the kitchen clock. It was 6:35 a.m. A few minutes later, the vehicle moved on. *What was that about?*

Two hours later, I was on my third cup of coffee and lost in the State Association for the Preservation of Iowa Cemeteries website. I'd started a vague internet search to read about methods of finding bodies lost in natural disasters, but it hadn't taken long to wander off topic.

My main takeaway was it would require a butt-load of time to determine where the graves were located in the Bishop Cemetery and an even bigger butt-load of money to put up new markers when—if—I found them. Legally, I wasn't obligated to do anything with the burial ground, other than not wreck it any more than it already was, but its presence on my land came with a self-inflicted sense of responsibility. That was sacred ground, and the people interred there were a part of Fox Hollow's history.

Seeking a respite from thinking about death, I pulled on my coat and trekked down the lane to get the mail. Raider ran ahead, grabbing mouthfuls of leaves and flinging them around with joyful abandon. Suddenly, he plowed to a stop. He lowered his head toward something on the ground, and just as he opened his mouth for a lunging gulp, I screamed, "No!"

Raid froze and looked at me with such obvious canine disappointment it would have been funny if my heart hadn't stopped in my chest. I grabbed his collar and dragged him backward.

Chunks of bloody meat the size of my hand littered the gravel where Cat's Back Road met the farm lane. I remembered the early morning headlights, and an icy hand squeezed my heart.

I pulled out my cell and called the sheriff's department's non-emergency number. I didn't need a lights and sirens response, but Fox Hollow was too far off the beaten track for this to be accidental.

The dispatcher assured me a deputy would be there soon. As I dropped my phone back in my coat pocket, my fingers brushed a dog waste pick-up bag, standard equipment in every jacket I own. On impulse, I shook the bag open, slid one hand into it like a mitten, and picked up the nearest piece of meat. It was coated with a smear of brown goo.

Peanut butter? What the hell?

I pulled the bag back over my hand, tied it shut, and tucked it into my pocket just as a white Tahoe slowed to turn into the lane. I stepped into the vehicle's path to keep it from running over the evidence.

Raider growled as Brad stepped out. Of course. It had to be Brad.

"Are you all right, Jessie?"

"I'm fine," I snapped, fear overriding petty annoyance. My fingers clenched Raid's collar. With my free hand, I pointed at the ground. "I think someone tried to poison my dog."

Brad walked across the end of the lane, studying the ground. Blood oozed into the gravel dust where it formed red-black sludge around the meat.

"Have you seen any unfamiliar vehicles out here?" he asked.

"Someone stopped about 6:30 this morning, but it was too dark to see the car."

Brad nudged a chunk of meat with his boot. "Why do you think it's poisoned?"

I bit back my irritation. "Why else would someone throw raw meat where my dog would find it?"

"Why would someone want to poison Raider?"

His use of my dog's name, like they had ever been buddies, grated like nails on a chalkboard.

"No idea."

To scare you into leaving, the voice in my mind hissed. That was ridiculous, but just because I wasn't paranoid didn't mean someone wasn't out to get me.

Brad pulled gloves and an evidence bag from the back of the Tahoe. He picked up several lumps of meat and dropped them into the bag, then turned to me. "I'll have the lab guys take a look at this. Probably kids playing a practical joke. Last night was Halloween, after all."

By now I was holding onto my temper with both hands, and his mansplaining dismissal of the incident irritated me even further, if that was possible.

"It didn't happen last night, it happened this morning, and if they meant to kill Raid it's not a joke."

As usual, Brad ignored any input that conflicted with his assessment of the situation.

"I'll let you know when I get the results. It'll take a day or two." He closed the hatch on the Tahoe and hesitated. He took a deep breath and scuffed the toe of his boot through the gravel.

"Look, I'm sorry about what happened between us last spring. I think we deserve another chance." His tone held just the right amount of contrition and his smile was hopeful. "I'd like it if we could get together, maybe for dinner?"

I stared at him. A few months ago, when the wounded part of me wanted nothing more than an apology for that night's judgmental words, I would have welcomed the olive branch. Now, I saw the truth like sharp rocks at the bottom of a clear stream. There was no *we* in his intent. He only *intended* to give me a second chance to realize the error of *my* foolish ways.

I looked past the arrogant confidence I'd once found attractive. A spoiled boy whose sense of entitlement was amplified by badge and uniform looked back.

"No."

Brad's face went hard with surprise, then too quickly shifted to hurt, a practiced look that had probably gotten him everything he wanted since he was little.

"Why?" His mouth tightened.

A million reasons flooded my mind. I chose the simplest one. "I'm not interested."

Brad Jennings was good at a lot of things, but handling rejection was not one of them.

"If that's how you want to play this," he said in a

tone edged with ice.

"I'm not playing anything. I've moved on. You should, too." Listen to me, giving relationship advice. At my side, Raider coiled like a steel spring, feeding off my tension.

"With your neighbor? That's convenient."

"That's none of your business."

For a second, I thought Brad was going to demand I give his flowers back, then he got in the Tahoe and slammed the door. Gravel sprayed from the tires as he gunned the engine and disappeared down the road.

I knelt, and Raider dived into my arms. He buried his muzzle against my chest, and I held him, breathing in his warm animal scent. If anything happened to him, I would take the person responsible apart piece by piece.

I dusted off my jeans and swore I wasn't calling the sheriff's office again for anything short of a zombie apocalypse. Back at the house, I shut my disappointed dog inside and drove back down the lane with a garbage bag and shovel. I scooped up the remaining chunks of peanut butter-smeared meat and the blood-stained dirt around them, then poked around in the grass until I was satisfied I'd found them all.

I'd just dropped the bag in the sealed trashcan in the garage when my phone rang. Kerri didn't bother with hello, just a desperate, "You have the photo album, right?"

I went into the kitchen. The album was where I'd left it, but it had opened again to the same picture. I didn't mention that. Kerri didn't need to know a ghost had been messing with one of the Lenox County Historical Society's artifacts.

"Yeah, it's here," I assured her. "Hey, I'm coming into town. Meet me at Mare's in thirty minutes."

DR. DIANE Griffith at the North Willow Veterinary Center was a tall woman in her late forties with short, ash blonde hair and a no-nonsense attitude.

"What's up? Is Raider all right?" She ushered me into an exam room and closed the door. My nutty dog is one of her favorite clients by merit of being well socialized and easy to handle. I also pay my bills on time and in full without complaining, a quality vets find endearing. I knew she'd do me a favor.

"He's fine." Pulling the plastic bag out of my coat pocket, I tossed it on the stainless-steel exam table where it landed with a splat. "I think this has been tampered with." I told her the whole story, ending with, "I'd like a second opinion."

Dr. Griffith poked the bag with a neatly trimmed nail. "I'll call you as soon as I know something."

THE RELIEF ON Kerri's face was palpable when I handed her the album, wrapped discreetly in a plastic grocery store bag. She locked it in her van, and we went into A Likely Story.

Mare had switched the Halloween décor for bunches of Indian corn and miniature pumpkins trimmed with raffia ribbon. The chalkboard near the door sported the date and time for the chamber of commerce's annual pre-holiday kick-off in a few weeks. Customers were queued up in a noon hour rush, so Mare ushered us to a small corner table and brought a tray with mugs of hot chocolate and a plate of molasses cookies.

"This isn't your usual clientele," I said, noting the high school kids in line.

"Brewed Awakenings probably closed early again," Mare said. "Bev has been doing that a lot. She can't keep staff. The kids are coming here now for a sugar fix."

After two molasses cookies and half a mug of cocoa, I told her and Kerri about the morning's events.

"Brad wrote it off as kids playing a prank. He said he'd have the meat analyzed, but I took a sample to the Vet Center for a second opinion." I grimaced. "It gets worse. He asked me out again."

"You're not going, are you?" Kerri looked horrified.

"Oh, hell no. I can't believe I wasted nearly a year of my life on him. At least he didn't try to kill me when we broke up," I said, then chided myself immediately. Dan had been blunt about Hannah's mental breakdown and subsequent attack, but that wasn't the sort of thing I needed to go around telling everyone.

Kerri blinked in confusion. I told her how Dan's broken engagement led him to Iowa.

Mare nodded. "He told me about that shortly after I met him. He was pretty up-front when I asked what brought him here."

I breathed a sigh of relief. When I'd asked him

the same question the night of the housewarming, he'd brushed it off as needing a change of scenery. In hindsight, I suspected he didn't care to review that particular chapter of his life at what was meant to be a happy gathering of friends. I doubted he'd truly gotten over what Hannah did to him, since moving on from almost being killed by someone you loved was not a process with a clearly defined end date. Either way, I was glad I hadn't blurted out something that could have damaged the trust growing between him and me. Friends don't gossip about friends.

"His ex could find him again if she really wanted to. No one can hide, thanks to the internet," Kerri said, then laughed. "I wondered why he was single. Heck, I wondered if he was gay."

"He's not." I said it without thinking. Would I ever learn to keep my mouth shut?

Mare smiled. "And you know this how?"

"I don't," I stammered. "Not really." But last night, the warmth of his arms around me when Sarah threw her temper fit sparked a simmering heat between us that had nothing to do with an impatient ghost. I'd been too caught up in the crisis of the moment to acknowledge it beyond brushing off his apology for ending up with a hand under my shirt—a hand he'd had plenty of opportunity to remove, if he'd chosen. I could still feel every glowing fingerprint.

"You don't think Hannah's the one who tried to poison Raid? Because you and Dan are, um, whatever you are?" Kerri said carefully.

"She didn't like dogs, but Dan says she's out of his life for good." I ignored Kerri's implication.

"By the way," Mare said, "we're discussing one of Dan's novels at book club now. I thought maybe you'd like to come. Bev told me I'd need to find someone else to lead the discussion since she's interviewing baristas and can't be there tonight."

"Thanks, but no thanks."

I appreciated the invitation, but going to the meetings only because Bev wasn't there sounded like a whole lot of avoidance behavior. I'd rather enjoy Dan's writing in the peace and quiet of my own living room. With a ghost reading over my shoulder.

"If Bev wasn't such a battle axe to work for, she'd have better luck keeping employees," Kerri said. "Ryan's girlfriend, Amanda, worked there over the summer and said Bev was so obsessed with her genealogy project she kept leaving the part-time girls in charge of the shop while she left to do research. Then she'd come back and yell at them for not doing things the way she wanted them done. Amanda quit and got on at the Handimart instead."

None of that surprised me. The fact Bev had been willing to turn her business over to part-time employees did surprise me. Bev liked to be in control—of everything and everyone—all the time, for all the good it did. Now she didn't have enough staff to keep her business open.

Kerri stood and said, "I have to get that album back to the museum before they notice it's gone." She took a cookie for the road and left.

I left A Likely Story a few minutes later, stopped at the grocery store, and ran smack into Bev in the dairy section. Damn it. I was going to have to start doing parking lot recon before making bread and milk runs.

"We've missed you at book club," she said, eerily echoing my conversation with Mare. I cursed small town grocery store etiquette that demanded I acknowledge her. Still, she was making an effort at civility. Was Brad's attempt at reconciliation more genuine than I'd thought? Maybe he finally stood up to his mother and told her to play nice.

"I've been busy." I held her pale blue gaze and noticed purple bags under her eyes that even Estee Lauder couldn't conceal.

"I'm sure that house needs a lot of work." Judgement dripped from every word.

So much for playing nice.

"I heard Brad was called out to your place again," she continued. "Everything okay out there?"

Good lord, was the woman psychic? Then I remembered the police and fire scanner that resided in Bev and William Jennings' kitchen. The thing squawked out an endless barrage of city, county, and state law enforcement call outs and status updates. It was standard equipment in a family where a father and two sons wore the uniform, but I secretly thought Bev had it so she could keep track of Brad when he was on duty.

"Not a big deal," I said with forced casualness. "Kids playing a Halloween prank."

"That's good." Her smile didn't reach her eyes.

My phone rang. "Excuse me," I said, checking the caller ID. Bev moved on.

"Hi, Jess, it's Diane at the Vet Center. That meat you brought in had been laced with warfarin and the peanut butter contained xylitol."

I nearly toppled into a display of pumpkin pie filling as a thousand horrible scenarios flashed through my mind. As if rat poison wasn't bad enough, the artificial sweetener was deadly to dogs.

"If he'd eaten any of it, it would have been fatal." Diane's words confirmed my worst fears.

I thanked her for the quick response and clicked off. My hands trembled on the steering wheel as I drove home. The meat had been a one-two punch delivered with deadly intent. Rat poison was available at every farm supply store in the state. A simple internet search would reveal xylitol would kill a dog, and it was common in everyday food items from peanut butter to gum and candy. But why would someone try to kill Raider?

I circled back to Dan's comment after the incident on the road. *It sounds like someone doesn't want you living here.* There was no rational reason for anyone to want me out of Fox Hollow. The house had been on the market for months, and when I bought it, there hadn't exactly been a bidding war.

I didn't have any professional or personal enemies. I've never written scandalous news stories exposing public figures' aberrant behavior. My divorce was conducted in icy silence. I took back my maiden name, and Michael and I never spoke again.

My following relationships imploded one way or another, and all parties involved moved on.

Except for Brad, but I couldn't see him doing this. He was an arrogant jerk, but he wouldn't hurt an animal. Bev made it clear she had no use for me after I dumped her son, but her style of retribution was more about condescending looks and a general air of superiority. Which was how she treated me when Brad and I were together, for that matter.

Lost in thought, I turned into the lane but didn't realize a vehicle was behind me until my eye caught a motion in the rearview mirror. My heart accelerated, then I recognized Dan's pickup. My heart accelerated again for different reasons.

He waited while I pulled into the garage and let Raider out of the house, then he let Ruby out of the pickup. The dogs immediately started a chase game. I envied their carefree lives. Raid had no idea how close his had come to ending only hours earlier.

"Something happen this morning?" Dan asked by way of greeting. "I saw Jennings' Tahoe go past my place earlier."

"That was three hours ago," I said. "I could be dead by now."

He looked me up and down in appraisal. "You're not the damsel in distress type. I didn't figure you needed rescuing."

I collected my groceries, Dan whistled for the dogs, and we all trooped into the house. I put things away while he leaned against the counter, booted feet crossed at the ankles. He cared enough to come check on me. Again. I closed a cupboard door with more force than necessary. Things that seemed too good to be true usually were.

"Someone tried to poison Raid," I said.

"What the hell?" He looked at the dogs, who were making happy, snarly faces at each other.

I told him about the mysterious car at the end of the lane and the meat. "Brad was the responding officer. He wrote it off as kids playing a Halloween prank, but he took a sample to analyze."

"How do you know it had been poisoned?" Dan asked.

"Because I took a sample to Raid's vet, and she called thirty minutes ago to tell me the meat was spiked with rat poison and there was xylitol in the peanut butter. Either one would have killed him."

Dan issued a single, eloquent expletive. "Who would do that?"

"No idea. On top of it all, Brad apologized for how we ended things six months ago. He wants to get back together."

Dan's face went blank. "You don't think he planted the meat, do you? Some kind of twisted plan so he could come play the hero?"

"It would have backfired in spades if Raid had eaten any of it." My voice wavered and tears threatened. I could deal with the other weird stuff that had happened recently, but trying to kill my dog was too much. The tears won, and I wiped my face with my sleeve. "I don't know what to think anymore."

Dan uncrossed his legs, opened my refrigerator, surveyed the contents, then pulled out two beers.

"It's five o'clock somewhere," he said. He popped the caps off and handed me one, then folded himself back against the counter. Raider leaned on him, and Dan studied the dog. "If they're going after Fangs, it's getting personal."

"I thought it was personal when someone ran me off the road."

I tried to sound irritated, but I liked that he took the attempt on my dog's life seriously. And that he hadn't pursued the will-you-give-Brad-a-second-chance angle. I would run screaming from anything that looked like another relationship with Brad Jennings, but I wasn't ready to unpack everything else spinning around in my head.

"Do you want to borrow a gun? I've got an extra nine-millimeter I could loan you."

I blinked. An *extra* nine-millimeter? I'm not against guns. I'm against feeling like I need a gun. Fox Hollow is my happily ever after, not an armed compound.

"What about your ex-husband?" Dan took my lack of answer for an answer.

I shook my head. "His family was frantic to keep things quiet after the Brittni incident, so I'm pretty sure he's forgotten I exist."

Dan smiled. A slightly crooked eyetooth made that irrepressible grin even more intriguing. He leaned forward and tapped his bottle against mine. "You'd be hard to forget, McCallister."

My cheeks warmed, but I didn't look away. For one reckless minute, I allowed myself the luxury of him. His face was a study in hard angles—jaw, nose, chin—but laugh lines bracketing his mouth emphasized the full curve of his lower lip.

"The ghost that's run everyone else out of here wants me to stay, but now it appears there's a criminal element trying to get rid of me," I finally said.

"Life was a lot quieter before you moved out here, you know that?" His easy smile didn't falter. "You're an absolute lightning rod for weird stuff."

I forced air into my lungs and raised my bottle. "Here's to weird stuff."

AFTER DAN LEFT, I prowled through the house, looking for a project that would get my mind off visions of meat oozing dark, poisoned blood. My to-do notebook presented a detailed list of options, and I was getting a YouTube education about tile restoration when my phone rang. Tile restoration is exactly as exciting as it sounds, so I jumped at the distraction and answered. I should have known better.

"Jess! It's Logan Barnes. How ya doin'?"

"I'm fine." I knew what he was going to ask before he asked it.

"Hey, I'm doing a follow up on the treasure hunting book story, focusing on the Bishop Trading Post and that hidden gold legend, and hoped we could sit down for an interview. The historical society's been a ton of help, but I'd love your input, too, since you own the land where its hidden." He paused. "Allegedly hidden."

"Look, Logan, I came here from Benton County,

and I'd never heard that story until the day I moved in. You probably know more about it than I do."

"I'd still love to talk to you about what it's like to own a historic property with rumors of buried gold that's featured in a nationally released book."

"I'm not crazy about having my property in the spotlight. So yeah. No. Sorry."

Undaunted, he pushed on. "Would it be okay if I took some pictures of where the trading post used to be? You could show me where to get the best shots."

"I don't even know where the trading post was." I relented slightly. "You can take pictures from the road if you want, but if I catch you out there, I'm calling the sheriff." It was a hollow threat, and we both knew it. I could nail no-trespassing signs to every tree in the timber, and people would come and go as they pleased.

"Can you give me a quote, at least?"

He sounded so disappointed, I said something generic about not being familiar with the tale and doubting the gold was still there, if it ever had been, and reminding people to ask permission before entering private property. For all the good that would do.

Logan had the grace to thank me before he hung up. I went back to YouTube tile videos and thought about changing my phone number.

By late afternoon, I was heartily fed up with tile. I grabbed my jacket and hat, and Raider and I went on a slow meander around the pasture. When we reached the tree line along the river bluff, we inspected several relatively flat spaces that seemed likely sites for a trading post. The only interesting thing we found were the mummified remains of a dead raccoon.

I cut through the trees and stood on the bluff overlooking the Iowa River valley. The floodplain below was dotted with clumps of driftwood and willow, a still life in shades of faded sienna. The gentle curve of the hills beyond had been stripped bare as autumn marched toward winter.

The decades that followed the vision Sarah showed me on Halloween saw the land sculpted by water, wind and the inexorable movements of the earth. A hundred years later it looked nothing like it had on that storm-blasted afternoon. I could hike down there for a better perspective, but it was too late in the day for such an adventure. I turned back toward the house, frustration gnawing at me with sharp teeth. Was paranormal communication always one step forward and two steps back?

The sun slanting through the trees cast everything in gold. I blew out a breath and relaxed, enjoying the play of light and shadow and the peace that comes from living in the moment. I'd think about finding Luke tomorrow. Just call me Scarlett O'Hara. Raider hurdled the remains of the stone wall into the cemetery and snuffled noisily among the leaves.

I followed him in the fading light. Here and there, my boot stubbed against stone under matted grasses. I imagined how the cemetery might look with the saplings and encroaching vines removed, the grave markers reset and the stone wall rebuilt in a tribute to the area's early settlers.

My heart caught in my throat.

The new hole was partially—and poorly—disguised with leaves. The shovel marks remained sharp in the loamy soil, unblurred by rain or dried by exposure to air. Dirt lay in untidy heaps nearby.

Damn it to hell. Did this mean the initial holes yielded nothing, driving the digger to come back for further exploration? Or had the digger returned because he was finding what he wanted?

The damp soil was cold against my knees as I knelt, and the earthy scent of rotting vegetation filled my nose. I scuffled my fingers along the surface near one end of the hole. No headstone. Maybe this wasn't a grave. Or maybe it was, and the marker crumbled away long ago.

Leaning in, I scraped aside the accumulated leaves. If my fingertips brushed the decaying wood of a coffin lid, I'd pee my pants. Swallowing hard, I convinced myself any coffin would be buried the standard six feet down. I pulled out my phone, flipped on the flashlight, and tried again. I saw nothing but dirt. Were my fingers only inches from buried treasure? Or had someone come close to tampering with a pioneer's eternal rest?

Anger boiled through me at the sense of violation. Raider pushed in close, and I put an arm around him. The golden light had given way to dusk as shadows stretched into the woods.

I climbed to my feet. This was still consecrated ground, no matter how neglected it was. I should have addressed the situation the first time I realized someone was messing around out here, but it had been easier to write it off as a minor annoyance and ignore it in light of more pressing issues.

It was after five p.m. The situation wasn't an emergency, nor did it merit an after-hours call to the sheriff's non-emergency number. It would be dark soon, anyway. It would have to wait until morning.

FRIDAY, NOV. 2

I CALLED THE sheriff's department in the morning and reported the vandalism. To the dispatcher's credit, she didn't laugh when I said someone was digging holes in my cemetery. All personnel were tied up with a multi-vehicle accident in the southern part of the county, but she promised to have a deputy contact me as soon as possible.

I spent the rest of the morning immersed in laying tile in the upstairs bathroom. The tedious precision occupied my entire being, and when my phone rang at noon, I jumped and cracked my head on the underside of the pedestal sink.

"Hi Jess, this is Stephanie at the Lenox County Sheriff's Department," said a brisk female voice. "Deputy Jennings asked me to let you know the meat he collected from your property yesterday tested negative for any tampering."

Sinking dread replaced the pain in my skull. It would have been easy for Brad to switch the samples before sending them to the lab, but that implied he knew they were tainted in the first place. If he knew that, he knew who did it.

Or maybe he'd flat out lied about the results. Or maybe he'd picked up a piece that hadn't been tainted. Or maybe I'd been wrong about my assessment of him being a jerk but not a psychopath. Or maybe Dan's idea had been right—Brad was trying to play the hero.

That one was pretty thin. If Raider had eaten any of the meat, any attempt by Brad to save the day would have come far too late. Maybe that had been his intent, and he expected me to fall into his arms for consolation. That was a lot of maybes, and none of them answered any questions.

I thanked Stephanie and asked for an ETA on a deputy to respond to my earlier request. She said the accident scene had been cleared, and someone would be at my place within the hour. I considered requesting it not be Brad but let it go. The county employed four full-time deputies and the sheriff. What were the odds?

On an impulse, I called Dan. "Can you come over?" I bit my lip in the ensuing silence. The man had to be working under a deadline, and here I was, making demands of his time at my convenience.

"Should I bring anything? A bottle of wine? Ghost-catching equipment?" His tone held an undercurrent of resigned amusement.

"No, I'd just like your opinion on something."

There was a long pause during which I imagined editors yelling about word counts and re-writes that would not be addressed by mucking around in an abandoned cemetery.

"I'll be there in ten."

CHAPTER 14

THE SOUND OF A VEHICLE coming up the lane sent Raider bounding to the window. His initial cheerful woof turned into a growl as Brad stepped out of the white SUV. Seriously? I groaned so loudly Raid looked at me with concern.

"You reported vandalism?" Brad asked, glancing dismissively at the house and barn as I stepped onto the porch.

My hackles went up. With its peeling paint and air of shabby chic, Fox Hollow wasn't a *Better Homes and Gardens* cover, but I resented the implication he couldn't tell if anything had been intentionally damaged.

"Yes."

"Where?" He was deliberately obtuse. I'd given the dispatcher the specifics.

"The old Bishop Cemetery," I said and pointed across the rolling expanse of open field.

He jerked a thumb at the Tahoe. "Can we drive out there?"

"Yes." The pasture was rough, but the old farm lane could be easily navigated with four-wheel drive.

"Get in," he said and started for the Tahoe.

I'd never have made a career of the military because I do not take orders well. "No."

Brad turned, impatience etched in every line of his body. "Do you want to report property damage or not?"

"Dan's coming. He'll be here soon."

Brad gave me the irritated look I'd come to know so well in the final days of our relationship. I folded my arms across my chest and mirrored it.

Dan's pickup rattled up the lane a minute later. He parked and got out. In the cab, Ruby wagged her tail and bounced back and forth across the seat.

"Hey, McCallister." He flashed me a grin and gave Brad a civil nod. Brad's glare deepened, but he returned the acknowledgement.

I gave Brad my sweetest smile. "We can go now."

Brad got in the Tahoe and slammed the door. Apparently, my orders to ride with him had been canceled.

"Let's go," I said to Dan. "You're driving."

"Where are we going? And why is he here?" Dan nodded toward the Tahoe as he started his truck.

"There's been more digging in the cemetery. Go through the pasture gate and follow the fence line east."

Dan eased the pickup into the pasture and Brad followed, both vehicles bumping slowly along the rough track.

"More digging?" he asked. "Are they taking things out or putting things in?"

"What?" I stared at him across the sea of canine tails and ears.

"You're talking about holes in a cemetery. Your options are limited. And you didn't answer my question—why is Lenox County's finest here?"

"Jealous?" I said without thinking.

The truck hit a rut and lurched violently. The

rear end slewed sideways as Dan punched the accelerator and the tires dug for purchase. I slid halfway off the seat, smashed into the door, and ended up with both dogs on my lap. Dan got the truck straightened out and continued like nothing happened.

"Where'd you learn to drive?" I muttered as the dogs regrouped between us.

"Kandahar," he said. "You didn't answer my question."

"You didn't answer mine, either."

"I forgot what it was."

I gave up. "Brad's here because I called the sheriff's office to report new vandalism, and God knows why but they sent him. Again. Your turn."

Dan didn't say anything for a long minute as he concentrated on navigating the faint track.

"No," he said with a husky blend of sarcasm and amusement. He didn't look at me.

"No, what?"

"No, I'm not jealous that a guy you dated and is apparently still interested keeps showing up every time you have a problem."

"I could say the same thing about you," I fired back.

"No," he said mildly. "I show up because I can't wait to see what the hell kind of mess you're in this time."

The warmth of his laugh sent a little flame dancing through me. I didn't know what to do about that so I ignored it.

"Stop here," I said. We'd reached the flat space

where I imagined the trading post once stood. We got out of the truck, and without waiting for Brad, I led Dan through the trees to the cemetery. The dogs raced around, doing wild dog things.

A muffled curse made me glance over my shoulder in time to see Brad trip on the loose stones of the tumbled wall. Maybe I should have told him they were there. Arms flailing, he regained his balance and strode through the leaves like nothing happened. He looked at the fresh hole and scowled. You'd think I'd called him out here just to ruin his day.

Brad had probably known about the hidden gold legend since he'd played cops and robbers with his brothers as kids. The Jennings family loved local history. It gave them a reason to talk about people and highlight the achievements of all the Jennings ancestors.

Dan whistled for the dogs and wandered off, scuffing his boots through the leaves and looking at the few remaining vertical tombstones.

"When did you first notice the damage?" Brad asked, nodding at the cemetery in general. He pulled out a small notebook and pen.

"Two weeks ago."

"And you're just now reporting it?"

"It didn't seem like a big deal at the time. But after that story about the treasure hunting book ran in the newspaper, I think someone's looking for that gold."

And when I found the first hole, no one had run me off the road or threatened me in the middle of the night or tried to poison my dog.

Brad surveyed the new dig site. I pointed out the

other two holes, now semi-re-filled and covered with leaves. I left out the part about falling into one of them.

"They just dug in these three places?" he asked. "Nowhere else?"

"I don't know. With all this leaf cover it's hard to tell."

A few yards behind Brad, Dan knelt to examine something. He caught my eye and raised a finger to his lips. He needn't have worried. Brad was ignoring him so loudly I could hear it.

"Is this an actual grave or just a hole in the ground?" Brad asked. "There's no headstone."

"It could be a grave. Some of them would have had wooden markers, which would be long gone." I tried to sound like I knew more than I did.

Dan ambled off to lean against the trunk of a cottonwood tree. He shoved his hands in his pockets. He looked bored. Brad squatted on his heels and made a show of inspecting the hole, running his hand along the straight shovel lines.

"This hole was dug carefully," he pronounced. "Vandalism is generally more haphazard. Whoever did this took their time."

"Of course they took their time," I snapped. "They can come and go as they please. No one can see this place from the road."

Brad stood. "I wouldn't worry about a few holes in the ground." He flipped the notebook closed, indicating the situation didn't merit further questions.

I resisted the urge to shove him in the hole.

"That's not the point! I don't want people poking around out here. What if someone breaks their neck and decides to sue me?"

"Since that book is getting so much publicity, you could try posting private property signs by the road." His voice was cool.

"This started before Dr. Aldrich's book hit the media." This was going nowhere. I renewed my vow not to call the sheriff again for anything short of zombies dragging their rotting carcasses onto my front porch.

"There's a guy down by Millers Grove we charged a year ago for digging in places he shouldn't, looking for Native artifacts. This looks like something he'd do. I'll have a chat with him."

The arrogance in Brad's voice reminded me he had resources to mitigate an unpleasant situation if he chose to. I doubted anyone was digging for flint points in Bishop Cemetery, but if Brad wanted to have the last word, it wasn't worth my breath to argue.

He took a step forward, expecting me to move out of his way. I didn't. He made an exaggerated circle around me and the open hole and left.

I looked at the cemetery with a sinking heart. Was the whole site destined to become a minefield of gaping holes plundered by would-be treasure hunters?

Dan strolled over as the Tahoe rolled away through the pasture.

"You could have joined us," I said. "He'd appreciate your opinion as much as mine."

"He'd push me off the bluff and make it look like an accident."

"Take a number and get in line," I said. "This is the third time he's been out here. One of the dispatchers must have it in for him. *'Hey, let's send Jennings out to his ex-girlfriend's place. That'll be fun.'*"

"You really don't think he's doing it on purpose? Taking the calls to impress you?"

"He's so impressed with himself it would never occur to him he needs to try."

Dan laughed and motioned me toward the cottonwood tree. "Come look at this."

I followed him as he knelt and brushed back the leaves. Two dull copper rods lay on the ground. Each was about two feet long and bent at a ninety-degree angle a quarter of the way from one end.

I blinked. "Are those...?"

"Dowsing rods."

"Isn't this evidence? Shouldn't you have said something to Brad?"

"Do you think Dudley Do-Right would have taken them away for fingerprinting?"

I heard Dr. Griffith's voice telling me the meat was laced with rat poison and xylitol, overlaid by Stephanie from the sheriff's office telling me the meat tested negative for tampering. "Even if he had, I bet they'd have come back clean. Are those expensive? Do you think whoever left them will come back to look for them?"

"They might, but you can buy them on Amazon for twenty bucks. Or maybe they found what they're looking for and don't need them anymore."

"Exactly how do they work?"

"They pick up disturbances in the soil composition that indicates something's been buried or there's underground water. You hold one in each hand and the wires cross above the site. The scientific community isn't crazy about their accuracy, but folklore and anecdotal evidence says otherwise," Dan said.

I lifted the rods from the leaf mold. "You want them?"

"They might be fun to mess around with. I've always wanted to find the old outhouse at my place."

"You're kidding."

"I shit you not," he said and grinned broadly when I groaned. "They call it privy digging. I worked construction with a guy who was into it. People dumped all kinds of cool stuff in their outhouses back in the day—bottles, old kitchenware, even guns. They're like miniature landfills."

"I'll loan you these any time you want. But you're on your own for digging up the outhouse." I gripped each rod loosely by the handle, extended my arms and stared at them. Nothing happened. "I guess it's something you have to practice."

Unlike the previous day's gilded light, the afternoon had gone a muddy shade of gray that caught the cemetery in a gloomy web. Any dowsing practice would have to wait.

"This whole thing is nuts," I said when we were

back in the pickup with the dogs. "If anyone dug up so much as a chamber pot out here, they couldn't keep their mouths shut. Everyone in the county would know about it."

Dan guided the pickup toward the house through the fading light.

"The story doesn't specifically say the gold was buried in the cemetery," I continued. "Maybe whoever is digging is looking for something else entirely."

"Like what?"

The options were too awful to think about, and for a horrible moment I wondered if some whack job was actually digging up bodies. When I didn't say anything, Dan said, "Speaking of dead people."

"No." I slumped back against the seat.

"I haven't asked the question. You can't answer a question I haven't asked."

"Yes, I can. You were going to ask if I'd done anything about finding Luke. The answer is no. I've read through those news clippings Kerri brought. I don't know anything more now than when I started. The river bottoms were a mess after the tornado. Searchers could have walked within feet of his body and never found it." I thought of the cow I'd seen in Sarah's vision. "And not to be morbid, but there was full of dead livestock. The stench would have been unimaginable."

"Aren't you the good news fairy."

We rode the rest of the way in silence. When Dan stopped in front of my house, he said, "I've got supper in the slow cooker. Want to come over?"

My stomach growled at the suggestion, pushing away any macabre remnants of our conversation.

"I'll take that as a yes."

"I need to shower first," I stammered.

He gave me a fast once-over. "No, you don't. You look fine."

"Yeah, I do," I said, pretty sure I did not look fine.

"Then hurry up, I'm hungry."

He drove off, and I bolted into the house, Raider at my side. I glimpsed my reflection in the bathroom mirror as I yanked on the tap in the shower. My hair was a wild tangle and my faded sweatshirt sported a collection of tiny rips, courtesy of Raider's puppyhood. I appreciated Dan's come-as-you-are invitation, but a girl has her standards.

I set a new speed record for showering, then hopped one-legged across my bedroom, pulling on clean jeans while agonizing about what to wear. This wasn't a date. It was just supper with a friend at the end of a long day. There was no need to read more into it than that. I finally settled on a flannel shirt under a navy blue down vest.

Too impatient for anything resembling styling, I damp-dried my hair and let it fall in loose waves. I rummaged to find my makeup, then swore. This was not a date. I didn't want to spoil the comfortable ease of our friendship by trying to be someone I wasn't.

I shoved my feet into boots, grabbed a jacket that wasn't covered with mud and Malinois fur, and headed out before my head exploded.

AT MY KNOCK, Dan yelled, "Come in, it's open," and I stepped into his kitchen. Ruby greeted me as if she hadn't just seen me half an hour earlier. Dan glanced at the clock.

"Twenty-four minutes to shower and change. I'm impressed."

"Twenty minutes," I corrected. "Plus two for convincing Raider he had to stay home and two to drive over here."

He gave me one of those absolutely not subtle appraisals followed by a smile that made my breath come quicker. *Not a date*, the little voice reminded me. Just friends sharing dinner.

He'd showered, too. The fresh scent of soap lingered as he moved around the kitchen, pulling things out of the refrigerator and setting the table. His jeans were old but clean, and the sleeves of his faded flannel were rolled up to the elbows.

With a classic rock station playing in the background and the faint tang of sawdust drifting from another room, the house resonated a comfortable masculinity. Dan handed me a plate and motioned toward the stovetop, where a vintage slow cooker perched. He lifted the lid and the fragrant steam made my stomach growl again.

"Hope you like beef and noodles," he said. "It's one of the three things I can make."

I ladled thick egg noodles with generous cuts of beef and brown gravy onto my plate and sat down at the table. Dan added a loaf of bread, cut in ragged slices, to an array of deli salad containers, and we ate likc royalty.

"Do you think whoever is digging out there could be somebody you know personally?" he asked between bites. "Someone who overheard you talking about the gold story?"

I shook my head. "Anders Linder, one of the guys in my Tuesday night dog training group, went to hear that author speak at Mare's shop last spring. I guess everyone in the group knows about it, but I can't see any of them getting involved in that kind of nonsense."

"Maybe the bigger question is, who's had unlimited access to your property?"

I made a wry face. "Anybody who wanted it. Susanne had a few open houses because it's a historic property, but otherwise, the place sat empty all summer."

"Susanne is your real estate agent? What about her?"

"She's barely the walking-in-the-woods type, let alone the hole-digging type."

"Who else is interested in the story?"

I did a quick review, starting with additional members of the HDTC training group, dismissing names as quickly as faces flashed through my mind.

Conn and TJ? No, our friendship went back years. If they wanted to dig for treasure, they'd ask permission and insist I come with them. Kyle Montgomery, with a landscaping business full of shovels and dirt-moving equipment at his disposal? Ridiculous.

Alf and Clara, seeking to enhance their retirement pensions? Absurd.

Brad? Even more absurd. The candidate for the next sheriff of Lenox County wouldn't take the chance of tarnishing his golden boy image. Beverly? Too obsessed with running her business and her genealogy research, not necessarily in that order. Who else would be interested enough to sneak out there?

"Dr. Aldrich," I blurted.

"The guy who wrote the book?"

"Yeah. The story in the paper said he tried contacting the owner of Fox Hollow for more information, only it was between owners at the time, so maybe he decided to take advantage of nobody being around."

"He's a professor at the University of Oklahoma," Dan countered. "It's not likely he'd take off in the middle of a semester to drive across two states to dig in your cemetery without contacting you. Even if he did it on weekends, the latest hole showed up when? Thursday?"

My shoulders sagged. "But what if he had information he chose not to include in the book because he intended to find it himself?"

"He's an academic. Getting public recognition is what college professors live for. If he went off the rails and found something out there, he wouldn't be able to tell anyone. Plus, getting arrested for criminal trespass would wreck his credibility."

I sighed. Being suspicious of everyone I knew was tiring. No one else had shown more than a casual interest in the topic, let alone asked me if they could go out there. No one except—

"Logan Barnes."

"Who?"

"He's a reporter at the *Sentinel*. He's been bugging me ever since I moved in. First, he wanted to do a ghost-hunting story before Halloween, then he did a story about that book and wanted to do a follow up with me about the treasure."

"You turned him down?"

"Yeah, both times. He wasn't happy about it."

"Means, motive, opportunity." Dan ticked off points on his fingers. "Whoever is doing this is familiar with the story and physically able to hike in there and dig. They think they know where it is, and want it badly enough to risk getting caught because they didn't stop after you moved in. They know if they drive through the ditch into the trees, they're invisible."

"What am I supposed to do, sit out there in a lawn chair with a rifle across my lap like Clint Eastwood and yell 'Get off my cemetery?'"

"Maybe you could find the treasure yourself and put an end to it." Meal finished, Dan started to clear the table. I rose to help him.

"I'll do that right after I find Luke." Frustration spilled out as sarcasm. "Find a body, appease a ghost, dig up a treasure, stop the trespassers, try not to let anyone kill my dog. I'm all over it."

"You've got a problem for every solution, you know that?" Dan's eyes had gone the deep blue of storm clouds. I stood at the sink, holding my plate and silverware, and just for a second, allowed my mind to imagine a thousand what-ifs.

His friendship felt like an invitation to open a door and find an unexpected new world waiting on the other side. All I had to do was cross the threshold. Then I clamped down hard on that nonsense. I didn't have time for it.

I scrambled for safe territory. "What are the other two?"

"The other two what?"

"You said you could only make three things. What are the other two?"

"You'll have to come back to find out." His grin was just short of flirting, his eyes still dark as sin.

Great. I didn't need Dan Sinclair complicating my life, but I wasn't sure I wanted to stop him.

SATURDAY, NOV. 3

THE CONTRACTOR MATT recommended came out in the morning to give his opinion on refinishing the dining room floor. We talked about the scope of the project and haggled over the price. He agreed to start next week.

After he left, I rolled up my sleeves and started scraping what Kerri called the Victorian boudoir wallpaper in the first-floor bathroom. Since I was making changes to the house, I expected Sarah to have an opinion, but the air remained quiet, as if her explosion of energy on Halloween left her drained.

When my phone rang mid-afternoon, my hands were slimy with old wallpaper paste. I answered it, fumbled the device, dropped it, and picked it up again, swearing.

"You okay?" Dan asked with dry amusement.

I glanced in the mirror over the sink. Tattered scraps of paper stuck in my hair like vintage confetti. "How do you feel about scraping wallpaper?"

"Firmly in favor of someone else doing it." Without pausing, he continued. "Hey, can I come over tonight? I have something to show you."

"Um, sure. What is it?" I stammered, caught off guard.

"I'll explain later. See you around seven." He hung up.

I reined in the annoying little part of my mind that had gone galloping off into options beyond friendship again. I wasn't interested in being a convenient booty call. My relationship with Dan was like a coin spinning end over end in the air. I loved being single and alone. I loved doing what I wanted, when I wanted. But it was a short trip from being alone to being lonely, and I couldn't keep the coin in the air forever.

I took my frustration out on the remaining wallpaper, showered, fed Raider, and ate supper. Shortly before seven, I knelt to build a fire, but when I reached into the antique coal scuttle that held tinder and kindling, my fingers closed over a ball of calico fabric. I looked up at the mantel. The remaining balls sat tidily in their bowl. This one could have been a victim of gravity, but nothing in this house happened by accident. I cupped the dark indigo fabric in my hand, and my fingers tingled as if I'd touched an electric current. I tried to drop it but wasn't fast enough.

Raw emotion blindsided me so suddenly it stripped the breath from my lungs. I struggled to get above it, but Sarah was relentless. The pain she felt at Luke's loss twisted savagely with everything from my unrequited high school crushes to the repeated failures of adult relationships, and I was overwhelmed with the weight of desperate, lonesome despair. The living room faded as my vision swirled to black and my mind screamed for escape. I had no idea where Sarah was taking me, but I did not want to go.

Slowly, the darkness was replaced by sunlight. As if through a soft-focus camera lens, I saw her, wearing a blue calico dress, kneeling in the township cemetery. There was no freshly turned earth marking a grave, only a simple granite marker, gleaming in autumn sunshine.

Luke Jamison Bauer
March 19, 1899 – July 4, 1919
Son of John and Martha Bauer
Beloved of Sarah Cameron

A keening sob like a wounded animal split my head. Gone. He'd been taken from her forever, and she'd been denied even the cold comfort of laying his body to rest. Grief knifed so deeply into her heart she wanted to join him in death.

The scene shifted. I watched as Sarah cut the blue calico dress into long strips and methodically wound them into balls. She'd sewn it for that special evening when he'd ask her to share her life with him. Instead, she'd worn it to weep at an empty grave that offered neither closure nor comfort.

The torrent of pain eased, like water trickling from a spigot, replaced by numbness. She drifted in a cold fog of loss, considered taking her own life because there was no reason to keep living without him. Her days held only dreams that cut like broken glass.

The flickering glow of a candle flame wavered through the dark. The whiskery velvet of the horses' muzzles, their big heads lowered in greeting, brushed away the fatigue of sorrow. The sounds of steel-shod hooves and creak of harness leather was music to her ears. She drew strength from her family's legacy.

Her mind filled with joy as she studied pedigrees and planned breedings, and her heart soared in delight with each new foal. She gentled colts, trained yearlings and cared for the massive teams that tilled the soil in the spring and hauled laden wagons during harvest.

Farmers came from surrounding counties to purchase Fox Hollow Belgians. Her days were full and rewarding. Years passed, then decades. The internal combustion engine worked longer hours without being fed or watered or rested. The demand for draft horses faded, and so did her purpose for living. Dark memories returned along with the razor-sharp pain of her loss.

"McCallister?"

I blinked, disoriented.

"Jess? Where are you?"

The living room swam back into focus. Footfalls sounded in the hall, and Dan appeared in the doorway. Raid bounded ahead of him to snuffle anxiously at my face.

"I knocked, but you didn't answer." Dan gripped my arms and pulled me to my feet. "Are you okay?"

"I'm fine."

"You're a bad liar, sweetheart. What happened?"

I caught my breath at the unexpected endearment, and for a minute, I was speechless. Then the words came in a torrent. "She made the cloth balls out of the dress she'd worn to his funeral. She loved him so much it nearly killed her when he disappeared. She can't escape that pain until he comes home."

Dan wrapped his arms around me. I stepped into him and buried my face against his chest as my breath came in ragged gulps. I was so tired of crying over a tragedy that happened a hundred years ago, but Sarah's pain was part of Fox Hollow and now, by extension, part of me.

Dan held me until the waves of raw emotion stilled, replaced by the steady beat of his heart. Finally, I took a reluctant step back, swiping at tears with my sleeve. Ghosts didn't haunt places, they haunted people, and I was Exhibit A.

"And you know this how?" He was so calm we could have been talking about the cattle market or the winter weather outlook.

I told him about the vision. "Here." I held out the calico ball. Slowly, he extended his hand.

"Be careful. It's loaded." I tipped it into his palm. His hand was steady, but tension radiated from his body.

Nothing happened.

"Guess I'm not on her wavelength tonight." Dan put the ball back on the mantel with the others. "You have more trouble with dead people than most of us do with live ones. Come on. I brought something that might help."

Before I could ask if it was alcohol or chocolate, he wrapped an arm around my shoulders and steered me to the kitchen. I caught a glimpse as we passed the hallway mirror. My eyes were too bright, my face taut, but at least I didn't look like I'd been ugly-crying. I took deep breaths and focused on the comfortable warmth of his body against mine. I was disappointed when we got to the kitchen and he let go.

He pointed to a stack of eleven- by seventeen-inch printed sheets lying on the kitchen table.

"What's this?" I asked.

"Maps. I have a friend at the FSA office."

My bruised mind couldn't fathom what the United States Department of Agriculture's Farm Service Agency had to do with my life.

"I told him what I wanted, and he printed these." Dan arranged the sheets of paper on the table, shuffling them like giant puzzle pieces. The satellite photos showed fields, timber and intersecting roadways. Meandering through it all was a river.

"You didn't have to do this, whatever it is. We could have looked it up on Google Maps," I said, still confused.

"Call me old school. This will have more impact than a laptop screen. There." He stepped back from the table. "It's the land between Fox Hollow and what used to be Walnut Bluff. I thought it might help us figure out where Luke is."

Us? When had that happened?

"But these are modern maps," I protested to cover a jumbled rush of feelings. "Don't you think we need ones from 1919?"

"You think the land has changed that much since then?" He braced his palms on the edge of the table, and we stood shoulder to shoulder, looking at the photos. The roofs of the houses and outbuildings at both Fox Hollow and the old Bauer farmstead were easily identifiable. The two-dimensional maps flattened the topography, but my mind's eye saw the rise and fall of the pasture, the sharp drop from bluff to river and the flat, flood-scoured plains below.

I pointed. "Yeah, it kinda has. The tornado re-routed the river. The channel today isn't the same as it was a hundred years ago."

"Why does that matter?"

"I don't know. It just feels important." I slumped as the lingering tendrils of Sarah's grief twisted through my mind. Finding Luke was like training dogs. The more I learned, the more I realized how much I didn't know.

"You got any of my beer left?" Dan asked.

"Your beer? It's my beer."

"It was my beer first."

I was not going to win this argument.

"Grab a couple," he said, taking my silence for defeat. "I'll start the fire."

When the flames caught, he dropped down on

the couch. I tucked my feet under me in my recliner. Raider rolled around on the floor, upside down, clacking his jaws in Malinois bliss. Dan considered him.

"Know anybody with a cadaver dog?" he asked.

"No. Are they even trained to find bodies that old?"

"I read somewhere they were using dogs to find mass burials in Europe. Some of them were centuries old. Might be worth a shot."

"Even if I could find a handler willing to help, I wouldn't know where to start." I was back to square one. "What if—and this is awful—but what if his body literally rotted away, like the carcasses of the livestock I saw in the vision on Halloween? And his bones were scattered by wild animals or flooding? What if there's nothing left to find?"

"If that were the case, Sarah wouldn't have asked you to do it. She knows he's out there, and she wants him brought home. Hell, maybe if you find him, she'll show you where the treasure's buried." Dan looked at me expectantly over his bottle.

"I'd be happy if she'd just stop ambushing me. Besides, how would she know about the gold? That happened almost fifty years before her parents bought the land. And if they'd known where it was, they would have dug it up themselves."

"Maybe they did."

"And didn't tell anyone? Not likely." I shook my head. "Sarah wants me to bring Luke home, that's all. She doesn't care about anything else."

We both looked around the room, waiting for

affirmation. The calico balls had nothing to say.

Dan stretched his stocking feet toward the fire. "That piece of crockery means someone found something out there, and they're looking for more."

"But it's a felony to mess with a burial site," I protested.

"It's only a felony if they get caught. How often do you go out there?"

"Almost every day if the weather's good. That's one of the reasons I bought this place—so Raider and I would have a place to hike."

"You're driving whoever's digging nuts. They can't come and go as they please. They have to figure out what you're doing first."

"You think that's why someone tried to poison Raid? So if I didn't have a dog to walk, I wouldn't go there? Or I'd be so upset I'd move out?"

"It's a thought. If they hadn't found something, they wouldn't be harassing you."

The unidentifiable threat hung in the air like a storm building on the horizon, but I had more pressing matters on my mind. In the vision on Halloween, the bluffs were behind me and I was facing the river.

"I still think we need maps from before the tornado." I was clinging to a hunch I couldn't explain. "I want to compare the river channels before and after 1919."

"Then what are you going to do—excavate the entire river bottom?"

"Maybe." I said, because I didn't know what else to say.

Dan looked at his empty bottle. "You want another?"

"You're awfully free with my beer."

"I think your pet ghost justifies a two-beer night."

"She's not my..." I started, then held his gaze, unable—or unwilling—to break away. The firelight accented the contours of his face and highlighted the sensual promise of his mouth. That particular train of thought had nowhere to go when it left the station, and I watched it derail with a pang of disappointment. "Sure. Thanks."

Dan was back a minute later, only to find Raider had taken his spot on the couch.

"Move over, Fangs." He shoved the dog out of the way. Raider grumbled but moved. Dan handed me a bottle. "You think Jennings is involved in all this? Every time you have a crisis, he can't get here fast enough."

"I thought about that, but why? He can't be the one digging in the cemetery. You saw him yesterday—he tripped over the wall and nearly fell on his face. He'd never been out there before."

"Could have been an act."

"Not likely. Brad's always been Mr. Look-How-Cool-I-Am. He couldn't fake being clumsy if he tried."

I savored the cold malt tang of the beer. "I ran into him in the hardware store the same day I got run off the road, but it wasn't his truck that ran me off. That phone call wasn't his voice. He's a jerk, but he's not a psycho, he wouldn't poison a dog. At least I don't think he would. Besides, he's a political climber. He'll run for sheriff soon. He wouldn't take the chance of wrecking his reputation by doing anything sketchy."

"You're assuming the reckless driver, the prank caller, the meat poisoner, and the digger are all the same person."

"Do not tell me there's a whole gang of people trying to get rid of me."

"What about some coat-tail descendant of Sarah who thinks you stole the family legacy?"

"Sarah probably left this place to Ian or his kids, but I'd guess none of them wanted it. If the family wanted it back, they've had plenty of chances in the last five years. And the people who owned it before me didn't leave because they got run off the road or someone tried to kill their dog. They left because Sarah wouldn't leave them alone, whether they admitted it or not."

"Ever wish you'd bought a nice little house in town?" His face was serious, but I caught the small twitch at the corner of his mouth.

"No." *Because then I'd never have met you.* Not for the first time, I wondered if Sarah was orchestrating more than her quest to bring Luke home.

"You don't do anything the easy way, do you?"

"Thanks."

"That wasn't a compliment." Dan laughed, and I joined him. For a moment, the living room was a bubble of warmth and security in an uncertain world.

"Thank you," I said again. "I mean it."

"For what?"

"For not running in the opposite direction when weird shit happens here."

He dismissed it with a shake of his head. "Anything for you, McCallister."

His eyes lingered on mine, but our friendship felt like a luxury I shouldn't get used to. If—against all odds—I found Luke, would Dan fade out of my life when the crisis that drew him into it no longer existed?

Dan stood. "It's late. I should go."

We walked to the kitchen and stared at the aerial photos still spread on the table.

"Guess this didn't solve anything," he said.

"No, it was a good idea," I said firmly. "I'll go to the historical society tomorrow and see if the pre-tornado version helps me figure anything out." I waved my hand at the maps like I was brandishing a wand, waiting for Disneyesque sparks to emerge from the tip and reveal a hidden answer.

Dan pulled on his jacket, then threw an arm around my shoulders and gave me a quick squeeze. Without thinking, I turned into him and slid my arms around his waist, reluctant to let the evening end. His hands were warm as he pulled me in.

It was the second time he'd held me that evening, and since I hadn't just been ambushed by a grief-stricken ghost, I appreciated it with more clarity. His hands were quiet, his body solid and warm against mine, not advancing, but not retreating either. I sank into the unexpected intimacy of the moment, wrapped in a feeling of being both protected and cherished.

Cherished? Where had that come from? It had been a long time since such physical closeness meant anything more than a prelude to a tumble between the sheets. Then Raider shoved between us, and Dan stepped back. Both of our hands dropped to the dog, our fingers tangling.

"Lock the door," he said and left.

CHAPTER 15

Monday, Nov. 5

When I called the historical society, Esther Wetterling said yes, they had maps of Sand Creek Township from both 1918 and 1920, and yes, she would be happy to pull them out for me. I thanked her and spent the rest of the morning attacking wallpaper. I had no idea what I expected the comparison to reveal. It was like trying to scratch an itch that was just beyond my fingertips.

Kerri's minivan was in the museum parking lot when I arrived mid-afternoon. Bev Jennings' sedan was parked next to it. Just my luck.

Half a dozen teens armed with rakes were doing yardwork on the museum grounds. Kerri was in the office, drinking a Coke and chatting with a couple of historical society members. I glanced around for Bev but didn't see her.

"Don't you ever work?" I asked Kerri.

"It's Mustang clean-up day." She referenced the high school's annual community service event. "I volunteered to supervise the kids working here."

"Yeah. I see that."

Esther appeared with the maps I'd requested and spread them atop a counter.

"So good to see you again, dear. Doing more research?"

Her query held the palpable air of someone dying to know why I wanted one hundred-year-old maps.

Kerri had the same look but kept her mouth shut.

"Just a little history project I'm working on." I smiled. "Which one is from 1918?"

Esther tapped the corresponding sheet. I oriented myself, finding Cat's Back Road, Fox Hollow and the Iowa River. A little thrill went up my spine to see Gavin and Moira Cameron and John and Martha Bauer listed as owners of my property and Dan's, respectively. I traced the river channel as it meandered through the Bauer farm onto Cameron land, then compared it to the map drawn the year after the tornado.

Yes! I was right! I curled my toes inside my boots to keep from jumping up and down.

"Could you make copies of these, please?" I asked, and Esther bustled away.

"Hey," Kerri said idly as we waited, "are you doing anything the weekend of the 24th and 25th?"

"Probably not. Why?" I looked around, sure Bev was lurking somewhere, but I still didn't see her.

"I need an extra handler at the Marshalltown shows. Matt's working overtime to get a new build framed before it snows, the boys have an FFA event that weekend, and I've got three dogs entered. You can borrow my teal suit."

Kerri takes the breed ring dress code seriously. I made a face. "Are you sure that skirt will fit me?"

"As long as you can bend over without flashing your panties, that's all that matters." Seeing my hesitation, she added, "Just get around the ring without falling down, the dogs will take care of the rest."

"You're not asking for much." I handled dogs for her now and then, but the breed ring with its emphasis on flawless presentation wasn't my skill set. "You need me both days?"

"Yes. And I want to stay for the breeders' seminar Saturday after best in show so plan to get home late."

"All right. I owe you for helping me paint."

Bev Jennings breezed out of the museum's reading room under full sail, cutting our conversation short. Her smile of acknowledgement was oddly ingratiating. "Hello, Jess."

Wow. She even used the correct form of my name. She couldn't possibly think Brad was making progress in winning me back or be pleased about it. She barely tolerated me the first time.

Bev brandished a folder of papers. "They have a whole collection of letters from my mother's side of the family. They're fascinating." She flew out the front door without waiting for our opinion.

"Everyone needs a hobby," I muttered. Bev's dedication to her family tree was admirable, but given the labor shortage at her business, I wondered how she justified the time.

People who live in glass houses. I had a to-do list that involved house restoration, body location, spirit appeasement, and putting a stop to whatever was happening in Bishop Cemetery. And here I was, planning an out-of-town dog show trip with Kerri that would have us leaving at the crack of dawn and not getting home until after dark.

Esther returned, and I paid for the copies. Kerri

gulped the rest of her Coke and followed me outside. She looked pointedly at the maps.

"It's three-thirty, school's out. The kids are on their own time now," she said. "Let's go see Mare, and you can tell us what you're doing."

"MARE'S IN THE kitchen. Go on back," Becca Scott, the assistant manager, called from behind the counter.

We bypassed a queue of teenage customers and pushed through the swinging door at the back of the shop to find Mare in the compact commercial kitchen amidst a swirl of cinnamon and vanilla. Steam rose from apple pies cooling on racks, and several trays of leaf-shaped cookies awaited the oven.

"Here." Mare scooped cookies onto a saucer and poured two mugs of coffee. "Maple brown sugar cut-outs. They're selling like hotcakes." She nodded at the sheaf of papers I was holding. "What's that?"

I told them about Dan's FSA print-outs and our attempts at brainstorming where Luke's body might be. I arranged the maps next to the pies and added a single sheet from Dan.

"This is Sand Creek Township in 1918. Look." I tapped the paper. The line designating the Iowa River formed a horseshoe-shaped loop in the section of land with Gavin and Moira Cameron's name written in old-fashioned script.

"That's directly below the highest point on the bluff, the spot Sarah showed me on Halloween," I explained. "Here it is again in 1920. Look at the river channel. It's straight as an arrow now."

"And you think that's where Luke is?" Mare asked.

"Yes, but it's still a huge area," I said, struggling with clues that revealed just enough to be annoying.

"Have you shown these to Dan?" she continued.

"No. I just got them."

"Let him help you, Jess. He's a good man."

I had nothing to say that didn't sound like denial at best—*He's just a friend*—or an outright lie at worst—*I'm not interested.*

"What are you going to do now?" Kerri stuck another cookie in her mouth, probably to stop herself from telling me I was an idiot for not welcoming Dan's help with Luke or anything else.

I wasn't sure if she meant what I was going to do about Dan, Sarah, Luke or the hypothetical treasure hunters. I told them about the incident with the calico ball, how Sarah hijacked my emotional energy to share the kaleidoscope of her own memories. I left out the reassuring strength of Dan's arms around me afterward. No sense pouring fuel on that particular fire.

Dan's involvement in my search for Luke was uncharted territory. I couldn't remember the last time a guy had offered to help me with something that didn't directly benefit him one way or another. Dan had nothing to gain from my ghost hunting. Maybe he was just angling for a quick roll between the sheets, but that didn't feel right either. Nothing about him felt superficial.

We all ate another cookie. The door chimes

jingled and the cash register played a symphony of electronic beeps.

"You're crazy busy," I said to Mare. "Is this your normal afterschool rush?"

"Didn't you hear? Brewed Awakenings closed yesterday. All the high school kids are coming here now. They're a little disappointed I'm not set up for fancy coffee drinks, but the cookies are flying out of the case."

"Closed? But we just saw Bev at the museum," I said. "I figured she must have hired enough help for her to take the afternoon off."

"The kids told me the sign on the door says closed due to electrical problems, but there's more to it than that." Mare lowered her voice. "Bev and I share a couple of the same suppliers, and one of them told me he'd stopped delivering to her because she was months past due on her account."

"How is that possible?" I asked. "Brewed has been part of the town square for years."

"She's been having so much trouble keeping help, she may have put herself out of business," Kerri said.

"Whatever happened, it's good for me," Mare said pragmatically. "It's been a revolving door here all day. Now unless you two want to put on an apron, get out."

I DON'T KNOW how authors approach their craft in terms of working hours, but when I called Dan, he was at my house in less than ten minutes. Either he wasn't busy or I'd wrecked his work schedule so thoroughly he'd just given up. When I let him into the kitchen, he looked relieved I wasn't sobbing in a pile on the floor.

"What's on your mind, McCallister?"

I indicated the table. It was still covered with the satellite photos he'd brought the night before, but now I'd placed the copied plat maps from the historical society next to corresponding areas.

I pointed. "Look. Same area, one before the tornado, one after. See how much the river changed?" The importance of this twisted and looped through my mind like the old-fashioned script on the paper, slipping away each time I tried to get a firm hold on it.

Dan studied the 1920 map, his face a mask of concentration.

"Maybe they couldn't find Luke because he'd already been buried," he said finally.

"Who would have done that?"

"I don't mean someone actually buried him. Isn't the Fox Hollow story all about how the tornado miraculously stopped before it hit this house?" He tapped the map. "All the debris it was carrying would have dropped in this area when the system fell apart."

My idea began to take shape, and a sense of conviction poured through me as the hair rose on the back of my neck. I pointed at horseshoe-shaped section of the river on the 1918 map, then at the same area from 1920 and the current satellite view.

"Here. I've seen it from the top of the bluff, but I've never gone down there. It's all floodplain with lots of washouts. That's where he is." My words were almost a whisper. "The storm dropped him in the old riverbed and backfilled that channel when it tore the new one."

I couldn't look at Dan, afraid he would tell me I was crazy, or worse, agree just to humor me. A bright ribbon of energy danced through the room, and the maps on the table stirred as if in a breeze. I gripped Dan's hand. His fingers twisted through mine and we waited. The tension in the air relaxed, as if letting out its breath.

"Even if you focus on what used to be that horseshoe bend, that's still a couple of acres," Dan said.

The implication hung between us. An acre is roughly the size of a football field. It would be a Herculean task to search the entire area with any degree of precision. "If you had access to ground penetrating radar, you might stand a chance of finding him."

I sighed. "I might as well use the divining rods."

"Maybe you should just go out there and look."

"For what? A skeletal hand sticking out of the ground?" I paced the length of the kitchen and back.

"Sarah thinks you can do it. You kind of volunteered, after all."

"More like I was volun-*told*."

Dan leveled a dark blue gaze at me. "Of all the people who have lived here, she chose you to find him." He stepped forward, and I thought he was going to pull me into a hug, but instead, he squeezed my upper arms and left. I watched as the taillights of his pickup flashed at the end of the lane before turning west.

"She chose you, too," I whispered.

What would happen if I did find Luke? Would Sarah drift away like thinning smoke until her music and energy and temper were only memories? What about Dan? Once the rush of discovery was over, would he retreat to his own reclusive lifestyle and leave me to putter around in my old house like the proverbial spinster aunt? I'd moved here for precisely that reason, but suddenly, being alone felt less like desirable and more like lonesome.

CHAPTER 16

I TOOK ADVANTAGE of a damp, gray morning to fill out the cemetery survey I'd downloaded from the State Association for the Preservation of Iowa Cemeteries (SAPIC) website. If I pursued grant money to restore Bishop Cemetery, it would be handy to have the paperwork already prepped.

I filled in exactly three spaces—legal name of cemetery, contact person and owner of record—before I hit a wall. I'd have to drag out the property deed to find out what section of Sand Creek Township it occupied, and I had no idea what the latitude and longitude were. I had no idea what a UTM zone was, either, let alone what terms like easting and northing meant. I skipped all of that and soldiered on.

Stones present (if yes, complete the following: number of markers; number of graves occupied/unoccupied.)

All right, skipping that one, too. Yes, there were stones but the whole occupied/unoccupied thing was rather vexing.

Note any hazards imperiling the cemetery's existence. I hesitated. Lunatics with shovels probably wasn't an appropriate answer.

The next section didn't get any better.

Accessibility to the public: unrestricted; restricted (explain).

Definitely unrestricted. I got another cup of coffee and was eating chocolate chips straight out of the bag when Dan pulled in.

"It's open!" I yelled before he knocked. Raider launched himself across the room, caught Dan in the upper chest with his front paws, and knocked him back against the wall, his tail lashing and a maniacal gleam in his eyes.

"I thought you said you were a dog trainer." Dan regained his balance and untangled himself from Raid.

"I never said I was a good one. Want some coffee?"

"Sure." His eyes narrowed when he saw the semi-sweet chips on the table. "Are you eating those straight out of the bag?"

"Don't judge."

He didn't. Instead, he held out a copy of *The Des Moines Register*. "Figured you hadn't seen this."

"You still get the paper delivered?"

"Old school, remember? Page two, upper right."

The headline caught my eye immediately.

Treasure hunting couple arrested on theft, vandalism charges

Onawa, IA—An Iowa couple who claim to be professional treasure hunters has been charged with vandalism and theft after they allegedly damaged an exhibit at the Monona County Heritage Museum.

Scott Carlson, 38, and his wife, Melanie Carlson, 37, claimed they were searching for a hidden document rumored to have been signed by Abraham Lincoln in Monona County in 1854. The document in question was referenced in historian Dr. Peter Aldrich's book, *Treasure Hunting in the Heartland*, due to be released in December.

The couple also faces a charge of fifth degree theft for stealing an advance copy of the book, which had been sent to the museum as thanks for that organization's help with Dr. Aldrich's research.

The sinking feeling in my gut had nothing to do with how much chocolate I'd eaten.

"The crackpots are at it already," Dan said.

"I hope there's a foot of snow on the ground when that book is released. No one's going to come out here and mess around in the winter." If I said that often enough, maybe it would come true.

"If the person doesn't find what they're looking for this fall, they'll start again in the spring. What's that?" Dan gestured to the cemetery form on my laptop.

"I'm jumping through hoops so I can apply for a restoration grant for Bishop. If it's a legit historic site, maybe the nut jobs will stay away. But I don't know what half this stuff means."

Dan pulled my laptop toward him and scanned the screen. Thirty minutes later, the form was nearly completed, and the bag of chocolate chips was empty. In my defense, it wasn't full when I started.

Dan told me UTM stood for Universal Transverse Mercator, a mapping system that assigns coordinates to locations on the surface of the Earth. He showed me how to use my phone to find a site's longitude and latitude. All I had to do was stand in the middle of the cemetery and open the mapping app. He pushed the laptop back to me.

"Does it strike you as odd that you're dealing with a site that contains forgotten human remains, while at the same time you're looking for human remains people still talk about?" he asked.

"Nothing strikes me as odd anymore. And I'm not exactly looking." A pang of guilt poked me in the ribs. "Sarah's going to have something to say about that if I don't get started."

"Ghost whisperer."

"Call me that one more time and I will hurt you."

"Try it, sweetheart."

He held my eyes for a minute too long and my heart skipped a couple of beats. I blamed it on too much coffee and semi-sweet chocolate. Was he deliberately sticking his foot across the line in the sand of our friendship to see what would happen? It would be easy to flirt if he didn't have any intention of following up. Conversely, it would be easy to flirt if he did intend to follow up. I bit the inside of my lip. This modern dance of overthinking everything made my head want to explode.

"I've got to get back to work." Dan gave Raider a parting scratch, then let himself out. I watched him walk to his pickup, the slight limp visible only because I knew it was there. I reread the story in the

Register, wondering why the past was so determined to get tangled up with my present. The present was tangled enough.

Still not ready to tackle the day's to-do list, I scrolled through the cemetery preservation sites I'd bookmarked. An archived story about volunteers assisting Iowa's state archaeologist in exhuming remains from a pioneer plot to accommodate a highway expansion sounded intriguing even though it wasn't recent. I clicked on the photo gallery. The site had been cleared of vegetation and reduced to a series of neatly trenched grids. The cemetery was so old, its inhabitants had been laid to rest in wooden coffins that deteriorated over time, leaving the workers to unearth bare bones. The dirty, sweaty volunteers all looked absurdly happy regardless of their morbid task.

A photo of several T-shirts and blue jeans-clad people lifting a headstone caught my eye, and the kitchen tilted on its axis. It was my own shocked response this time, not any of Sarah's doing. I gripped the edge of the table and stared in confusion. The body carriage and facial expression of one of the workers was immediately familiar despite the passage of time.

No. It wasn't possible. I enlarged the photo. The image blurred slightly, but the facial features were unmistakable.

I scanned the rest of the gallery. The figure was in several more shots, each making me squint in confusion. I closed the laptop and stared out the window as my mind struggled to superimpose those features from the past on a current face.

It had to be a coincidence. There was no other explanation.

THE EVENING SPENT channeling Raid's reckless energy into competitive obedience skills at the HDTC workout made me feel guilty about not doing more with him than our rambling daily walks. I resolved to buckle down this winter and address our training deficit or we'd never get into the show ring come spring. I was having a hard time shifting from Sarah/Luke/Dan/Brad/Bishop Cemetery problems to heeling/retrieving/scent discrimination problems, though.

"You look like you're a million miles away," Kerri observed as Raider and I came off the training floor after a lukewarm attempt at a retrieving drill.

"Trouble focusing. Life is weird." I tossed Raider's tennis ball in my gear bag.

"*Your* life is weird." Kerri sank into the chair by her crate. Tangle leaped into her lap, and she disappeared momentarily behind a cloud of blue merle fur.

"Won't argue that." I sat down next to her, and Raid flopped his front end across my lap. I was happy to be back at the club building, with its familiar faces and routines, but as Kerri and I watched Conn help Susanne fine-tune Cannon's heel position, my mind drifted to the odd list of priorities I'd accumulated in the last month.

In the adjacent ring, Clara was busy imparting wisdom gleaned from all the dogs she'd never trained to Kyle, who was politely ignoring her. The photos from the cemetery excavation clicked through my mind in review. Kyle had access to all manner of earth-moving equipment, either hand-held or motorized, but his weren't the facial features I'd recognized. I couldn't prove anything and wasn't about to start making baseless accusations.

Before I started seeing graverobbers everywhere, I collected Raider and his tennis ball and headed back into the ring. Susanne and Conn were deep in conversation, but as I passed, Conn said, "Hey, I saw in the paper where your place is featured in a book."

"That Confederate gold story is getting a lot of press," I said.

Conn started to say something, but Susanne stepped into the conversation.

"How are things with the house? Any ghost sightings?" She laughed, then added hastily, "I don't believe in them, but some people do." Her voice trailed off.

"No ghost sightings," I said, which was true. As far as it went. I hadn't seen Sarah as a ghost. I'd seen her as a real, live young woman, devastated by loss. "I've done some painting and a few repairs. It's definitely a long-term project."

And getting longer by the minute because my current project involved neither painting nor repairs.

Later, as we packed up to leave, Kerri nodded at Susanne. "Why does she keep asking you about the house?"

"She's just showing professional courtesy. She tried really hard to not sell me Fox Hollow, but only because the price was so low. She kept pushing a higher priced property she wanted to move, but it wasn't what I wanted."

"I still think there's still something she's not telling you," Kerri said.

FRIDAY, NOV. 9

WHY DON'T YOU just go out there and look?

Dan's words echoed in my mind as I stood on the edge of the bluff overlooking the Iowa River. Below, where the former horseshoe had once looped at the base of the rock face, the channel made a ninety-degree turn to angle northeast.

I worked along the bluff's edge, peering over and pulling dizzily back until I found a navigable downward slope. Raider scrambled ahead of me as I half-walked, half-slid behind him until we emerged on the wide floodplain between the base of the bluff and the river.

I paused to get my bearings. I was standing approximately where the old river channel would have been.

Driftwood washed downstream by decades of floods littered the desolate stretch of weather-beaten scrub. A few low-lying areas formed miniature wetlands edged with stands of native willow and cattails gone to fluff. Record flood crests on the Iowa the previous spring had gouged deep rifts through the soil as Mother Nature reinvented herself.

I set off at a cautious distance from the biggest of the washouts, not trusting its unstable bank. Intermittent drizzle dampened my confidence in the outcome of this mission, but Raider ranged ahead, bringing me sticks to throw and leaping driftwood obstacles with graceful athleticism, oblivious to the chill and occasional spits of rain.

After about a quarter mile of climbing over logs and pushing through tangled vegetation, I stopped to catch my breath. I'd thought about bringing the divining rods but decided against it as I didn't know how—or where—to use them. Sarah had directed me here, but beyond that, I had nothing. There was no X marking the spot. All I'd have to show for this was a lot of sore muscles tomorrow.

I wandered for another half an hour, admiring the starkness of late autumn. The only things I saw in the sandy loam were tracks of deer, wild turkeys, and an army of raccoons. Raid continued his stick campaign, fetching and delivering with fervor. I let his joy override my anxiety about making zero progress on finding anything useful.

A heavy overcast cloaked the afternoon in dull pewter light as the intermittent drizzle grew steadier. Without warning, the clouds opened in a downpour that diluted the landscape into a watery blur as wind scoured the river bottoms. Damn Iowa's turn-on-a-dime weather. That was exactly what got Luke Bauer killed.

I whistled for Raid and turned for the trek home. Once I reached the top of the bluff, it would be a cold, wet slog back to the house. I should have insisted Dan come with me. This had been his idea, and if I was going to be miserable, I might as well have company.

I stomped along, disillusioned in the day and grumbling about the weather and not paying any attention to my footing as I skirted a huge tangle of driftwood edging the big washout. It shouldn't have been a surprise when my left boot sank into a small, burrowing animal's front door, and my ankle folded painfully under me. I crashed into a stand of fuzzed-out cattails in a graceless landing. Raider stuck his cold nose in my cold ear and whuffed with concern.

My ankle blazed with pain, but experimental flexing determined I'd only rolled it. I swore loudly and without apology and was about to get up when a small disc on the ground only inches from my nose came into focus.

I sat up gingerly and picked it up. The surface of the coin was pitted with age. I thumbed off loose dirt to reveal a woman's worn profile. The only women on modern coins were Sacagawea and Susan B. Anthony, and this was neither. I clenched it in my fingers and stared at the ground through the slashing rain.

A second coin was half-buried in the scuff of soil I'd dislodged in my landing. I immediately recognized the Indian head penny. What years had those been minted?

"Ouch!" Tiny ice pellets stung my cheek as the rain changed to sleet. Raider's judgmental look and flattened ears said this was no longer a pleasant adventure. A scan of the nearby dirt revealed nothing more, although I was fast becoming too cold to care. I could come back when the weather cleared.

I struggled to my feet and pocketed the coins, then reoriented myself. I was a few yards south of the massive driftwood deadfall parallel to the biggest of the washouts. I could easily find this place again. The smashed cattails served as Mother Nature's crime scene tape.

The wet fabric of my jacket clung to my shoulders like an icy compress, and my fingers stung with cold as I started to limp homeward. I took a few more painful steps and rethought the situation. If I cut through the trees to the east, it was only about seventy-five yards to the road. I pulled out my phone.

Dan answered on the second ring.

"Can you give me a ride?" I asked. "I'll be up on the road about a mile east of the house."

"What are you doing out there in this weather?"

"Freezing to death." A little exaggeration never hurt.

"Anything for you, McCallister."

I limped out of the timber just as he parked along the side of the road. He didn't say anything, just scrambled through the shallow road ditch, slung an arm around my waist and half carried me back to the truck. Raider leaped in and licked Dan's cheek to express his gratitude.

Dan grumbled and flipped the heater on high. He didn't give me a chance to speak. "What were you— no, let me guess—you were looking for Luke. Did you find him? No. But you apparently broke your ankle."

"I just rolled it. It'll be fine."

"Then why'd you call me?"

"Because it hurts, and I didn't want to walk home in the rain."

"You should have thought about that before you went out there."

"It wasn't raining when I left the house. And that's a bit rich, coming from the guy who told me to go out there."

I shivered. Dan scowled. We rode the mile back to Fox Hollow in silence broken only by the slapping of the windshield wipers. When he pulled up in front of the house, he said, "You owe me another pie. And my truck smells like a wet dog."

I narrowed my eyes. "Don't you dare tell me this is the first time your truck's smelled like a wet dog."

"Go warm up before hypothermia gets you. I don't have time to haul you to the emergency room."

"Thanks." I tried to sound grateful, which was hard because my teeth were chattering. "I mean it."

"So do I. Your lips are turning blue."

I toweled Raider off in the laundry room, rubbing him from nose to tail until his fur stood up in damp little tufts. Then I filled the claw foot tub in the second-floor bathroom and sank blissfully into the steaming water. Heat tingled through my toes and fingers in a delicious counterpoint to the icy rain hissing against the window. Warm to the core after a long soak, I climbed out and dried off. I pulled on fleece-lined leggings, thick socks, and a blue and white North Willow Mustangs hoodie. When I gathered up my sodden jeans for the laundry, the coins clattered from the pocket onto the tile floor.

I studied them. Were they significant, or did my need to find Luke make them seem more important than they really were? If they pre-dated 1919, it was possible they'd fallen from his clothing when the storm dropped his body. A century of freeze-thaw cycles and erosion could have brought them to the surface.

I bit my lip. Even if they pre-dated 1919, that proved nothing. They could have been dropped by anyone who'd hunted and fished in the river bottoms over the years or been carried downstream by decades of flooding. I put the stopper in the sink and rubbed the coins under running water.

I held my breath as dirt sluiced away from the larger coin, the one with the woman's face. The date was 1910. The penny was worn and harder to read but I could just discern 1...9...1...4.

Yes! Realistically, both could have been in circulation the year Luke vanished.

Heart pounding, I clenched the coins in my palm. They were the first physical clue I'd found. With a whoop of excitement, I called Dan. He was going to seriously regret giving me his number.

"Can I come over?" I shoved my feet into dry boots and winced as my ankle protested.

"Um, sure," he said, but I was already in my Jeep, leaving a baffled Raider behind. Minutes later, I limped through the rain onto his back porch. I've never mastered a level of comfort at knocking and walking into someone's house except Kerri's or Mare's, but I did it without thinking.

"Sinclair!" I yelled.

Ruby barreled into the room, hackles up, then launched herself at me in a spiral of canine delight. Dan's face was a mask of resignation as he appeared from the direction of his office.

"Now what?" he asked.

"Look!" I felt a pang of guilt. My repeated interruptions couldn't be doing his writing any good. I tumbled the coins onto the kitchen table. "I found these this afternoon where the old river channel used to be." As he turned them over in his fingers, I shared my theory.

"Hypothetically, they could have fallen from Luke's pocket and hypothetically, erosion could have brought them to the surface," he said. "But there's no way to prove these were his."

Undaunted, I pocketed the coins. "I'm going back again tomorrow."

He scowled. "With that ankle?"

I was standing with all my weight on my right leg, using the table for balance. "It's fine."

"I doubt that. Sit down." He left the room. Cupboard doors banged in the bathroom, and he was back in less than a minute, carrying a white first aid kit. "Thought I told you to sit down."

"Are you always this bossy?" I asked, but sank into a chair.

He pulled a chair opposite me and gestured. "Foot."

I unlaced my boot and peeled off my sock. Streaks of purple and red bruising circled the swollen joint.

Dan snorted. "Did you plan to ignore that?"

"I've done it before. It'll be better in the morning."

"Before you rub some dirt on it and walk it off, let me wrap it. Then go home and elevate it with an ice pack." Dan produced a roll of lime green self-adhesive wrap from the first aid kit.

"Vet wrap? Really? Is that your first aid kit or Ruby's?"

"Yes," he said. Without asking, he grasped my foot by the heel and lifted it. I winced. He rolled my legging up and out of the way. I winced again. His hands were warm, his fingers quick and sure as they wrapped a compression bandage around the injured joint.

I wished he weren't quite so efficient, that he would slow down so I could enjoy his touch a little longer. I'd stopped wincing. Again, he was doing something for me without expecting anything in return, the increasing number of pies not-withstanding.

What did it say about me and my past relationships that I found this simple act of kindness so novel? Anytime I got involved with a guy, I immediately started trying to be what he wanted and ignored the fact that behavior was never reciprocated. With Dan, there wasn't time to try being someone else. I had to be me—the delightful, sarcastic, dog training, ghost wrangling hot mess that I was.

"There." He tore the wrap off the roll and gently squeezed the end down on my leg a few inches above my ankle. "That will help keep the swelling down." His hand lingered. "I'll go out there with you tomorrow if you want me to."

"That would be great." I bit down on my delight that he was going with me, if only to haul me home when I broke something for real. "We can start where I found the coins. I don't know exactly where to go from there, but you're the one who told me to go look."

His lips curved into a reluctant smile. "I suggested you go look. If I'd told you to do it, you wouldn't have gone near the place." He rolled the cuff of my legging down and straightened. "Go home, McCallister. Ice and elevate. Lieutenant Hanson's in a mess of trouble and I can't deal with both of you at the same time."

CHAPTER 17

Saturday, Nov. 10

"How's the ankle?" Dan asked. I climbed into his pickup and Raider scrambled in after me.

"As long as I don't run any sprints, I'll be fine." My foot was still tender, but the swelling was down. Now I was wearing my tallest pair of hiking boots, laced tight, and the river bottoms called like a siren's song.

"It won't be hard to find the spot where I found the coins. It was on the south side of a huge pile of driftwood. We'll start there and look for... something." My crack about a skeletal hand poking out of the ground didn't seem quite as funny as it had a few days ago.

The storm had blown itself out, leaving the afternoon chilly but sunny. Dan drove to the spot where he'd picked me up yesterday and parked on the side of the road. As we walked through the trees onto the river terrace, Raider brought me a stick. I gave it a toss and let him retrieve it until he found a different one he considered a greater prize. Ruby didn't share his obsession with sticks and hunted field mice in the tangled grass.

We worked our way along the big washout, skirting muddy depressions holding remnants of yesterday's rain. My ankle twinged occasionally, but my rising anticipation overrode the discomfort.

"It's just up here." I pushed through a stand of willow scrub and stopped short. Ahead, part of the washout's western face had fractured off like a calving glacier. The twisted jumble of driftwood I'd detoured around yesterday, along with the adjoining soil, now lay in a tangle at the bottom of the deep ditch. A cold lump of disappointment formed in my stomach.

"The bank collapsed from the rain," I said. "The place where I found the coins is gone."

"Are you sure this was it?" Dan asked. I didn't blame him for questioning my orienteering. One water-carved washout looked pretty much like another.

"Yeah." I pointed at the crushed cattails. "That's where I fell."

The dogs sniffed around, inspecting the freshly disturbed earth before navigating the slope to the bottom of the wash. A minute later, Raider raced back with a new stick clamped in his jaws. He shoved it at me, and I took it without looking, still numb with disappointment. It felt like I was back to square one. Again.

I drew my arm back to chuck the stick, and Raid danced in anticipation, clacking his jaws for me to hurry. At least one of us was having fun.

"Jess, stop."

Dan sounded like I was about to step on a landmine. I froze. "What?"

"Don't throw that."

I looked at the stick. It was more than a foot long, smooth and stripped of bark, the surface stained brown. Knuckle-shaped protrusions formed one end.

"That's a human tibia."

My fingers opened without conscious thought, and the bone fell to the dirt with a soft thud. Raider made a grab at it.

"No, dog, leave it," Dan said. Raid pinned his ears in annoyance but backed away. We all stood there, staring at the not-a-stick.

"You know that how?" I choked.

"I looked at a lot of X-rays when I had my leg put back together. Didn't you take anatomy in high school?"

I had, but in all fairness, I'd never expected to see human bones outside the context of the articulated skeleton hanging in Mr. Garland's classroom. Could this piece of human remains, delivered so casually by my dog, be part of what I was desperately looking for?

I stepped back to look over the edge of the washout where the dogs had disappeared again, and without warning, the saturated soil gave way under my feet. I toppled backwards, landed hard on one hip, and slid sideways down the embankment on my butt. A chunk of weathered driftwood stopped my wild descent.

Ignoring the impact, I scrambled upright. My jeans were filthy and my ankle throbbed, but nothing was injured except my pride. Raider bounded over to me, tail wagging, waiting to see what fun thing I'd do next.

Dan looked over the edge. "Way to go, Grace."

"I'm fine, thanks for asking."

An almost tangible feeling of rightness hummed through my body like an electric current. I tried to get my bearings, no easy task since I was below ground level. Was I standing in the old river channel, carved anew by the spring's repeated flooding? Perhaps a geologist could have figured it out, but that knowledge was above my pay grade. I scanned both banks for a clue but saw only crumbled earth and flood debris.

"Anything there?" Dan called.

Like the other two hundred and five bones that comprise a human body?

"No." If my dog brought me a leg bone, he could at least have the good manners to show me where he found it.

Raid hiked a leg on the tree trunk I'd crashed into and showed no signs of having good manners. Dan stretched out a hand to help pull me up. I grasped his wrist and set a boot against the bank, but our combined weight made the soil crumble again. I let go, and he backed up hastily as I slid back to the bottom.

I set off toward a gentle grade of undisturbed ground ten yards away that promised better footing, my jaw clenched with frustration. Was my theory about Luke being buried in the old river channel correct, or did the bone belong to a resident of Bishop Cemetery? If it was the former, where was the rest of him? If it was the latter, had someone been digging up bodies and dumping them in the river bottom? To what end? Raider trotted happily along with me, oblivious to my mental agitation.

Sunlight flashed on something white protruding from the bank, and I caught my breath, only to let it out with a sigh. It was a shard of broken china. Disappointed, I wiggled it free and brushed away the clinging dirt.

My breath caught again. Gold sparkled along the rim and what remained of the pink rose design looked like it had been painted yesterday.

It was a fragment of the plate I'd seen perched delicately atop the mud amid chaos and death when Sarah dragged me into the post-storm river bottom on Halloween. I let it fall to the ground. It was just a random artifact that had been buried by the passage of time, not an impromptu grave marker.

I picked my way through the ditch, getting dirtier with each step and trying not to feel claustrophobic. Here and there slabs of dirt had sheared off in miniature landslides, exposing cross sections of a soilscape that rose above my head. Dark loam on the surface gave way to underlying substrata of brown, red and gray tints that reflected soil composition. There was even a deposit the color of old ivory.

I froze.

Iowa soil comes in a lot of different shades. Ivory isn't one of them.

The curve of cranial bones jutted from the exposed bank. A dirt-packed eye socket stared blindly toward the sky. I stumbled backward and slammed hard against the opposite bank, feet backpedaling but taking me nowhere, like a cartoon character suspended over a precipice. My mouth opened, but my tongue couldn't form words. The skull, which was tipped slightly toward me, mirrored my silence.

A wave of vertigo pushed me toward the bones, as if some unseen force was playing tug of war with my body. I flattened my outstretched palms on the earth in front of me for balance, dislodging another cascade of dirt that revealed the curve of a ribcage.

I jerked back, upright but swaying like a drunk. The sun slid behind a cloud, and the bones gleamed dully in the two-dimensional light.

I closed my eyes, took several deep breaths, and opened them again. As they grew accustomed to the shades of earth and bone, I made out more of the skeleton. It lay on its back under six feet of soil, right side partially exposed, the left still trapped in the earth. The right leg was missing below the femur.

The clouds pulled apart, and sunlight sparkled off something near the skeleton's right hip. I reached out a trembling hand. When my fingers touched the rust encrusted framework of a tiny box, it crumbled in a shower of oxidized flakes. A gold ring tumbled into my palm.

Barely breathing, I rubbed away the dirt. The oval sapphire was flanked by a small diamond on either side.

My heart surged into my throat. Joy tinged with the bitter pain of loss slammed through me with so much power I couldn't move. My fingers clenched the ring as if it were a talisman connecting two dimensions.

"Jess?" Dan's voice reached me from across

several yards and an entire century. When I didn't answer, he took the most expedient route and slid down the ten-foot drop with more style than I had.

I opened my hand. The sapphire blazed with blue fire. Dan looked from the ring to the bones and back to me. He issued a single reverent swearword and wrapped an arm around my shoulders. I slid my arm around his waist in return. The dogs joined us, standing on their hind legs to sniff the exposed bones. I whistled Raider to my side before he could take off with anything else.

The weight of expectation I'd carried since Sarah's Halloween revelation had been replaced by euphoric buoyancy. If Dan's arm hadn't been around me, I might have floated right off the ground.

"I suppose you should call the sheriff," he said finally. When I didn't respond, he added, "When you find a body, you're obligated to notify law enforcement, even if it's a hundred years old." When I still didn't respond, he said, "I'll call the sheriff."

Reluctantly, I let go of his waist. He dropped his arm from my shoulders, and his fingers sought mine. Electricity sparked through me at his hard, reassuring squeeze, then he stepped away to pull out his phone.

I opened my other hand. The ring's setting was caked with dirt except for the smooth facet of the sapphire. It had been documented in the newspaper articles, part of the legend of young lovers and a long-anticipated betrothal ended in tragedy. The ring would establish Luke's identity, but I couldn't bear to see it sealed away in an evidence bag. I put it in the front pocket of my jeans.

Dan clicked off his phone. "Sheriff Gray will be here as soon as he can contact the coroner."

I looked away from the bank. Staring at the bare bones protruding from the earth felt like an invasion of privacy. I'd rather remember Luke as the handsome, smiling man in the faded photographs, not this broken collection of organic remains. I closed my eyes as past, present and future whirled in a carousel of time and emotion.

"What are you smiling about?" Dan asked.

"Now Sarah can—" I stopped. With Luke accounted for, the tie that held her to Fox Hollow had been released. What would happen to her? Disoriented, I reversed the question. "What are you smiling about?"

His mouth curved with amusement, white teeth against dark stubble. "You. Do-it-yourselfer by day, ghost whisperer by night."

"Stop."

"Communing with spirits and hunting buried treasure. You could write a book. Hell, you could launch your own TV show."

"Seriously, stop." I jabbed an elbow in his direction, which he easily evaded. "Sarah pestered me until I came out here and fell in a ditch. I practically landed on the—landed on Luke. I don't think that constitutes communing."

We stared at each other, both of us grinning insanely, standing in the mud two feet from the lead story on the evening's six o'clock news. A dozen things I wanted to say stampeded through my mind but were tangled into silence before they reached my tongue.

I wanted to tell Dan how glad I was that he was here with me in this moment. I wanted to tell him Sarah was happy he was here, too, and that I suspected she'd deliberately forged him into the chain that linked her past with my present.

But while Dan accepted Sarah meddling in my life, I had no idea how he felt about her fiddling with his. If I told him I thought she'd united us in the quest to find Luke for reasons not entirely related to that end, the bubble that held the mess of my emotions would burst, splattering both of us with all the things I didn't know how to handle.

Dan squeezed my arm. "I'm going up to the road to meet the sheriff. Try not to fall in the river while I'm gone." He gave me a quick, lopsided smile and left, Ruby at his heels.

I sat down on a piece of driftwood and tangled my fingers in Raider's fur. I didn't know if I was sorry I hadn't followed my impulse to spill my heart all over the afternoon, or if I deserved a medal for keeping my mouth shut. The day was out of my control now, either way. Once the media caught wind of this, it was going to be one striped tent short of a three-ring circus.

CHAPTER 18

Saturday, Nov. 10

"Miss McCallister! Do you believe you've found Luke Bauer's remains?"

I didn't answer the reporter immediately. Cat's Back Road looked like someone had kicked over an ant hill. Four vehicles from the sheriff's department and an Iowa State Patrol cruiser clogged the narrow gravel, their lights slashing through the late afternoon sun. The white coroner's van sat behind them.

Satellite trucks from local television stations crowded the emergency vehicles as closely as they were allowed. Broadcast journalists, print reporters from the Cedar Rapids and Iowa City metro dailies, and Logan Barnes from the *Sentinel* hummed like a hive of bees, shooting footage and posting to social media feeds. Sheriff Adam Gray had confirmed the discovery of human remains near the Iowa River but refused to speculate about their identity.

I took a deep breath and focused on the reporter holding out a microphone. "I know many of you have heard the story about the man who disappeared in this area a hundred years ago, but I can't confirm anything." My skill at lying was commendable, but it took a conscious effort not to touch the ring in my pocket.

Sheriff Gray stepped forward. "Despite the obvious age of the remains, this is still an active investigation. I can't release any further details at this time, but my department will share further information as it becomes available."

His disclaimer put an end to the press conference. I ducked into the blockade of law enforcement vehicles barring access to the river bottom. Randy Simmons, one of the local deputies, nodded me through without question. I escaped behind the state patrol cruiser and called Kerri, trying to condense the madness into reasonable sentences.

She was incoherent with excitement. "You found him? How—where?"

Raider growled at my side.

"Jess?"

I ignored the familiar voice and tightened my grip on Raid's leash. The last thing I needed was him taking a chomp out of Brad Jennings in front of a half dozen news cameras.

"I can't talk now," I said to Kerri. "Can you come out? Call Mare and ask her to come, too. The DCI already has a team here to remove the bones. I'll be back at the house soon." I put the phone in my pocket and turned around. Brad stood right behind me.

"I was on a car accident at Stone Run or I'd have been here sooner," he said, as if his absence had been my biggest concern. His eyes flicked across the river bottoms. "What were you doing out there?"

His accusatory tone sent a ripple of unease through me, but I had no time for whatever Brad-centric agenda he was pursuing.

"Walking." I learned early in my journalism career that single word answers are a quick way to kill an interview. I'd been on the receiving end of that technique and employed it now without hesitation.

"By yourself?"

"No."

His lips tightened. "Did you find anything besides the body?"

"No." The ring burned icy hot in my pocket.

"Have you been in Bishop Cemetery today?"

"What are you talking about?" I let irritation burn the words to ash. "What I found has nothing to do with the cemetery."

Brad glanced toward the river. The white glow of halogen lights around the site cut through the gathering dusk. He took a step closer. Raider curled his lip and a growl vibrated up the leash. Brad stepped back.

I'd had enough of whatever he was playing at. "Excuse me."

"Wait! I need to know—"

"I don't care what you need." I spun on my heel and walked away, trying not to limp. Brad didn't follow.

I made it twenty feet before Logan Barnes popped out from behind one of the deputies' vehicles. He'd either sneaked past the officers or they'd recognized him as local media and given him unrestricted access. My bet was on the former.

"Jess! Glad I caught you. Can I ask you a few questions?" He had a pen and notebook in one hand, a cell phone in the other, and a digital SLR camera slung around his neck. He looked like energy drinks still constituted his main food group. "Everybody thinks this is the guy who disappeared in that tornado, but is there a chance the remains could be connected to the vandalism at the cemetery?"

I stared at him in confusion. This was the second time in five minutes someone had asked me about the cemetery.

"Bishop Cemetery," he repeated. "You know, because someone's been digging there?"

"How did you know about that?"

He shrugged. "Heard the vandalism call on the scanner at the office. I recognized your address and, well, everyone knows about the cemetery."

I took a deep breath and let it out slowly. "This has nothing to do with Bishop Cemetery. This body was buried under six feet of dirt in what I think was the old river bed. The only reason I found it was because it had been exposed by erosion. No one dug it up. I can't tell you anything else because I don't know anything else."

Logan looked so disappointed I felt sorry for him. This was a big story, and if he handled it well, it could be a major stepping stone in his career.

"I'll give you a call as soon as I know anything, I promise," I said. I wondered how I was going to relate the story without involving ghost messages from the afterlife. Hopefully no one would look too hard at my "I-went-for-a-walk-and-fell-in-a-ditch" explanation.

That seemed to satisfy Logan. He left to take

more pictures of the river bottom with an absurdly long telephoto lens.

Raider and I found Dan sitting on the tailgate of his pickup with one arm around Ruby as he watched the tide of reporters, cameramen, and law enforcement ebb and surge. The brim of his hat was pulled so low he was almost a caricature of someone trying not to attract attention.

"What did Jennings want?" he asked.

"To know why I was walking around on my own property." I hiked myself up on the tailgate next to him.

"And you said?"

"Excuse me." My voice held the same burning frost as when I'd told Brad our conversation was over. "What's so funny?"

Dan's lazy smile deepened. "I like a woman who can tell a sheriff's deputy to fuck off."

"I didn't say that, exactly."

"If you said it in that tone, you meant it, exactly."

He had a point.

We shared a bottle of water and a dusty package of granola bars from the pickup's glovebox. My hip ached from crashing into the tree trunk, and my ankle throbbed from overuse, but I didn't want to go home. It seemed wrong to abandon Luke after I'd just found him.

When Sheriff Gray promised to keep me updated on the DCI team's progress, I surrendered to my pain and left with Dan and the dogs. Back at the house, Dan followed me inside.

I didn't protest when he took off his coat and

muddy boots and pulled two beers out of the refrigerator. We'd just settled at the kitchen table when the first reporter knocked on the back door, setting off Raider and Ruby like the hounds of the Baskervilles. I limped to the door and politely declined the woman's request for an interview.

After she left, Dan parked his pickup across the foot of the lane to prevent any more media from descending on the house. Shortly after that, Kerri called and asked if he'd parked there deliberately or if the truck had finally died a natural death. Dan moved it and let her in. Twenty minutes later, Mare called to say she'd brought supper and would someone please move that junk heap so she could get through.

Seated in front of a crackling fire, we ate heaping plates of spaghetti with meatballs from Pasta Ranch and watched the evening news.

"A century-old missing persons case may have been solved today," said a blonde reporter wearing a red wool pea coat and matching beret, standing on the road at the edge of my property. "Jessica McCallister, who owns the historic Lenox County property known as Fox Hollow, was walking her dog this afternoon when she found skeletal human remains near the Iowa River.

"Authorities wouldn't confirm, but the Lenox County Historical Society has suggested the remains may be those of Luke Bauer, a man who disappeared in a tornado that devastated the area on July 4, 1919. His body was never found. The Iowa DCI is working with the Lenox County Sheriff's

Department to exhume the remains."

The screen cut to footage of Sheriff Gray addressing the assembled media earlier that afternoon, then to me, awkwardly answering a few questions. The camera cut back to the reporter.

"This isn't Fox Hollow's first appearance in the spotlight. Be sure to watch our ten o'clock newscast for a segment on Dr. Peter Aldrich's book on treasure hunting in the Midwest and its link to this property. Reporting live from Lenox County, this is Julie Harrison, KCRG TV9."

I shut the television off.

"That book is going to have people flocking out here like crazy," I grumbled. "I'll have to fence the place with razor wire to have any peace."

"One problem at a time," Kerri said. "What happens now?"

"I know it's Luke, but the sheriff isn't going to rely on a ghost story to establish a positive ID," I said. "The state medical examiner will determine age and sex. They could pull DNA from the teeth or bones, but they'd have to find relatives for comparison. I don't know where the other Bauer brothers went after they sold the family farm."

"What are the chances it's not Luke but some other poor schmuck who ended up under six feet of dirt by accident?" Mare asked.

I pulled out the ring. "This was next to his right femur, like it had been in his pocket." I handed it to her. Mare took it with the reverence of someone receiving a holy relic.

"Shouldn't you have given that to the sheriff?"

Kerri asked. She examined the ring and offered it to Dan, who held it so the firelight danced off the stones before he gave it back to me.

His fingertips were warm as he pressed it into my palm, and I heard a faint, sweet ripple of music. Dan's fingers jerked almost imperceptibly, and our eyes met.

"Probably," I said, oddly reluctant to pull my hand away. "When the sheriff finds Luke's next of kin, I'll give it to them. I couldn't stand to see it disappear into some dusty evidence locker if Gray can't track them down."

We were lingering over Mare's maple butterscotch cake when my cell rang.

"Jess, this is Adam." The sheriff's tone was informal. "We've finished up out here."

"Already?" I looked out the window. It was full dark now. A sliver of crescent moon hung low on the horizon.

"The ground was soft from all the rain and the DCI team didn't have any problems collecting the skeleton," Gray continued. "We found some coins, all pre-dating 1919, and a pocket watch. It's engraved L.J. Bauer WBHS 1917. We checked with the historical society and your missing man graduated from Walnut Bluff High School in 1917. The watch was probably a gift. Unless the state medical examiner says the bones are more recent, or a woman's, you're right. It's him."

I let out a breath I hadn't realized I was holding. Gray assured me he would be in touch regarding next of kin. I thanked him and hung up.

"They've got him," I said. "I've already told the sheriff I'll pay the burial expenses if they can't find Luke's family. Sarah wants him laid to rest properly, and if he ended up stuck in a box at the morgue there'd be no living with her."

DAN LEFT HIS TRUCK across the end of the lane to block any more reporters. Even if they parked on the road, no one was likely to navigate the distance to the house on foot in the dark.

"You're good?" He paused, hand on the kitchen door. Kerri was gone, and Mare was waiting in her car to give him a ride to his house. I'd drive his truck back to him in the morning.

"I'm fine." Exhausted, aching and euphoric but fine. "I'm going to bed."

"Ice your ankle."

I looked down. I was standing on one leg again as the injured joint throbbed with a dull ache.

"Go home already. Tell your agent or editor or whoever he can blame me for putting you behind schedule."

Dan looked around the kitchen as if seeing more than the room. "She knows, doesn't she?"

"Yeah." A faint hum of joy echoed through the house like sunshine sparkling through rain. "I can feel it."

"Me, too."

Impulsively, I reached out and caught his hand. His fingers slid into mine without hesitation.

"What happens with her now?" His voice was husky.

"No idea." A thousand things that had nothing to do with Sarah Cameron tangled in my mind. Dan was close enough I could see faint flecks of gray in the stubble on his cheeks. There was a small white scar along his lower jaw I'd never noticed. War wound? Damage from Heather Wintergarden's assault?

There was so much I didn't know about him, so many things I wanted to ask, to say, but I didn't because all I could think about was how this wouldn't have to end if it never started. It would end now anyway. We'd found Luke. The mission goal had been achieved. Dan could retreat into his writing where there wasn't a risk of having savage memories ripped out by a grieving ghost or being plagued by his crazy neighbor asking him to go look for a body to appease said ghost. We'd go back to just being whatever we were before this all started.

I didn't expect Sarah to linger now that she'd gotten what she wanted. I didn't hold that against her. I still wondered if her pulling Dan into this whole adventure had been less about a need for assistance from the two people living in the sites that were critical to her own life story and more about her recognizing two damaged souls who needed a little push to find each other.

That was ridiculous.

It also left it up to me to take the first step with Dan, but I hesitated. Happily ever after was a mirage I'd chased too often before, only to see it vanish as I reached for it.

Dan squeezed my hand and stepped back.

"Go," I said. "I'm fine."

"I doubt that," he said and left.

I iced my ankle for fifteen minutes, took ibuprofen and a hot shower and crawled into bed. Raider joined me, turning three times clockwise before curling against my hip. The creak and groan of the house settling for the night was like a lullaby.

Drowsy warmth tugged me toward sleep as I relived the day's events. Sarah's joy bubbled through me like champagne, defying traditional rules governing life and death. I would see Luke laid to rest in the township cemetery, his stone no longer marking a century of uncertainty.

"I'll take care of him," I whispered into the darkness. "I'm so happy for you both."

That sounded stupid, but I meant it. The realization I'd written the final chapter in the story of Sarah and Luke's lives made me wonder if it was time to apply some of that effort to my own situation before Dan eased out of my life.

Just as I started to poke at the edges of that idea, Brad marched into the middle of things.

"Wait! I need—"

Fed up with his never-ending self-importance, I hadn't cared what he needed. But what if he'd wanted to tell me something that actually mattered? What if I should have listened?

CHAPTER 19

Tuesday, Nov. 13

The state medical examiner confirmed the remains were of a male aged 18 to 25. The C1 vertebrae, as well as the lower back of the skull, had been crushed, consistent with an injury from windblown debris. Death would have been instant.

Sheriff Gray put me in touch with Luke's great-great-nephew in Vermillion, South Dakota. Ironically his name was also Luke Bauer. Luke 2.0 and I began the process of planning his namesake's second funeral.

A sense of peace settled over Fox Hollow as autumn faded toward winter. Raider tore the downspout off one corner of the house, trying to catch a ground squirrel. I hired Kerri and Matt's boys to help me work the neglected lawn into shape before it snowed. Mare delivered mulch so I could tuck the flowerbeds in for the winter.

Indoors, the house smelled of wood dust as a two-man crew from Cedar Rapids began sanding the dining room floor. Kerri accompanied me to an architectural salvage warehouse in Des Moines where I picked out a vintage porcelain sink for the first-floor bathroom and replacement hinges for the broken ones in the butler's pantry. Dan helped me install the new old hinges, offered unsolicited advice on wrapping heat tape around exposed water lines in the basement, and held the ladder while I re-hung the downspout from which the ground squirrel had escaped, unharmed.

I was grateful for his continued presence but wondered, was this my life now? Renovation help and friendly beers with a guy who had the most heart-twisting smile I'd ever seen?

I told myself it was no big deal. We were grown adults with commitments that went beyond whatever Sarah had hoped to ignite between us. Dan had a publisher waiting for a completed manuscript. I had to make a legit effort on my six-month deadline to decide if home restoration was truly in my skill set. If re-grouting loose tile on the fireplace surround or patching plaster walls turned out to be nothing more than mind-numbing drudgery, I might as well move into one of Susanne's turnkey homes and spend my extra time training Raider.

In any event, Sarah was gone. With Luke's body released to a local funeral home and plans underway for interment in Sand Creek Township Cemetery, the energy that pushed her into my dimension faded. The calico balls stayed where I put them. Raider's tennis balls rolled only when he pounced on them. At night I listened for footsteps in the hall but heard only the quiet settling of the old house.

Raid and I walked almost daily to the little cemetery on the river bluff. There'd been no more digging. Perhaps Brad's chat with the trespassing artifact collector had put a stop to it, although I doubted it. If that angle had panned out, Brad would have told me, just so I knew how much influence he wielded.

My life settled into an easy rhythm filled with friends, dogs, and house projects, and I relaxed into it. I was a fool to think it would last.

TUESDAY, NOV. 20

KYLE MONTGOMERY WAVED me over as soon as Raider and I walked into the Heartland building for open training. His black Lab, Dash, thumped her tail in greeting.

"Hey Jess, Anders told me you're restoring the Bishop Cemetery," Kyle said. "I've done a lot of landscaping masonry. I'd be happy to rebuild that wall when you get to that point."

"Thanks," I said, surprised but appreciative. I'd need all the help I could get when—if—I tackled that project. "Anders may have the cart in front of the horse, though. I'm still working on funding."

That was a stretch, but at least I had the SAPIC form nearly filled out. I kept forgetting to record the longitude and latitude.

Kyle shuffled his feet. "When I was in high school, my friends and I used to go out there and mess around. We thought we'd find that gold and be set for life." He looked sheepish and added hastily, "That was a long time ago."

My smile froze. Maybe it had been a long time ago, but it meant he had familiarity with both the site and the legend. Well, neither were exactly a secret. If I suspected everyone who knew the story, the list would have a thousand names.

I added Kyle to my collection of pseudo suspects even though I doubted he'd be so bold as to offer help restoring a site he'd been vandalizing. Still, murderers were known to help search for the victim while the body was cooling in their trunk. Maybe this was an olive branch to banish any latent guilt about digging there. If he'd already found what he was looking for, it would be easy to play the part of a civic-minded business owner willing to donate time and equipment for a historic cause.

We chatted briefly about Dash's Open-level training and Raider's Utility-level training and the challenges inherent to both, then parted company.

"What was on Kyle's mind?" Kerri asked when I dropped my gear bag on Raider's crate.

"He offered to help with work on the cemetery. And he said he'd played treasure hunter out there with his buddies in high school."

"More like went out there to drink beer where he wouldn't get caught," Kerri replied. "I'm sure he's not the only one."

"You graduated from North Willow High School. Did you go out there?" I challenged.

Kerri's eyes sparkled. "No. Matt and I had better things to do, and we weren't doing them in a cemetery."

WEDNESDAY, NOV. 21

A SHARP CRACK outside the house woke me from a dream in which the living room reverted to its previous horrible color no matter how often I painted it. Next to me, Raid growled. I pushed back the blankets and swung out of bed. Beyond the window, the night was ink-black. The security light between the house and barn was out. I looked into the hallway, but the soft glow of the nightlight in the bathroom assured me the electricity was still on.

Boots sounded on the front porch. Unexpected footsteps weren't anything new in my world, but this wasn't Sarah. Her ethereal footfalls had always been light and brisk, coming from nowhere and fading into nothing. These heavy treads made no attempt at stealth. Fury clouded reason as my heart leaped into overdrive.

With one hand in Raid's collar, I slipped out of the room on bare feet. The measured tread of footsteps on the porch continued. The rational part of my mind told me to call 911, but anger obliterated anything resembling good sense. Damn it, why couldn't I just enjoy living out here without attracting idiots? I suddenly regretted dismissing Dan's offer of a firearm, but with my luck, I'd shoot out a window or put holes in the woodwork, and that would make me madder than I already was.

I reached the head of the stairs and stepped down into shadows. In the entryway below, the knob on the front door rattled violently. I froze on the landing. Under my hand, Raider coiled like a steel spring. We could have stood there for ten seconds or ten minutes.

The front door crashed open in a cacophony of splintering wood and glass. Raid wrenched free and lunged down the stairs, nearly dislocating my fingers in the process. I screamed, but not from the pain. Unarmed, barefoot and clad in a T-shirt with a sunglasses-wearing cartoon Malinois on it, psychological warfare was the only weapon I had at hand. I screamed as if channeling the entirety of Clan McCallister charging into battle on an ancient bracken-covered moor.

The sound ricocheted eerily off the high ceiling, bouncing and echoing and coming back from every direction at once. Before it died away, I pulled in a deep lungful of air and cut loose again. If the intruder dropped dead from fright, I would feel zero remorse.

Raider's harsh barks cut off suddenly, replaced by the sound of a body slamming into the wall and a human scream. A metallic crash was followed by cursing and muted snarls. I hobbled blindly down the remaining steps and across the hall. Fumbling for the light switch, I misjudged its location and rammed my knee into the marble topped walnut parlor table instead.

Through blinding tears of pain, I saw a figure silhouetted against the darkness of the open doorway. Raider's jaws were clamped on its forearm, his body twisting as the intruder thrashed to dislodge him. With a swarm of obscenities, the figure staggered out of the house, my dog clinging to its arm with single-minded purpose.

The hallway light snapped on, momentarily blinding me. My hand was six feet from the switch. The front porch light blazed to life, then lights in the dining and living rooms came on. Outside, Raider let go of the intruder, and I glimpsed the fleeing figure as it hurled itself over the fence and vanished into the darkness.

I picked my way through the shattered glass and stepped over the threshold onto the front porch, too loaded with adrenaline to register the cold. Raid stood, hackles up and body rigid, in front of the open doorway as if guarding it. His ears flicked in response when I said his name. For a terrifying second, I thought he was going to go after the now invisible intruder, but he turned and stalked inside with me, fur bristling.

I picked my way back to the foot of the staircase and dropped onto the steps.

"Good dog, you're a good dog," I whispered, cradling his head. I checked Raid from nose to paws. He was unhurt. I'd walked through the glass without any damage, although a bruise was already blooming purple on my knee. Icy air blew into the house as the front door hung uselessly in its ruined frame.

The adrenaline left my system as fast as it had come, leaving me shaking with a sense of violation. Somewhere beyond the end of the lane, a car engine roared to life, then faded.

Raid accompanied me as I limped up the stairs. I sank onto the bed, longing to crawl back under the warmth of the blankets and pretend none of this happened. It was 4:07 a.m. I picked up my phone.

"McCallister, this better be important." Dan's voice was rough with sleep.

"Someone broke into the house."

"You okay? Are they still there?" All traces of sleep vanished.

"Yes. No. Raider chased him off." My voice was shaking as badly as my hand.

"Call the sheriff. I'm on my way."

I hung up and dialed 911. When the dispatcher's voice came on the line, I recognized her immediately. We were nearly on a first name basis by now. Minutes later, I'd yanked on jeans and a sweatshirt when headlights bounced up the lane. I let Dan in through the kitchen, avoiding the mess in the front hallway until law enforcement arrived.

"You good?" He gripped my shoulder with his left hand and inspected me from top to bottom. Satisfied, he pulled me into a tight, one-armed hug. I wrapped my arms around him and buried my face against his shirt. For one long moment, everything was right with the world.

"I'm good." I looked down at Dan's right hand where a pistol gleamed dully. "The guy's gone. I don't think you'll need to shoot anyone."

"So call me a Boy Scout. Do you know every light in the house is on?"

"Yeah...Sarah's back." I wobbled slightly. My knee ached, and residual shockwaves from the violent intrusion sent tremors of nausea through me.

Dan steered me to a kitchen chair. "Are you sure you're not hurt? Now you're limping on your other leg."

"I ran into a table in the dark. Bruised my knee."

"Did you call 911?"

When I nodded, he indicated his gun. "I'm going to put this back in the pickup. If Barney Fife shows up, he'll just get excited." He disappeared out the door.

I tipped my head back and stared at the ceiling. Barney Fife, indeed. I wasn't up to dealing with Brad at four-thirty in the morning. I hadn't heard from him since the day I found Luke. Whatever he needed to say—or whatever nosy question he wanted answered—hadn't been important enough for him to follow up. Or maybe he'd gotten it through his thick skull I truly wanted no part of his or his family drama.

Dan returned and appointed himself chief coffee officer. He was pouring water into the machine when the now-familiar white Tahoe stopped in front of the house. The light bar wasn't flashing. The early hour must have suppressed Brad's flair for the dramatic.

I opened the door and was surprised to find Sheriff Adam Gray on the back porch.

"Good morning. I hear you had some uninvited company." His uniform was crisp, his voice brisk. I wondered if the man ever slept.

I grabbed Raider before he could do anything rude, and we all made our way to the mess by the front door. Splintered glass glittered across the dark wood of the entry. The floor sander had been knocked over in the melee, and the refinishing crew's tools and supplies were strewn helter-skelter. I recounted the events of the last hour as Adam snapped a few photos with his cell phone. He knelt and inspected the floor, then stepped onto the porch and looked at the ruined door jamb.

"Whoever did this was an amateur or they intended to do as much damage as possible. Or both.

You said you interrupted the guy?"

"My dog interrupted him. I never saw his face."

"Did you cut yourself?" Adam indicated the broken glass.

I shook my head.

"What about your dog?"

"No. He's fine."

"There's blood on the floor." He indicated dark smears on the glass and wood. "Did your dog bite him?"

"Yeah. He was hanging off the guy's arm when he ran."

Adam gave Raider an appraising look.

"Good dog," he said. Raider looked smug. Adam went back to his vehicle, then returned with an evidence bag and collected several pieces of bloody glass. "I've put area hospitals on alert, but that's a long shot," he said. "No one's going to go to the ER for a dog bite at this time of the day—too many questions."

We went back to the kitchen. I took over coffee detail, my hands going through the familiar motions while the sound of heavy footsteps and shattering glass looped endlessly through my mind.

"Any reason someone would threaten you?" Adam asked as I set steaming mugs around the table. "Issues with personal or professional relationships?"

I was the poster child for issues with personal relationships but failed to see how they had any bearing on the current situation.

"I've been divorced for a couple of years," I said.

"I haven't been involved with anyone since, um, Brad."

Adam nodded but diplomatically didn't say anything. I'm sure my name had been all over the sheriff's department when I told Brad explicitly what he could do with the Jennings family legacy.

"Do you think your ex-husband is capable of something like this?" he asked.

I shook my head. "I don't think so. We didn't stay in touch."

"What about you?" The sheriff turned to Dan.

Dan shrugged. "My ex-fiancée tried to kill me five years ago, but I think she got over it."

Adam's slow blink was the only indication he'd been caught off guard.

"Could this have been someone threatening Jess because of her relationship with you?" he asked Dan. The unspoken implication dangled in the air, waiting to detonate. Dan laughed, and I choked on my coffee.

"We're not—it's not like that—" I started, then stopped. Dan was at my house at four-thirty in the morning. It looked exactly like that. Dan grinned and shrugged. I rolled my eyes. Adam looked back and forth between us, again chose discretion, and moved on.

"My department has had more calls to this address in the last month than it has in the last hundred years." He looked around the room. "I read the piece in the newspaper about your property being included in that treasure hunting book."

"No one's going to find any treasure in my house

at four in the morning," I snapped, then sighed. "Sorry. I moved out here for peace and quiet, and so far, I've had everything but that."

I could hear professional grade law enforcement gears turning in Adam's head.

"That old tale has floated around for years," he mused, "but that's all anyone does, just talk about it."

"They've stopped talking and started digging in Bishop Cemetery," I said. "This place sat empty for months before I bought it. God only knows what someone could have found out there." Given that I had presented the man with a century-old skeleton only two weeks prior, he seemed open to outlandish possibilities. I got the crockery shard from the pantry.

"I found this in the cemetery. I think it came from one of those holes. And I think whoever dug it up believes there's more of whatever it is out there. And I think they want me to leave because I'm in their way." It was a lot of thinking balanced on a razor's edge of speculation.

Adam didn't say anything, and I got the feeling he knew more than he was letting on. He inspected the outside of the house before leaving. Broken glass at the base of the security light's pole showed the bulb had been deliberately broken, probably by a rock. The leaf-strewn ground provided no useful evidence. He recommended I look into an alarm system and left.

Dan helped me clean up the mess in the hall. I swept up glass while he dragged the door back into its ruined frame and covered the broken window with a piece of cardboard. I'd call TJ as soon as her shop opened and see if she could replace the beveled antique glass pane. Matt would fix the damaged frame if I asked him. I almost asked Dan to do it, but I felt bad enough about dragging him out of bed before sunrise with my latest crisis du jour.

"So, your pet ghost is back," he said.

"She's not—" I started automatically, then broke off at his crooked smile. "Yeah. She's back. Maybe she never really left."

"So help me God, if she wants you to find another body, tell her I don't have time. Lieutenant Hanson's in the brig and facing court martial. If I don't get this manuscript wrapped before Christmas, my agent is going to drive out here and chain me to a radiator until it's done."

"Maybe she just showed up to protect the house," I said, feeling even guiltier about imposing on his time.

"Do ghosts even do that?" he asked and left before I could answer.

I watched the pickup's tail lights fade at the end of the lane. I knew exactly what she wanted. And that was asking a lot, even from a ghost. It was what I wanted, too, but I didn't know if I was ready to let it happen.

CHAPTER 20

SATURDAY, NOV. 24

"YOU'RE LUCKY THE JERK who did this only broke the glass, not the trim. This hundred-year-old stuff would have been hard to remake." TJ tapped the final piece of curved, polished window trim into place with a tiny finishing nail and stepped back. I admired the custom, oval-cut glass with beveled edges sparkling in the repaired front door.

"You're amazing." I ran a finger along the repair site. "This looks more original than the original."

TJ smiled at the compliment. "I thought Dan might be here, you know, helping."

"I didn't ask him. He's on deadline with a manuscript."

"You'll know."

"I'll know what?"

"If you two are supposed to happen, it'll hit you. Just like that. Conn and I knew each other for almost a year, then boom!" TJ pulled on her jacket.

"But he's too good to be real," I blurted. "Hot, straight, intelligent, sense of humor, loves dogs, loves old houses." I threw my hands in the air. "Has nothing better to do than come over here and get mixed up in my crazy."

"You deserve every bit of that. Why are the two of you not a thing?"

It was a straightforward question, but I couldn't answer her. A million empty excuses flooded my mind. Because we were both too busy for a thing. Because we both had trust issues, thanks to truly rotten previous things. Because I'm scared to take another chance.

TJ picked up her toolbox. I expected some kind of philosophical observation like "life's too short" or "you don't know what might happen tomorrow."

"Don't get in your own way," was all she said.

I paid her and helped carry her tools to her van. The Glass Slipper's logo, a sparkling crystal slipper in front of stained-glass windows entwined by a floral border, adorned each side. Glass slippers only led to happily ever after in fairy tales.

After TJ left, I tackled a list of domestic chores. Kerri was at the dog show in Marshalltown, the one I'd agreed to attend as an extra handler. After the break-in, she'd been adamant I not be gone for extended periods of time in case some other idiot made an attempt on the house. Matt adjusted his work plans so he could go in my place despite my protests.

Thanksgiving was next week, and Mare was busy with the North Willow Chamber of Commerce's holiday kick-off event. With my friends occupied and Dan immersed in his writing, I looked forward to an uneventful weekend that didn't include any degree of chaos, paranormal or otherwise. Especially paranormal. Sarah had gone back to keeping a low profile.

I vacuumed the floors and scrubbed Raider's nose prints off the windows and brooded about what TJ said. I wasn't getting in my own way, was I?

It was so easy to operate at surface level with Dan, enjoying the borderline flirting with no intention of letting the slightly too-long looks and casual embraces slide into anything more. But we couldn't do that forever.

Was I ready to cross my self-imposed boundary into a journey that, for the first time in my adult life, was built on honest friendship and respect? Or had the insecurities that snarled my previous relationships left me unwilling to ever take that chance again?

None of the household chores proved a respite from thoughts that were like an itch I couldn't scratch. I grabbed my jacket and whistled for Raider. I still hadn't recorded the cemetery's latitude and longitude. It was late afternoon, but if we went out there right now, I could finalize the SAPIC form this evening and launch the pursuit of a restoration grant.

I put my phone in my pocket and, on a whim, picked up the divining rods. Messing with them in the cemetery might be a pleasant diversion, although I was under no illusion they'd reveal anything. Or what I would do if they did. Things in cemeteries were meant to stay in cemeteries.

I thought again of the photos I'd seen online of people exhuming bodies from an old pioneer plot and the familiar facial features of one participant. I'd thought about it six ways from Sunday, and it still didn't make any sense.

I followed Raider's cheerful tail across the pasture and reveled in the chilly air. The branches of the trees along the bluff were etched starkly against the sky in a scene worthy of Ansel Adams. My mind wandered between what kind of rug would look best on the now gleaming red oak dining room floor and how big of a mess I'd make if I pulled up the worn vinyl in the laundry room to expose the wood plank flooring underneath.

Raider disappeared into the trees ahead of me as we reached the sagging fence line separating pasture from timber. Lost in my daydreams, I jumped when he erupted with a volley of barks. I hustled through the trees, praying he wasn't doing something that would have me calling Kerri for her de-skunking shampoo recipe.

The breath slammed out of my lungs, and I stopped as if my feet had grown roots. Two figures stood in the cemetery with their backs to me. They faced Raider as he circled, hackles up and tail stiff. Sunlight and shadows dancing through leafless trees cast the scene in an ever-shifting camouflage.

One of the figures held a shovel in both hands, jabbing it with enough power to crush bone as my dog danced just out of range. A tarp near a gaping hole was piled with earth. Next to it sat two ten-gallon salt-glazed crocks. Dirt caked their exteriors, and the wooden tops were sealed with dark wax.

Raid's angry barks echoed off the trees. He circled the figures, never taking his eyes off them, stopping when he reached my side. The trespassers pivoted slowly as if my dog and I were magnetic north on a compass. I stared at them for a long, horrible moment as I struggled for comprehension, my mind creating explanations and discarding them as fast as they came. Then white-hot anger overrode confusion.

"What the hell are you doing!" I exploded.

Susanne Bartachek shifted awkwardly, her eyes darting from me to Raider to the person at her side. Her lips moved, but no sound came out. Next to her, the face that was so familiar from the photos on the archaeology website stared back, unflinching. The features were older now, but the blue eyes were the same.

I looked around the cemetery, moving from one thing I didn't want to see to the next. The mound of dirt on the tarp came into focus like pixels resolving into a clear image. It wasn't just dirt. A jumble of what looked like earth-stained sticks protruded at odd angles. Unlike the discovery of Luke's remains, this brought no joy. I looked away, sickened.

"How dare you!" I spat. I wanted to scream and shout and hurl accusations, but the words caught in my throat like barbed wire.

The picture from the website flashed again through my mind, a younger version of the woman in front of me standing in a trench at the cemetery excavation site. I added forty years, the crumbling control over her children's lives, the decline of her business and an all-consuming obsession with family history, but the pieces didn't mesh with who I saw now.

"You weren't supposed to be home," Bev Jennings said. Her knuckles clenched white on the shovel. "You're supposed to be out of town with

Kerri Grimm."

My mind flashed back to encountering Bev at the museum the afternoon I'd gone to get the maps. It seemed like a hundred years ago. Still unable to process what was happening, I turned to Susanne. "You flat-out lied to me when I asked if you knew anything about this cemetery. All the while you were out here doing this?" I had no idea what *this* was.

"I tried to stop you." Susanne's voice was sulky, like a child wrongly accused. "I told you it was the wrong house for you but you wouldn't listen."

Uncertain which front to attack first, I let my anger target Bev. "It was you! Did you really think you could scare me off with those little stunts? That I would just run away so you could...?"

Words failed me. I jabbed a finger toward the disinterred remains on the tarp. Had she actually found the gold and these poor souls were collateral damage? Or was she looking for something else? What else was there?

An acid mix of anger and fear churned in my stomach. Bev's lip curled in a condescending sneer that reminded me so much of her son I could have vomited. My mind screamed at me to shut up and get out of there.

I could bolt into the trees and call 911. But if dispatch sent Brad, he'd wave his badge and the whole situation would disappear and possibly take me with it. He wouldn't let a little thing like his mom committing a felony spoil his bid for the sheriff's seat in next year's election.

Raider began circling again, teeth bared in silent warning. Bev jabbed the shovel at his head, but he dodged easily out of the way.

I pointed at the bones on the tarp. "What the hell is that?" More appropriately, it should have been *who* the hell is that, but I wasn't in a position to fuss over syntax.

Bev's laugh sounded like old cloth ripping. "They've been dead so long nobody cares." She swung the shovel toward the crocks, her eyes narrowed with proprietary greed. "I can't wait to see how much is in those two."

My heart simply stopped. She'd found the gold.

Except that was insane. It wouldn't be hidden in pickling crocks. It would be in a rusty strong box or rotted leather bags.

"In those two?" I snapped. "How many others are there?" The idea she'd been doing this long enough to have unearthed multiple containers virtually under my nose was staggering. "How many graves have you destroyed?"

"I have a collector who will pay top dollar." Bev ignored my questions.

A tiny part of my brain protested she couldn't flood the collectors' market with Confederate States of America gold pieces without someone in a position of authority sitting up and taking notice. It couldn't be the gold, but what else was there?

Bev glanced at the divining rods, which were clenched in my nerveless fingers. A tattered scrap of laughter fell from her lips.

"What were you going to do, try finding the

treasure yourself?" Her eyes glittered, half-mad. "Those don't work for crap. That's how we ended up with him. Them." She cast a sideways glance at the bones in their disjointed heap. "Thought we could tell the graves from the stash. Right about half the time. Oh, don't worry, we would have dumped them back in a hole when we were done. You'd never have noticed. Everything in its place." Her voice took on an eerie singsong quality, as if she were encouraging a child to tidy his room.

I turned to Susanne. "How did you—I don't understand—why?" Confusion blunted my anger. If I could get the facts straight, maybe I'd discover this had all been a terrible misunderstanding.

"I'm sorry," Susanne whispered. "We—I—never meant it to come to this."

"You didn't mean it? You tried to kill my dog!"

Susanne flinched as if someone had struck her. "That wasn't my idea."

"But you didn't stop it." My own hackles went up, but I bit down on further accusations. Susanne stood hunched with her arms wrapped around her middle as if she was trying to disappear.

I turned back to Bev. She might be older than me, but she was taller and muscular. And armed with a shovel. And crazy. I had nothing remotely resembling a weapon except my dog, and I wasn't about to sacrifice him to save myself.

I'd spent the last month hiking these hills. I knew every rise and hollow between here and the house like the back of my hand. If I ran, I could get through the trees and into the pasture, then call 911 while I kept moving and tell the dispatcher to send anyone but Brad. Raider and I would be back in the house behind locked doors before Bev could do anything.

I backed slowly away, wrenching my eyes from the exposed things on the tarp. If I could put a few more yards between me and Bev, I could vanish into the trees. Twilight fell fast in these pre-winter days. In my dark jacket, I'd be just another shadow.

"Sit down," Bev ordered. She pointed at a fallen tree trunk.

"No." Still not good at taking orders. I shifted my weight to the balls of my feet.

It was now or never. I flung the divining rods with as much force as I could muster and bolted. Raider sprinted ahead of me. Bev cried out as the cold metal struck her face, but I didn't look back. I should have.

I barely made it ten yards before I heard the obscene metallic click of a pistol being cocked. I glanced over my shoulder to see Bev taking aim at me.

Disbelief and terror mingled in equal, poisonous amounts as momentum carried me inexorably forward. My brain kept screaming *run!* Surely the woman wouldn't shoot me in cold blood. Just a few more yards and I'd be out of her direct line of sight.

I'd have made it if I hadn't tripped over a headstone. I fell sideways and my left ankle folded in a searing wrench of pain. I landed hard, scrambled to all fours, and tried to push to a stand, but my ankle refused to cooperate this time. I fell back, biting down on a litany of four-letter words.

Beverly approached slowly, gun trained on me. Raider darted to my side, licked my face and took off before I could grab his collar. He ran to the edge of the cemetery, barked once, then turned to face me and held his ground.

Well, hell. The best defense is a good offense.

"You ran me off the road." The accusations came fast and easy. "And tried to poison Raider. And broke into my house." Razors of pain sliced through my ankle, which had already started to stiffen. I'd done more than just roll it this time, and the pain made me even madder. With a monumental effort, I lurched to my feet. Damned if I was going to kneel like I was begging for mercy. "You volunteered on that cemetery excavation in northeast Iowa. Digging up human bones isn't anything new for you."

Bev jerked in surprise, and I realized, belatedly, surprising a crazy woman pointing a gun at me might not be in my best interest.

"That was forty years ago. How'd you know about it?"

"I saw it on a website when I was researching cemetery restoration." I didn't give her a chance to reply. "Did you think you had the right to come out here and do whatever you pleased?"

Her curling lip, a mirror of her son's expression of superiority, said she thought exactly that.

"I found what I needed," she said.

For one macabre moment, I thought she meant the scattered bones on the tarp. If she had resorted to collecting human remains for some dark ritual to restore her life's balance, she was crazier than I thought.

"What's so important it justified that?" I pointed at the bones. She ignored me. Again.

"They were in the way," she said dismissively. "If you'd have listened to Susanne in the first place, we could have avoided this. Now you've made things complicated." She leveled the pistol at my chest in a two-handed grip like she meant business.

I quit caring what was in the crocks and swayed, balancing on my good leg.

"You can't shoot her!" Susanne said. I jumped. I'd forgotten she was there.

Before Bev could prove her wrong, my phone rang. Reflexively, I reached for it, but Bev waved the pistol and shook her head. I lowered my hand to my side. The ring tone continued, bright and artificial amid the trees. The caller let it ring until it went to voice mail. Time stood still as my universe narrowed to the ugly little opening at the end of the gun.

"This is all your fault," Bev hissed at me. Her hand trembled, and my mouth went dry.

"No!" Susanne cried. "We had a deal. You said no one would get hurt. We'd just dig up the—"

"The deal's over," Bev snapped, cutting her eyes to Susanne but not taking her aim off me. "You didn't hold up your end of it. How hard is it not to sell a haunted wreck in the middle of nowhere?"

"I never promised you the property wouldn't sell." Susanne's voice was petulant. "You had all summer to finish this while no one was living here."

"I had a business to run too, didn't I? And I didn't

know it was here for sure until September. And then it took a lot of trial and error." Bev scowled at the bones on the tarp. I waited for her to say it was their fault, too, for getting in the way.

"I told you to stop it when Jess bought the property. I said it wasn't worth it." Susanne clenched her fists. For a second, I thought she was going to take a swing at Bev. "Now see what happened. And you still haven't—"

"Shut up! Don't lay it all on me. You couldn't sign up fast enough when I promised you half the money." Bev's words dripped scorn.

"I wanted out when you tried to kill her dog."

Bonus points for Susanne, but I failed to see how that would help my situation.

"Too late for that, partner," Bev sneered.

I tried to take advantage of their distraction to edge further away, but my ankle had seized into a leaden cramp. Raid trotted to my side and leaned against my right leg. His weight threatened my balance, but I appreciated his closeness.

"Now look at this mess." Bev looked around the cemetery. "We're going to finish this if we have to work until morning."

Susanne's eyes darted to me, then away, with the panicked look of a small creature trapped by a predator. I felt sorry for her. Almost.

"What's that damned dog barking at? Make it stop before I shoot it." Bev's attention snapped back to Raider, who alternated between barking at the two women and barking toward the trees. She aimed the gun at him, and my heart turned to ice.

"Raid, be quiet." My voice was a choked whisper, but he complied.

Twilight drifted into the cemetery. Something scuffed against the matted leaves just out of sight, but I didn't bother to look. I'd lived with a ghost long enough to think it was normal to hear noises when there was nothing there to make them. I shifted, easing weight off my worthless ankle. Running was out of the question. The best I could do was keep Bev talking.

"Whatever you think you're going to do, you won't get away with it," I said with confidence I didn't feel. There were a number of things she could do, and all of them ended badly for me.

A soft noise sounded in the dark behind me. Coyote? Bobcat? Maybe a cougar? A chill unrelated to the gun pointing at me ran down my spine. Iowa isn't known for large predators, but mountain lions occasionally wander in from other states, following the whitetail deer population. I kept my eyes straight ahead.

Bev gestured with the pistol to the edge of the bluff. "Go over there. Move!"

"What happens if I don't?"

She lowered the gun and fired. The bullet hit the ground in a spray of dirt only feet from Raider. The dog snarled but didn't flinch.

"I'd rather they find his body with yours, the loyal dog who fell to his death with his owner, but I'll shoot him and dump him in a ditch if I have to." Bev's words were shaky as her breath clouded in the evening chill.

The threat to Raider spurred another reckless verbal attack. "I knew you were involved from the start, and Kerri knows all about it, too. If I disappear, you'll be the first one they look at." I was whistling through the graveyard, literally, but if anyone was qualified to do that, it was me. I'd never suspected Bev of being anything more than an overbearing, financially desperate business owner distraught at the prospect of losing her community status, but if I could plant even a seed of doubt, it might gain me a few more precious minutes.

Bev sneered. "The first person they'll look at is your boyfriend. Brad will make sure there's a clear evidence trail."

"Dan's not..." I started, then grabbed the bigger picture. "Brad knows what you're doing?" Bev was truly delusional. Brad wasn't above throwing his status around, but he'd never condone a murder or cover one up. But I hadn't thought a grown man would side with his mother when it came to adult relationships, either.

"Family takes care of each other." Bev's gun arm rose until the pistol pointed directly at my head. "Move."

"Stop it!" Susanne begged. "Just stop it, please, you can't—"

"Shut up!" Bev swung the gun toward her, her arm trembling with rage or nerves. She turned back to me. "I should have known you'd ruin everything."

"I'm not responsible for any of this shit show," I said. This was like riding an out-of-control merry-go-round, spinning faster and faster as my fingers lost their grip. I looked at Susanne. "Why are you doing this?"

"I need the money," Susanne said. "Ron wants to take Cannon away from me."

For a heartbeat, I was in complete sympathy with her. If someone tried to take Raider from me, I'd do anything to prevent it.

"When I had the listing for Fox Hollow, I used to let my dogs run in the pasture after the open houses." Susanne continued like this was the optimal time for full disclosure. "The place was listed for months, and I was out here a lot. I ran into Bev in the cemetery." Her voice faltered, and she looked furtively at the other woman. "We made a deal."

"That's right. We made a deal," Bev said with icy calm. "That you'd keep your mouth shut and steer people away from buying the property." She turned on me. "Then you bought it and started wandering around out here, sticking your nose in things that weren't your business."

I refrained from pointing out as the owner, everything on—and under—Fox Hollow was my business.

"What kind of deal? Why didn't you just report Bev for vandalism?" I asked.

Susanne's face took on a crafty look. "It would have been a shame if the mother of the popular candidate for next sheriff of Lenox County got arrested for digging up bodies. I kept my mouth shut and discouraged buyers and I get half."

Half of what I wanted to scream.

Anger etched Bev's face, and she gestured again with the gun. "Move. You're a complication I should have gotten rid of a long time ago."

A twig snapped in the dark behind us. Bev spun toward it. Susanne lunged forward and tried to knock the gun from her hand, but she was too slow.

Bev shot her.

Whether it was from calculated rage or a twitchy finger on a hair trigger, the result was the same. Susanne's face registered disbelief before she crumpled to the ground.

Darkness edged my vision, inviting me to escape into oblivion. I considered faking a faint or giving in to the real thing. Maybe if I played possum, Bev would cut her losses and run.

No. She'd shove me over the bluff first.

Bev stared at Susanne, who lay unmoving. "Fuck!" She pinched the bridge of her nose. "What am I supposed to do now!" She spun back to me. "Move!" Her voice broke as she screamed the word.

In a slow-motion nightmare, I hobbled toward the spot she indicated, directly above the river channel's ninety-degree turn. Raider paced at my side. I didn't look over the edge. It was at least a hundred feet to the water below.

Bev lowered the gun. Was she going to give me a sadistic choice—jump or be shot? There was nothing to break my fall. My body would bounce off the rock face, bones snapping like twigs until the dark water closed over my head.

"If the fall doesn't kill you, you'll drown." Her

smile scared me more than the gun.

They say your life flashes in front of your eyes in times like these, but I wasn't seeing memories of the past, only things I'd left undone. All the words I hadn't said, the feelings I hadn't acted on because I was scared to take the chance, galloped through my mind in a stampede of aching regret.

"Is a handful of gold really worth your soul?" I demanded. The longer I argued, the longer I lived. "That cemetery was sacred ground. The dead will walk now that you've disturbed them."

Bev's aggressive posture faltered.

"What do you think they'll do to someone who defiles consecrated ground? Add my blood on top of it and they'll make you pay." This all sounded like a script from a vintage horror movie, but I didn't care.

"That's bullshit." The older woman's breathing was ragged.

"Is it?" I let the doubt hang between us. "You believe in the undead, don't you." It was a statement, not a question. "You've felt them out here. They know what you've done." If she was going to make my last minutes on earth hell, at least I could return the favor.

She aimed the pistol at my chest, her finger on the trigger, and I stopped breathing. I wondered who I'd see first when I got to Heaven. I wondered what they'd say.

"Drop the gun, Beverly."

That wasn't what I expected.

CHAPTER 21

Dan stepped out from behind a burr oak tree. The Glock in his steady, two-handed grip was aimed at Bev.

"Stand down, Bev, and we'll sort this out." He glanced at me. "You all right?"

"I'm fine." I was alive and breathing. In my immediate world, that constituted the pinnacle of health, although there were entirely too many guns pointed at people for my comfort. "But she shot Susanne." My voice trailed off. The realtor's body lay, unmoving, where she'd fallen.

"You won't shoot me," Bev said. Her gun hand trembled visibly.

"I don't want to shoot anyone," Dan said, "but Iowa's a stand your ground state. I have the right to use reasonable force to protect myself or others. You're in a law enforcement family, you know that." He took one step forward, and Bev shifted her shaky aim to him.

I must have made a noise, because Bev's attention snapped back to me and she pointed the gun at Raider. "Keep backing up or I shoot the dog. One, two—"

I took a hobbling half-step backward. The cold breeze rising from the river enhanced the sense of vast nothingness behind me. Bev raised her gun to chest height. I released Raider's collar. The impact of a bullet would knock me into freefall, and I wouldn't drag my dog down with me. If her fragile self-control snapped, she wouldn't miss at this distance.

"Jess! Stand still! The sheriff is on his way," Dan continued, the calm voice of reason amid madness. "Put the gun down, Bev. It's over."

"The sheriff? How—?" She didn't get to finish.

The second her head turned toward Dan, Raider launched from my side, his powerful muscles driving him forward like a target-locked missile. Bev tried to re-aim the pistol, but he hit her with the momentum of sixty airborne pounds and took her off her feet.

Writhing, snarling shadows filled the night as the tangle of dog and woman rolled toward the cemetery. Dan rushed toward them. I stood paralyzed with fear and pain, my eyes straining into the darkness, but the thin slice of crescent moon overhead showed nothing.

The first gunshot was obscenely loud. After a second of silence, the snarling continued, punctuated with grunts and the sound of impacting bodies. Another shot sounded, this one muffled, followed by a guttural scream.

Breaking the horrified inertia that held me, I lurched forward. I managed one whole step before the ground crumbled, and the edge of the bluff fell away under my feet. Off balance with all my weight on one leg, I toppled sideways. My heart rate shot into the red zone.

If I screamed, I didn't hear it. The roar of blood in my ears obliterated everything else. I flung myself forward. My fingers smacked painfully against rock as I clawed for purchase on a tangle of tree roots. Gravity set its teeth in me like a starving beast, and I slid another foot before my left boot clipped a protrusion in the cliff face. Knives of pain stabbed through my entire leg, but my downward slide stopped. I clung to the rock face, barely daring to breathe, terrified the slightest movement would send me plummeting. My left leg was useless as I tried to push upward from the tenuous foothold, my damaged ankle unable to respond to my brain's frantic demands.

The fibrous tree roots I'd been clinging to broke loose, and I jerked back reflexively to avoid a cascade of dirt and small rocks. My foot slipped from its perch. I clawed at rough stone to no avail, abrading skin and clothes alike. The more I struggled, the faster I slid, gaining deadly momentum. I screamed this time, as if a panicked torrent of words could stop the inevitable.

Except it did.

Like a summer breeze through tall grass, a warm updraft of air wrapped around me. Strong hands settled on my waist, and the downward rush toward death slowed, then halted. My right foot snagged on an outcropping. I sucked in a tiny breath, testing the stability of what could be no more than a few inches of granite. I was suspended God only knew how many feet above icy water. There was no one here to catch me. My overloaded circuits were inventing things, but the invisible hands stabilizing me persisted. A soft chuckle sounded, not in my ear, but in my mind.

Hang on, girl, a quiet male voice said, *he'll be along for you in a minute.*

The shock of it nearly sent me catapulting backward.

"Luke?" I whispered. The night swallowed his name. The only reply was the hoot of a hunting owl. I clung to the rock face like a bug, focused on nothing more than breathing. The voice rang quietly in my head. *Hang on, girl.* It couldn't be Luke. He'd never spoken to me before, not even when I found his body, and I had no reason to think he'd start now. Maybe aural hallucinations were common before death.

"Jess? Where are you?"

That was not a hallucination.

"Here," I whispered, then louder, "down here!" I scrunched my eyes shut and focused on digging my nails into the rock despite the burning muscles in my arms and shoulders.

Something rustled above. I dared to look up. Dan's fingers waggled in my peripheral vision.

"Give me your hand, sweetheart, you're missing all the fun."

Paralysis bound me. "If I let go, I'll fall."

"If you don't let go, you'll fall anyway."

That didn't help.

"I swear to God..." What, exactly, he swore went unsaid as his words trailed off into muttered curses. "Give me your hand. Now." The steel in his voice made it impossible to refuse.

Blindly, I reached up with my right hand. Warm fingers closed hard and fast around my wrist. The good news was I couldn't have slid very far if Dan could still reach me. The bad news was if he lost his grip, I had a long way to go.

Cautiously, willing myself to defy gravity, I wormed my way upward. My knees and thighs hugged subtle protrusions in the rock I hadn't noticed before, my determination reinforced by a desperate will to live.

"Give me your other hand." This time I complied without hesitation. Dan's fingers clamped like iron around my left wrist. As our collective weight shifted, the edge of the bluff crumbled further, and I slipped downward again, pulling him with me. I fought gravity like a demon. My boots clawed at rock as I ignored the pain that stabbed from everywhere at once.

"I'm pulling you over. Let go," I gasped. Maybe if I weren't in freefall, I could manage a controlled descent, not the previous bloody slip and slide.

"No." His words ground through clenched teeth. "Shut up and climb."

I shut up and climbed, my brain laser focused on a single thought. This fierce refusal to give up was only one of the things I loved about Dan Sinclair.

I loved him.

I loved him!

Not just the desire for a fast hook-up, to feel his mouth on mine and explore the contours of that lean body, but something soul-deep and honest that ignited when he walked into my crazy life and wouldn't leave.

The shock of this realization was overwhelming.

It released me to an entire new world of possibilities. Euphoria filled me, made me want to laugh out loud in the moonlight, to wrap my arms around Dan and delight in the simple pleasure of being alive.

If we both didn't die first.

I pushed everything but survival out of my mind and concentrated my whole being on vertical motion. One painful inch at a time, I scrabbled upward. After what felt like hours but couldn't have been more than a few desperate minutes, Dan hauled my upper half onto solid ground. He let go of one wrist and grabbed the back waistband of my jeans. His fingers were cold against my bare skin as he pulled the rest of me over the lip of the bluff. We staggered back to solid ground and collapsed.

We landed in a tangle of limbs, my arms tight around his waist. I couldn't let go, as if releasing him would create a vacuum that would pull me back into the abyss. He dragged me awkwardly onto his lap, and Raider pressed close in typical Malinois fashion, trying to occupy the same space. None of us moved. Dan's heart pounded in time with mine, and I buried my face against his neck. He smelled like dirt and blood, or maybe that was me.

"Jess." Just my name, a single word like a sacrament. He cupped the back of my head with one hand, the other between my shoulder blades. I didn't open my eyes, just pushed into his warmth while my heart ricocheted around in my chest like a crazed butterfly.

"You good?" he asked finally.

"Yeah." When the adrenaline wore off, I'd feel like I'd been hit by a truck, but now it didn't matter. "You?"

"I'll do."

More silence.

Then he started talking. His voice was muffled since he was speaking directly into my hair, and I couldn't understand half of what he said.

"—think you were doing—out here alone—didn't answer your phone—Gray called—walked—damn near got shot—stupid thing to do—what the hell—"

I pulled back. He was still talking, but my mind had gone somewhere there was no need for words. "Sinclair?"

"What?" He glared at me.

I kissed him.

My lips skimmed his, asking for nothing more than the moment. If he didn't return my feelings, I could write it off as a thank-you-for-saving-my-life kind of kiss, and we could go on as if it hadn't happened. Well, he could. I'd crawl off somewhere and die.

For agonizing seconds, he didn't move. My heart seized. Then his fingers tangled in my hair, and electricity surged through every battered inch of my body as his mouth took mine. The kiss was brief but not tentative. When we broke apart, his eyes were indigo, his face cast in hard relief by the moonlight. Dried blood crusted one cheek.

"Damn it," he whispered and kissed me again. He was rougher this time, or maybe it was me, emotion spilling into physical expression. My lips parted, inviting the kiss to deepen, wanting affirmation that—at least for the moment—he felt the same way. He took the invitation. The scent of his skin mingled with the crushed leaves and dirt and blood rising around us on the cold night air, and for a long, glorious moment, the world stopped turning.

Breathless, I pulled back and rested my forehead against his. Raider gave an annoyed snort and wiggled his way between us.

"You scare me, McCallister. Are you sure you're okay?"

The use of my last name signaled a return to somewhere emotionally neutral. I took a deep breath and let it out, reluctant to let go of that sparkling moment when everything, despite everything, felt unarguably right.

"I'm fine. Really." This didn't seem like the right time to start cataloging everything that hurt.

Dan gently shifted me off his lap and stood. Blood seeped through the torn knee of my jeans. My left ankle was a throbbing knot of pain. I looped an arm around Raider's neck, and the dog leaned against me with reassuring warmth. Across the clearing, Bev sprawled on her side.

"Is she dead?" My interest was purely academic. I didn't care.

"She shot herself in the leg," Dan said, which didn't answer my question.

Bev groaned and rolled to face us. She clutched her ripped coat sleeve and snarled, "That fucking dog bit me!"

"That fucking dog will bite you again if you do

anything stupid," Dan assured her.

She lashed out with a string of invectives but didn't move. In the distance, sirens wailed, followed by the barely audible moan of a wounded animal. I lurched up on my knees and sat back down just as quickly. "Susanne!"

Dan stepped over the fallen stones of the cemetery wall and knelt to check for a pulse.

"She's alive, but there's blood everywhere," he said. Returning, he pulled me upright. I nearly toppled over.

"What the hell? You said you were all right."

"I lied."

Dan half carried, half dragged me to a solid portion of the stone wall and deposited me on it. The gentleness of his hands was at odds with the snarl on his face.

Raider snugged in close, still keeping an eye on Bev.

"What were—how did—?" I gave up. "What are you doing out here?"

"Rescuing a damsel in distress." He sat next to me and put an arm around my waist. "I went to Mare's holiday gig this afternoon to sign a few books and stopped at your place on the way home. You weren't there, so I figured you'd gone for a walk, but then it got dark and you didn't answer your phone. You're such a lightning rod for weird shit, I came looking for you."

The sirens drew closer. Emergency lights pulsed along the road from the east. "I called Gray before I headed out here and told him you might be in trouble. He was on his way to Bev's house with a search warrant." He jerked his head toward Bev. She huddled with her face buried in her knees, all the fight gone out of her.

"A search warrant for what?"

"No idea."

"She found something out here but I don't think it's the gold." I gestured toward the crocks. "I thought she was digging up bodies.

"You have a morbid imagination."

"She *was* digging up bodies, but they were collateral damage. Is that why Gray had the warrant?"

Dan shook his head. "Jennings had gone to Gray about a month ago, said he was concerned about his mother's mental health. Her obsession with genealogy research was sending up red flags."

"Lots of people are genealogy nuts, why would that send up red flags? And what's that got to do with this?" I waved an arm to indicate the carnage surrounding us.

"Did you know Bev is descended from the family who owned the Bishop trading post? And the land where this cemetery is located?"

I stared. "No. So she thought that gave her the right to come out here and do whatever she was doing?"

"Gray wouldn't tell me more, other than he was concerned for your safety. He said he'd tried to link Jennings to all the problems you've had out here, because of your history with him. Gray also knew Bev had a strong influence on her son, but he couldn't make a connection."

"It had to be Brad who broke into the house," I said. "Raider hates him."

"No," said a faint voice.

"Susanne!" I shifted on the wall and leaned toward her.

Dan used the flashlight on his phone to scan her body. The right side of her coat was stained dark crimson.

"Help is on the way," he said, pressing her gently back down as she tried to rise. "Lie still, or you'll make the bleeding worse."

She ignored him. "Not Brad. She paid a guy. Same guy who...ran you off the road. Wanted to scare you. Brad...doesn't know... about things."

Brad didn't know? Not effing likely.

Susanne inhaled raggedly. "Bev...said she'd cut me in. Had to keep quiet...not supposed to sell the house until she was done."

It was probably rude to yell at someone who'd just been shot but I couldn't help it. "Done with what?"

"Finding..."

"Finding what?"

"When she tried to poison...Raider...too much. Please...I never wanted to hurt..." Susanne's dry whisper faded away.

My head reeled. The story had grown more absurd without explaining anything.

"You were in it just as deep as I was!" Bev screamed from the near darkness. I jumped. Raider growled. "You wanted that money as bad as I did."

"I didn't want to kill anyone to get it." Susanne's words were so soft I could barely hear her.

Dan rose and shone the flashlight on the two dirt-caked crocks near the cemetery wall. They looked as vulnerable as the disinterred bones lying nearby.

"What's in those?" he asked Bev. "How many of them have you found? How did you know they were here?"

She clamped her lips together in stony silence. Susanne made no sound. The sirens wailed to a stop on the road, and flashlights slashed blue-white arcs through the darkness.

"Lenox County Sheriff's Department! Call out!" Adam Gray's voice rang through the trees.

"Over here," Dan shouted, then cradled my face and said, "Just once, I'd like to spend an evening with you that didn't involve law enforcement and dead bodies."

I wanted to tell him I felt the same way, to tell him everything I thought I'd never have the chance to, but all I could manage was, "No promises."

SHERIFF GRAY WAS joined by three deputies, the Lenox County ambulance crew with both rigs and the same state trooper who'd caught the call when I found Luke.

Susanne was loaded into the first ambulance, which drove away with sirens wailing. Bev remained silent while Gray read her rights. She would be charged with attempted murder for shooting Susanne and trying to shoot Dan, criminal trespass, interfering with a burial ground, multiple counts of desecrating a corpse and vandalism. He also charged her with intimidation for the last six weeks of crap she'd pulled on me. Gray looked like he believed me, however, when I told him I'd fallen off the bluff by myself. Granted, I wouldn't have been standing on the edge of it if Bev hadn't been waving a gun in my face.

"It belongs to me!" Bev screamed as they loaded her—handcuffed—into the second ambulance. "It's mine!" She was still yelling as a deputy shut the doors.

I let the paramedics check me over, but there wasn't anything wrong a hot bath and a lot of ibuprofen wouldn't fix. They advised me to have my ankle X-rayed. Dan, too, was battered but not broken. Raider didn't seem any worse for the wear and stuck to me like a burr.

We finished our preliminary statements and promised Gray we would stop at his office for a more thorough debriefing in the morning. He drove us back to my house.

As I limped toward the back door, a second white Tahoe pulled up. I sighed with relief when two deputies, Randy Simmons and a deputy I recognized, stepped out.

"Where would you like us to put these?" Randy called as he opened the SUV's rear hatch.

"Put what?" I asked.

"Gray told us to drop these off," the second deputy said cheerfully and pulled a stoneware crock from the back.

"Garage," I said numbly, focused on the

mechanics of staying upright. I sagged against the side of the porch while Dan opened the garage door for the men. The deputies deposited the two crocks from the cemetery.

"Don't you need those for evidence or something?" I asked.

Randy shook his head. "Since they were found on your land, they're your property. Gray would like you to open them, since the contents have a bearing on this case and Mrs. Jennings won't tell him what's inside. But you don't have to do it tonight."

"Unless it's body parts or illegal drugs, you can keep it," said the second deputy.

I took a wobbly step toward the crocks.

"They can wait." Dan caught me around the waist. I didn't resist as he helped me into the house and deposited me in my recliner.

"Don't move," he said, as if I were a flight risk, and vanished into the kitchen. I closed my eyes and inhaled the sun-dried flower essence of the house as its warmth and quiet wrapped around me. Raider tried to climb in my lap. I kissed his nose.

My dog kept a vigilant watch as I gingerly unlaced my boot and, with a whimper, pulled it off. I peeled my sock down. My ankle was a garish wash of purple-blue streaked with red and swollen to twice its normal size.

Dan reappeared and handed me a bottle of water and four ibuprofen tablets. Without speaking, he pulled the blanket off the couch, folded it, and gestured for me to lift my leg. I did and he slid the blanket under it, then settled a plastic zip-seal bag filled with ice across my ankle. I washed the ibuprofen down and set the water bottle on the end table.

"Thank you." The words were totally inadequate considering the last few hours, but they were all I could muster.

"Anything for you, McCallister." He dropped onto the couch and tipped his head back. "Lightning rod." He rolled his head slightly in my direction. "You. Weird shit." He closed his eyes.

The lines of his face were etched with residual tension. I wanted to kiss them away, to tell him I loved him, but I couldn't say it out loud. The thought of exposing my raw emotions was paralyzing, like hanging from the edge of the bluff again.

"Oh," I said, startling with sudden memory.

Dan opened one eye. "What?"

I couldn't explain. It was too odd. That made me laugh because my entire life had become so odd, the incident seemed almost reasonably acceptable. Of course, I was trying not to fall to my death at the time so that may have tempered my perception. When I didn't say anything, Dan leaned forward.

"Are you sure you're all right? Did you hit your head? How many fingers am I holding up?"

I held up one very specific finger. He laughed, and I knew if I told him what I'd remembered, he'd believe me.

"Luke was there tonight," I said quietly. "He stopped me from falling, before you pulled me up." I told him about the strong hands steadying me, and the encouraging words in my mind. "He told me to hang on, you'd be there soon."

Dan's eyes were storm blue, his jaw set. His torn, dirty clothes and the blood streaking his face combined with his standard three-day stubble made him look like he'd just come off a tour of duty. Which was what dealing with me was turning into.

"The ghost of a guy whose body you found showed up to save your life?"

Family takes care of each other. Bev's words, but tempered in a different light. Family was more than blood.

"Yeah. Pretty much."

"Ghost whisperer." His tone burned through me like summer lightning. I wanted to kiss him until neither of us could breathe, but I couldn't get out of my chair.

Instead, I fumbled for my phone and called Kerri. I gave her the condensed version of the latest crisis du jour, and she, Matt and Mare showed up within half an hour. Kerri and Mare hugged me fiercely and fussed over my ankle and scraped hands. Matt even hugged me and refrained from rolling his eyes.

Mare rummaged around in the kitchen and returned with a smaller ice pack for Dan's bruised cheek. He groaned theatrically, then caught my eye and winked. Everyone petted Raider and told him he was wonderfully brave.

Slowly, amidst questions and exclamations, the story unfolded.

"No wonder Susanne was always asking how you were getting along with this place when she came to Tuesday night training," Kerri said when I finished.

"I thought it was just professional courtesy, but she was trying to figure out if I suspected anything more than kids messing around in the cemetery." I shifted the ice pack on my ankle. It was comfortably numb. The rest of me felt like I'd been dragged through a hedge backward.

"It sounds like Bev was selling whatever they dug up as fast as they could get it out of the ground. Will the authorities be able to recover any of it?" Mare asked.

"Maybe," I said. "Sheriff Gray had a search warrant for her house."

"What's in the crocks?" Kerri asked. "Did she actually find the gold?"

"I forgot about the crocks! Let's go look." I heaved myself upright, wincing as my body protested.

"You're not going back to the cemetery tonight!" Kerri yelped.

"No, but two of the crocks are in the garage." I levered my way out of my recliner, swayed and gripped the chair for support. "I won't be able to sleep until I know." I probably wouldn't be able to sleep anyway, but this was one thing I could check off the list.

"Sweetheart, you can't even stand up by yourself," Dan said. The whisky roughness of his voice curled around me like a caress, then settled firmly in the part of my mind reserved for things that would keep me awake later.

He wrapped an arm around my waist, and I returned the gesture with what had become comfortable familiarity. Just once, it would be lovely to enjoy his touch without having to survive some kind of trauma first.

Dan and I limped down the hall, out the back kitchen door and into the garage with Kerri, Matt and Mare following. Raider trotted happy circles around all of us, still on duty and determined to keep his people gathered tightly.

The dark blue maple leaf stamp of the Western Stoneware Company was barely visible through the dirt on the crocks. The numeral 10 painted on each in matching dark blue indicated their capacity in gallons. The tops were covered with circular pieces of wood, cut to fit and sealed with thick layers of wax. Their mysterious appeal almost made me forget someone had been willing to kill me over their contents.

"That's it!" The shadows that had been drifting through my mind since leaving the cemetery snapped into clear focus. "My grandma had a huge collection of crocks like these. I thought they were cool and when she let me pick out a couple for my own, I researched them. The Western Stoneware Company wasn't founded until the early 1900s."

"So?" Kerri asked.

"So, the gold was buried at the end of the Civil War, forty years before Western Stoneware existed. Whatever Bev found can't be the gold, unless someone dug it up and reburied it, and I don't see that happening."

"Here." Dan handed me a screwdriver from the tool bench. "Do the honors."

I took the tool and started to kneel, but my left leg screamed. I handed the screwdriver back to him. "You do it."

I leaned against Mare, who braced me with an arm around my shoulders. Kerri bit her lip. Matt stepped closer.

Dan used the screwdriver like a utility knife to loosen the seal around the lip of the nearest crock. The age-darkened wax crumbled away in chunks. Raider crowded against him, sniffing enthusiastically.

"Get out, dog." Dan pushed him back gently, then pried up the wooden lid and let it fall to the floor. The sour odor of mold wafted upward. We all leaned in, and I caught my breath in surprise.

"I'll be damned," Dan said.

"What is that?" Kerri queried.

"You've got to be kidding me," Mare said.

Matt burst into laughter. "Didn't expect that."

I reached into the crock where a dozen glass bottles nestled amid folds of rotting burlap sacking. I pulled one loose, and held it up to the light. The worn label on the dull green glass proclaimed Dr. Simon's Soothing Syrup. I shook the bottle. The contents sloshed merrily.

Dan pulled out a second bottle, this one made of clear glass. Dark amber liquid was visible inside. He tipped it toward the light and read aloud, "Restorative Elixir for Ladies."

"Patent medicine?" Mare asked.

Dan unscrewed the cap and held the open bottle under his nose. He pulled back, blinking. I twisted the cork out of my bottle and cautiously sniffed the contents. Alcohol fumes seared my sinuses. Dr. Simon's Soothing Syrup smelled like it was one hundred and ten proof liquor.

I pulled more bottles out of the crock. They were mismatched but of a uniform size and all contained the same amber liquid.

"Why would someone bury a bunch of patent medicines?" Kerri pondered.

"These aren't the original contents," I began. "I think it's—"

"Home brew," Dan finished.

"Sarah was a moonshiner?" Kerri looked stunned.

"The timeline fits," Matt said. "Prohibition ran from 1920 to 1933. It's possible she had a side hustle."

I shook my head. "Sarah was managing a farm and raising draft horses. She wouldn't have had time to run a distillery."

"You'd be surprised what people can find time for when it comes to making money," Dan said. "She could have set up a still out in the timber, or looked the other way if someone else did and taken a cut."

"I've got a couple of books about Prohibition at the shop," Mare said. "Lenox County wasn't exactly a hotbed of bootleggers, but there is documented evidence of local families who brewed their own private stock. A lot of the stuff was rotgut, but a few local producers distilled a fairly high-quality product. They used the river to transport it to Iowa City, safer than going by road. From there it could be moved to bigger markets."

"What was it doing in Bishop Cemetery?" My mind was still struggling with the idea of my resident ghost as a bootlegger.

"Maybe whoever brewed it was feeling the heat," Dan suggested. "They stashed this batch, intending to come back for it later but never did." He held a bottle up to the light and swirled the contents. "I wonder if it's still good."

Matt uncorked a bottle and sniffed it appreciatively.

"Matt Grimm, if you drink that, you'll be blind by Tuesday," Kerri warned.

Matt reluctantly recorked the bottle. He and Dan opened the second crock, which contained more of the same. They removed several bottles, reading labels as they went: J.D. Wickersham's Liver Tonic, Eli Englebreit's Rheumatism Remedy, Mrs. Meyers Cordial for Colicky Children.

"Clever. Back in the day, every household in America had this stuff in their cupboards," Mare said. "If you brewed up a batch of homemade hooch, what better way to camouflage it?"

"Did you hear about those guys in New York state who found a stash of Prohibition-era whisky in the walls of their house while they were remodeling?" Matt asked. "It was all over the news last year. Those bottles went for over a thousand dollars apiece at auction."

I looked at the motley collection of antique glass.

"That must have been what Bev was hoping for, but I can't see these being worth much," I said. "The bottles those New York guys found had original labels from a documented distiller. Without any provenance, these are just a curiosity."

"Bev claimed to have a private buyer. Some people pay big money for crazy things," Dan said.

"I think Bev had lost touch with reality by the time she found these." I paused. "I need to call Adam and tell him about this. And the Lenox County Historical Society. And maybe the State Historical Society, too."

Dan shook his head. "You're not doing any of that tonight." His eyes held mine, and the warmth in them felt so damn good all my aches and bruises vanished for a minute.

"Come on. The guys can empty the rest of it." Mare took my elbow and steered me back into the house while the men pulled the remaining bottles from their cocoon of rotted burlap and lined them up on the garage's workbench.

"Spill it," Kerri said, the second we were in the kitchen with the door closed. "What else happened out there?"

"What do you mean?" I put on my best poker face, which wasn't saying much.

Mare scrutinized me. "You're glowing. Something happened between you and Dan, didn't it?"

"Maybe."

"Maybe, my ass," Kerri hissed. "Tell us, or we'll ask him."

"I might have kissed him."

"You two are a thing now? Finally!" Kerri said

with exasperated affection.

"I don't know what we are," I said. "He'd just pulled me back over the edge of the bluff, and we were all tangled up, and I kissed him."

"But he kissed back, right?" Mare clarified.

"He did." I couldn't keep the grin off my face, but the sparkling heat of that kiss was the only thing keeping me from dissolving into a puddle of pain and exhaustion.

"Then it's time for us to get out of the way," Mare said.

"Oh please." I rolled my eyes, unable to think about anything but a hot shower and falling into bed. Alone.

Kerri collected Matt, who was still in the garage with Dan, contemplating what one-hundred-year-old homemade whisky buried in a cemetery would taste like. If either of them had actually tried it, they weren't telling. Mare and the Grimms departed amidst a whirlwind of assurances for me to call if I needed anything.

"Are you going to be okay here?" Dan asked when their taillights faded at the end of the lane.

I wanted to say yes, I was fine, everything was fine, but again, the words wouldn't come. The thought of him leaving was unbearable, as if it meant this horrible, wonderful night had never happened and he would never be anything more than my neighbor down the road.

I stood there, trying to say something that didn't sound totally stupid. I failed. No one had ever threatened my life before, and I wasn't prepared for the emotional backwash. On top of it all, I'd gone and fallen in love in spite of my resolve not to engage in that nonsense ever again.

Dan took my lack of reply as an indication I was incapable of caring for myself.

"Go take a shower," he said. "You really need a hot soak in the tub, but I'm afraid you'd drown." He steered me down the hall to the bathroom and paused in the doorway. "I'll bring you clean clothes if you tell me where to find them."

I stared at him, unsure if our newfound intimacy extended to my lingerie drawer. He laughed at my hesitation. "Do you own a bathrobe? How about I get that?"

I told him where to find my robe and he turned toward the stairs.

"Hey," I put my hand on his arm. "Would you stay here tonight?" My voice was barely a whisper.

He flashed an unconvincing leer.

"Stop it." I poked him in the chest, unable to hold back laughter that had a mildly hysterical edge.

Dan wrapped his arms around me. "I'll stay, sweetheart. Let me go home and feed Ruby, then I'll come back." He looked around the bathroom. "I don't think you can hurt yourself in here, but for the love of God, please don't do anything I can't fix with a Band-Aid."

"That's what I like about you, Sinclair," I said, my words muffled against his chest. "You're all heart."

I waited until he brought my robe down from upstairs. He insisted I lock the kitchen door behind him, and I insisted he take my spare house key. I cranked the tap over to incendiary and stood under the steaming water long after the blood and dirt disappeared down the drain. My mind wouldn't stop manufacturing endless scenarios that ended with Dan and Raider dying violently at the hands of Beverly Jennings, who kept saying it was all my fault.

The ibuprofen reduced my twisted ankle to a dull throb, and I was limping around in my robe twenty minutes later when Dan's key sounded in the kitchen door. His hair was damp from a shower, and he brought Ruby with him. He announced they would sleep on the living room couch. I said my bed was plenty big enough for all of us.

"After everything, you shouldn't have to sleep on the couch," I said and thanked God it didn't sound like the worst come-on line of all time. The truth was, having him close kept my demons at bay. He helped me navigate the stairs and waited outside my bedroom while I pulled on pajama pants and a T-shirt.

"I'm decent," I called, and he came into the room as I slid under the blankets.

"I usually sleep nude. Mind?" He started to pull the T-shirt over his head, and damned if he wasn't watching me watching him. I had an intriguing view of lean abs and faded flannel pants riding low on his waist before he tugged the shirt back down. "Just kidding."

"Smart ass," I said. No, I wouldn't have minded. The only thing keeping this from being ridiculously awkward was the fact neither of us was in a condition to do anything but sleep. When he didn't move toward the bed, I asked, "Are you okay?"

Dan rolled his left shoulder and massaged the base of his neck. "I'll be fine. Wrestling crazy women armed with guns and rescuing damsels in distress is a lot easier to do on paper than in real life." He gave me a sideways glance. "You're not going to argue about being called a damsel in distress?"

"No. In my book, being threatened with a gun and falling off a cliff qualifies as distress."

He climbed under the blankets, rather over-doing the point of staying on his side. Then both dogs leaped up and tromped on us indiscriminately as they situated themselves. I turned off the lamp. The ibuprofen and steaming shower, combined with the resolution of the last month's madness, sent me drifting in drowsy warmth where anything was possible and nothing hurt if I didn't move. I was acutely aware of Dan's presence in the darkness, and my heart leapt when he leaned across Ruby and brushed my hair back from my face.

"Good night, McCallister," he said.

Impulsively, I caught his hand and kissed the palm. It was rougher than I expected for someone who makes their living with a keyboard. Without thinking, my lips moved to the inside of his wrist, brushing the pulse point as I inhaled the scent of his skin.

"Careful." The husky timbre of his voice held a warning I didn't want to heed. I shifted toward him, still adrift on possibility, but the pain that lanced upward from my ankle jarred me back to reality.

"I'm always careful," I said and settled back into my pillow. His quiet laugh was the last thing I remembered until morning.

CHAPTER 22

I woke up with Raider snuggled against my stomach and Dan's arm over my shoulders. Ruby was in there somewhere, but we were all so tangled up it was hard to tell where the humans ended and the dogs began.

The remnants of a dream drifted through my mind like tendrils of fog, and I fought a wave of vertigo as the bluff crumbled under my feet, hurtling me toward dark water. I rolled over and curled into Dan's warmth, my face against his chest. Everything felt right. The sun was rising on a new day, one that wouldn't involve threats against anyone I loved.

There it was.

I was waking up with the man I loved. While that should have said all that needed saying in polite society, it felt wonderful and terrifying at the same time. Sharing a near-death experience, a smoldering kiss, and a bed didn't automatically translate to happily ever after, no matter how badly I wanted it to. I was contemplating this, and the bruised curve of Dan's lower lip, when one dark blue eye opened.

"Morning, McCallister."

"Morning, Sinclair." I shifted up on an elbow, unable to hold back a smile.

"See anything you like?" His voice was rough with sleep, but there was heat in the words.

My world tilted on its axis again, leaving me unsure how to find solid ground.

"How do you feel?" I asked. That seemed like safe territory.

Dan stretched experimentally and fell back against the pillow. "Like I'm three days dead."

I touched his lip gently with my index finger, then stroked his skinned cheek. He caught my hand and slid his fingers through mine, studying my general disarray.

"How do you feel?" he asked.

Aside from my ankle, which didn't hurt if I didn't move, the rest of me was one big, aching knot.

"I hurt in too many places to be dead."

"Good. This house doesn't need another ghost." He looked at his phone. "Come on. We told Gray we'd meet him at nine o'clock."

I didn't remember making any such commitment. Dan seemed sure of himself though, so with a great deal of groaning, we got out of bed like two people in their geriatric years and shuffled off to start the day. Another steaming shower and more ibuprofen jogged my memory enough to recall Gray asking us to come in make an official statement. I needed to tell him about the moonshine in my garage and hoped he'd have a few answers regarding Bev and how the universe had conspired to achieve last night's mayhem. Dan went home to change clothes, then picked me up. Low clouds spat a rain-snow mix when we arrived at the Lenox County Law Enforcement Center in North Willow.

When we were seated in Sheriff Gray's office, I

pulled out my phone and showed him photos of the bottles from the crocks. He chuckled and shook his head.

"I didn't believe it when Beverly finally told me," he said, holding up a hand to forestall any questions. "The whole story is absolutely bizarre."

After taking our statements, Gray brought us up to date. Despite firing point blank, Bev had missed Susanne's vital organs. She was in serious condition but expected to recover. Given the severity of the charges against Bev, the judge had denied bail and she remained a guest of Lenox County. Susanne faced a number of lesser charges.

The blood on the broken glass Gray collected after the break in belonged to Chip Halgren, a local ne'er-do-well whose rap sheet included previous counts of breaking and entering. Facing jail time, Chip had been happy to tell Gray all about Bev paying him to run me off the road, "get rid of that damn dog," and "get inside the house and give that girl a scare."

Given Susanne's willingness to testify against Bev, the eye-witness accounts, and amount of evidence at hand, Gray doubted it would get as far as a trial. Bev would enter a plea and go quietly off to the women's state reformatory at Mitchellville.

These matters were all well and good, but I couldn't stand it any longer.

"Why was she digging in the cemetery in the first place?" I blurted. "Was she looking for the gold, or was she intentionally digging up the whisky?"

Gray tossed the pen he'd been holding onto his

desk and pushed his chair back. "It's one of the strangest things I've seen in my twenty years as sheriff in this county."

I held my breath.

He steepled his fingertips. "It started when Bev found some old letters while she was cleaning out Maisie Porter's house."

I scrambled to place the name. From more than one Jennings family dinner, I recalled Maisie Porter was Brad's great-great-aunt on his mom's side, but I couldn't pinpoint her significance amidst the twists of Jennings family achievements. She died before Brad and I met, but her estate granted her house in North Willow to Beverly while we were dating. That was about the time Bev started going seriously nuts on her genealogy project.

"What kind of letters?" I asked.

"The kind that revealed Maisie Porter was Maisie *Bishop* Porter. That's when Bev found out she was related to the original owners of the land where the trading post and cemetery were located. It was sold to Gavin and Moira Cameron in the 1890s, and you know the rest."

I nodded, trying—but still failing—to connect the dots.

Seeing my confusion, Gray continued. "I think her genealogy research started innocently enough. The Porters were a prominent family in North Willow. Maisie's husband, Milvoy Porter, was a state senator in the 1920s. The couple moved back to North Willow in the 1940s after he lost a bid for governor. When they died, their kids left their papers to the historical society."

Their papers? That sounded important. I sat forward.

Gray answered my question before I could ask. "It was mostly letters from Milvoy's constituents and other family communications. The Porters ran the feed store here in town. Nothing exciting, but the kind of stuff genealogy buffs can't get enough of. Plus, there were journals and letters from the 1800s, when the first Bishops settled here.

"I talked to Esther at the historical society this morning, and she said Bev started spending a lot of time in the research library last spring, reading every single piece of it. Bev volunteered to pay for the conservation materials and organized what she called the Bishop-Porter archives. Esther said they were delighted at her donation of time and materials and gave her free rein.

"At some point, Bev found out the Bishop family operated a stop on the Underground Railroad. That must have been about the same time that professor gave his treasure hunting program at Mare Mac-Gregor's shop."

He paused and laughed. "My wife went to that and came home ready to go out there and start digging. It stirred up a lot of fresh interest in an old folk tale, but Bev took it more seriously than most. She quit reading letters from Maisie to her sisters about fashions and recipes and did a deep dive into the journals from a few generations earlier, in the 1800s. She was convinced she'd found references to the gold being buried in the cemetery."

I nodded. "Kerri told me Bev was at the research library constantly during the summer. So that's why."

"If there was written evidence of the gold being in the cemetery, why didn't someone from the Bishop family dig it up themselves?" Dan asked.

Gray shook his head. "Maybe they did. People take secrets with them to their graves. After the trading post burned, the Bishops sold the land and moved on. If they had the gold, they could have created a new life for themselves far from here."

"But someone had to have told someone through the generations, otherwise the story wouldn't have lasted all these years," I reasoned.

"We'll never know who said what, but Bev convinced herself she'd found some kind of veiled reference to the location." Gray shook his head doubtfully. "Those journals were a hundred and fifty years old. Ink fades and handwriting can be hard to decipher. Someone could have written *cold* or *old* in reference to the cemetery, and she was so focused on gold, that's the word she saw. By the time she started digging, it was early summer."

"When the Weldons moved out," I murmured. "Then the house sat empty until mid-October."

"Bev found the first whisky cache by accident in September. She went back to the museum library, desperate to find more clues from the Bishop archives about the gold. In the meantime, she was convinced the whisky was valuable and someone would buy it, so she kept digging. That's what she was doing when Susanne walked into the middle of things. Bev told her she was close to finding a fortune and would cut Susanne in if she'd keep quiet.

"A month later, you moved in, and Bev hadn't found the gold. By then, both she and Susanne were convinced the whisky would bring top dollar if they could find the right buyer. Susanne wanted out when Bev started pulling those stunts to get you to leave, but Bev said no, if Susanne backed out, she'd go to the authorities and tell them Susanne was the one doing the digging. As the wife of the former county sheriff, the authorities would take her word over Susanne's. Susanne could lose her real estate license. Ron had just told her he was filing for divorce, and she was desperate for money."

"Bev flipped the blackmail back on Susanne," I murmured.

Dan spoke up. "We counted forty-seven bottles packed in those crocks. Who buries that much whisky and then forgets about it? It must have been worth a small fortune back in the day."

The sheriff laughed out loud. "We know there was some low impact moonshining going on in the area in the 1920s, but we don't know much else. I thought we might find records of Sarah Cameron being run in on bootlegging charges, but I put a deputy on it and he came up empty handed. I'm not saying it wasn't hers, but since it was on her land..." He shrugged, dismissing the past. "Whoever buried those crocks probably intended to come back for them, but for whatever reason, they never did."

A tiny part of me sighed with relief. Even if I

never found out where the homemade hooch came from, I was glad Sarah's legacy hadn't been tarnished by illegal activity. Or maybe it would have only added another layer of mystery to Fox Hollow.

"Did Bev really think she'd get rich by selling the stuff?" I asked.

"She'd seen a story about Prohibition-era whisky bringing a high price at auction and decided until she found the gold, the whisky cache was the answer to her financial problems," Gray explained. "She wasn't about to admit she'd driven her business into bankruptcy by her own mismanagement. She managed to sell half a dozen bottles to a guy in Cedar Rapids who collects odd things, but he didn't pay as much as she wanted."

"Where did Brad fit into all of this?" I asked, reluctantly curious.

"I truly believe he didn't know what was going on," Gray said. "I questioned him last night, and he knew about the letters proving his mom was related to the original owners of your land and about the journals and the gold rumor, but that was all. He suspected something was going on, especially after you reported the cemetery vandalism, but he couldn't pinpoint it.

"And honestly, no one in law enforcement would suspect their mother of doing what she did. He thought she was going all in on the genealogy stuff because she had time on her hands after his siblings and their families moved out of state."

"Will he be charged with anything?" Dan asked.

"No. As bizarre as this whole thing is, I can't

prove he had prior knowledge or involvement with any of it. But his political career in this county is shot to hell, which is a shame. He's a decent cop."

Gray cleared his throat and looked at me. "The story and Bev's mug shot are all over the news this morning. Brad's taken a leave of absence to deal with it, and then I expect he'll resign. He'll find a place with another department. In another state."

I felt the tiniest bit of sympathy for Brad. He was an egocentric jerk, but he didn't deserve to have his life ruined by his mother's delusions. "What happens now?"

"The coroner's office collected the remains from the cemetery. Someone will contact you soon about reinterment." He smiled broadly. "This generated a lot of interest in the Bishop Cemetery. It should practically guarantee you a restoration grant."

"I would have been fine with going through normal channels," I muttered.

After settling a few more housekeeping details, Gray thanked us for our cooperation. Dan stood and gestured at me. "Come on. I'm taking you to the hospital to have your ankle X-rayed."

CHAPTER 23

"HAVE YOU BEEN taking it easy?" Kerri asked as she bustled into the kitchen, grocery bags dangling from each hand. "Icing and elevating?"

"Yes, Dr. Grimm. What's all that?" I gestured at the bags.

"I was afraid you were going to do something stupid like drive to town and go hobbling around the store by yourself." She began putting bread, milk, and eggs away.

"I could have managed. I'm not a complete invalid." My ankle wasn't broken. It was a grade two sprain, and I was stumping around in an immobilizer boot, swearing at my own clumsiness and the forced downtime.

"Here." Kerri plunked a Mason jar of amethyst crystals on the table. "Mare sent these bath salts, some kind of woo-woo stuff a friend of hers makes. She swears they have healing powers."

"That was thoughtful. What's new in town?"

Kerri heaved a dramatic sigh. "Nothing like attempted murder by a former sheriff's wife, disturbed graves, and homemade whisky to put Lenox County on the map. The phone at the historical society has been ringing nonstop with reporters." She leveled me with a glare. "If you'd answer your phone, they wouldn't bother us so much."

"I've been turning it off by noon every day. There's only so much I can take." As expected, the media had gone nuts over the latest chapter of the Fox Hollow chronicles. I'd finally granted Logan Barnes an interview, and his story had been surprisingly accurate, but I was over the publicity.

"How are things with you and Dan?"

"He was here this morning," I said. He'd brought my mail to the house but didn't linger. Thanksgiving was in two days, and Kerri had invited both of us to join the Grimm clan for a day of overeating and football. I'd hoped to tell him about it, but he hadn't stayed long enough for me to bring up the subject. Or anything else.

"That isn't what I asked."

"He's on deadline with his manuscript. It's my fault he's so far behind, so I'm staying out of the way." Wow. That sounded lame. There were things I wanted to say in the few brief minutes Dan and I shared each day, but the words got so tangled in unexpected emotions they never made it past my lips.

"You slept with him."

"We slept in the same bed," I corrected. "There's a difference."

"You kissed him," Kerri said with the patience of someone dealing with the mentally impaired.

"Once. Well, a couple of times."

Those kisses in the timber replayed in my dreams like fireworks, exploding hotter and brighter each time, as if my life and Dan's woven together would be greater than our individual journeys. Yet that dream was still a coin tumbling end over end as it spun through the air, giving no indication of how it would land.

Sensing she'd hit a stone wall, Kerri changed the subject. "I read in the *Sentinel* that Brad resigned from the sheriff's department."

"He'll find a job somewhere far away from here. If he wants a career in law enforcement, it would be hard in a county where everyone remembers your mom digging up bodies and 'threatening the life of historical renovation expert Jess McCallister.'"

"Who called you that?"

"A reporter from *The Des Moines Register*. At least he didn't call me a paranormal activity expert."

"Speaking of which, how are things with Sarah?" Kerri looked around the kitchen.

"She's been really quiet. She walked up the stairs and down the hallway last night, and that was the end of it."

"Do you think she'll always be here? Or once Luke is buried, she'll be gone?"

"I don't know." Sarah Cameron was as much a part of Fox Hollow as the hardwood floors and leaded glass windows. I would miss my ghost if she just up and left.

"If you ask me—" Kerri began.

"I didn't."

"If you want my opinion—"

"I don't." Kerri's opinions tended to make me think about things I'd been trying to avoid.

"I think she's hanging around until you and Dan figure out you're meant for each other."

"Don't be ridiculous. Ghosts don't play match-maker." Did they? While Kerri had been quick to proclaim Dan and I were now a thing the night Bev tried to kill me, that *thing* had remained in a holding pattern since.

"Then why is she still here? You found Luke and the funeral arrangements are in place. She could go wherever ghosts go when they're over it."

I laughed at the thought of Sarah being over it, but if Kerri's matchmaking theory was right, it put everything I didn't want to think about right back on my shoulders. The last woman Dan loved tried to kill him. That would create a great big roadblock when it came to making that kind of commitment again, no matter how Sarah—or I—felt about the situation.

"Ghosts are always here for a reason," Kerri said and crossed her arms with finality.

I CELEBRATED THANKSGIVING with the Grimms. Dan declined the invitation, citing pressure to finish his manuscript. Kerri insisted on fixing him a plate loaded with turkey, mashed potatoes and gravy, cornbread dressing, green bean casserole, and dinner rolls, and another with three different slabs of pie.

When I delivered them, Dan's distracted air said he was somewhere in the Southwest Pacific Theatre in 1943. Unsure if he would actually stop to eat, I reheated the food and insisted he take a break. When he finished the meal, he gave me a fast, hard hug, then stepped back, holding me at arm's length.

"Thanks for thinking of me," he said.

"No problem." I forced a smile. Damn it, damn it, damn it. This was going right back to neighbors looking after each other. Just country folks being friendly, nothing else on the table.

Finally, he broke the awkward silence. "I have to get back to..." He glanced toward his office, squeezing my upper arms so hard it hurt. We stood there, staring at each other across a chasm filled with words that refused to come.

SUNDAY, DEC. 2

THE BISHOP CEMETERY story should have died a natural death, but the media refused to move on. Without a convenient political scandal or celebrity sexcapade to distract them, reporters continued to wring every detail out of the attempted triple homicide by a local sheriff's deputy's mother who'd unearthed a century-old whisky stash in an abandoned cemetery—along with several of its residents—while pursuing a legend of hidden gold.

To top it off, *Treasure Hunting in the Heartland* had been released ahead of schedule in anticipation of Black Friday sales. Every reporter who'd called about Bev trying to kill me now called back and wanted to talk about hidden gold and home brew whisky.

I didn't give a damn. Whatever might or might not be out there could just stay where it was. I wasn't convinced the gold had ever been there in the first place, and if the historical society had documents revealing Sarah as bootleg royalty of

Sand Creek Township, it could stay buried in their dusty archives. I wasn't going looking for it.

When my phone was still ringing with reporters by mid-afternoon, I shut it off and took a long, hot soak with Mare's miracle bath salts. The stuff really worked.

The first heavy snowfall of the season fell silently past the windows, cocooning the house in pearl-gray twilight as I built a fire. While the flames caught, I yanked the Velcro tabs loose on the immobilizer holding my ankle captive and extricated my limb from the contraption, pleased it only twinged at random when I flexed it.

Raider barked, and I looked out to see headlights cutting through the snow as a vehicle made its way up the lane. Boots sounded on the back porch, then the kitchen door opened and Dan called, "It's just me." I hadn't asked for my key back.

"In here!" I said and added a few more logs to the fire.

I hadn't seen Dan since Thanksgiving night when he'd kept me, literally, at arm's length. We'd exchanged daily texts but recognizing an author caught in the momentum of a home-stretch run, I stayed out of his way. At least that's what I told myself.

Raider ran to the kitchen, then trotted back into the room in tandem with Ruby. I gave the cattle dog a friendly scratching. She picked up one of Raid's toys, flopped in front of the fireplace, and snarled at him when he tried to take it back. Undeterred, he lay down nose to nose with her, tail wagging.

Glassware clinked in the kitchen and Dan appeared, carrying a bottle and two glasses. He wore faded jeans and an untucked, equally faded flannel shirt. He hadn't shaved for at least a week.

I eyed the bottle. "That better not be the cemetery whisky."

"It's good to see you, too." He showed me the bottle, a sweet red from a local winery. The cemetery whisky was still lined up on the tool bench in the garage, since I had no idea what to do with it, and neither did anyone else.

"I tried calling, but you didn't answer," Dan said. "Thought I'd come see if you needed rescuing."

"I shut my phone off. Reporters won't leave me alone about that book. Do you always bring alcohol on rescue missions?"

He dropped onto the couch. "We're celebrating." He set the glasses on the low trunk that served as a coffee table, splashed wine into them, and held one out to me.

"Celebrating what?" I took the glass and turned toward my chair. Ruby was sitting in it, now with two of Raider's toys. I folded myself onto the end of the couch instead.

"I finished my manuscript."

"That's wonderful. Congratulations. What happens now?" With the excuse of *I'm giving him space to work* no longer readily available, our paths again loomed uncertain.

"My agent reads the final chapters and points out everything that needs changed, and I think about doing something else for a living. Then I start the revision." Dan raised his glass with a tired grin and tapped it against mine. The crystalline chime hung in the air a little longer than I thought it should have, as though time itself stretched like molten glass.

"What's this?" He picked up the scrapbook lying on the trunk.

"Kerri scanned all the pictures in Sarah's photo album from the museum. I had them printed and made myself a copy of the album while I was sitting around with my foot up."

Dan opened the cover and flipped slowly through the pages. I slid closer to admire my handiwork. He paused on a photo of Sarah and Luke, then looked around the room.

"She's still here, isn't she?" he said.

I pulled my mind back from where it had wandered to the gentle pressure of his thigh against mine. The wine, the fire, the snow falling outside, all were a dance choreographed for other purposes, but here we sat, talking about a ghost.

"I hear her walking at night sometimes. And there's that." I pointed to the calico balls on the mantel. Five were in the bowl. One was perched absurdly atop the glass chimney of a kerosene lantern. "But she's stopped doing those mental ambushes."

"What else is there for her to do?"

"No idea." I tried not to think about Kerri's theory.

Dan turned to the photo of Sarah and Luke with the Belgian foal. Their faces glowed with happiness, and I smiled as I studied them.

"They had the world at their feet. They were ready to start a new life together," I said. "When I was their age, all I could think about was what to wear to the bars on Saturday night."

"And now you can barely get out of your rocking chair."

I elbowed him lightly. "Stop it. You're no spring chicken, either."

"Old enough to know better, young enough to do it anyway." His grin was unrepentant.

On impulse, I flipped my index finger through the hint of gray above his ear. "Is that how you got this gray hair? Doing it anyway?"

"Hey!" He tried to look offended, but the sparkle in his eyes invited more. "What about this?" He caught my wrist and held it while rifling the curls at my temple with his other hand. "Where'd you get this gray streak?"

"That's not gray! That's a blonde highlight, bought and paid for." I tried to sound indignant but was having trouble thinking about my hair. Dan's fingers were warm on my wrist. I didn't fight it because I was afraid he'd let go, and we'd both slide back into whatever we'd been before that night on the bluff, both of us afraid to step into anything more complicated.

That was a lie. If I didn't step across my own self-imposed line in the sand and capture the mirage before it evaporated, it would be my own damn fault. I couldn't bear it.

I leaned toward him and realized at the last impossible second he was already lowering his mouth to mine. The kiss was a whisper of summer wine, sweet and ripe and effervescent. It rippled through me like a rush of wind and when it ended, Dan's lips curved in lazy pleasure against mine for a long moment before he pulled back. I lost myself in the planes of his face, the set of his jaw and the invitation in his eyes.

I hadn't fallen in love with him that night on the bluff when he saved my life—I'd been falling in love with him since he knocked on my back door and started teasing me about things that went bump in the night. Every time he showed up at Fox Hollow, he walked a little further into my heart whether I'd wanted him there or not.

"I think...I'm...I love you," I whispered. The words swirled like ink spilled into water between us, impossible to contain now that they'd been set free.

He brushed his thumb over my lower lip. For a heartbeat, I was terrified he'd parrot the words back out of obligation—hollow and meaningless—and I would shatter. I stopped breathing.

"You're distracting as hell." His voice was rough, almost angry. "You find dead bodies like some people find loose change. I spend more time fixing stuff in this house than I do in my own, and when I'm not with you, I can't get you out of mind."

He pulled me close and buried his face in my hair. "I thought I was going to have to shoot someone to keep you alive, then you damn near killed yourself anyway."

"I'm not that easy to get rid of." Oxygen poured

into my lungs again in a heady rush.

"I'm not trying to get rid of you," he growled. "I can't get enough of you."

"I come with a lot of baggage."

"So do I, sweetheart." His words rolled out low and bitter. "So do I."

Neither of us moved. A log crumbled in the grate, sending sparks soaring upward like fireflies on a summer evening. I wondered how long the dark image of Hannah Wintergarden would lurk in his shadows.

"Your baggage is worse," I said softly.

He quirked an eyebrow, inviting explanation.

"My ex-boyfriend's mother tried to kill me. The woman you planned to marry tried to kill you. Fewer degrees of separation. That makes your trust issues bigger than mine."

"You walked in on your husband doing the cheerleading captain. That didn't cause trust issues?"

"Yoga instructor, *former* cheerleading captain," I corrected. "And technically, she was doing him, if you know what I mean."

"Lord, McCallister." He laughed, the sound pulling me into a warm, easy place where we could laugh at betrayals no one else would find funny.

"Promise me something?" He twisted a lock of my hair around his index finger.

"What?" My heart clenched. I loved him, but I wouldn't reinvent my life to keep him in it.

"No more ghosts and skeletons or crazy women in cemeteries. Maybe we give normal a chance?"

Somewhere in my heart, a lock inexplicably opened, letting all the doubt and fear and anger of every wrecked relationship I'd ever had burn away with a white-hot flame that left no ashes behind.

"You wouldn't know what to do with me if I was normal," I said. "I think you like my ghosts and skeletons and cemeteries."

"I love you too, Jess."

I managed three seconds of stunned silence before I tried to say too much all at once. The result was an incoherent mumble that made him press an index finger against my lips, then he kissed me again, slow and deep. It felt like coming home to a place where I'd wanted to be for a long time but hadn't given myself permission to go until now. I wasn't sure if the tingly feeling low in my belly was from the wine or the last shred of self-control leaving my body.

My lips broke from his to skim along his jaw and down his throat as his heartbeat echoed against them. I pushed his shirt aside and kissed my way into the hollow of his collarbone, inhaling the scent of his skin.

"Don't start something you can't finish." His warning sent another jolt of molten heat through me.

"I don't think I started this," I whispered. I'd thrown a leg over him, my thighs straddling his. All right, maybe I had started this.

He slid a hand into my hair to pull my mouth down to his, but I was already there. He kissed like a summer storm sweeping across the fields, and I gave myself to that rush of power. His hands slid under my shirt and circled my waist, stroking my back from shoulders to the base of my spine, fingertips leaving heat simmering wherever they touched. My eyes locked on his as his hands explored, fingers warm and rough, and the easy smile on his lips reflected his pleasure.

One finger traced the upper swell of my breasts, then slid lower, across my belly, and I startled at the dizzying rush of sensation.

"If this isn't what you want, tell me to stop." His low tone held unhurried promise.

"No." My answer was instant, breathless.

"No, stop?" His lips brushed the corner of my mouth, then along my neck with a lightness that set every nerve tingling. "Or no, don't stop?"

I kissed him, making my choice clear.

Neither of us said anything for quite a while after that. When Dan spoke again, his voice was husky against my neck. "Does your bedroom door latch?"

"Mmm."

"Is that a yes?"

"Mmm." My hand was on the inside of his thigh, fingers playing along the heat radiating through his jeans. I wasn't sure how it had gotten there, but it was occupying all my attention.

"Good. We don't need an audience."

I tipped my head back slightly. Raider and Ruby watched intently from where they sprawled near the hearth, as smug as if they'd orchestrated the whole evening. Wordlessly, I slid off Dan's lap and held out my hands. He took them and together we walked up the stairs. As we tumbled onto my bed, I thought I heard a woman's footsteps pause in the hallway, a quiet sigh of satisfaction as she walked past the door. But it could have just been the wind.

ACKNOWLEDGEMENTS

When I sat down to write *How to Live with a Ghost*, I had no idea what I was doing. And it showed. I was a newspaper reporter, not a fiction writer. The collective guidance, encouragement, and exasperation of everyone who helped me make this book a reality far exceeds my ability to express a sufficient amount of gratitude.

In no particular order, I want to share my genuine and heartfelt thanks with:

Everyone who ever said, "You're so good with words. You should write a book." Thanks for throwing me into years of existential angst.

Mare Chapman, author of the Neville-Mackenzie Adventure series, for telling me I was a writer when I had doubts. She also told me I'm not normal, so there's that.

Jill Morstad, for reading the horrible first draft of *Ghost* and still being willing to crate next to me at obedience trials.

For Cathy Essick, Susan Schild, and Diana Horel, friends across time and space, who listened to me talk about this book for years. Like, seriously, a lot of years.

J.O. and Debbie Parker and the All-Iowa Writers' Conference, for giving me enough inspiration to keep blundering happily along, imagining "what if?"

Nick Narigon, one half of Hayseed Press and fellow survivor of community journalism, who emailed me during the COVID-19 pandemic in 2020 and said, "I'm bored. Send me your manuscript so I can read it." I did, and he did. His suggestions launched my collection of words on the journey to where they are today. And he's still talking to me, too.

Kristi Murdock, beta reader extraordinaire, for reading the twenty-seventh almost-but-not-quite final draft that was less horrible than anything that preceded it and saying encouraging things.

Misty Urban, Madwriters Editing Services, who read my manuscript when things started to get real and said, "This really needs to be a book."

Christoph Truemper for working his magic with the cover design in spite of me throwing random bits of artwork and ideas around like glitter.

The whole crew at Pearl City Press who took me on as their project, made things happen, and put up with me acting like I was back in the newsroom and trying to get tomorrow's paper printed yesterday.

My Belgian Malinois, Phoenix (OTCH. Carousel's Call of the Wild, UDX, OM, MX, MXJ and a bunch of other alphabet soup), who was the prototype for Raider's character. His memory still sparkles, especially when tennis balls roll across my office floor for no reason.

And finally, my husband, Jeff, who spent a lot of years asking, "Aren't you done with that book yet?" Yes, honey, I am finally done with that book. And I've started another one.

ABOUT THE AUTHOR

Melinda Wichmann is a third generation Iowa farm kid who earned a bachelor's degree in journalism and mass communication from Iowa State University. After a thirty-five-year career in community journalism, she decided to write a novel, despite having no idea what she was doing. Melinda lives on a family farm near the Amana Colonies in Iowa with her husband, Jeff, and two Australian shepherds who bark at things no one can see and do as they please in the show ring. *How to Live with a Ghost* is her first novel.